Bend IN THE RIVER

Judy Lennington

By:
Judy Lennington

Copyright © 2017 by Judy Lennington.

HARDBACK: 978-1-947620-47-6
PAPERBACK: 978-1-947620-46-9
EBOOK: 978-1-947620-48-3

All rights reserved. No part of this publication may be reproduced, distributed, or transmitted in any form or by any electronic or mechanical means, without the prior written permission of the publisher, except in the case of brief quotations embodied in critical reviews and certain other noncommercial uses permitted by copyright law.

Ordering Information:

For orders and inquiries, please contact:
1-888-375-9818
www.toplinkpublishing.com
bookorder@toplinkpublishing.com

Printed in the United States of America

Thank you, Dave Lennington,
for the best years of my life.
I love you very much.

I dedicate this book to the girls that meet for lunch regularly.

Essie Barnard
Edith Anderson
Vivian Sell Culler
Nancy Bowers
Patricia Guy
Lois Esenwein
Susie Steeves
JoAnn Ludt
Christina Bowers Flickinger
Sandra Sell
Bonnie Bennett
Gwenn Schmidt
Cindy Butler Lortz
Teresa Robison
Shirley Martin

I would like to thank Debby Rogers Mora, Jim Plunkett, and the Wellsville Historical Society for their help and assistance. God has blessed me with good friends, and I thank God that you are some of the best.

It was a warm spring day in Wellsville, Ohio. Lester Gideon shuffled his feet as he made his way down the dirt street toward the wooden boardwalk that bordered the store fronts of the main street. He watched his grandson, Jack, as he skipped ahead, kicking the dust into the air as he went. Lester walked with the aid of a cane he carried in his right hand. His knees ached and at times he found himself massaging his muscles in his back as he struggled to keep up with Jack.

Jack would pause from time to time to look back at his grandfather. He climbed the steps of the wooden sidewalk that went down the street in front of the businesses that lined both sides of the main street. Jack sat down to wait for his grandfather. Lester panted as he began to climb the steps. He rustled Jack's brown hair as he reached the top.

"Why do you need a cane, Grandfather?" Jack asked.

"Because, I'm old and my legs are weak, Jack," Lester explained. They had reached the door to the mercantile. Lester opened the door and held it for Jack to pass through.

"Just imagine if you didn't have any legs," Jack began, "or maybe if you had a wooden leg."

Lester sighed and replied, "I knew a man with a wooden leg once when I was about your age."

"Good afternoon, Lester," Rosalie Dodge said with a smile.

"Good afternoon, Rosalie. How is the mister these days?" Lester asked.

"Tell me about the man with the wooden leg, grandfather," Jack said.

Lester looked down at Jack and smiled, "Not now, Son. It will keep for another time. I'm having a conversation with Mrs. Dodge. You look around and mind that you don't touch anything."

Jack sighed and hung his head as he turned to walk away. Lester smiled over at Rosalie Dodge as she stood behind the counter watching the young boy. "I apologize, Rosalie. He forgets his manners sometimes."

Rosalie nodded her head and said, "I remember when my son was his age. Don't give it a second thought, Lester. Boys will be boys."

Lester smiled, "I remember when I was that age."

Rosalie nodded her head and wiped the dust from the counter. "What can I do for you this morning, Lester?" she asked.

"I need to mail this here letter," he placed a letter on the counter. "And I need a bag of salt for Delores," he said, with a nod of his head. He leaned his weight upon the cane.

"How is Delores this morning?" Rosalie asked.

"She's fine. She is baking a batch of bread now. I brought Jack with me to keep him out of her hair," Lester said.

"Ah, it's quite different with the grandchildren, isn't it?" Rosalie asked.

"It is at that," Lester said. "Of course, it isn't the same as raising your own. Sheldon comes home tired after working over at the Stevenson Company."

"It's a sad thing, the boy's mother dying of pneumonia at such an early age. Poor Sheldon is a very lucky man that you and Delores were able to take them in the way you did," Rosalie said, speaking softly and shaking her head. "Yes Sir, mighty lucky indeed. Of course, you two being up in years and all; it can't be easy for you looking after a boy his age."

Lester glanced over at Jack, who was inspecting a jar of licorice sticks. He smiled and said, "It isn't so bad. He comes in pretty handy at times."

Rosalie smiled and nodded her head as she placed both hands on the wooden countertop. "Can I get anything else for you this morning, Lester?" she asked.

Lester nodded his head in Jack's direction and said, "You can give Jack one of those licorice sticks. I think he deserves a treat this morning."

Rosalie walked around the counter and approached Jack. "Would you like a licorice stick, young man?" she asked him.

Jack's eyes widened and he smiled as he nodded his head. He looked over at his grandfather, seeking permission. Lester nodded his head and Rosalie removed the cover from the jar, lowering it to where Jack could reach inside. After selecting the candy of his choice, Jack went to stand next to his grandfather. He remained there, holding the candy in his hand until Lester paid Rosalie for the candy. Lester rustled Jack's hair and they walked out of the store together.

"May I eat my candy now?" Jack asked as they descended the wooden steps and proceeded to walk the dirt street toward home.

"You may," Lester replied.

Jack moved along slowly as he walked at his grandfather's side. Lester thought it strange as the lad usually skipped ahead. Lester continued to move along, relying upon his cane as they moved through the dusty streets toward the rows of smaller houses that lined a back street. "You said you knew a man with a wooden leg, Grandfather. Who was he?" Jack asked.

"Oh, he wasn't anybody special, and again, he was a very special individual," Lester said smiling down at Jack. "I suppose that doesn't make much sense, does it Jack?"

Jack shook his head. "No, it doesn't, Grandfather."

"Well, he wasn't a famous pirate, as you might imagine him to be. I remember the first time I saw him, I thought he was a pirate. I was about your age, and the only people I had ever heard of having wooden legs were pirates," Lester laughed. "He was not anyone famous. However, he was more special than most people thought."

"Special how, Grandfather?" Jack asked.

They were climbing the steps to their front porch. "Maybe some other time, Jack. You run along and play now. I need to speak with your grandmother," Lester said with a nod of the head.

Jack's shoulders slumped with disappointment. He turned and began to walk away, leaving the aroma of licorice lingering in the air. Lester smiled and opened the door that led into their kitchen. His wife, Delores, turned around briefly to look at him. "What's happening downtown?" she asked, as she went back to kneading her bread dough.

"Not much of anything is going on downtown this morning," Lester said. "I suppose that is a good thing. Jack is eating a licorice stick, so I suppose he won't be hungry for a spell."

Delores sighed, but said nothing. She began to pat the large dough ball and placed it in large, white, porcelain, wash pan that she had carefully scrubbed just for this purpose. She covered it with a cloth and began to wipe her hands on her apron. "I suspected as much," she said, pushing a loose strand of hair up under her white cap. "You spoil that boy, Lester."

"Awe, Delores, he's just a boy. He doesn't ask for much and he isn't any real trouble. A treat now and again doesn't hurt anything. It isn't like he eats candy every day," Lester said. He slowly lowered himself to sit upon a wooden chair near the window where he could watch Jack standing under a large tree inspecting the buds that were forming from the warm spring sunshine. "He doesn't ask about his mother. Do you find that strange?" he asked.

"Sheldon tells me he asks about her at times before he goes down for the night," Delores said. "I suppose he feels more comfortable talking about it with his father."

"How long has it been since Sara passed?" Lester asked.

Delores stopped what she was doing and closed her eyes as she thought before responding. "I reckon it's been almost a year now. I recall the trees were in blossom because she remarked upon how beautiful they were from her bed near the window. I believe the hardest thing a parent must go through is leaving a young child behind when their time comes. Sarah was too young. Her poor lungs just couldn't handle the strain anymore. Once that pneumonia took hold of her, she went quickly, and I thank God, every day for that. Watching her struggle to breath surely broke my heart," Delores said, shaking her head.

"Well, she's in a better place now," Lester said turning his head to watch Jack who had finished his licorice stick and was pondering the thought of climbing the tree he stood under.

Judy Lennington

Lester put weight upon his cane and rose to his feet. He went to the open door and called out, "Jack, come wash your sticky hands."

Jack turned to look back at his grandfather. He flexed his fingers and determined that they were, indeed, sticky. He ran toward the front porch. As he passed his grandfather in the doorway, Lester said, "I seem to recall the branches of those trees calling to me when I was your age. It's a perfectly normal thing for a boy your age to want to climb a tree, but I would prefer you fight the urge to climb that tree. The branches are too small and if you don't break your neck, you will break a limb."

"What is so special about that tree, Grandfather?" Jack asked.

"Well," Lester began, "that particular tree is a plum tree. We rely upon those plums for food. If you break a limb off, that is a jar or two of jam we won't have to get us through next winter." Lester laughed and winked over at Delores who stood drying her hands on a towel.

Jack seemed satisfied with the response, as he washed his hands. Delores handed him the towel and he dried his hands as he walked to stand in the door. "What trees can I climb?" he asked.

Lester sighed and shuffled to stand near his grandson. "Well, let's see now, I suppose that is a safe tree to climb." He pointed to a large Maple tree with his cane. "I wouldn't want you going up too high. A smart man knows his limitations. Never go so high that you might break something if you fall."

"I might break my neck and die," Jack said, looking up at his grandfather.

"That is true," Lester said, smiling down at Jack.

"Then I would go to heaven and be with mother," Jack said.

Lester frowned. "Well now," he began, "think about how sad you feel about your mother being gone, Son. That's how your father, grandmother, and I would feel if you went to heaven. What would we do without you?"

Jack shrugged his shoulders. "I don't know." He grew quiet and gazed out across the yard toward the river. "I reckon I wouldn't want to leave Daddy all by himself." He narrowed his eyes and seemed to drift off in thought.

Lester rustled his hair and laughed, "Let's go for a walk and see what old Hermon Griffin is up to this morning." Jack nodded his head and smiled as he skipped out the front door. Lester looked over his shoulder at Delores who waved them on. Jack stood in the yard waiting for Lester to make his way off the front porch by leaning upon his cane in one hand, and holding onto the porch railing with the other. "I'm coming Jack. I'm slow, but I'll get there."

"It is okay, Grandfather," Jack said. "We aren't in any big hurry." Jack slowed his pace to walk beside Lester as they moved westward.

They passed the widow, Mavis Cartwright's house. Mrs. Cartwright was a school teacher. Jack was one of her students. In fact, he was one of only three third graders she taught in her school. Vivian Gardner and Lewis Tully were the other two. Jack was the only boy his age in Wellsville. Although Lewis Tully was in the third grade, he was older than Jack by a year. Jack hated that fact and two second grade girls teased him about it daily. Lynette Raines and Milly Thompson were mean to Jack in particular. He was glad that this was Saturday. He had made up his mind that he would get the most out of the day. Tomorrow they would go to church, which wasn't much different than going to school, for both Milly and Lynette would be there, waiting to taunt him. After

Judy Lennington

church, they would have a nice meal together as a family. It was the only day of the week that his father did not work. Perhaps his father would take him fishing down by the river's bank after dinner. Jack loved fishing down by the river's bank. The time seemed to stand still and he could talk to his father about his mother all afternoon and there wouldn't be anyone to disturb them. That was Jack's favorite thing to do. Jack's father said that when he was Jack's age, Lester would bring him and his brother, Dallas, down to the river to go fishing on Sundays. It was sort of a family tradition. Now Dallas was married and had four children of his own. They lived in the big city somewhere in Pennsylvania. Jack had never been there, nor had he met his cousins. He only knew what he heard his father and grandparents say about them. He often tried to picture what they may look like, but each time his vision was different. He had many cousins he had never met before. Lester and Delores had four children and Jack's father was the only one that stayed in this area.

Jack's Aunt Ruth Ann married Leonard Gable and had two children, Rachel and Wilbur. Aunt Nancy married Daniel Reeves and had eight children, Michael, Amelia, Mary, Helen, Thomas, Edith, Paul, and Raymond. They were all much older than Jack. Uncle Dallas married Aunt Paulette and they had four children, Charles, Dallas II, George and Harriot. Jack's father, Sheldon, was the youngest and Jack was his only child. Jack often wondered if his mother had not become so ill, perhaps he would have had a sister or better yet, a brother. It didn't matter if they were much younger than Jack. It would be someone he could play with. Better yet, someone who could share in his adventures. Jack spent a lot of his time dwelling on the possibilities. What would it be like to have his cousins living close by? He wouldn't mind a Sunday, now and again, when they would all go down to the river fishing. Climbing trees would be more fun if he had someone to share in the exploring. Jack was lonesome. He was anxious for school to be dismissed for the summer. His grandparents would let him go off to explore the neighborhood on his own a couple of hours a day. He had only one restriction and that was the river. Jack was never to play along the river's bank. Although there were places where one could walk across the river, it often had currents that could sweep a boy Jack's size off his feet. He was a good lad and always obeyed. He knew the consequences all too well, if he didn't.

Jack walked alongside his grandfather. He resisted the urge to skip ahead. He was hoping his grandfather would feel like talking, and perhaps tell Jack more about the man he knew with a wooden leg, as Jack was very interested in learning more about this man. Grandfather said he wasn't a pirate. Jack thought only pirates had wooden legs. He looked up at his grandfather as they moved along the dusty street toward Herman Griffin's house. Herman and Lester had been friends for many years. Herman used to visit Lester daily until his wife became ill. She had something they called dementia. Jack wasn't sure what that was, but knew that Herman could not leave her alone.

They had reached Herman and Hilda Griffin's house. Jack stood by patiently waiting for Lester to climb the three wooden steps that led onto the front porch. Lester knocked on the door with his cane. Herman opened the door and smiled. "Hello there, Lester. I see you brought Jack with you. How are you doing this fine Saturday morning, young Jack?" Herman asked.

"I'm fine, Sir," Jack replied politely.

Judy Lennington

"Come in and sit a spell," Herman said, opening the door wide for them to enter. Jack waited for his grandfather to pass through the door first, and then he followed.

Hilda Griffin sat at the square wooden table in the center of the kitchen. Her hands were folded to rest on the table top in front of her. Her gray hair had been braided in two braids and wrapped around her head, secured tightly on the top. She wore a white lace head covering; much like the one Jack's grandmother wore every day while indoors. When she ventured outdoors, she wore a bonnet to cover her head. Hilda's shawl had fallen behind her back. As Herman moved toward his chair, he paused to pull the shawl up around her shoulders. Jack noticed that he squeezed Hilda's shoulder before moving to sit on a chair.

"Jack and I went down to mail a letter a little while ago and thought it was such a nice morning for a walk," Lester said. "How are you doing this morning Mrs. Griffin?" he asked, smiling over at Hilda.

Hilda smiled back at Lester and looked over at Jack. She winked and pointed her finger in his direction. "You've been climbing trees again, I see," she said.

Jack looked from his grandfather toward Herman. How did she know this? Had she been watching down the street?

"Yes Ma 'am," Jack replied.

"This isn't Wayne, Mother," Herman said, patting her arm. "This is Jack Gideon, you remember, Sheldon Gideon's boy? He lives with Lester and Delores. You remember Lester and Delores Gideon, don't you Mother?"

Hilda frowned. She appeared to be confused. She glanced over at Jack again and smiled, but Jack could tell by her eyes that she didn't understand. Apparently, she thought Jack was her son,

Wayne, at a much younger age. Wayne was a fully-grown man now with a wife and four grown daughters of his own. One of his daughters still lived at home, but the others had married and moved away. Wayne and his wife, Louise, lived in a big brick house over on Water Street. Jack passed their house every Sunday when he went fishing with his father, down along the river's bank. He had often wondered what it would be like to live in one of the grand brick homes that lined the right side of Water Street. The left side was open to look down upon the Ohio River.

Hermon patted her arm once again and she looked away from Jack to stare off into space. "She gets confused sometimes," Herman explained. "She doesn't seem to understand how much time has passed since the children were young. You must excuse her, son; she is having a difficult day."

Jack nodded his head. He glanced over at his grandfather and swallowed hard. He felt his face growing warm. "Yes Sir, I understand," he said, politely.

"So, tell me about your trip to the store, Jack," Herman said, smiling. "Did you get one of those delicious licorice sticks Mrs. Dodge keeps in a jar?" Jack nodded his head and smiled. "I recall getting a licorice stick for myself when I was your age," Herman said, laughing. "How about you, Lester, don't you mind how delicious those licorice sticks were when you were his age?"

Lester laughed and nodded his head. "I do recall. Old Mr. McCall used to hide one inside the wrapping paper of my father's purchases. He would wink at me to let me know what he did. Of course, I think my father knew all along what was going on," Lester replied.

"Yes, he did the same thing with all of the kids in the area. He was a fine old man that Mr. McCall," Herman said.

"Who was Mr. McCall?" Jack asked.

"Mr. McCall owned the mercantile when we were lads. Mrs. Dodge was his daughter," Lester began to explain. "Rosalie grew up and stayed local. When her father got too old to look after the store, she took over. Then she married Howard Dodge and he stepped in to run the place while Rosalie raised a family. That store has been in her family since Wellsville came into existence, I reckon." Lester teased.

"I can't say as I ever knew when or who started the place," Herman said.

"Nor I," Lester replied.

"They kept their licorice in a jar when you were boys?" Jack asked.

"They certainly did," Mr. Griffin said. "They kept the jar in the same place too."

Jack frowned as he pondered the conversation.

"I see the buds are starting to form on the fruit trees. It won't be long now, and the weather will be warm enough to sit out on the front porch in the mornings. That's what I look forward to these days," Lester said.

"Yes, Lester, I know what you mean. It seems every winter is longer than the last, the older I get," Mr. Griffon said.

"Do you suppose it's the same licorice sticks?" Jack interrupted.

"What's that, Jack?" Lester asked, looking over at his grandson.

"The licorice sticks in the jar at the mercantile. Do you suppose they are the same ones in there as when you were a boy?" he asked.

Mr. Griffin broke out in such laughter that he caused Mrs. Griffin to jump. He reached over and patted her arm.

Bend in The River

"Oh no, Son, those licorice sticks are long gone by now. I think Mrs. Dodge makes them herself," Lester said, holding back his laughter.

"Oh, that is comforting to know," Jack said.

"It certainly is," Mr. Griffin said, snickering.

Mrs. Griffin tapped the table and pointed toward Jack again. "You stay out of those trees, boy. You might break a leg or worse yet, your neck."

Jack looked over at Mr. Griffin who was stroking Mrs. Griffin's arm gently. "He'll be fine, Mother. He's just a boy and boys climbing trees is a fact of nature," he said, winking over at Jack.

"He should be in school with the other boys his age," Mrs. Griffin said.

"There isn't any school today, Mrs. Griffin. It is Saturday," Jack explained. That seemed to appease her, as she smiled and nodded her head. She interlocked her fingers again and went back to staring at her hands.

"She'll be alright, Jack. You never mind her, she gets mighty confused at times," Hermon Griffin said.

"Yes, Sir," Jack replied.

Lester placed his hand upon Jack's shoulder. "Jack is a pretty good boy. He is doing very well in school they tell me."

"So, you like school do you, Jack?" Hermon Griffin asked.

"I wouldn't say that," Jack began, "there aren't any boys my age in school. In fact, there isn't another boy my age in all of Wellsville. I only have two other classmates. There are these two girls at school, Lilly Thompson and Lynnette Raines are their names. They stick together, and have a way of making my life miserable."

- 13 -

Judy Lennington

Again, Hermon Griffin burst into laughter. "Now I can see how that might be a problem for a lad your age," he said.

"Yes Sir, it is a problem alright," Jack replied. "I'd certainly like to whoop on them girls sometimes, but Father and Grandfather both tells me it isn't something a boy should do, so I stand there and takes it. I don't like it much, though."

"I understand, but the fact that you do take it, shows me what a fine man you are going to grow up to be. A man, who raises his hand to hit a woman, or girl, isn't much of a man at all. It's a coward's way," Mr. Griffin said.

"Yes Sir, that is what I hear," Jack replied.

"It's a little hard at times, isn't it Jack?" Lester asked.

"Yes, it is, Sir. Very hard, indeed, I might say. Sometimes, it makes me sick to my stomach because I want to let them have it so bad," Jack said, clenching his teeth.

"Well, I am mighty proud of you," Lester said. "You are going to be a fine man."

"Hey Lester, mind what old Limpy had to say about a mouthy woman once?" Hermon asked.

Lester nodded his head, "Yes I do. He said, "If she can't mind her place, she ought to stay in the kitchen." He snickered. "Old Limpy had something to say about everything."

"Who is old Limpy?" Jack asked.

"Why, your grandfather hasn't told you about old Limpy? Lester, here, and old Limpy were nearly inseparable at one point. I'm surprised he hasn't mentioned him to you," Hermon said, laughing.

Lester nodded his head and looked over at Jack. "Limpy's real name was Charles Woodward. He was from Bedford, Massachusetts," he explained.

"Where is Bedford, Massachusetts?" Jack asked.

"That's up north. It's almost to Canada. Do you know where Canada is, Jack?" Lester asked.

Jack frowned. "I recall Mrs. Cartwright showing us a map of the United States, and Canada was at the top. It borders the United States. Mrs. Cartwright said it is a whole other country," Jack replied, while obviously deep in thought.

"That's right, Jack," Lester said, smiling. "Well, Massachusetts is a state up north, out near the ocean. It's a big fishing port, I'm told. They fish for everything up there, even whales."

"Whales? I saw a picture of a whale once in school. It had a picture of an elephant and a man standing beside it. It was huge! What kind of line holds something that big?" Jack asked.

"Well, apparently, they have a line to hold a fish that big because old Limpy was a fisherman of whales. They called themselves Whalers," Lester explained.

"Whales are technically mammals, Grandfather. They aren't fish," Jack corrected.

"Well, you would know more about that than I would, Son," Lester explained.

Hilda Griffon pointed at Jack again and narrowed her eyes as she said, "You stay away from old Limpy, Lester. My Mamma said he is a no account, and we are to stay away from him."

Hermon placed his hand over her pointed finger and said, "That's not Lester, Hilda. That is his grandson, Jack. Lester is all grown up now and Limpy has died years ago. Don't you mind when old Limpy died, Hilda? He was buried at sea."

"Limpy was buried at sea?" Jack asked.

"Yes, he was," Lester said, nodding his head. "It was his wish. Hermon's father took me and old Limpy's body out on the river and had a ceremony before lowering him into the water."

"But the Ohio River isn't the same as the sea," Jack said, looking up at his Grandfather.

"It is the closest thing to the sea here in Wellsville," Lester said. "We took him out to the deepest part of the river and said a prayer over him. Then Mr. Griffon and I lowered him into the water. We had big rocks tied around the body so it would sink to the bottom."

"I wasn't there," Hermon said. "As I recall, I was down with the chicken pox at the time."

"I never heard this story before," Jack said.

"Oh, you would have liked old Limpy, Jack. We were good friends, despite the difference in our ages," Lester said. He rubbed the top of Jack's head. "You say your goodbyes to Mr. and Mrs. Griffon now. We shouldn't overstay our welcome." Lester pushed himself to his feet and stood waiting for Jack to shake hands with Hermon Griffon. He nodded his head politely toward Mrs. Griffon and went to stand near the door while Lester shook hands with his friend, Hermon. Mrs. Griffon smiled over at Jack and watched him until they were outside.

As Lester and Jack made their way back toward their house, Jack asked, "Why did Mrs. Griffon think I was you, Grandfather?"

Lester took a deep breath. "Sometimes, as we age, we get confused. That's what has happened to Mrs. Griffon. Sometimes she may think you are Jack Gideon, and other times she may think you are someone else, altogether."

"Kind of like, whatever she is thinking of at the time," Jack mumbled.

"Kind of like that, I suppose," Lester replied.

"Do I look like you when you were my age?" Jack asked.

"Not so much. You look more like your mother. Something about you reminded her of me when I was your age, I suppose," Lester said. He was breathing heavily, as they neared the porch. "I'm going to sit out here a spell and catch my breath. You run along and play. Mind what I said about climbing those trees, Jack."

"Yes, Grandfather. I don't think I will climb any trees before dinner. I'm going to explore the hillside if you don't mind," Jack said, standing in a patch of green grass, looking up at his Grandfather as he lowered himself to sit on the porch steps.

"Okay, but mind the snakes. It's that time of year when the copperheads are crawling out to catch the warm sun," Lester said.

Jack waved to his grandfather as he turned to run toward the steep hill behind the rows of houses. He followed the dirt roads that the horse and wagons traveled as they made their way from the riverboat docks toward the Great Lakes, heavy with wares and goods to be delivered to destinations that only Jack could dream of.

Jack climbed the steep hillside a while and turned to look back upon the town below. The river was wide, and the water seemed to flow slowly. In places, green grass grew in the shallow spots. For the most part, it was deep enough for the heavy boats, laden with supplies, to dock and pull away. Men would wait in their horse pulled wagons, near the dock, for their turn to unload the boat's contents into their wagons and pull away. Jack watched a while and then resumed his climb of the hill. He was going to explore the hillside. It was a warm Saturday and it was spring. Soon school would be out for the summer. Jack looked forward to spring for that reason. He didn't like school much and often thought he would prefer to quit school and take up an occupation of some sort to earn money. There was no real reason for him to continue

Judy Lennington

with his schooling. He certainly did not look forward to going to school every day and be tortured by Milly Thompson and Lynette Raines. He hated girls. They were mean, wimpy creatures that always managed some sort of devious act which always resulted in them crying and Jack getting in trouble for it. He dusted his dirty hands upon his pant legs. Some day he was going to have a job and money of his own. He would wear fine clothes and maybe take a trip on one of those fancy paddle boats that went up the river. He would never look back.

Then Jack thought about his father being left behind, all alone. Jack was all Sheldon had now that Jack's mother had died. Well, of course, there was Grandfather and Grandmother. They were getting up there in years and Sheldon helped a lot around the house when he wasn't working. It seemed the only real time Jack had to spend with his father was on Sunday mornings after church when they went down to the river's bank to do some fishing.

Jack squat low and rested his elbows upon his knees as he looked down upon Wellsville stretched out below him. He thought he caught a glimpse of two little girls twirling in the grassy yard along Water Street. He felt his face warming as he thought of Milly and Lynette. He rose to his feet and turned to climb higher. He glanced over his shoulder a couple of times as he made his way up the rocky incline. He was nearly to the top now. He turned once again and looked down. He could see the rows of horse drawn wagons pulling away from the docks and following the Wellsville turnpike toward Lisbon with their wagons full of wares on their way to Niles. More wagons came from the eastern route as they were arriving from as far as Bedford Massachusetts. Jack watched a while. He wondered if old Limpy arrived from Massachusetts by way of this route.

A squirrel caught his attention as it chattered, annoyed at his presence. Jack shook the stick he carried at the squirrel. He put the stick to his shoulder, making believe it was a gun. "Bang!" Jack said out loud. The squirrel climbed the tree higher and stopped to look down at Jack. He pretended to shoot at it again, leaving the squirrel to canter off down a limb and jumping to another tree to get away from Jack.

Now Jack turned and surveyed his surroundings. The leaves had matted upon the ground after being covered with a heavy blanket of snow all winter. A hint of green seemed to surround him as nearly all the trees had new leaves sprouting forth. He took a deep breath and closed his eyes. Soon the smell of lilac and honeysuckle would fill the air. Here and there the ground would be covered with wild Mountain Laurel vines, Lily of the Valley, and Morning Glories. It would also mean he would have to be on the lookout for Poison Ivy and Poison Oak. Jack remembers a couple of times he had a bad reaction to the green foliage that blanketed the hillsides and forest floors, as well as vining up the trees that he liked to climb.

Here on the hillside, he didn't climb trees. The bank was too steep and required his full attention just to keep his footing. Once he began to slide it took a full-on collision with a tree to stop him. He never ran into anyone else on the hillside. Up here he could be totally alone with his thoughts. There were paths that ran along the side of the hill, but not up this far. Up here there was nothing but nature and Jack. He paused to think back to a time he might have seen someone other than himself up here, and could not think of a soul. From up here he could see nearly all of Wellsville and most of the surrounding area. He could see the building where his father worked. They built brick-making machinery there. Jack's

Judy Lennington

father worked hard six days a week, often coming home after dark to find dinner sitting on the table covered with a cloth to keep it warm. Even after working all day and coming home late, Sheldon Gideon found a moment to stop by Jack's bed to say goodnight before retiring at the end of a long day.

Jack was lucky to have a father like Sheldon. Milly Thompson taunted Jack once about almost being an orphan. She said that orphans lived in big brick buildings that were filled with children of all ages and the heat was turned down low because they couldn't afford to buy wood to keep the woodstove's burning day and night. She told him how all the children had to care for each other and they had to work every day, all day long, for their keep. They were underfed, under clothed, and unloved. Jack recalled a time when she got up into his face and said, "You better hope nothing happens to your Daddy, or you would be a full-blooded orphan." Jack covered his eyes at the thought. He could see Milly's face as if she were standing right in front of him. Milly Thompson and her friend Lynette Raines were the reason Jack hated girls. He uncovered his eyes and grabbed a tree for support as he hoisted himself higher up the hill. He felt the need to stand at the very top on a jagged rock that was surrounded by pines. From that spot, he could see, eastward, all the way to East Liverpool and westward to the bend at Yellow Creek.

Jack was sweating by the time he reached the large sandstone rock that jutted out of the top of the hill. He looked to his right at the wooded area of Yellow Creek. He recalled his grandfather and father telling him the story of an Indian they called Logan. Settlers moved into the area on the other side of the river and killed Logan's family. Logan, being a prominent Iroquois chief, went on a rampage and began killing white people all up and down the river banks. Jack could picture what Logan must have looked like. He spun from side to side, shooting his imaginary foes with his imaginary rifle. From time to time, he would swing the stick in a sword like fashion. Jack could play for hours in this manner.

After some time, he paused to sit upon the sandstone and rest. He would lay back and place his hands behind his head. He enjoyed his time up here, alone from the prying eyes of vicious little girls who taunted him and older boys who bullied him for the sake of looking tougher or because they were incapable of withstanding a pulping from someone their own age or size. Jack covered his eyes with his right arm, but did not drop the stick he held tightly in his hand. It was his only weapon, should he find himself able to defend himself.

He missed his mother. He imagined that he could still smell her hair falling over her shoulders and tickling his face at night when she kissed him goodnight. He could still hear her voice as she sang while going about her chores. When she first became ill, she would allow him to lay in the bed next to her while she told him stories of her life as a girl and sometimes she read to him from the many books she kept in a chest against the wall. He could still see her green eyes twinkling in the light of the fireplace in their little house where they lived together as a family. Jack often inquired about her freckles that he seemed to have inherited. She would tell him it was where the sun had kissed their noses and left little flecks of sunshine behind to bless them. Jack liked that story. He liked everything he remembered pertaining to his mother, except the last few days.

Jack fought the memory, but it flooded back regardless of his intentions. His mother was confined to her bed, coughing relentlessly, and his grandmother sitting at her bedside every day while his father was at work. They would chase him from the room, but Jack often huddled near a place where the boards parted only slightly and he could see inside. His mother would cough up blood and finally she drifted off to sleep and barely breathed at all. This lasted nearly an entire day. Jack's father came home from work and sat on the side of her bed crying as he held her hand. Jack could still hear the wheezing sound she made with every breath she took. His grandmother sat in a chair near the bed praying and reading from her bible. Then they both rose from where they were sitting and covered his mother's face. That was when Jack's father told him his mother had died and gone to Heaven.

For weeks Jack felt angry that they both spent her last moments at her side, but would not permit him in the room. His father said he was too young to understand the concept of death. He understood perfectly well. It was the end of all life. Grandmother said that his Mommy was with him always and that every time he thought of her she was alive in spirit. Jack didn't know about that, but he would certainly like to hear her voice occasionally. Tears were beginning to well up in Jack's eyes. His chest felt tight and his nose began to run slightly, causing him to sniffle.

He looked down the hill toward the Stevenson building where his father worked. They made steam machines that powered the paddle boats that traveled the river. His father had told him that the factory had been there since 1836. It was a decent job and it provided security for Jack and the family. Yet, Jack recalled his grandfather once saying that nothing lasted forever. What would he do if something happened to his father? He was almost an orphan now. If his father was to die or become ill, he would be an orphan and must go live in an orphanage. His grandparents

Bend in The River

were too old to care for a boy his age. Jack grew anxious at the thought of being homeless.

As Jack sat up on the rock looking down the hill, he saw people walking about the dirt streets below him. They had no idea they were being watched. Perhaps he could be a guardian of Wellsville. A vigilante like Robin Hood in the tales his grandfather often told him. He rose to his feet and swung the stick in a sword like manner again. From time to time, he would release an arrow from an imaginary bow. His stomach growled and he decided it was time to go home for something to eat.

Jack darted from tree to tree as he quickly made his way down the hill. At one point the loose shale underfoot began to slide and Jack dropped to his butt as he continued to slide. He let go of the stick, and opened his eyes wide. The warning about the copperheads, his grandfather had spoken earlier, came rushing back at him. This was a perfect day for snakes to come out and sun themselves. If a snake should happen to be in his path, there would be nothing he could do to stop himself. He continued to slide until his foot happened to line up with a large Elm tree. It halted his descent long enough for him to get a grip on the tree and pull himself to his feet again. Jack resumed making his way down the hill from tree to tree until he reached the path that wound around the hillside. From here, he thought it best to follow the path back toward the dirt road beneath him.

Jack hurried toward the porch. He could smell the bread his grandmother was baking from the front yard. As he entered the house his grandfather looked up from where he sat at the kitchen table. "Where you been, Jack?" Lester asked.

"I was exploring, Sir," Jack replied.

"Well, you have sense enough to come home in time to eat," his grandmother said, placing a bowl in front of him.

Jack stared down into the bowl of chicken broth and noodles. He smiled up at his grandmother as she handed him a fresh baked roll. Lester slid the butter dish in Jack's direction. Jack began to butter his warm roll while his grandmother sat down on the chair across the table from him. She cleared her throat and Jack put the roll down and bowed his head while his grandfather recited grace. It grew quiet as they ate their noon day's meal.

As they were finishing their dinner, Delores smiled over at Jack and said, "I could use some help bringing wood in after you've finished."

"Yes Ma'am," Jack replied. He rose from where he had been sitting and began to help clear the table. His father had always told him it was important to be helpful as his grandparents took care of his needs and provided them with a home. He went outside and filled his arms with wood that was stacked inside a wooden box on the end of the porch. He carried it inside and placed it in another, smaller, wooden box that sat next to the fireplace. He made several trips until the box was filled. The wood would dry from the heat of the fireplace and by supper time, it would be ready to use.

After making the last trip, Jack paused near the water bucket for a cold drink of water. "Jack, I have something for you," Lester said, reaching into his pocket. He pulled out a wooden horse he had carved from a piece of dried wood.

Jack's eyes widened as he took the carving in his hands and inspected it. "Thank you very much, Grandfather. This is a fine horse. I can see every detail of his face." He smiled up at his grandfather. "Would you teach me to carve something?" he asked.

"Maybe when you are a little older," his grandfather said, winking at him. "I don't think your grandmother would approve of you using a sharp knife at your age."

Jack felt disappointment. Why did he have to wait until he was bigger to do anything? He sighed and said, "Thank you Sir. It is my favorite toy."

"You run along now and play outdoors," his grandmother said. "It is too nice out there for you to be indoors."

"Yes Ma'am," Jack replied as he turned and ran toward the door. He skipped along the path along the side of the house that led to the dirt street. Here he turned left and proceeded around the corner of the house. That was when he ran right into Melvin Riley. "Oh," Jack said, backing up slowly while keeping his eye on Melvin.

"Watch where you're going, Punk!" Anthony Patrone said.

Jack did not look over at Anthony Patrone. He kept his eyes upon Melvin, who narrowed his gaze and puffed up his chest. Jack knew what was coming and was helpless to avoid it.

Melvin shoved Jack, causing him to fall backwards onto the ground. "Yeah, watch where you're going, Punk!" He stood over Jack daring him to get up.

Jack remained on the ground. He knew if he got up, Melvin would just knock him down again.

"What do you have there in your hand?" Anthony asked, reaching down and twisting the wooden horse from Jack's grip. Anthony held it up for Melvin to look at. He smiled down at Jack who found himself unable to speak. "Where did you get this?" he asked.

Jack opened his mouth, but words would not come out. Melvin took the wooden horse from Anthony and smiled down at Jack.

"Thanks runt, I've been wanting one of these." He laughed out loud and said, "Come on Anthony, let's go." Melvin turned and began walking away. Anthony kicked dirt at Jack and followed his friend. Jack remained on his back until he was certain the bigger boys would not return to have another go at him.

Jack felt tears welling up in his eyes as he rose to his feet and dusted himself off. What was he going to tell his grandfather? He didn't even get to keep the horse for one full day. He went back the way he came. He could hear his grandparents talking in the house as the front door was open. Jack went to the plum tree and sat down under it. He allowed his head to fall back against the tree as he looked across the yard at the row of small houses that lined the streets.

Melvin and Anthony were in the sixth grade. They were always together. They picked on all the younger kids and the kids that were bigger picked on them. That was how it was here. It seemed everyone was picked on by someone and everyone picked on someone smaller. Everyone with exception to Jack, that is. Jack's father and grandparents preached at him regularly about how unchristian it was to mistreat others. Jack listened and he obeyed, however, it left him in some very precarious positions many times. He remained under the tree until dusk, when his grandfather called him inside.

"Jack, you'll catch a chill out there in the evening air without a sweater," his grandmother said, as he came inside.

"Leave the boy be, Delores," his grandfather began, "he was playing with his new toy, weren't you son?"

Now Jack was in a predicament. He had been taught not to lie. How was he to explain what happened without sounding like a whining little baby? He felt his face and neck turning red and the lump in his throat threatened to shut off his air.

"What's the matter, Jack?" Lester asked, taking Jack by the shoulders.

"The toy, Sir," Jack managed to get out with a crackling voice.

"What about the toy? Did it break?" Lester asked.

Jack shook his head. "No Sir, it didn't break."

"Then, where is it?" Lester asked.

"Melvin Riley and Anthony Patrone took it from me," Jack thought he was going to cry. He fought the feeling. It was bad enough that two bullies took his toy away from him, but he couldn't let his grandfather see him crying like a baby. He just couldn't. He wiped at the tears and swallowed the lump in his throat.

"Two bullies took the horse away from you?" Lester asked.

Jack nodded his head. "Yes Sir."

"Lester," Delores said, softly.

"It's alright, Grandmother," Jack began. "I wanted to fight for it, but those boys don't have anything. I felt sorry for them, so I let them keep the horse." Well, it wasn't really a whole lie, only partly a lie.

Lester took a deep breath and nodded his head. "It's alright Son. I understand and I'm proud of you for being so gracious. There is plenty of wood lying around here. I can always make another one."

"Thank you, Sir," Jack replied.

"You wash up now and get ready for dinner," Lester said, patting Jack on the back.

Jack began to remove his shirt. Delores filled a pan with warm water and Jack went near the fireplace to wash his face, neck, arms, legs, and feet. This was something he did every evening

Judy Lennington

before dinner. He pulled his shirt on again and was pulling up his suspenders when his father walked in the door. Jack smiled up at his father. This was his favorite time of day. Jack ran into Sheldon's arms. "Daddy," he said.

Sheldon held Jack in his arms. He rose, lifting Jack off the floor. "How was your day?" Sheldon asked his son.

"It was fine, Sir," Jack replied. "How was yours?"

Sheldon chuckled. "Mine is the same every day, Jack. I go to work, I eat my lunch and go to work again, then I come home. Day in, day out, it's always the same old thing. But, hey, I get paid every Saturday and do you know what day it is?" he asked, smiling widely.

"It's Saturday," Jack said, laughing.

"It is Saturday," Sheldon said, reaching into his pocket and pulling out an envelope.

"Well, now that you are a rich man, how about washing up for supper," Delores said, without looking back at them.

"Yes Ma'am, Momma," Sheldon said, going to the wash pan. He wrinkled up his nose and asked, "Who left all this dirt in my wash pan?"

Jack giggled. "I'll empty it, Father," he said, taking the pan from his father. Jack carried it out onto the porch and tossed it over the side. He carried the pan back inside and handed it to his father. Sheldon smiled and poured warm water into the pan and began rolling up his sleeves.

"Anything new happening in town today?" Sheldon asked, with his back to them.

Jack looked over at his grandparents and froze with fear. He prayed they did not tell his father about Melvin and Anthony taking the wooden horse from him.

Lester winked at Jack and said, "Not much happening today. I guess that is a good thing. Are you and Jack going fishing after church tomorrow?"

"If it doesn't rain," Sheldon said. He carried his dirty water outside and tossed it over the side of the porch as Jack had done only moments ago. Then he placed the pan on a nail that hung over the water bucket and went to sit at the table. They were having the same chicken soup and bread for supper. Jack didn't mind for it was one of his favorite meals. After dinner Jack dressed for bed and waited for his father to tuck him in for the night.

Jack slept well that night. The anxiousness he felt earlier in the evening seemed to take a toll on him and, by the time his father blew out the candle, he was exhausted. Jack prayed that it didn't rain, for he waited all week for Sunday afternoon when he and his father went fishing. He smoothed the covers of his bed and hurried down a ladder that led to the kitchen from the small loft he shared with his father. Sheldon was usually a little slower about getting up on Sunday's. Jack went out onto the porch. The sun was coming up and the sky was cloudy. Jack said another silent prayer that it didn't rain, then he went back inside where his grandmother was busy making flap jacks.

Jack was placing plates on the table when his grandfather made his way to the kitchen table. By that time, Delores was pouring coffee from the blue and white porcelain pot, Sheldon was climbing down the ladder wearing his long johns.

"Sheldon, the least you could do is dress for breakfast," Delores said, frowning.

"I'm going to dress after breakfast for church, Mother. Why go to all the trouble for an hour or less?" Sheldon winked over at Jack.

"Suppose someone should drop by," Delores said.

"Who would drop by this early on a Sunday morning?" Sheldon said, raising the coffee cup to his lips.

"I'm going to change for church too, Grandmother," Jack began, "Why can't I dress after breakfast?"

Sheldon tapped Jack's arm. "You listen to your grandparents, Jack. They are older and wiser. Your grandmother is right; I should have dressed for breakfast. It is a matter of respect."

"Yes Sir," Jack replied.

"Hey, are we going fishing today?" Sheldon asked.

Jack's face lit up at the thought. He nodded his head. "Should we invite your grandfather to come along?" Sheldon asked. Jack didn't want his grandfather to come. He enjoyed his time alone with his father. His grandfather was slow and cumbersome. Jack looked up at Lester who was watching him, waiting for his answer. Jack swallowed the lump in his throat and nodded his head.

"Now that is real nice of you boys to invite an old man to share your day, but I don't get around like I used to. I might stumble and fall in that old river and drowned," Lester said, smiling. "I thank you for the invite, but I believe I'll hang around the house and keep Delores company today."

"Well, you certainly are welcome to join Jack and me if you change your mind," Sheldon said with a mouth full of flap jacks.

By this time, Delores had finished cooking and sat down at the table to eat. Lester began talking about all the events that happened throughout the past week in town. Jack found the conversation boring as he had heard it many times the last few days. He listened politely as his father would ask a question and a whole new conversation would arise. Soon he had finished his breakfast and sat with his hands in his lap, waiting for his grandfather to finish talking. When Lester paused between sentences, Jack asked, "May

I please be excused?" Sheldon nodded his head and Jack left the table.

They went through their normal Sunday morning routine and soon they were walking together down the dirt street toward the church. Others walked ahead of them, and behind them, as nearly all of Wellsville gathered inside the building to praise God for their humble lives.

Jack sat quietly in a pew between his father and grandmother. Lester sat next to the aisle nodding his head now and then as the preacher recited his sermon. Jack often turned his head to look out the filmy windows at the sky. Dark clouds had moved in. He prayed it didn't rain for this was the one day every week when he had his father all to himself as they fished down by the river's bank.

They stood and sang a hymn together, and waited patiently for the minister to finish the final prayer. It seemed to go on forever as Jack shifted his weight from foot to foot. As they were leaving the church Jack noticed Melvin Riley walking with his widowed mother. He smirked at Jack and held up the wooden horse he held tightly in his hand. Jack noticed that the horse now only had three legs. Jack quickly looked to the ground as they made their way back to the house where he would change clothes and eat a slice of day old bread with butter and sugar before going to the river.

Jack and his father found an isolated spot near the river's edge. The water seemed to be moving slowly by them as the dark clouds overhead reflected upon the water like a silvery painting. "You are awful quiet this morning, Jack," Sheldon said. Jack shrugged his shoulders. "Is there something you would like to talk about?" Sheldon asked.

Again, Jack shrugged his shoulders. "I suppose I have a heaviness weighing upon my shoulders this morning," Jack replied.

Sheldon smiled and nodded his head. "Is it something you would like to talk about?"

Jack watched out over the top of the flowing water. "It's that mean Melvin Riley and his friend Anthony Patrone," he began, "Grandfather whittled a horse for me from a piece of wood. I didn't even get to play with it when that mean old Melvin and his friend happen upon me and took it from me. I hate them boys, and I hate Milly Thompson and Lynette Raines too. I can't help it, that's how I feel. I'm sitting in the house of God, this morning and they are in there with their parents and I know it is wrong to hate, but I can't help it."

"Well, hate is a powerful thing, Jack. It's not as powerful as love, I suppose, but powerful none the less. I guess nearly every person in church this morning prayed that God would help them with some sort of sinful thoughts. I reckon you aren't any different than the rest of the folks around bouts. I'm thinking that you could pray to God to help you out with the way you feel. I'm sure he would listen and with a little time and patience, I think you may find yourself feeling differently in the future," Sheldon said, with a sigh.

"I don't think that will work because they are just too mean and evil. I don't see how God could take my mother and leave such mean people behind to make my life miserable," Jack busted out.

"Well, maybe God was merciful by taking your mother, Jack," Sheldon said. He pulled his line in and put a new worm on the hook before tossing it into the water again. "Tell me something, do you remember your mom the last days of her life? She struggled for every breath of air she took in. She was suffering so, that when death came, as much as it hurt to see her pass, I was glad that she was not suffering anymore."

Jack looked up at his father with tears in his eyes. "I remember, but God could have healed her so she wasn't suffering. Then she could have stayed with us," he said, wiping at his eyes with his sleeve. "It isn't fair, Daddy. The preacher said God hears all our prayers. We all prayed for Mommy to get better. Why didn't he make her better? If he didn't hear our prayers, then what makes us think he hears them now?" Jack was sobbing now.

Sheldon put the pole down and placed his arms around his son. "Jack, I know it is hard. I miss her very much too. Your mother and I had made many plans for your future, and I wasn't prepared for any of this. I wish there was something I could have done to save her, but there was nothing anyone could do." He buried Jack's face into his chest and took deep breaths to fight back the tears.

Jack pulled back and wiped his eyes with his sleeve again. He pointed to Sheldon's pole that lay on the ground behind them. Sheldon jumped back and grabbed the pole. "I think I got a big one," Sheldon said.

There was no more talk about Jack's mother today. Sheldon pulled on his line until he managed to get his catch to the bank. It was a catfish. They decided that a catfish was as good as anything and after the sky grew darker, they headed up the bank, and home. They would be having fish for supper.

That evening Jack was quiet. He tried not to dwell on the conversation he had with his father at the river. It only made him cry, and he didn't want his grandparents to see him crying. He didn't want to see the day end. Tomorrow his father would return to work and Jack would return to school. As he lay in the loft listening to his father and grandfather snoring, he recalled his mother's labored breathing from where he peeked through the crack in the boards of their house. After his mother died, Sheldon sold the house and he and Jack moved in with Jack's grandparents. Jack needed someone to look after him and Sheldon would not be available to do so. He worked from sunrise to sunset six days a week.

Jack appreciated his grandparents taking care of him. He was well fed and wore clean clothes. There were other children who went to school in far worse condition, and they had two parents caring for them. Jack had been most fortunate to be with them. They were both up in years and someday they would be gone too. Jack prayed for their health. His grandfather worried him. Lester did not get around well and he tired easily. This worried Jack. Milly Thompson's taunting about his nearly being a full-blooded orphan came rushing back to him. He prayed to God to forgive him for hating her and prayed that God would punish her for being evil.

"Jack!" a voice from far away called. "Jack Gideon, get up and get dressed for school."

Jack sat up. It was his grandfather calling from below. "I'm up Grandfather," Jack called down the ladder. He dressed quickly and descended the ladder to find breakfast waiting for him on the table.

"Thank you, Grandmother," Jack said. He had prayed and prayed. His father told him to be patient. He had no choice but to give it a try. He would be kind to others and as helpful to his grandparents as he could be. Perhaps God would smile down upon him and resolve his problem with those who taunted him. As he saw it, he had no choice in the matter.

Jack ate his breakfast slowly. He knew he would have to rush to make it to school before the last bell, but he dreaded the thought of walking into the schoolyard when the others where outside. He did not want to run into the girls or Melvin and Anthony.

"You better hurry up Jack," his grandmother said.

Jack was aware of his grandfather watching him closely. Jack kept his eyes averted to his bowl of oats. "Are you alright this morning?" Lester asked his grandson.

Jack nodded his head without looking away from his nearly empty bowl of oats. "Yes Sir, I am fine," he replied.

"Perhaps you wouldn't mind if an old man walked with you to school this morning. I need to exercise these old legs of mine and today would be a perfect day to start," Lester said.

Jack could only nod his head. He had told his grandfather about Melvin taking the horse from him. Did he suspect that Jack didn't want another run in with Melvin? Jack couldn't find the words, so he remained quiet. When he had finished, Lester stood up and said, "Come along, let us walk together."

"He's going to be late, Lester and you will only slow him down more," Delores said, wiping her hands on her apron.

"Don't worry, Delores. If he's late, I'll talk to the teacher and explain that it was all my fault. We will be fine." Lester smiled down at Jack and smoothed his hair. "Are you ready?" he asked. Jack nodded his head and forced himself to smile up at his grandfather. Lester leaned heavily upon his cane this morning as they made their way along the dirt streets toward the school.

"That was some nice catfish you boys caught yesterday," Lester said, as they moved along.

"Yes Sir, Daddy caught it. I didn't catch anything all day," Jack said.

"Well, we all have had those days," Lester said. "It reminds me of old Limpy. He told me once that it isn't so much what you catch, it's the experience."

"Limpy was the man with the wooden leg?" Jack asked.

"He was. He was a good friend of mine. Old Limpy was up there in years when we first met, but we became the best of friends and remained so until he died. When Old Limpy passed away, I thought my world had ended. You see, I was in the same boat as you are now. There weren't many boys my age in these parts at that time. Hermon is a year my senior. We didn't become friends until we were in eighth grade. Hermon started hanging around and he got to know old Limpy pretty well, but it wasn't long after that Old Limpy died," Lester explained.

"How did you meet old Limpy, Grandfather?" Jack asked.

"Well, that is another story all together. We are coming upon the school yard and there isn't time for me to tell you, so it will keep for another time," Lester said. "Will you be alright from here?"

Jack nodded his head. "Everyone is inside and the bell hasn't rung yet. I'll be fine. Thank you for walking with me Grandfather."

Lester patted the top of Jack's head. "Would you like me to meet you after school and walk home with you?"

Jack thought about that for a moment. He rather liked the idea, and smiled up at his grandfather. No one would dare challenge him in front of his grandfather.

"I'll meet you right here after school," Lester said, nodding his head. "Now you run along before that bell rings.

Jack ran toward the schoolhouse door. Mrs. Cartwright was ringing the bell just as he passed through the door. She smiled and nodded her head as she noticed him hurrying to his seat. Jack stopped dead in his tracks as he approached the seat he normally sat in. A big boy with wild curly red hair and freckles everywhere sat in his seat. He glared up at Jack with smoky blue eyes. Jack forced himself to smile as he went to sit behind the boy. As he sat down, he noticed that the boy totally obliterated his view of the blackboard.

"Good morning students," Mrs. Cartwright said, from a position Jack could not see. There was a long pause before she continued, "Children, we have a new student with us today. His name is Collin McCauley." Mrs. Cartwright paused and said, "Mr. McCauley, perhaps you would like to stand and tell the class a little about yourself."

Jack watched the back of Collin McCauley's neck as it turned a fire red color. Jack noticed a tightening in the neck and shoulder muscles. After a pause, Collin McCauley rose to his feet and clenched his hands into two tight fists that were double the size of Jack's. Jack noticed that the freckles covered every inch of the boy's body from what he could tell. It was after Collin stood up that Jack could see Mrs. Cartwright standing at the front of the class.

There was a long pause of silence before Mrs. Cartwright said, "Perhaps you could start with where you came from, Mr. McCauley."

"I lived in Jackson, Mississippi and after that we lived in Hanover, Ohio. My father worked on building the canal there. He doesn't work there anymore so we moved here. Me Dah is hoping to find work on the docks," Collin said.

The class began to snicker and Anthony Patrone said out loud, "What's a me Dah?" Then the entire class began to snicker. All but Jack, that is, for he felt sorry for this newcomer.

Judy Lennington

"Class, class," Mrs. Cartwright said tapping her desk with a wooden stick she used as a pointer on the blackboard. "That will be enough!" The class instantly went silent. Jack watched as Collin allowed his head to fall forward so that he could only see the floor. "Mr. McCauley is obviously Irish. For those of you who are unfamiliar with the Irish, I will tell you that they often use words that are quite different than ours. There is nothing wrong with these words, we are merely unfamiliar to them. Dah is a word used to describe Dad, Daddy, or Father. Some of you use the term Ma to describe your Mother. They use the same term. Their language isn't all that different than our own and I will expect each one of you in this classroom to use respect and manners regarding Mr. McCauley," she said. "You may have a seat, Collin."

Just as Collin sat down, Mrs. Cartwright said, "Excuse me Collin. Would you mind terribly trading places with Jack? He's the boy sitting behind you."

"Trade places Jackie boy," Anthony said, sneering.

"That will be enough Anthony Patrone! Another word spoken out of turn from you will result in your sitting in the corner for the remainder of the day," Mrs. Cartwright said. With that statement, the class giggled. "That is enough class," Mrs. Cartwright said, striking the desk with her wooden stick.

Jack and Collin traded places then. Jack sat at his desk with his hands folded in front of him. Now Mrs. Cartwright gave the class a reading assignment so she could start her lessons with the first grade. She would work her way across the room, each row being a different grade until she reached the last row. It would be recess time after that, and she would begin again when they returned from recess. Then they would eat their lunch and play until the afternoon bell rang. Mrs. Cartwright would work her way across the room one last time before the bell rang to excuse the class for the day.

The first recess bell rang and Jack held back as the rest of the children made their way out the door. It was a chilly spring day. Mrs. Cartwright took this time to erase the black board and prepare for class to resume. Jack noticed Collin standing by two oak trees watching the other children playing. He began to approach the new boy when he noticed Melvin Riley and Anthony Patrone walking that way. Jack held back and watched. The boys taunted Collin, and Collin stood there taking it. Jack saw a lot of himself in Collin McCauley. He wanted to go to his aid, but fear kept him from moving. Just when it looked like Collin McCauley had had all he was going to take; the bell rang and everyone ran for the door. Jack watched as Collin McCauley waited for the others to enter the school house before he began walking in that direction. Jack followed at a distance.

As Mrs. Cartwright worked her way to the row of four third graders, they were asked to take turns reading from their reading books. When Jack's turn came, Milly Thompson turned in her seat and stuck her tongue out at him. The class snickered and Mrs. Cartwright immediately called for order. Jack read his paragraph and sat down. Now it was Collin's turn to read. His paragraph was a short one and that was a good thing, for Collin McCauley had to sound out every word in the paragraph and often Mrs. Cartwright was required to assist him in figuring out what the word was. Jack really felt sorry for Collin, for he knew this young man was going to be taunted twice as much as Jack was. He decided that it would be in his best interest to stay away from the new kid. His life was miserable enough as it was.

Judy Lennington

Mrs. Cartwright wrote some spelling words upon the blackboard and instructed the third graders to write each word ten times on their slates. Now she moved to the fourth graders in the next row. Jack began writing and as he concentrated on every letter, he forgot about his problems and the new boy, Collin McCauley the Irish boy with orange hair and freckles.

The bell rang and Jack reached under his desk for his lunch tin. He knew he would find a thick slice of bread all buttered and sprinkled with sugar wrapped in a cloth napkin. There would also be an apple that his grandparents kept in wooden barrels buried in the cellar wall throughout the winter months. Soon the trees would sprout new blossoms and shortly after they fell off, the new fruit would begin to grow and ripen. Jack liked apples. His grandmother could make so many good treats out of them. He carried his tin outside and sat down under one of the large trees to eat. As he did this, he scanned the playground, looking for Collin McCauley. He found him sitting on the steps that led up into the schoolhouse. He was holding a stick and slapping it against the wooden banister. He was not eating any lunch and Jack didn't see any signs of a lunch tin around him anywhere. He knew the Christian thing to do was to offer the lad some of his lunch. He also knew that by doing such a thing, the others would pounce upon them both with taunts that would bring tears to Jack's eyes. Jack had been through this so many times lately. It seemed he was the prime target in the playground. If those nasty girls didn't get to him, Melvin and Anthony did. He usually ended up crying, as much as he hated himself for it. He even cried when he was alone and remembering. Why did he have to be so darn sensitive? Well, hopefully all that was in the past. Maybe, just maybe, the new kid would become the prime target and they would leave Jack alone.

As Jack watched, Milly Thompson and Lynette Raines skipped over to stand in front of Collin. Jack could not hear what was being said, but from Lynette's mannerisms he assumed they had begun taunting him. Collin jumped to his feet and placed both hands upon his hips. He leaned close so that his face was only inches away from Lynette's. Jack rose to his feet and moved closer for a better view of what was transpiring. He was not the only one. Nearly the entire playground occupants had stopped what they were doing and began to circle them.

"What do you know?" Collin asked. "You're nothing but a stupid girl. Everyone knows that girls are stupid. Go play, stupid girls. Go on before I give you a good thumping." Collin was holding his fist in the air.

"You're not supposed to hit girls!" someone from the crowd yelled out. Jack moved closer. He watched as Collin stood nose to nose with Lynette Raines, clenching his fists tightly.

"You're the one who is stupid. You can't even read," Milly Thompson shouted.

Now Collin turned to face Milly. Again, he stood with his fists clenched. "Get away from me you stupid girls!" he shouted.

"Stupid Collin McCauley. Stupid Collin McCauley. He can't read. What else can't you do stupid Collin McCauley?" Milly taunted.

Jack caught movement in the background. Mrs. Cartwright had heard the commotion and was coming to the door. It was at that exact moment that Collin took a deep breath, unclenched his fists, and shoved Milly Thompson hard. She stumbled backward and fell upon her back on the ground. She saw Mrs. Cartwright in the door and began to cry hysterically, "He shoved me. He hurt me. That big meanie hurt me."

Mrs. Cartwright grabbed Collin by the ear and began to pull him up the steps and inside the school house. Collin winced in pain, but made no sounds. Everyone gathered just outside the door, watching.

"Bend over the desk, young man!" Mrs. Cartwright demanded.

Collin did as he was instructed, gripping the edge of the desk with both hands and looking toward the crowd that was watching him.

"I don't know how things are done in your home or where you came from, but here in Wellsville, Ohio, we do not hit, shove, or bully little girls," Mrs. Cartwright said, taking the large wooden paddle in both hands. She swung and the crack could be heard distinctly from where Jack stood. His eyes were fixed upon Collin McCauley's face. He showed no emotion. Mrs. Cartwright swung again, and again, Collin continued to stare at the crowd watching with only a blank stare. Mrs. Cartwright gave Collin six good whacks, and it didn't seem to have any effect on the lad.

Jack couldn't believe what he was witnessing. Even Melvin Riley squealed like a girl when Mrs. Cartwright wacked at him with that heavy oak slab. Mrs. Cartwright rang the bell and everyone hurried to their seats. Jack hung back and watched as Collin stood up straight and walked to his seat like nothing had happened. Jack walked up the aisle to the third desk in the third-grade row. He looked down at Milly who pouted, with her bottom lip sticking out. Jack knew it was all for show. As he walked past Lynette, her lips curled up into half a smile. She was taunting him. He looked up at Collin McCauley, who stared him straight in the eye. He had a look of defiance upon his face. At that moment, Jack knew that he was going to do everything in his power to become Collin McCauley's friend. The third-grade boys would have to stick together.

The rest of the day went quickly. Jack studied his spelling words, for they were having a test tomorrow. He wrote every word ten times. He did his multiplication tables twice and only got three of them wrong. Mrs. Cartwright rang the bell and Jack grabbed his lunch tin. He turned to say something to Collin, but he brushed past Jack quickly as he made his way to the door. Jack hurried and followed Collin outside. He looked around and saw his grandfather making his way up the dirt street toward the school yard.

Melvin Riley began to taunt Collin. Jack followed at a distance, watching Collin closely. Collin turned and looked back at the schoolhouse. Mrs. Cartwright was standing on the steps watching the children leave. Collin clenched his fists and began to walk toward the street, facing Jack's grandfather. Jack followed at a safe pace. All the while, Melvin continued to dart about Collin, taunting him. Anthony Patrone came running out of nowhere and began to join in the taunt.

Jack noticed that Collin was just a little bigger than both Melvin and Anthony. He appeared to be about the same age, but he was only in the third grade. It dawned upon Jack that Collin must have failed a few years and was held back, for he surely looked to be the same age as Melvin and Anthony.

Collin looked back again. They were out of sight of the school yard now. Mrs. Cartwright could no longer see them. Collin turned quickly, and before anyone knew what was happening, he punched Melvin Riley in the face, hard enough to put him on the ground. Melvin's nose was bleeding profusely. Anthony stopped and stared down at his friend. Collin jumped toward Anthony and he turned to run away. Collin stood over Melvin with both hands on his hips. "You cause me any more problems, boy, and I'm going to give you another go," Collin said, through clenched teeth.

Lester was close now. "Jack, Jack, come here," Lester called out.

Jack looked back at Collin and smiled. "What are you looking at Punk?" Collin asked.

"I'm Jack. Jack Gideon," Jack said. "I'd like to be your friend."

Collin stood watching Jack with his eyes narrowed. "Jack, come on, it's time to go home now," Lester called.

"I'll see you tomorrow, Collin," Jack called out as he ran toward his grandfather. He looked over his shoulder and saw Collin making his way down the dirt street alone, while Melvin Riley lay on the ground holding his bleeding nose and crying like a girl.

"What was going on back there?" Lester asked, placing his arm around Jack's shoulders.

"It had nothing to do with me, Grandfather. We have a new kid in school. His name is Collin McCauley. He's Irish. He was just getting acquainted with Melvin and Anthony," Jack said, with a big smile.

"I could see that," Lester said. "It appears they are going to be great friends."

"I hope he is going to be my friend. Nobody will pick on me anymore if Collin is with me. I won't have to worry about having my toys taken from me or about being called names either," Jack said.

"Well, Jack, I wasn't aware it was that bad for you," Lester said.

"Oh, it won't be bad anymore, Grandfather. Not anymore it won't," Jack said, smiling.

The evening went by slowly. Jack cleaned his plate up and when his father got home he sat at the table telling him every detail of what happened. Sheldon listened and at times, Jack caught a glimpse of a smile trying to creep across his father's lips. Finally, Jack finished the events of the day. Sheldon carried his plate to the porcelain dish pan and washed it. He dried it and returned it to the shelf with the others. "I think I saw that McCauley boy's father in the shop today looking for work. He's a big brute with orange curly hair. I didn't get a chance to talk to him," Sheldon said, turning to look down at his son.

"Are they gonna hire him, Daddy?" Jack asked.

"Are they going to hire him?" Sheldon repeated. "I don't know. I do not have access to that information. He certainly looks like a hard worker, I'll give him that. They don't hire many Irishmen, Jack."

"Why not, Daddy?" Jack asked.

"Well, they like their drink too much. Often, they don't make it to work on time. The Irish are a smart lot, but they have a reputation for being brawlers and drunkards," Sheldon explained.

"I think Collin is a brawler. I don't see anything wrong with that. It comes in handy sometimes," Jack said.

"Yes, that may be so, but it's the drunkards that give them a bad name," Sheldon said rustling Jack's hair. "Now off to bed with you. I'll be up in a minute."

Jack climbed the ladder to the loft. He covered up and waited for his father to say a prayer with him before he, too, went to bed. Jack laid there staring up at the wooden lathed ceiling. He hoped Collin's father found employment in Wellsville somewhere. If he couldn't, they may move on and Jack would be right back where he was before Collin came to town. He fell asleep, anxiously awaiting morning and another day of school.

Jack stirred when his father climbed down the ladder to go to work. He forced his eyes open to find it was still dark. He closed them again and went back to sleep. He did manage to rise before his grandfather called up the ladder to him. As he climbed down the ladder he found his grandmother stirring the oatmeal in a pot that hung over the red embers in the fireplace. "You're up early, Lad," she said.

"Yes Ma'am. I slept well enough, I reckon," Jack replied. "Where is Grandfather?"

"He's out at the privy. He'll be in shortly," Delores said.

It was at that moment the door opened and Lester entered the kitchen. "Phew! It's starting to rain a little out there," Lester said. "You best wear some extra clothing to school today, Jack."

"Yes Sir," Jack said dancing about. He darted out the door and ran toward the narrow building at the side of the house. He closed the door behind him and stood listening to the rain pelting at the roof as he relieved himself. He closed his eyes and looked upward as he fastened his breeches. He pulled his suspenders up over his shoulders and opened the door. The rain began to fall harder now. It was coming straight down. Jack took a deep breath and darted toward the porch.

As he entered the kitchen, Delores was pouring him a cup of tea. "You drink this hot tea before you go off to school, Jack. I don't think your Grandfather is going to go with you this morning. He can't move along fast enough with his bad knees and he'll be soaked through before he gets far. Besides, he'll slow you down and you will arrive at school soaked through too."

"Oh, that's okay, Grandmother," Jack said, sipping from the cup of tea. "I don't need Grandfather to walk me to school anymore. I can manage on my own."

Lester smiled as he pulled out a chair and slowly lowered himself to sit upon it. "Jack, here, has a new friend at school. It appears there are newcomers in Wellsville and they have a boy in Jack's class," he said.

"Oh, I hadn't heard," Delores said. "What is his name?"

"Collin McCauley," Jack replied.

"McCauley?" Delores asked looking over at Jack.

"Yes, that's right, Grandmother. Do you know the name?" Jack asked.

"I know it's an Irish name," Delores said, sitting down across from Jack.

"Yes, he's Irish. He's a big Irish boy too. I think he must have failed a few years, because I am certain he is older than I am. However, he is in the third grade and I hope to make him my friend," Jack said, reaching out to clasp his grandparent's hands. Lester Gideon said the morning prayer. Jack looked across the table at his grandmother. "Is there something wrong with having an Irishman for a friend, Grandmother?"

"Oh no, Jack," Delores said, shaking her head. "They are God's children too."

Jack ate his breakfast and stood near the door looking out at the pouring rain. "I suppose it wouldn't hurt for you to be a little late today," Lester said.

"Oh no, Grandfather. I must be on time today. I don't want to make Mrs. Cartwright angry with me," Jack replied.

"I don't think Mrs. Cartwright will be angry with you if you are a little late due to the adverse weather," Delores said. "After all, she lives right next door."

"I know that, Grandmother, but she expects all of us to be on time for class. Besides, maybe Milly and Lynette won't go to school today. I look forward to a day without them two girls sticking their tongues out at me," Jack said.

Judy Lennington

Lester smiled up at his wife from where he sat at the table. "I suppose you know best," he said to Jack. "Just try not to get too soaked."

"Don't worry, Grandfather. Mrs. Cartwright will have the stove hot when I get there. She makes us all hang our coats on pegs on the wall around the stove. By the time, I come home, my coat will be nice and dry," Jack said, without looking back.

"Well then, you better be off with you," Lester said.

Delores placed Jack's coat around his shoulders and held his lunch tin while he pulled it on. He buttoned his coat and took the lunch tin from her. "Thank you, Grandmother," he said, smiling up at her. He went to stand on the porch and stared out at the pouring rain. While Delores and Lester watched from the window he bolted out into the pouring rain and disappeared down the street.

"Well, I seem to recall doing the same thing a time or two in my day," Lester said, working his way back to the table. "I don't think I'll be doing it again though."

Delores giggled. "It's a good thing you can't because I know I wouldn't be able to keep up with you." She began to pour him another cup of coffee.

Jack darted through the rain and reached the school house in hardly any time at all. He was out of breath and soaked through to his undershirt by the time he arrived. There weren't many students there this morning. Jack looked at the second-grade row and noticed that it was empty. He was happy to see that the girls were absent, but disappointed to find that Collin McCauley was not there, either. He placed his tin on his desk and removed his coat. He had no trouble finding an empty peg to hang his wet coat on, for over half of the seats were empty this morning.

Harry Moser was placing more wood in the fire. He was the only eleventh grader and the oldest student in school. Most of the other young people his age had long since quit school to either marry and raise a family, or go to work somewhere to prevent being a burden upon their family. Harry's family wanted him to graduate and go on to college. He was going to study law and become a lawyer. Only two other people had ever graduated from school in Wellsville up till this point. Times were hard and families struggled to make ends meet. Harry was tall and thin. He had thick dark hair and hairy arms and chest. Jack thought he was perhaps the hairiest person he had ever seen, leaving Jack to wonder if that had anything to do with the name his parents gave him. Jack watched as Harry poked at the fire with a poker before closing the door and going to his seat.

Mrs. Cartwright hit the desk with her pointed stick. "Alright, children. Take your seats please," she called out above the rumble of young voices. The door opened and in walked Collin McCauley, soaked to the skin. He wore no coat or shoes. His pants were dripping water and his red hair was pasted to his head, dripping water into his eyes. Mrs. Cartwright smiled and nodded her head in his direction. He went to sit at the desk behind Jack.

There were two empty rows to Jack's right as the Huffman twins, who were the only first graders, were absent and the only second graders, Milly and Lynette, were also absent. Mrs. Cartwright stood at the front of the row and said, "I'm going to read off your spelling words and I want you to write them down on your slates. Are you ready?"

Jack nodded his head. He couldn't see Collin behind him, but he assumed he had nodded his head also. "Let us begin," Mrs. Cartwright said. "Program." Jack wrote quickly. He did not have

Judy Lennington

to think about it. He had been writing his spelling words all week. "Direction," she said. Mrs. Cartwright called out ten words that had been their weekly lesson and Jack knew every one of them. When she finished calling out the words, she took Jack's slate and studied what he had written. She marked the slate with and "A" and moved to Collin's slate. Jack did not turn around, but he heard her writing on the slate. It seemed she wrote a lot. Collin must have gotten a lot of the words wrong. She went to stand at the front of the row again. "Now for your next assignment, I want you to arrange those spelling words in alphabetical order," she said. She went to the row where the seventh graders sat. Only two of the four seventh graders had made it to class today.

Jack worked diligently on arranging his words in alphabetical order. He listened for the sound of chalk on slate behind him. It was quiet, and Jack assumed Collin was having trouble with the assignment. He didn't dare turn around. If Mrs. Cartwright saw him she would assume he was copying from Collin and they both would get an "F". Jack finished his words and sat with his hands folded upon his desk until Mrs. Cartwright finished with the older students.

Jack's mind would wonder and then something Mrs. Cartwright said would catch his attention. "General George Washington made his way down the Ohio River from Pittsburgh with a soldier named William Crawford in 1770. Jack sat up straight. General George Washington? Was that the same George Washington that was president? How interesting the older classmate's studies were. Jack couldn't wait until he was old enough to study such things.

Mrs. Cartwright was making her way back toward his row now. "Collin McCauley!" she said sharply. Jack jumped and he felt the desk behind him jolt as well. "We do our sleeping in the night, young man. That is not why we are here. Perhaps if you spent more time studying in class and less time sleeping, you would not have failed your spelling test."

The room was quiet. Jack could not help but think that if the girls had been in class today they would have been giggling. For that matter, so would Melvin and Anthony.

"Now, let's have a look at your spelling list," Mrs. Cartwright said, walking up the aisle to stand behind Jack's desk. "My, oh, my," she said. "I am afraid you are going to need to stay after school every day until you catch up with Jack here." Before Jack realized what was happening, his hand was in the air. "What is it, Jack?" she asked.

"I don't mind helping Collin. I would stay after school to help him, Mrs. Cartwright," Jack said.

"What have you to say on the matter, Mr. McCauley?" Mrs. Cartwright asked. Collin sat staring down at his desktop. "Well? Which is it going to be, Collin?"

Collin nodded his head. "I'll study with Jack," he said.

Mrs. Cartwright turned to look down at Jack. "You will need to bring written permission from you father, Jack. I will need his permission to keep you after school."

"What about permission from my grandparents, Mrs. Cartwright?" Jack asked.

Mrs. Cartwright nodded her head and said, "That will do." Then she turned and walked to the front of the class. She turned quickly and looked back at Collin. Jack assumed it was to ensure that he was still awake. Jack wanted to turn around and tell Collin that he was looking forward to working with him and becoming friends, but he knew better. Mrs. Cartwright would be watching. It would have to keep until recess.

The recess bell rang and everyone jumped from their seats. Jack turned to speak to Collin, but he brushed past Jack as if he wasn't even there. It was still pouring down rain outside. The older boys that made it to school today began to move the school desks to the side of the room. Someone got the long rope that hung on a peg and they began to play high jump. This was the game they usually played on rainy days. Two students would stand on opposite sides of the room with one end of the rope in their hands. Everyone would form a line and jump over the rope. When the last student crossed the rope, it was raised a little higher, and they would jump it again. As this continued, the rope got higher and higher. If you did not have a clean jump over the rope, you were disqualified until there was one person left. That person was the winner and got to ring the recess bell at lunch time.

Jack had never won this game. He was too little. Usually it was Harry Moser who won. He was the oldest and had the longest legs. Jack was disqualified after the sixth pass. He stood along the side and watched, as Collin McCauley was still in the competition.

On bad days, such as today, Mrs. Cartwright would let the recess run into overtime. Today it would last until the game had ended. It wouldn't be much longer, as there weren't that many students present today.

The competition was down to two last contestants, Harry Moser and Collin McCauley. Around and around they went, both clearing the rope. Finally, it got so high that the two students holding it couldn't reach any higher. Mrs. Cartwright declared it a draw and announced that the desks were to be moved back to the center of the room.

Harry sulked, as he had never been beaten before. He was a quiet lad, and wasn't one to gloat, but he wasn't happy about the possibility of being defeated by the new kid. Collin didn't say much either, but he kept glancing over at Harry as they moved the desks. Soon Jack was sitting in his usual spot waiting for Mrs. Cartwright to give him another assignment.

Collin avoided Jack at lunch time as well. Jack felt disappointed. He was hoping Collin would be his new friend. He knew there was an age difference, but they were in the same grade. They had so much in common. They both hated the girls. As the day wore on, Jack became fretful of how to approach Collin at the end of the day. The rain had slowed down to a light drizzle. Everyone's coats were warm and dry from hanging near the wood stove all day. Jack pulled his coat on and looked over at Collin, who pulled his collar up around his bare neck. He did not wear a coat. He also wore no shoes. Jack began to approach him, as Collin darted through the door and made a dash for home in the rain. Jack took a deep breath and gripped his lunch tin tightly as he darted out the door as well. He ran in the opposite direction. He didn't stop running until he was on the porch of his grandparent's house.

Lester was placing a block of wood on the fire in the kitchen when Jack entered. "Hang up your wet coat, boy," he said, without looking up.

Jack placed his lunch tin on the sideboard and proceeded to remove his coat. He hung it on a peg near the door. When he turned around, his grandmother was waiting with a slice of bread, buttered and sprinkled with brown sugar. Jack smiled over at her and went straight to the table to eat his snack.

"How was your day?" Lester asked.

Jack chewed to empty his mouth before answering. "It was fine. Actually, it was a good day because the girls weren't in school today. Me and Collin McCauley were the only third graders there today." Jack took another bite of his bread and spoke with his mouth full, "You should see that Collin jump, Grandfather." He looked over at his grandparents frowning at him speaking with his mouth full. "Sorry," he said. He swallowed and quickly took another bite. He ate until the bread was gone. Then he began to explain his day.

"Collin fell asleep in school. He failed his spelling test and Mrs. Cartwright said I need a note from one of you, or from Daddy, giving me permission to stay after school to help him catch up with the rest of us. He don't know nothing, Grandma. He can't spell, he can't cypher and he doesn't even know how to put words in alphabetical order. He needs help really bad," Jack said, looking across the table at his grandparents.

"Well, now Jack," Delores began, "some of those Irishmen move around a lot. It is quite possible that he never really went to school much before. You really shouldn't blame the boy. I reckon it wouldn't hurt for you to help him out some, but I think we should discuss this with your father first."

"I don't see Daddy minding if I was helping someone out. He is always telling me to be kind to others. Collin doesn't have any real friends, and I aim to make him my friend. The way I see it, he and I have a lot in common beings we both hate Milly and Lynette. Those girls are mean to both of us. Collin gave Milly something to remember when he shoved her to the ground. I'll bet she thinks twice about teasing him from now on. And you should have seen the way he thumped old Melvin Riley. Collin bloodied his nose real good. Yes Sir, I aim to make Collin my friend. The way I see it, if you have a friend like Collin with you, there ain't nobody going to mess with you," Jack explained.

Lester took a deep breath. "I saw that Irish boy punch the Riley boy in the nose. I am not sure that is the kind of friend you should link up with boy."

Jack had a puzzled look on his face. "Grandfather, I am tired of being picked on all the time. Everyone is either much bigger than me or they are girls who I'm not supposed to combat. Didn't you wish, just once when you were my age, that you had someone who could look out for you?"

Delores looked over at Lester and raised her eyebrows. Lester's face flushed and he squirmed in his chair. "I didn't have anyone bully me when I was your age," he replied.

"Nobody? Were you the bully?" Jack asked.

"Of course, not, Jack," Lester replied. "I had friends, but there wasn't as many children here in Wellsville when I was your age."

"I know Mr. Griffin was your friend. I remember his saying so. I remember you had that Limpy guy for a friend too," Jack said.

"Limpy wasn't a boy, Jack. He was an old man when I met him. You best go get out of your school clothes. You can help me put new soles on my shoes when you come back down. I've been shuffling my feet so much, I plum wore a hole in the bottom of my shoes," Lester said.

Jack wanted to ask more questions, but knew better. He rose from his chair and climbed the ladder to the loft where he proceeded to remove his school clothes. He hung them on a peg and put his play clothes on. He stood in the center of the room and tried to imagine this loft when his father was his age. Sheldon was the youngest of four children who slept up here. He had one brother and two sisters. Jack shook his head at the thought of having two sisters. He hated girls. He wasn't happy being an only child, but if it meant having sisters, he was happy

Judy Lennington

with the way things turned out. He thought about Collin and wondered if Collin was an only child. He knew nothing about Collin McCauley. He hoped to change all that and he would start tomorrow. Jack climbed the ladder down to the kitchen once more. His grandfather had already removed the soles from his shoes and was working on smoothing out a piece of cowhide.

"You draw an outline of my shoes for me Jack, and I will cut it out," Lester said, pointing at the shoes with the knife he held in his hand.

Jack placed the floppy shoe on the flattened leather and began to draw an outline with a charred piece of wood. It put down a black mark around the shoe. Lester began cutting it out while Jack outlined the second shoe. "Go wash your hands," Lester instructed, when Jack was finished.

"You want me to help you do some cutting?" Jack asked.

"No, I can do that part, Son," Lester said. "See if your grandmother needs any help with supper."

Jack stood up and went to the wash basin. He washed his hands good and dried them on a towel that laid folded next to the basin. "Dump that dirty water, Jack, before it gets spilled on my floor," his grandmother said.

Jack carried the basin outside and tossed the water over the side of the porch. It was a chilly evening and the sun was beginning to disappear behind the dark clouds. It would be dark early tonight. Soon school would be out and Jack would be playing outdoors until it got dark. He carried the basin back inside.

Lester was still working on his shoe when Sheldon got home from work. He put his labors aside and sat at the dinner table bare footed. It was Jack's turn to say grace this evening. He knew better than to rush through it even though he was very hungry. When he finished, his grandmother nodded her head in approval. "How was your day?" Lester asked Sheldon.

"It was alright. We hired a couple new guys today. I think the one might be that Irishman we were talking about," Sheldon said, before taking a bite of his dinner.

Jack perked up in his chair and asked with a mouth full, "Is his name McCauley? Collin's last name is McCauley." Everyone was watching him. Jack knew he spoke out of turn and he spoke with a mouth full of food. "Excuse me. I'm sorry," he said, swallowing hard to get it all down.

Sheldon had a fork full of food, all ready to put in his mouth. He paused and said, "I don't know the guy's name, but he's definitely Irish. You can't miss that curly red hair."

Jack swallowed before saying, "I hope it is Collin's dad. I think he needs a job bad. Collin doesn't even have a pair of shoes."

"I can relate to that," Lester said, laughing. It grew quiet while they ate.

After some time, Delores said, "Jack here thinks he might like to become friends with Collin McCauley. He thinks he might come in handy as an ally against the bullies."

Sheldon frowned and looked over at Jack. "Are you still having trouble with the Riley and Patrone boys?" he asked.

"Yeah, they pick on Collin too, but he fights back. He gave them a good go of it and I don't think they will mess with him anymore. The way I see it, if he's my friend, they might just leave me alone too. Why he even had a round with the girls. I think they are afraid of him. I see that as real helpful too," Jack said, before scraping his plate with the last bite of bread.

"I'm not so sure that is a healthy reason for a friendship," Sheldon said, looking over at Jack.

"You ain't the guy getting thumped all the time," Jack said, looking up at his father. "Excuse me Sir, I meant no disrespect, but there isn't another boy my age in Wellsville. A guy needs to protect himself anyway he can. At least, that's the way I sees it."

A smile crept over Sheldon's face as he looked down at his plate. "Well, I suppose a new guy could use a friend. Just don't let me hear you getting into trouble because of your association with this boy. As I understand it, he is a lot older than you."

"I don't know how old he rightly is, Daddy, but I think he's probably about the same age as Melvin and Anthony. They look to be about the same size and all," Jack said.

"Mrs. Cartwright has asked permission for Jack to stay after school every evening to tutor the McCauley boy. It appears he is behind in his lessons," Delores said.

Sheldon looked over at Jack. "Do you want to stay after school every evening?"

Jack nodded his head. "The way I see it, it won't be so bad. We only have a few more weeks of school anyway. Collin could sure use the help. He can't spell or cypher. I don't think he knows his ABC's either. He could use all the help he can get."

Sheldon sighed. "Well, I suppose it can't hurt. Mrs. Cartwright will be there too. I guess it will be alright," he said.

"You will need to write a note for Mrs. Cartwright," Jack said. "She told me I need written permission."

"I can do that. I'll do it right after dinner," Sheldon said.

"I have to finish my shoe," Lester said. "I can work on the other one tomorrow." He rose from his chair and shuffled his way back to the three-legged stool near the fire place.

"Help your grandmother clear the table, Jack," Sheldon said, pushing his chair back.

"Yes, Sir," Jack replied. He jumped to his feet and began carrying the dirty dishes to the sideboard where his grandmother stood scraping the plates before she washed them. When the table was cleared, he washed it off and returned to his chair.

Delores was washing the dishes in the basin on the sideboard. Lester was working on his shoe near the fireplace, and Sheldon sat at the table staring into the flickering flames. Occasionally, an ember would snap and fly out onto the wooden floor, burning a black spot on the boards. Jack sat on a chair near his father, kicking his legs as he daydreamed.

"What are you thinking about Jack?" Sheldon asked, as he lit his pipe.

"I was thinking about tomorrow. Everyone will probably be back in school tomorrow. I hope I manage to warm up to Collin early on, so I don't have no trouble with Melvin and Anthony," Jack replied.

"I believe you don't want any trouble with Melvin and Anthony," Sheldon said, smiling over at Jack.

"Yeah, that's right, I don't," Jack said.

"No Jack," Sheldon began, "You said you don't want no trouble with Melvin and Anthony. The correct phrase would be you don't want any trouble with Melvin and Anthony. If you are going to tutor your new friend after school, you might want to brush up on your studies, yourself," Sheldon said.

"Ah, right. You're right, Father. I'm sorry," Jack said.

"I'm also not certain your reason for wanting Collin McCauley for a friend is a very valid reason. Have you given any thought to what he is getting out of being your friend?" Sheldon asked.

"What do you mean?" Jack asked. "I'm going to help him with his studies, Father. That should get Mrs. Cartwright off his back."

"But, if you weren't being bullied at school, would you bother with Collin McCauley? Would you try to be his friend, if there wasn't something in it for you?" Sheldon asked, puffing on his pipe.

"Your father has a valid point, Jack," Lester said.

"I don't know, I might, I suppose," Jack replied.

"A friend is something very special. It is something that you take with you for the rest of your life," Lester said, without looking up.

"Without Collin McCauley for a friend, I might not have a very long life," Jack said.

Sheldon smiled. "I doubt those boys would kill you, Jack. If you were dead, who would they pick on? Did you ever stop to think that maybe they get bullied by boys older than they are?"

Jack frowned and replied, "I've never seen them being bullied by anyone. Maybe the girls sometimes, but they bully everyone. They are just dumb old girls."

"Careful there, young man," Lester said. "Your grandmother was a girl once, and I don't think I recall a time when she was dumb."

"I'm sorry, Grandmother," Jack said.

"No offense taken, Jack. Besides, I know that there will come a time when you will feel quite differently about girls," Delores said, as she dried her hands on her apron.

"It seems to me you spend a lot of time fretting over something that might happen tomorrow and less time worrying about what occurred today," she said, as she began to stack the clean dishes on a shelf.

Sheldon removed the pipe from his mouth and asked, "Do you have homework, Jack?"

"No Sir," Jack replied.

Bend in The River

While gripping the pipe tightly between his teeth, Sheldon stood up and said, "I'm going to bathe before bed. I feel like there is ten pounds of grit hanging on my arms tonight." He went to the kettle of hot water hanging on a hook over the fire. He dipped out some hot water into a basin and added some cool water from the bucket. Jack went back to staring at the flickering flames. At times, he thought she saw faces or figures in them.

"Your grandfather could tell you a thing or two about real friendships, Jack," Sheldon said, as he pulled his shirt over his head.

Jack remembered his grandfather mentioning a man with a wooden leg. He sat up straight and asked, "Were you friends with the one-legged man, Grandfather?"

"I was indeed, Jack. We became the best of friends," Lester said, smiling.

"He was older than you, wasn't he?" Jack asked.

"Oh yes, he was much older than me. It wasn't anything like you and your friend Collin. Limpy was an old man when I first laid eyes on him. I wasn't much older than you are right now," Lester explained.

"What about you, Grandmother? Did you know Limpy?" Jack asked looking over at his grandmother.

Delores shook her head. "I didn't know either one of them very well. I was at the age when I didn't put much stalk in boys." She smiled and added, "I suppose I felt the way about boys that you feel about the girls, Jack. You see, it is something we all go through. Those girls that tease you aren't all that much different than you are, Son."

"What about Mr. Griffin? I thought he was your friend," Jack said.

- 61 -

Judy Lennington

"He was, but he was a year older than I was, and Limpy wasn't very popular back then. Not many of the kids in the area had anything to do with him. In fact, as I recall, most of them were instructed to stay away from old Limpy," Lester said, looking over at Jack.

"How did you come to meet him?" Jack asked.

"Well, let's see now;" Lester said, looking upward. "The first time I saw Limpy he was passed out in the doorway to McCall's Mercantile. The store was owned and run by Mrs. Dodge's father back then. It hasn't changed much over the years though." Lester took a deep breath and smiled. "Anyway, I was with my father and we were climbing the steps to the Mercantile. There was this heap of smelly rags blocking the door. Father poked at it with his cane, the same cane I'm using today, and it moved. Mr. McCall shouted from inside the store for him to get out of there. When he moved, I noticed he had a wooden leg."

"Did it go all the way up or just to the knee?" Jack asked.

"Oh, it went just above the knee, as I recall," Lester said.

"What did he do?" Jack asked.

"He limped off mumbling 'tween season voyage', I believe it was," Lester said.

"What did that mean?" Jack asked.

"Oh, that's a whaler's term, Jack," Lester began, "It means a short voyage."

"A short voyage," Jack repeated. "I don't understand."

"Limpy was always mumbling something nobody could understand. I suppose it meant he didn't get to linger long where he was," Lester replied.

"Was he drunk?" Jack asked. His grandmother turned sharply to look at him.

Bend in The River

Lester cleared his throat and nodded his head. "Limpy was always drunk in the early days."

"You said he was an old man, Grandfather," Jack said, leaning forward and placing his chin in his hands as he rested his elbows on the table.

"He was an old man Jack, but he wasn't from around here. He traveled a long way to get here," Lester said.

"Oh, I see," Jack said. "Tell me more."

"You've heard enough for one night, young man," Delores said. "You need to get some sleep. Off to bed with you, now."

Jack sighed and jumped to his feet. "Will you tell me more about Limpy, Grandfather?" he asked.

Lester nodded his head and said, "Some other time, Jack. You go off to bed like your grandmother said."

Jack began to climb the ladder that led to the loft. He paused and called down, "Don't forget to write that note for Mrs. Cartwright, Father."

"I won't forget, Jack. Good night Son," Sheldon called up to Jack.

Jack climbed the ladder and crawled to the spot where he slept. There were no windows in the loft. It was dark, with the exception to the flickering shadows put off by the candle. Jack pulled his clothes off and crawled beneath the blankets. He blew out the candle and laid staring up at the darkness that surrounded him. He was curious about his grandfather's friend, Limpy. But shortly his thoughts went to the prospects of having Collin McCauley as an ally. Collin wasn't very friendly, but Jack had to find a way to win his trust. He drifted off to sleep with visions of Collin punching Melvin Riley in the nose.

Jack's father was already gone when he descended the ladder the next morning. A note was folded neatly and waiting on the table for him. Jack smiled as he placed it carefully in his trousers pocket. He could hear the birds chirping outside as he laced his shoes. He made his way to the privy, while dodging the mud puddles. The rain had stopped and the sky was full of fluffy white clouds, with brilliant shades of red and gold behind them as the morning sun was rising. It looked like it was going to be a beautiful day. Unfortunately, that meant everyone would be in school today.

Jack dodged the mud puddles again as he made his way back to the house. He knew he was having oatmeal for breakfast because he smelled it when he got up this morning. His grandmother was placing a bowl on the table for him when he returned. Lester held a slice of bread affixed to a long stick close to the fire. Jack reached for the cream pitcher and began to pour it over his oatmeal. When the bread was toasted on both sides, his grandmother smothered it with butter and jelly. "Thank you," Jack replied very politely.

"It looks to be a nice day out there today, Jack," Lester said.

"Yes Sir, it does," Jack replied before taking a big bite of oatmeal.

"Will you be late from school today?" his grandmother asked.

"I'm not sure, Grandmother. I suppose it depends on Collin McCauley. I sure hope he starts his lessons today. He is behind in everything," Jack said.

"I wonder why the lad is going to school at all," Delores said, as she poured water into the pot that hung over the fire.

"It's the law, Mother," Lester said.

"I know that, Lester, but lots of boys his age is working in the mines. The law doesn't seem to care about them," Delores said.

Bend in The River

Jack listened to his grandparent's conversation as he ate his breakfast. At last it was time for him to leave for school. Lester placed the hat upon Jack's head and smiled down at him. "You have a good day today, Jack. We'll see you when you get home."

"Yes Sir," Jack said, nodding his head. His grandmother handed him his lunch tin and off he went.

Jack hung back, slowing his steps as he approached the school yard. Melvin and Anthony were picking on Lynette and Milly. Perhaps he could sneak past them unnoticed. He began to climb the steps to the school when Anthony turned and noticed him. "Look, there's Jack Sprat. What cha got in your lunch tin, Jack? Fat? Oh, no, you don't eat no fat, only lean," Anthony began to tease. Melvin began to laugh. Even the girls were laughing. Jack hung his head as he continued toward the open door. "Let me have a look," Melvin said, grabbing Jack's lunch tin.

Jack fought back the tears. He didn't want everyone to see him cry. That would only make it worse. "Give it back!" a voice boomed from behind Jack. He turned around to see Collin McCauley standing at the bottom of the steps. "I said, give it back!" he repeated.

Melvin handed Jack his lunch tin back. "Come on, Anthony," he said. As Anthony brushed past Jack he whispered, "I'll see you later when you don't have your hound dog to protect you, Punk!"

Jack closed his eyes. He was dead. Collin began to climb the steps and Jack noticed he was still barefooted. "Thanks," Jack said softly.

"I didn't do it for you," Collin said. "I did it because I don't like those two and I plan on making their lives miserable."

Jack smiled. "Well, that works for me," he said, following Collin inside the school house.

Judy Lennington

They took their seats. Jack tried not to look over at Melvin and Anthony as they sat near the front of the class in their row. Melvin sat in front with Anthony right behind him. The last student was Paul Harris. Nobody picked on Paul because his father was the constable. "He is lucky," Jack thought. "I wish my father was the town constable."

Jack knew his father was doing the best he could. There really weren't too many jobs to be had in Wellsville, unless you were lucky enough to have your own business. Melvin's father had died a long time ago, but that didn't seem to matter because he had Anthony for a friend. Anthony's father had a bar downtown. Jack noticed Melvin glancing over at him. He squirmed in his seat and sunk low, trying to avoid the stare.

Mrs. Cartwright began with the first-grade row. The Huffman twins listened to their instructions and from time to time they would nod their heads. She moved to the next row which was the second grade, with only two students, Lynette Raines and Milly Thompson. Now she had reached the third-grade row. She was looking straight at Jack. At that moment, he recalled the note in his pocket. He pulled it out and raised his hand high in the air.

"What is it, Jack?" Mrs. Cartwright asked.

"I brought the note you asked for, Mrs. Cartwright," Jack said.

Mrs. Cartwright walked past Vivian Gardner and Lewis Tully to take the note from Jack's hand. "Thank you, Jack," she said reading the note. She smiled down at him and looked behind him to where Collin McCauley sat. "Are you willing to stay after school to study with Jack, Mr. McCauley?"

"Yes, Ma'am," Jack heard Collin say.

Jack let out a sigh of relief. He smiled over at Anthony Patrone who was glaring at him. Now all he had to do was get Collin to be his friend.

Mrs. Cartwright walked to the front of the row and turned around. "I want you to write your multiplication tables from one through ten. There will be a test tomorrow," she said, looking straight at Collin. Jack turned and smiled at Collin. "Jack Gideon, turn around and mind your own business," Mrs. Cartwright said. Everyone burst into laughter. "That will be enough. It goes for all of you," Mrs. Cartwright said.

Jack felt his neck growing hot and his face flushing. He assumed everyone was watching him, however, he dared not look up from his slate. He began writing his multiplication numbers, pretending not to be affected by the scolding. Inside he was screaming out with embarrassment.

Mrs. Cartwright worked her way across the room until she came to the only twelfth grader in the school, Harry Moser. Next year Harry would go on to college to be the lawyer his father wanted him to be. Jack wondered how far he would go in school. It was true that most of the boys quit school to work in the coal mines around the area. Some worked on the docks along the river, but they only hired the older boys who could do the heavy lifting. The coal mines weren't that picky. In fact, the smaller you were, the better they liked it. Jack had even heard rumors that in some mines, they paid younger children, even girls, to work in the mines because they could get back in the smaller places. Jack didn't want to work in the mines. He wasn't too fond of going all the way to the twelfth grade, but he didn't want to work in the mines. He hoped he would grow more so he could work on the docks. Jack loved the river. He loved the smell of the water and the feeling of the heavy fog upon his face in the mornings. Most of all, he loved fishing on the bank with his father. That was his favorite thing about the river. He and his father had many interesting conversations while fishing along the river banks. Then there was the fish. Jack also loved the fish. They almost always had fish for dinner on Sunday's.

Jack finished his multiplication tables and folded his hands upon the desk waiting for Mrs. Cartwright to make her way back to his side of the room. He watched her as she stood next to Harry Moser's desk. They were having a discussion in soft voices. It appeared, to Jack, as though Mrs. Cartwright was helping Harry with a problem. Jack couldn't make out what they were saying. Mrs. Cartwright walked to her desk and picked up the recess bell. Jack's stomach told him it was lunch time, for it rumbled just as she began ringing the bell.

Jack had a favorite place to eat his lunch. He prayed no one else was there. In the school yard stood a large Elm tree with a humped air root that had been worn smooth from all the children playing on it over the years. Jack made his way to the root and sat down to eat his lunch, alone. He watched the girls playing a familiar game where they joined hands and skipped in a circle singing, "Ring around the roses." He looked to his left and noticed Melvin and Anthony sitting on the steps to the porch watching him. They were laughing and whispering. Something told him they were plotting some evil scheme against him.

He saw Collin step out onto the porch and walk up behind them. "Scram, you bums," Collin said. Melvin and Anthony jumped to their feet to let Collin past. Jack watched as Collin made his way straight toward him. Jack scooted over to allow room for Collin to sit down next to him.

"Hey Kid, are we doing this tutor thing after school today? I gotta know, cause I got things to do," Collin said.

"I think we should get started as soon as possible. School is almost out for the summer. There isn't much time and you have a long way to go to catch up," Jack said, swallowing hard. He hoped he hadn't insulted Collin. He didn't want to get on the wrong side of this young man.

"Okay, I'll stay after, but I have to be home before dark. I have responsibilities," Collin said.

"I understand. Mrs. Cartwright won't let us stay that late. She won't leave us here alone. Of course," Jack's mind was jumping ahead, "we could always meet after school anytime you want to work extra time on your lessons."

Collin narrowed his gaze at Jack as he thought about the proposition. "Humph," Collin sighed. "I'll have to think about that, Kid."

"You can call me Jack. If you want, that is," Jack said.

"Okay Kid, Jack," Collin said.

Jack took another bite of his sugar bread. His grandmother had sprinkled some shaved cinnamon onto the sugar this morning to make an extra treat. Jack noticed Collin had no lunch tin. He broke the bread in half and offered Collin a piece. Collin stared down at the sugary treat. Jack noticed he had a strange look as he stared at it. Collin took a deep breath and took the bread from Jack. He did not say thank you. He didn't say anything at all. He sat quietly next to Jack eating the bread. Jack wanted to smile, but refrained. Perhaps Collin would become his friend after all. Collin finished the bread and stood up. He walked off toward the privy without saying a word. Jack noticed the dastardly duo watching him leave. Once Collin was out of sight, Melvin and Anthony's attention went back to Jack.

Mrs. Cartwright stepped out onto the porch and rang the bell for them to return to class. Melvin and Anthony parted to allow the other children to climb the steps. Jack suspected they were waiting for him. He joined a group of children climbing the stairs in hopes that there was safety in numbers. He noticed Anthony stepping closer. Before Jack could respond, Anthony tripped him and he went face down in the soft mud left behind from the previous day's rain.

Jack felt the dampness soaking through his clothes. He stood up and wiped the thick ooze from his face. Everyone was laughing. "Hey Stupid, you have mud in your eye," Anthony said, leaning close. It was at that moment that Jack noticed Anthony's eyes bulging, and he began clawing at his collar. Collin McCauley had walked up behind him and was lifting him off the ground by the back of his coat.

"Mr. McCauley!" Mrs. Cartwright shouted from the porch above them. "That will be enough of that!"

Collin released Anthony and he dropped to his knees in the same mud Jack had fallen into. Melvin scrambled up the steps and disappeared into the school house.

"I will meet you at my desk inside, Mr. McCauley," Mrs. Cartwright said, pointing toward the open school door. Collin climbed the steps and disappeared inside the school house. Mrs. Cartwright stared down at Jack and Anthony, shaking her head. "You boys wash up before you take your seats. I'll not have all that mud in my school." She stood at the door and waited for Jack and Anthony to pass through before she closed the door behind them.

There was a half wall that separated the wash room from the classroom. A sideboard lined the wall and several pitchers of water and wash basins sat upon it. Anthony took the first basin he came to. Jack moved all the way down to the very last one, to be as far away from Anthony as possible. He could not see what was happening on the other side of the wall. It was quiet with the exception to the six whacks that Mrs. Cartwright was giving Collin. Jack pictured Collin taking the whacks as he had previously, with no cries or emotion. When Jack stepped beyond the wall he saw Collin sitting on a stool facing the corner to the right of the black board.

"Jack, you are soaked to the skin," Mrs. Cartwright said. She pulled a desk near the potbellied stove and pointed to it. "You sit here until you are dry."

Jack took a deep breath. He slid into the desk with his back to Collin McCauley and facing Anthony and Melvin. He tried not to look up, because he knew everyone was staring right at him. When he did look up, he noticed Melvin Riley and Anthony Patrone making faces at him. Milly Thompson stuck her tongue out at him. He looked over at Mrs. Cartwright who was writing on the blackboard and had her back to the class. He quickly looked down again. It was going to be a long afternoon.

At long last, Mrs. Cartwright rang the dismissal bell. Jack was dry by now, but remained at the front of the class. He turned around to see that Collin had not moved. He was still sitting up straight as a board with the cone shaped dunce hat upon his head. "You may be dismissed, Mr. McCauley. I hope you have learned a lesson today," she said.

"Yes Ma'am," Collin said, removing the hat and placing it on the stool.

"Jack, you do not have to tutor Mr. McCauley today if you want to go home and clean up," Mrs. Cartwright said.

Jack looked down at his dried, mud stained, clothes. "If it's alright with Collin, I would like to get started, Mrs. Cartwright."

"Very well, I'll leave it up to the two of you," Mrs. Cartwright said, sitting down at her desk. "I have papers to grade and you are welcome to stay until I've finished."

Jack looked over at Collin who nodded his head. They went to the back of the room near a window. Jack turned a desk around so that they faced each other. Jack wrote the alphabet on the slate, all in capital letters. "I'm going to teach you a song to help you remember the alphabet," Jack said. He pointed to each individual letter as he began singing softly, "A, B, C, D, E, F, G," on and on, until the end. Before long Collin was singing it along with Jack. Mrs. Cartwright's desk was behind Jack, but he noticed Collin looking in that direction often. Jack assumed Mrs. Cartwright was watching them.

Before long, Mrs. Cartwright called out to them, "You boys bring in some fire wood for tomorrow and then go home to your families."

Jack returned the desk to its rightful position and followed Collin outside to the wood pile. They carried several arm loads of wood inside and stacked it near the wood stove. Mrs. Cartwright was locking the door as they walked across the school yard together. "I'll see you tomorrow, Collin," Jack said, as they parted ways.

Collin frowned and asked, "How long before I can read and write whole words?"

Jack was surprised. "Collin, it has taken me three whole years to learn what I know, and I don't know all the words yet."

"I don't have three years. I need to larn to read and write whole words right away," Collin said, shaking his head.

"Well, we could work together more often, but it will still take a while for you to get where I am," Jack said.

"Tell you what, Kid, you help me larn how to read and write whole words, and I'll keep those two goons off your back. Deal?" Collin asked.

Jack smiled. "I'll do what I can. Working an hour after school every night isn't going to get you very far anytime soon. We will need to step up the studies. It may even require working all summer long."

"I'll do whatever it takes," Collin said.

"Why is it, suddenly, so important that you learn?" Jack asked.

"You don't need to worry about that, Kid. You just do your part and I'll keep them rats off your back," Collin said, frowning. "See you tomorrow, Kid."

He could hear Collin singing the alphabet song as he moved down the muddy dirt street toward home. He was humming when he entered the house. Lester was lifting a freshly filled bucket of water onto the sideboard. "You seem to be in a much better mood this afternoon, Jack. Had a good day, did you?" he asked, without looking over at Jack.

"Well, sort of. It started out kind of bad, but it got better as it went," Jack said.

Both Jack's grandparents had their backs to Jack when he entered. As they turned to look back at him his grandmother gasped. "What on earth happened to you?"

Jack looked down at his stained clothes and said, "Oh that, Anthony Patrone tripped me and I fell face first into the mud. That was the bad part of the day."

Judy Lennington

"I'll have to soak those clothes two days to get that stain out," Delores said.

"It's just mud, Delores. The boy isn't hurt, and that is what is important," Lester said, winking at Jack. "You best get out of those clothes and get a bath before your father gets home."

Delores was still mumbling as she carried Jack's stained clothes to the sideboard. Lester poured hot water into a basin and added some cool water from the drinking bucket. He handed Jack a bar of lye soap and a wash cloth. Jack began washing near the fireplace.

"What was the best part of the day?" Lester asked, sitting down on the stool near the fireplace.

"Oh, Collin McCauley and I are friends now. I might have to spend more time tutoring him, but we are going to be good friends, I just know it. He's also agreed to help me with my problem," Jack said, rubbing the soapy wash cloth over his face, ears, and neck.

"What problem might that be?" Lester asked.

Jack rinsed his face and began patting it dry as he replied, "Melvin Riley and Anthony Patrone. Collin is going to help keep them off my back. No Sir, I won't have to worry about those two anymore. They are afraid of Collin." Jack laughed. "Everyone is afraid of Collin."

"I see." Lester said, lighting his pipe. He looked over at his wife who was still mumbling about the muddy clothes. "It's good to see your friend is interested in learning, all of the sudden."

"I don't know why, but he is. He wants to learn to read and write as fast as he can. It seems awful important to him. I said I would do what I could, and I will. In return, he is going to keep

Melvin and Anthony from bothering me." Jack explained. He sat on the floor and began to wash his feet and legs.

"Dinner is likely going to be late, since I have this mess to clean up," Delores complained.

"Oh, Delores, I will help with dinner. As for the mess, all you need do is put those clothes in a pan of cold water to soak. Now stop complaining and just do it," Lester barked. He winked at Jack again. Jack smiled up at his grandfather.

"Grandfather, what was your friendship with Limpy like?" Jack asked.

"Oh, Jack, it was different," Lester began, "Limpy was an old man and I was a boy. My father wasn't too happy about my association with Limpy at all. My mother forbade it completely. I would sneak off to find Limpy lying in some corner out of the weather. He would be stone drunk and smell of stale urine and sweaty clothes. At first, I was afraid of him. He mumbled all the time. He used terms I had never heard before too. But that wooden leg seemed to be calling my name. I wanted to know how he got a wooden leg, what happened to him, and why didn't he have a home and family. My curiosity was so strong that I figured it was worth the risk of a trip to the wood shed. Limpy wasn't easy to find either. Although he moved around a lot, people were always running him off. I suppose it was the stench. It bothered me too in the beginning, but after I got to know him better, I convinced him to get a bath and wash his clothes. Of course, that took some fancy talking and some time. It didn't happen overnight, you see."

"How did he get his wooden leg?" Jack asked.

Lester smiled, "That is a story of adventure. I'll tell you some day when we have more time." At that moment, the door opened and Sheldon entered the kitchen.

"What happened to you?" Sheldon asked smiling over at Jack.

Before Jack could speak, Delores turned holding the pan of soaking clothes in her hand, "Just look at these clothes. I don't know if I can get this stain out. We may have to buy new clothes for him to wear to school. Lord knows you can't afford that and neither can we."

"Delores," Lester said, closing his eyes. "It wasn't his fault."

"What happened?" Sheldon asked.

"Anthony Patrone tripped me as I was going inside after lunch recess. I fell face first in the mud. It was wet and I got soaked through before I could get up. Mrs. Cartwright made me sit by the stove to dry," Jack explained. "I wasn't fighting or anything like that, Father. Anthony and Melvin Riley were waiting for me. I tried to avoid them, but I didn't manage too well."

"I see," Sheldon said, removing his jacket.

"It won't happen again," Jack said.

"How do you know that?" Sheldon asked.

Jack smiled, "Because Collin McCauley is going to be my friend. He said if I teach him how to read and write, he will keep those rats off my back."

"Jack Gideon!" Delores said. "Where did you learn such language? I know Mrs. Cartwright didn't teach you to talk like that."

"No, Ma'am, that is what Collin calls them," Jack replied.

"What did I tell you?" Delores said, looking over at Lester. "Well, we will not be using such language in this house," she said. "I don't think you should use it out there either," she said, nodding her head toward the door.

"Yes Ma'am," Jack said. "I don't know why Collin needs to learn everything all at once, but he sure wants to learn. I said I would work with him every spare minute I have."

"He probably needs to know how to read and write to get a job somewhere," Sheldon said.

"Did they hire his Daddy where you work?" Jack asked.

"I don't think so," Sheldon said. "I haven't seen him around. They tell me he is at the bars downtown nearly every night, but no one has seen him working anywhere. I suspect that is why Collin needs to get an education. Someone has to earn money to feed that family."

"Family?" Jack asked.

"I hear he has a wife and six kids," Sheldon said, from where he sat at the table.

"Collin is the only one in school. He never mentioned anything about brothers and sisters," Jack said, pulling on clean long johns.

"Well, he probably has a reason for not mentioning it," Lester said.

"Maybe I better not mention it. You know, kind of wait and see if he brings it up first. I wouldn't want him getting mad at me, or anything like that," Jack said.

"I suppose that would be a clever idea," Sheldon said.

"Are you going to help me get dinner on the table, or were you just putting me off?" Delores asked, looking over at Lester. Lester rolled his eyes and pushed himself to his feet. Without saying a word, he began helping his wife. "Jack, set the table," Delores said, with her back to Jack.

"Yes Ma'am," Jack said, smiling over at his father.

Jack listened to the conversation around the dinner table, but was not able to absorb the content. His mind kept wondering off to the events of the day. For two days in a row, Collin McCauley stood at the desk and took a paddling from Mrs. Cartwright. Today he sat in the corner for half the day. Jack wondered if this would deter him from pursuing his lessons. Jack wasn't so sure that he would continue to take a whacking everyday just to learn to read and write. Jack wondered about Collin's siblings. His father said he heard there were six kids all together. Were they all very young? Perhaps they were too young to go to school. Collin never talked about his family. Jack had assumed there was only Collin and his father. Would Collin quit school as soon as he could read and write?

"Jack, eat your green beans before they get cold," his grandmother said.

"Yes Ma'am," Jack said, spearing two green beans with his fork and stuffing them into his mouth. They were cold. He had been day dreaming and now his dinner was cold. He finished his meal and helped his grandmother clear the table.

Lester was proud of the new soles he put on his shoes. He had unlaced his shoes and removed them. He handed them over to Sheldon and began talking about how his father taught him how to put new soles on his shoes when he was a boy. Jack went to sit on the floor next to his father's chair and listened to the conversation.

"Was that before or after you met Limpy?" Jack asked.

"Oh, that was long after I met Limpy," Lester said.

"Did your father ever find out you were spending time with Limpy? I remember you saying he didn't like you associating with him. Did he ever find out?" Jack asked.

Lester nodded his head. "He did. I remember that day well," Lester said. "I had been sneaking off to see him almost every day. Limpy would tell me the most amazing stories about his whaling expeditions and the people he went to sea with. I couldn't get enough of the stories. I would hide some bread or other types of food in my shirt for him. It was raining and Mr. Griffin, that would be Herman's father, saw us behind the mercantile one day. Hermon's father was visiting with my father and mentioned it to him. I sat frozen waiting for Father to scold me, but he acted as if it was nothing at all. When Mrs. Griffin left, he called me inside. He closed the door, and I thought I was done for. My father sat me down at the table and asked me how long I had been sneaking off to see Limpy. He threw some questions at me and I answered everyone honestly. I figured I was going to get it anyway so I might as well get it for everything at once. He sat there with his hands in his pockets for a while and then sent me to bed. I laid in my bed all night worrying about what my father was going to do to me."

"What did he do to you?" Jack asked.

"Absolutely nothing," Lester said. "He didn't do anything. After a few days, he told me I should stop sneaking around. He told me to bring Limpy by the house now and then and stop stealing food from our table to feed him."

"Boy, oh, boy!" Jack said. "You got off lucky."

"I suppose I did. However, that was the kind of man my father was. He was stern, but kind. It wasn't too long after that, he passed away and it was just me, my brothers and sister, and my mother. Mother didn't permit Limpy to come by the house because people would talk, her being a widow and all. But she packed food for Limpy when she knew I was going to meet him somewhere." Lester explained.

"I didn't know your father died when you were a boy," Jack said.

Lester nodded his head. "Yes, it was a tough time for me and my family. Mother had four children to raise all by herself. She did it though. She washed other people's clothes, cleaned the mercantile at nights, and sat in at school when the teacher was

Judy Lennington

sick. She never re-married, although Mr. Brickert certainly tried to persuade her often enough."

"Who was Mr. Brickert?" Sheldon asked. He looked down at Jack and said, "This is the first time I heard about this."

"Mr. Brickert was a local business man. I don't recall what his line of business was, but I recall he always dressed in a suit and stove pipe hat. Oh, he was a fancy one, that Mr. Brickert was. He would drop by a couple times a week, and Mother would make him sit outside on the porch so all the neighbors could see him at all times," Lester said.

"Why did she want the neighbors to see him on the porch?" Jack asked.

"Well, because," Lester began, "it wasn't proper for a woman to have a man in her house. It was frowned upon in those days. It still is, as a matter of fact. No decent woman would allow a man to come into her house when her husband wasn't home. People would gossip and she would become shamed by everyone in town."

"I didn't know that," Jack said.

"Oh, Jack, there is so much for you to learn," Delores said, smiling. "But that is enough for today. Tomorrow is the last day of school this week. You don't want to end the week by falling asleep in class."

"Oh, no, Ma'am. I don't want to get whacked by Mrs. Cartwright in front of the whole class," Jack said, rising to his feet. He hugged his father and grandfather. "Thank you for the story, Grandfather. I want to hear more about Limpy." Then he embraced his grandmother before climbing the ladder to the loft.

Jack waited for his father to come to bed, while thinking about what he had learned that evening. He had so much in common with his grandfather. They both had lost a parent at an early age. Suddenly Jack realized that there was someone who understood what it was like to lose a parent. His grandfather had two brothers and a sister, growing up. How hard it must have been for all of them.

As he laid in the loft waiting for his father to climb the ladder, he tried to imagine what it would be like to have siblings. He wasn't fond of having a sister, but he would like to have a brother or two. If only his mother had lived longer. Jack never heard his father come to bed, for he fell fast asleep with his head full of thoughts.

The next morning, Jack woke early. He heard the door downstairs and knew his father had left for work. He rose and made his way down the ladder. His grandmother was busy preparing breakfast and his grandfather was outside paying his morning visit to the privy. Jack danced around the kitchen until his grandfather returned, and then he made a dash for the privy himself. Upon returning, he found his breakfast waiting for him on the table.

"Grandfather, there are no whales in the river. Limpy had to have been telling you tall tales about being a whaler," Jack explained.

"Now Jack, I thought I explained that to you. Limpy wasn't from these parts. He traveled here, from the East Coast, long after his whaling days," Lester said, raising his tin cup of coffee to his lips. "He was from Massachusetts. Do you know where that is?"

Jack pondered the question a while and shook his head. "No Sir, I don't believe I do. Is it near the ocean?" he asked.

"It is. It is part of the New England states. You have heard of them, haven't you?" Lester asked.

"Yes Sir, I've heard of them. That is where the pilgrims settled, Plymouth Rock to be exact. Was Limpy a pilgrim?" Jack asked, seriously.

Lester smiled and shook his head. "I don't think he was a pilgrim, Son. He did come here from England though. He had family in England. He signed on with the whalers to earn enough money to bring his family to the new world. He wasn't married, but he had parents and siblings that he wanted to bring to America. At least, that is what he told me. He was a young man when he went to sea for the first time. He found that it paid well, and he saved every penny he made toward passage for his family."

"Did he ever get them over here?" Jack asked.

Lester shook his head again, "No Son, he didn't get the chance to do that. He told me he had been on three whaling expeditions all together. The third one was disastrous. He said a bull whale rammed their vessel and sunk the ship. They scrambled to get into the life boats and the whale attacked them as well. There were only two survivors. Limpy and a mate named Joe, I believe, he said."

"What happened to his leg?" Jack asked.

"Well, we don't really have time for that this morning. It is a very interesting story, and I would like to tell it to you after school. Perhaps after you've finished tutoring your new Irish friend, we can talk about it some more," Lester said. "You best be off with you."

"Don't forget your lunch tin, Jack," Delores said, smiling. "I've put a little something extra in there for your friend Collin."

"Oh, Grandmother, thank you," Jack said, hugging his grandmother. She held his coat for him while he slipped his arms into it and pulled it up around his neck. He buttoned it all the way up to the top, and took the lunch tin from her. She hugged him

Bend in The River

and he nodded his head at his grandfather before rushing out the door. It was a sunny morning and the birds were extra vocal this morning. Soon school would be out for the summer. It wouldn't be long now.

Jack was looking forward to a new day with a new friend. He walked slower as he approached the school yard, looking for signs of Collin. He didn't see him, but saw the girls looking his way as he approached.

"Jack Spratt could eat no fat," they began to chant.

He stuck his tongue out at them and climbed the steps to the school house. He looked around carefully, just in case Melvin and Anthony were hiding in wait to ambush him. He was early this morning and they had not arrived yet. Jack hung up his coat and took his seat at his desk. He thought it was safer inside under the supervision of Mrs. Cartwright's watchful eye.

After some time, Mrs. Cartwright rang the bell and the children began to file through the door toward their seats. Jack's mouth dropped open when he saw Melvin and Anthony walking toward their designated seats. Both were sporting black eyes, and Anthony had a split lip. They did not look in Jack's direction, as they took their seats. As Collin walked past Jack, on his way to his seat, he smiled and winked. Jack took a deep breath and smiled. He was enjoying this very much.

Mrs. Cartwright was spending extra time with the Huffman twins, in the first row. She was helping them with their printing skills. Now she was moving toward Jack's row. Jack raised his hand.

"Yes, Jack, what is it?" she asked.

"Mrs. Cartwright, where is Massachusetts?" Jack asked.

She stood watching him for a moment, and then smiled. She turned and walked toward her desk where the atlas sat, and said, "Why don't you come up here and see if you can find it, Jack?"

Jack sighed. This was not part of his plan. He knew everyone would laugh at him if he didn't find it successfully. He slid from his seat and approached the desk. Mrs. Cartwright stood over him with her hands upon her hips. Jack remembered, his grandfather had told him, it was part of the New England states. Jack could find them well enough. He leaned close and looked down at the markings on the atlas. He smiled up at Mrs. Cartwright and placed his finger upon Massachusetts. She smiled and nodded her head. Jack looked at it closer. It was right next to the ocean.

"You may take your seat now," Mrs. Cartwright said. Jack returned to his seat. Milly Thompson stuck her tongue out at him as he glanced over at her. Collin sat at his desk with his head bowed. It appeared he was studying the alphabetical letters on his slate. Jack folded his hands on his desk, and Mrs. Cartwright nodded her head. "Now then, today we are going to work on our division. We will start simple."

Jack listened to every instruction carefully. He couldn't help but wonder if Collin was keeping up. He wanted, so badly, to turn around, but knew it would have dire consequences. He clasped his hands together tightly as he listened to Mrs. Cartwright. She nodded her head again, which was a signal for them to begin, and then she moved on to the next row of students.

By the time, Mrs. Cartwright made her way to the last row, it was lunch time. She rang the bell and stood next to her desk watching as each child removed their coat from the pegs that lined the wall nearest the stove. Jack and Collin were among the first students outside and quickly made their way to the air root of the large Elm tree.

"How did you do with your division?" Jack asked.

"I don't know nothin' about division. I can do me times tables up to seven. That Mrs. Cartwright is movin' way too fast for the likes of me," Collin replied.

"You need to work on your English too," Jack said, handing Collin a slice of bread. "My grandmother sent this for you. There is an apple in here too."

Collin frowned as he looked down at Jack. "Why would your grandmother do such a thing for me?"

"Careful…," Jack thought to himself. He smiled and replied, "She knew we would be eating together and wanted to make sure we both got our nourishment, I suppose." Collin thought about what Jack had said. He didn't reply, he merely took a large bite of the sugar bread. Jack could tell he was pleased. "Grandma knows you can't learn anything if your belly is rumbling," he said.

"Why do I need to work on my English? I'm an Irishman and proud of it," Collin said, with his mouth full.

"You are not supposed to talk with food in your mouth. It isn't proper. You should always swallow what is in your mouth before you speak. Sometimes, it's hard to remember," Jack explained. He took a deep breath and said, "You may be an Irishman, but you are in America. You should learn our customs and policies if you're going to stay here. If I were in Ireland, I would be expected to learn your language and customs, wouldn't I?"

Collin nodded his head as he chewed the last of his sugar bread. He held his hand out for the apple. Jack reached into his lunch tin and handed the largest one of the two red apples to his friend. Collin began to eat it rapidly. Jack couldn't help but get

Judy Lennington

the impression that Collin feared someone would take it away from him before he finished it. Collin ate the apple close to the core. Jack had never seen anyone eat an apple right down to the seeds before. Jack was only half way finished with his apple when Collin tossed his core into the high weeds. Jack took a deep breath, pretending to be full, and held his half-eaten apple out to Collin. Collin smiled and took it from Jack, and proceeded to eat it without giving it a second thought. Once again, he ate the apple close to the core, leaving the seeds exposed. "Tell your grandmother, I thank her for the food," Collin said when finished.

"She will be pleased to hear that," Jack said. "Now let me help you with your division."

The ground was dry today, so Jack took a stick and began marking in the soft dirt. He glanced up from time to time, watching for signs of Melvin and Anthony. They were nowhere to be found. He did see Milly and Lynette watching them from the swings that hung in the large Oak tree nearest the school house. Mrs. Cartwright stepped out onto the porch and rang the bell. Collin's head jerked upward to look in her direction. It seemed that the bell had startled him. The time went so quickly. Jack was hoping for an opportunity to ask him about his family and what had happened to Melvin and Anthony. Now it would have to keep until after school.

They returned to their seats. Melvin and Anthony were among the last of the students to enter the building. Jack wondered where they had been and what they had been up to. Were they plotting some scheme to get him alone? Perhaps they had plans to get even with Collin for the beating he gave them. Jack felt anxious as he waited for Mrs. Cartwright to make her way to their row.

"Now students, I looked over your work during recess and see that some of you need help. I don't want you to be discouraged by the low marks I gave you. I want you to continue working very hard. In time, you will catch up with the rest of your class," she said.

Was she talking about Collin? She did not mention any names. Perhaps Jack had made some mistakes. Jack felt his palms sweating as he continued to clasp his hands on the desktop in front of him. He noticed his desk was vibrating. That is when he realized that Collin was bouncing his leg nervously behind him.

Mrs. Cartwright handed Jack his slate and moved toward Collin. Jack heard her say softly, "Mr. McCauley, if you please?" The leg bouncing stopped immediately. She walked back to the front of the class, turning to face them once again. "I want you to fix your mistakes and continue with more division tables. There is no limit as to how far you can go. This is not a test. I want you to think carefully and concentrate on getting each one correct," she nodded her head and commanded, "You may begin."

Jack looked down at his slate. He had made two mistakes. He corrected them and proceeded on with his division problems. Once again, by the time Mrs. Cartwright reached the last row it was time to dismiss the class for the day. Jack watched as Melvin and Anthony hurried from the classroom. He and Collin went to the back of the class again to resume their studies.

"Tomorrow is Saturday," Jack said softly.

"Yeah, so?" Collin asked.

"We don't have school tomorrow. Do you want me to come to your house to help you with your studies?" Jack asked.

Collin quickly shook his head. "No, no, don't come to my house. I will come to your house. You tell me where you live and what time to be there. I'll be on time."

Jack sensed that he had alarmed Collin in some way. "Sure, that will be fine. I'll show you where I live after our studies. You can come over anytime. I don't have any plans for the day."

"We can meet Sunday, too, if you've a likin'," Collin said.

"No, Sundays are my special day to go fishing with my father. We go fishing down along the river bank every Sunday that it isn't raining. It's the only day we have to spend together," Jack explained. Collin nodded his head. "Do you and your father do anything special together?" Jack asked.

Collin shook his head and looked down at the floor. "No, me Dah isn't home much. He spends all his free time at the pub and bars. Me Ma fixes a fine meal on Sunday's, when we have the food," Collin said. He instantly realized that he had said too much and added, "It ain't like we don't have anything to eat, don't you know. We do well enough without me Dah. To tell the truth, we are better off without him."

Jack was speechless. He took a deep breath and crossed his fingers, as he asked, "Is it just you and your Ma, I mean, your mother?"

Collin closed his eyes and took a deep breath. "I need to get back to me studies, you know. I will never catch up if we keep goin' on about things that don't matter to me larnin'."

"Of course," Jack began. "It's just that we are friends, and friends are there to help one another and trust one another. I want you to know that you can trust me, Collin. If ever there is a secret you want to share with me, I want you to know you can count on me to keep it."

"I don't need friends, Kid," Collin said, leaning closer. "I need someone to help me with larnin'. That's all I be needin' from you."

Bend in The River

Jack swallowed hard and nodded his head. Perhaps it was not a suitable time to ask about Melvin and Anthony. "Okay, let's begin with your division. It isn't much different than your multiplication. It's kind of in reverse. Well, never mind that for now. Let me show you." Jack began explaining the division tables and for some odd reason, Collin seemed to catch on right away. Jack got the impression that math was going to be Collin's best subject. They worked until Mrs. Cartwright announced that it was time to bring wood inside for Monday morning.

As in the previous night, Jack and Collin carried several arm loads of wood inside and stacked them next to the wall near the wood stove. "Good night boys," Mrs. Cartwright said, as she began to lock the door.

Collin walked with Jack as they made their way to the street Jack lived on. Jack pointed his house out to Collin, before Collin turned to walk away without another word. He watched Collin as he moved away, thinking that he was a very odd character. Jack took a deep breath and ran toward his house. It was Friday night and he wouldn't have to go back to school for two whole days. He felt so light and free as he barged through the door. He stopped immediately when he noticed they had company.

On the chair sat the very large Mrs. Patrone. She was none other than Anthony Patrone's mother. Jack swallowed hard, for he instantly assumed he was in trouble. "Hello, young man," she said, looking over at Jack as he hung up his coat.

"Hello," Jack said, looking nervously at his grandparents.

"Mrs. Patrone is here on a private matter, Jack," his grandfather began, "would you mind changing your clothes and going outside to play for a while?"

- 89 -

"Yes Sir," Jack replied. He hurried up the ladder to change. He dressed quickly and quietly, for he strained to hear the conversation below. They were talking softly, and Jack could not make out their words. He climbed down the ladder and reached for the latch on the door.

"I'll call you when you can return," his grandfather said.

"Yes Sir," Jack said. He stepped outside and sat down on the porch steps. He knew he should go off and find a tree to climb or stream to skip rocks in, but his curiosity wouldn't allow him to leave the porch. He leaned back in hopes of hearing the conversation on the other side of the door, but was unsuccessful.

It seemed hours had passed when the door opened and Mrs. Patrone stepped outside on the porch. She smiled down at Jack and said, "Have a nice weekend, young man." Jack watched her as she moved down the street away from his house. He jumped to his feet and hurried inside.

"What did Mrs. Patrone want?" he asked.

"She was here about your friend Collin and his family," Lester said.

"Lester, I don't think we should discuss this in front of Jack," Delores said.

"Nonsense, Delores. Jack may have some insight on the matter," Lester said.

Jack's grandmother had started preparing dinner immediately after Mrs. Patrone's departure. She looked over her shoulder at her husband and shook her head as she mumbled, "I'm not so sure it is wise to involve the boy."

"Involve me in what, exactly?" Jack asked. The curiosity was killing him.

"Mrs. Patrone is concerned about the McCauley family. It appears as Mrs. McCauley is not in good health and Mr. McCauley spends all his time, and money, in the bars, or pubs, as she called it. She is concerned about the children's wellbeing. She suspects there isn't much food in the house and Mrs. McCauley needs medical care, which she is refusing. Mrs. Patrone believes it is because they haven't the money to pay for it," Lester explained.

"What is she going to do?" Jack asked.

"Well, she wants to have the children placed in a home where they will be cared for," Lester said.

"You mean the poor house? She wants to send them off to the poor house? Can she do that?" Jack asked.

"If she gets the right people involved, I suppose she can," Lester said.

"Lester, I think he's heard enough," Delores said.

"We can't let her do that, Grandfather. We must do something to help. They have a right to stay together as a family," Jack urged.

"See, what did I tell you? Now you have upset the boy. You shouldn't have told him, Lester. I warned you," Delores said.

"Quiet, Delores. Jack has a right to know," Lester said.

"Isn't there something we can do to help?" Jack asked, kneeling onto the floor beside his grandfather.

"Jack, we barely have enough to feed ourselves," Lester began, "how are we going to feed eight more mouths?"

"Maybe I could get a job to help," Jack said. He felt his voice crackling. He had to do something. He couldn't lose his new friend now. He did not want things to go back to the way they were before Collin came into the picture. Besides, if Collin were to leave now, it would be worse than ever for him. "Where did she say, they lived?" Jack asked.

Judy Lennington

"She said they lived over William Armstrong's chair factory," Lester said. "Mrs. Patrone said it is dusty up there and she suspects that is why Mrs. McCauley is sick all of the time. She thinks one of the children isn't well either." Before he could get another word out, Jack was on his feet. He grabbed his coat from the peg and ran from the house. He ran as fast as he could toward the chair factory. He saw a candle in the window. He climbed the stairs with his coat draped over his arm and pounded upon the door. The door opened a crack and Collin McCauley peered out at him.

"What are you doin' here, Jack Gideon?" he asked. "How did you know where to find me? Did you follow me home?"

"No, I didn't follow you, Collin," Jack said. "I have to talk to you about something, it is real important."

Collin looked over his shoulder and called out, "Ma, I'm steppin' out for a minute. I'll be right back now; don't you fret none."

Collin did not seem to be happy to see Jack. He pushed Jack along toward the steps that went down to the area between the chair factory and the building next door. When they reached the ground, below, Collin turned to tower over Jack. "How did you know where to find me?" he repeated.

"My grandfather told me where you live. He heard it from Anthony Patrone's mother. She dropped by to talk to my grandparents this afternoon. Collin, she wants to get a group of followers to place you and your siblings in the poorhouse."

Collin glared down at Jack. His anger was obvious and Jack could only hope that the anger he saw in Collin's face was not directed toward him. Collin's fists were clenched and his knuckles were white bone showing through his flesh. He turned so Jack could not see his face. Jack watched as Collin's chest rose with every breath. The air was beginning to get chilly and Jack began to put his coat on as he waited for Collin to say something. Finally, Collin turned and said, "I'll beat the snot out of Anthony Patrone for this.'

"I don't think that will help you any, Collin. We need to find a way that doesn't get Mrs. Patrone riled up," Jack suggested.

"Like what?" Collin asked. Jack noticed his fists were still clenched as he spoke.

"Well, maybe we could find your father a job. That might help," Jack said.

"Me Dah, has a job well enough," Collin said. "Well, at least he had one when he left the house this mornin'."

"Well, that should do it then," Jack said. "If he has a job and pays the rent, they certainly shouldn't be able to force you into the poorhouse."

"Me Dah is passed out cold on the kitchen floor," Collin began. "He got paid this mornin' and left work early for the pub. He spent every dime of his pay on the drink. I'm afraid there isn't any money for the rent or food either for that matter."

"What?" Jack asked. He wanted to inquire as to how his father could do such a thing, but knew it would only make Collin even more angry.

Collin sat down on the bottom step and placed his head in his hands. "Now you know why I need to learn to read and write. I thought if I could do that, I might get a job on the docks regardless of my age. Me mother thinks I'm too young to get a job. But I know the pickin's are slim when it comes to them that can read the shippin' papers and sign off on them. I've been hangin' round the docks and watchin' what goes on down there. I'm as strong as an ox and I'm bigger than most boys me age. I'm thinkin' I might be able to lie about me age."

"Is there no one else who can go to work?" Jack asked.

"Me Ma works at sweepin' floors in the chair factory after hours. But she got sick, and I've been doin' it for her so Mr. Armstrong don't find out. It's the only income we have. Me Dah finds work here and there, but he drinks up every penny he earns and there ain't any left when he gets home on pay day. We have to hide me Ma's money or he would drink that up as well," Collin explained. He shook his head. "I shouldn't be tellin' you this. It isn't your problem."

"Yes, it is my problem," Jack said sitting down next to Collin on the steps. "I would be at the mercy of Anthony and Melvin if it weren't for you. The way I see it, I must find a way to help you stay right where you are, and keep that nosey old Mrs. Patrone off your back."

"Aye, but how are we goin' to do that?" Collin asked.

"I'll think of something," Jack said. "I'll have to talk to my father about it. He will know what to do."

"I don't like folks knowin' our business," Collin said.

Jack stood up. "He won't tell anyone if we ask him not to. You can trust my father, Collin." He stepped close and placed his hand upon Collin's shoulder. "I'll see you in school Monday?" he asked.

Collin nodded his head. "Aye," he said.

"Okay, I hope your mother is feeling better," Jack said, as he began to walk away.

"Thanks for lettin' me know about Mrs. Patrone," Collin called out to Jack before going up the steps to the living quarters above the chair factory.

Jack ran toward home. The sun would be going down soon and his father would be returning home from work. He felt sorry for Collin. He pictured Collin's mother lying in her sick bed as Jack's own mother had done, not that long ago. He hoped Mrs. McCauley did not die. What would happen to Collin, and his brothers and sisters, if she did?

Jack ran inside and began to hang his coat upon a peg. He turned to find his grandmother standing with her hands upon her hips, with a very displeased look upon her face. "I suppose you went running straight to that McCauley boy and told him everything that went on here," she said angrily.

"Yes, Ma'am, I did," Jack replied.

Delores reached out and gripped Jack by the ear. She began pulling him toward the table. "Sit down!" she barked.

"Delores, let go of the boy!" Lester shouted.

At that moment, the door opened and Sheldon entered. He frowned and asked, "What is going on here?"

"Your son has been acting very strangely since his association with the McCauley boy," Delores said, as she placed her hands upon her hips again. "I am about to send him off to bed without his supper."

"No one is sending Jack off to bed without his supper," Lester said. "He didn't do anything that bad."

"What exactly did he do?" Sheldon asked, as he began to remove his coat.

"Mrs. Patrone paid us a visit. It appears the McCauley children are living in deplorable conditions. Their mother is sickly and their rent has not been paid in months. Her concern is for their well-being, and, she feels they may need placed in a safer environment," Delores said.

Judy Lennington

"You mean the poor house!" Jack said. He looked over at his father, "She is a nosey old busy body, who doesn't like the McCauley's because Collin beat up her son. That is why she is doing this, Father."

"So, what has Jack done?" Sheldon asked.

"Nothing, really," Lester said. "He merely did what he felt he should do for a friend." He looked over at Delores and shook his head. "I believe you should put dinner on the table, Delores."

Jack's grandmother took a deep breath as she stood glaring at his grandfather. "The boy is in our care, Lester, while his father is working. His actions will reflect upon us," she said, before turning toward the pot hanging over the red embers of the fire place.

Lester began to light the oil lamp that sat on the table. "Jack felt the need to forewarn his friend, Collin, of Mrs. Patrone's intentions. I see no harm in that, in fact, I would have done the same thing in his shoes. Now that I think about it, I have done the same thing when I was about his same age."

Sheldon pulled out a chair and sat down near Jack. "What did your friend, Collin, have to say when you told him?" he asked.

"They need our help, Father. Mrs. McCauley is sickly. She was sweeping and cleaning up in the chair factory every night, but now she is too sick. Collin has been doing it after school so Mr. Armstrong won't evict them," he explained.

"What about Mr. McCauley?" Sheldon asked.

Jack glanced over his shoulder in the direction of his grandmother. He shook his head, but said nothing.

"Well, what do you think we can do to help?" Sheldon asked.

"I don't know, but surely we can do something. We can't let them starve or get kicked out into the street." Jack looked over his shoulder again before saying, "We can't let Mrs. Patrone send them to the poor house either."

Sheldon smiled. "Mrs. Patrone can't send them to the poor house unless she has enough signatures on a petition from the locals. I think most of us here in Wellsville, have our own problems. By the time, Mrs. Patrone goes door to door and convinces people to sign the petition, the McCauley's situation may be changed."

"What if it isn't changed?" Jack asked.

"Well, perhaps we should all pray that it is," Sheldon said. He stood up and sighed. "I better wash up for supper. I think you should help your grandmother with setting the table."

Jack looked over at his grandmother who stood with her back to him. He could tell that she was still angry. He sighed and nodded his head as he stood up and began to set the table. While Sheldon was pouring water into the porcelain basin, Jack looked over at his grandfather and asked, "You said you warned a friend once Grandfather. Who was it?"

Lester smiled and placed both hands upon his cane. "It was old Limpy. The town folks were sick and tired of his sleeping in their doorways to keep warm and out of the rain. They were planning to run him out of town. I overheard Mr. Brickert telling my mother all about it, so I ran off to find Limpy and warn him."

"What did he do?" Jack asked.

"Well, I had to help sober him up some. I got Hermon Griffon to help me get him to a secret hide out we played in. We snuck some coffee out of Hermon's house and got him to drink it. Then we made him bathe. He wasn't too happy about that, because we didn't have any heat in our hide out. It was just an old shed that sat behind the Griffon's place. It was partially caved in and wasn't much of a shelter, really," Lester smiled as he recalled the event.

"Did it work?" Jack asked.

"I suppose it did, to a degree. He sobered up and we washed his clothes to get the stink of booze and sweat out of them. I remember cutting his hair." Lester began to laugh at the recollection. "That was a sight, as I recall. He never minded though, he kept mumbling something about a flurry. Turns out, that is a whaler's term for the struggle made by a dying whale," Lester's eyes seemed to glaze over as he said, "I remember that was the first time I ever saw old Limpy's stub of a leg."

"What did it look like?" Jack asked, scooting closer.

"Oh, it was taken off right above the knee. It was all wrinkly and the skin was darker than the rest of the leg. Hermon feared it, but not me. Limpy even let me touch it. It felt no different than touching your arm or leg." Lester explained.

"What happened to it, Grandfather? How did he lose his leg?" Jack asked.

"He was at sea with his mates. They had been out there for months, searching for a spray. That's when a whale surfaces to the top. It blows the water out of its blow hole so it can breathe in fresh air. They were hoping to find a Bowhead Whale. They produced the most oil. You see, Jack, it wasn't the meat they were after. It was the oil inside the whale that brought big money. Oh, most of the whale was used, but the oil was the most valuable commodity," Lester explained.

"Did they find one?" Jack asked. "A Bowhead Whale, that is?"

Lester shook his head. "No, they didn't find a Bowhead. They bobbed around out there in that big ocean for months. You see, whalers were everywhere in those days. They managed to kill just about every whale they came upon. It was widespread practice to let the young ones go, so they would grow and reproduce. It made no sense to kill them all, because they would put themselves out of a job. However, there were some unscrupulous whalers who even killed the young ones."

"Supper is ready," Delores said. Jack could tell that she was still upset with him, so he decided not to say anymore as they went to the table and ate their supper. Afterwards, he helped clear the table and washed up for bed. Even though there was no school tomorrow, he climbed the ladder at his usual time. He prayed for Collin and his family before crawling under the covers. Tomorrow he was looking forward to climbing trees and enjoying another spring day. As he drifted off to sleep, he thought that he may seek out Collin early in the day, and help him with his studies. There may be time in the afternoon for exploring. Perhaps he could teach Collin enough to get him a job on the docks. Jack drifted off to sleep with a sense of bobbing on the ocean, while looking up at the night sky full of stars.

Jack woke to find his father had left for work. Tomorrow was Sunday and it was a day when Jack and his father would spend the entire day together. Jack said another prayer for Collin and his family before descending the ladder, just for good measure. He approached the table cautiously, for he wasn't sure how his grandmother's mood would be this morning. "Good morning," he said, politely.

"Good morning, Jack," Lester said, smiling. "I'm going to the mercantile after breakfast. Would you like to walk along with an old man?"

"I would like that very much," Jack replied.

His grandmother placed a bowl of boiled oats on the table in front of him. Lester tore a slice of buttered bread in half and gave half of it to Jack. He winked at Jack as he took a bite of the bread. Delores didn't have much to say this morning and Jack thought it was best to keep quiet, as well. After breakfast, he and his grandfather pulled on their coats and hats and stepped out into the foggy morning.

"It's a chilly one today," Lester said, as he took the steps one at a time.

Jack waited for his grandfather to reach the ground before he commented. "Yes, it is," he said, watching his grandfather maneuver along with the aid of his cane. "You were telling me about Limpy's wooden leg before I went to bed last night. How did he lose his leg?" Jack asked.

"Well, I would like to finish telling you the story when we get back, Jack. It takes all my breath just to get me to the mercantile," Lester said.

Jack nodded his head and replied, "That would be fine, Grandfather." However, he felt very disappointed. He wanted to hear the story of how Charles Woodward, known as Limpy, lost his leg. Jack imagined swashbuckling pirates fighting with swords to steal the whaler's cargo of precious oil. Jack pictured men lying about with arms and legs cut off. Some were being cast overboard by the pirates who cheered. Lester had told Jack that the only survivors were Limpy and a first mate. He said a whale had attacked their ship. It was possible that a whale attacked them after the pirates looted the cargo. What an amazing adventure it must have been.

They had reached the mercantile and Jack waited for his grandfather to climb the steps, one at a time. They entered together to find Howard Dodge behind the counter and his wife, Rosalie, sweeping the floor. "Good morning, Lester," Howard

Bend in The River

called out. "Who is that you brung with you? Oh, good morning, Jack Gideon. How nice to see you this morning."

Jack smiled. "Good morning, Mr. Dodge. It's nice to see you as well," he said. He smiled over at Rosalie and nodded his head. "It's nice to see you as well, Mrs. Dodge."

"What a fine young man," Rosalie said, smiling. "Come over here and get a licorice stick from the jar, Jack Gideon. A fine young man, such as yourself, should have a good licorice stick every now and again."

As Jack reached into the jar his thoughts went to Collin and his siblings. He smiled over at Rosalie Dodge and pulled out a licorice stick. He shoved it down into his pocket. Rosalie had been watching, and she raised her eyebrows. "Are we saving it for later?" she asked. Jack nodded his head. "Are you going to share it with someone?" she asked, smiling. Again, Jack nodded his head. "Well, that is very kind of you. Perhaps, just this one-time, mind you, we could spare two licorice sticks." Rosalie smiled and nodded her head. "Go on, Jack Gideon, take another one for your friend."

Jack smiled and said, "Thank you Mrs. Dodge." He reached into the jar and pulled out a second licorice stick. He shoved it deep into his pocket.

"What a fine young man," Howard Dodge repeated.

"Yes, Jack is a good boy. Delores and I are blessed to have him under our roof," Lester said. He leaned upon the counter and said. "I have a list of things Delores needs. I'd also like a pouch of that tobacco that came in from South Carolina the other day."

"It's a good thing you came when you did, Lester," Mr. Dodge said. "We are nearly sold out of that particular tobacco already. Seems a lot of folks like that South Carolina tobacco. We have lots

– 101 –

Judy Lennington

of the other just sitting on the shelves back there. Folks have been coming in here asking for the new stuff left and right."

"It has a right nice flavor," Lester said.

Mr. Dodge smiled and said, "I wouldn't know. I'm not a smoker, myself. Never did take to the stuff. Tried it many times when I was younger, but never quite got the hang of it."

"Well, if you never liked it, you certainly wouldn't miss it much," Lester said, turning to watch Mr. Dodge as he went to the bin that contained the tobacco. As he lifted the lid on the wooden bin, Jack could smell the odor of the tobacco filling the room.

Mrs. Dodge spoke from behind Jack, "How are you doing in school, Jack?"

"Fine, Ma'am," Jack replied.

"It won't be long until you'll be out for the summer. Do you have any plans for the summer?" she asked.

"I hadn't given it much thought," Jack replied.

"Well, Mr. Dodge and I sure could use a boy about your age to help out around here. We are getting too old for climbing ladders to stock the higher shelves. Our son, Ralph, married a girl he met when he was in the military, and lives over in Kentucky. We don't see him and his family much. I'm sure he would help out if he was available, but since he isn't, I suppose we must hire someone," she said, looking over at her husband.

Mr. Dodge smiled and said, "Well, yes, Rosalie has a point. We were talking about that the other day. Jack is perfect for the job, if he's willing."

Jack looked over at his grandfather who was standing at the counter, leaning upon his cane. Jack's first impulse was to suggest they hire Collin McCauley for the job, but thought better of it. Folks around here didn't take to the Irish immigrant families very well. Lester nodded his head in approval. Jack smiled and said, "I would like that very much."

"Good," Mrs. Dodge said. "Maybe you could start working on the weekends and when school is out, you can work full time. I'm pretty sure we will have enough to do around here to keep you on full time." She looked over at her husband for approval. Howard smiled and nodded his head. "It is settled then. When would you like to start?' she asked.

Before Jack realized what, he was doing, he heard himself say, "I could start today."

"Well, that is exactly the kind of attitude we are looking for," Howard Dodge said. "If you need to go home and come back, you can. You needn't worry about a lunch. Rosalie always makes too much for the two of us."

"I do have one thing I have to do," Jack said. "It shouldn't take long."

"That will be fine. Just, whenever you are ready to start. We pay five cents a day," Howard Dodge said.

Jack smiled. "That sounds fine," he said.

"Five cents and two licorice sticks," Rosalie added.

"Thank you, Ma'am," Jack said.

"One for you and one for your friend," Rosalie said, looking over at her husband.

Howard Dodge placed the items on Lester's list into a sack, and Jack slung it over his shoulder. He walked alongside his grandfather at a slow pace. Lester huffed and puffed as he shuffled along the dirt streets toward home. He didn't say anything to Jack about the events that occurred while they were at the mercantile. Soon they reached the house and Jack waited while his grandfather climbed the steps and went inside.

"What took so long?" Delores asked. "I've been waiting for the sugar. Lunch will be a little late."

Lester winked over at Jack before saying, "We were busy."

"Busy with what?" Delores asked, looking over her shoulder.

"Busy getting our Jack a job at the mercantile," Lester said, sitting down near the fire.

Delores turned to her left to look at Lester. Next, she turned to her right to look over at Jack. She smiled. "Well, what do you know about that?" she commented. "It certainly will come in handy having some extra money coming in. I'm right proud of you, Jack."

Jack felt frozen where he stood. Surely, his grandmother wouldn't take the money away from him. He looked over at his grandfather for support. Lester sensed right away what Jack was thinking.

"Well, now, Delores," Lester began, "the boy can't be expected to turn over his earnings to us."

"Why not?" Delores asked. "Who feeds him, washes his filthy clothes when he falls in the mud, and looks after him every day?"

"Well, now, Sheldon is giving us money to do that," Lester said.

Delores turned to Jack and said, "Jack, you wait outside. I need to have a talk with your grandfather."

"Yes Ma'am," Jack replied as he stepped through the door and began to pull it shut behind him. "I have something I have to do," he called inside before pulling the door close behind him.

Jack jumped from the porch and began running toward the Armstrong Chair Factory. He had to tell Collin the good news. He climbed the stairs as fast as he could, and knocked on the door. The door opened a slight crack and a pair of smoky blue eyes appeared from within. "Is Collin here?" Jack asked.

A small red-haired boy shook his head. "He is downstairs," the little boy said.

"Thank you," Jack called out as he hurried down the stairs. He entered the chair factory to find Collin standing in a cloud of dust, holding a broom.

"I was going to come by as soon as I finished up here," Collin said, frowning. "I don't like folks coming by when I'm not expecting them."

"I'm sorry Collin, but I have news," Jack said, coughing. He covered his mouth and nose with his right arm and blinked the tears from his eyes, while waving the dust away from his face.

Collin leaned the broom against a long wooden table that had chair parts covering the top. "What news would that be?" he asked, walking toward Jack.

Jack kept coughing. "Is there somewhere we could go?" Jack asked, choking.

Collin nodded and pointed toward a doorway. "We can go out back." Jack followed Collin through the wooden door into the morning air.

"This is much better," Jack said.

"What news would you be havin' for me, Jack?" Collin asked.

"I got a job," Jack replied happily. "It only pays five cents a day, but it's a job. I was thinking I could split it with you until you got on your feet again."

Collin frowned. "I'm not about to be takin' handouts, Jack. We McCauley's are a proud lot, so we are. I'm happy you got a job, like you did, but I'll be lookin' for something of me own."

"Consider it a loan, Collin," Jack said. "You can pay me back when you get on your feet. We will keep up with your studies and soon you will be working down at the docks, or somewhere else.

The important thing is to keep you from going to the poor house and your brothers and sisters all sent to who knows where. You will be able to stay together as a family."

Collin frowned. "You would do that for the likes of me?" he asked.

"Sure, I would," Jack replied. "We have a deal. I help you out and you keep those two goons off my back."

"How are we goin' to do any studying if we are both workin'?" Collin asked.

"I haven't figured that out yet, but I thought if I talked to the Dodge's, they may let you hang around the store while I work. You could bring your slate and I could tutor you while I work. Of course, I must have their permission first," Jack said.

"Hmm," Collin rubbed his chin. "When do you start, again?"

"Today, I should get there as soon as possible," Jack replied.

Collin nodded his head, "I'll drop by when I've finished here. I'll pretend I'm just lookin' around. You give me a signal if you want me to leave or if it's okay to stay."

"Good idea," Jack said, smiling. He coughed again and said, "You should cover your mouth and nose with something when you are sweeping in there. I can see how your mother got sick from breathing that dust." Jack reached deep into his pocket and pulled out the two licorice sticks, handing them to Collin. "Here, if you break them in small pieces, there should be enough for all of you." Collin took the candy from Jack and frowned as he looked down at them. "I'll see you later," Jack said, before turning to run toward home.

He slowed down as he approached his house. He would tell his grandparents he was leaving and hurry to the mercantile to get started. He opened the door to find his grandfather sitting at the table. "I'm going to the mercantile now," Jack said.

Delores Gideon approached the door and said, "I suppose you were off with that McCauley boy." Jack looked up at his grandmother. "It's a good boy wanting to help out a family in need Jack. It's the Christian thing to do. However, you cannot expect to work every day to give your money to strangers. Even if they are strangers in need. Don't forget those who look after you every day. We could use the money at home as well."

"Delores, let the boy be," Lester called out.

"Yes, Ma'am, I will remember," Jack said, backing away from the door.

"That's a good lad," his grandmother said.

Jack turned and began walking toward the mercantile. His shoulders were slumped. He had been so happy to be able to help his friend. Now he worried that his grandmother would expect him to turn his earnings over to her. He bolted into a run. The morning fog was lifting and the air felt cold upon his face. He arrived at the mercantile in no time. Mrs. Dodge smiled as he came through the door. "Well, look who came back."

"Yes, Ma'am," Jack said.

"Did you get your business taken care of, Son?" Howard Dodge asked, as he came through the door carrying a box.

"Well, sort of, Sir," Jack said. "You see, I've been assigned to tutor someone at school. We meet after school every day and on weekends. I'm helping him learn to read and write. I was, well, I was sort of wondering if it would be alright if he dropped by here with his slate and I could tutor him while I worked? I promise not to let it interfere with my duties. I will keep working. He could just sit somewhere quietly working on his slate."

Judy Lennington

"I think that is a very honorable thing for a boy your age to be doing, don't you Rosalie?" Howard said. "What a fine young man you are, Jack Gideon. Your father and grandparents must be very proud of you."

"Yes Sir," Jack replied.

"I don't think it would hurt," Rosalie said. "This young man you are tutoring, I take it he is trustworthy?"

"Oh, yes, Ma'am," Jack said, standing up straight. "He is very honest and trust worthy. I stake my reputation on it."

Rosalie began to chuckle. "Well then, a reputation is a very important thing to a young man your age. If you vouch for him, I have no problem with you tutoring him while you work. Just understand that we expect you to work while you are here. We are paying you to get things done and that is what we expect of you. Your duty to us must come first. Do I make myself clear?" she asked.

"Yes, Ma'am," Jack said, nodding his head.

"You can start with these," Howard said pointing to the box. "I need this box of hinges put out. Just fill the wooden box with as many as you can get in it. Make certain they are neat. Then I'll carry the remaining hinges to the back."

"Yes Sir," Jack said. He lifted the heavy box into his arms and carried them to the wooden bins along the wall. There was a wooden bin with only six remaining hinges in it. Jack began to stack the hinges neatly in the bin until it was full. He lifted the box into his arms again, and carried it back to where Mr. Dodge had placed it.

"Excellent job," Howard said. "Now get down under the counter here and see if you can find a key I dropped earlier this morning.

Jack went behind the counter and dropped to his knees. He was running his hand along the edge of the counter when he heard the door open. "May I help you?" Howard asked. Jack popped his head up to see Collin standing inside the door. He kept his hand on the door knob, and it looked like he was ready to bolt any minute. Jack smiled and waved for him to come in. He noticed Mr. and Mrs. Dodge looking at one another.

"Is this the young man you are tutoring?" Rosalie Dodge asked.

"Yes, Ma'am," Jack said, "This is Collin McCauley."

"You are Irish aren't you, young man?" Howard asked.

Collin stiffened. Jack hurried to his side. "Yes, Mr. Dodge. Collin is Irish all right. He is respectable, and he wants to learn to read and write so he can get a respectable job here in Wellsville."

"Mrs. Patrone said your family is behind in their rent to Mr. Armstrong. She said you have no means of supporting yourselves. She said your father…" Rosalie did not finish her sentence.

Collin turned to leave. Jack took a deep breath and closed his eyes. "That is why it is so important that Collin learn to read and write. He needs to do it for his family. They need our help, and it is our Christian duty to help them if we can. You don't have to do anything. I will do it all. I will work hard for you. All you have to do is let him sit in the corner with his slate."

The door closed and Collin was leaving. Jack stood there looking from Mr. Dodge to Mrs. Dodge, pleading with his eyes.

"I suppose it can't hurt," Howard said. "Just so you know, we will be watching. I don't want to find anything missing at the end of the day. If I do, you both are out."

"Yes, Sir, I promise you will not regret it," Jack said. He turned and opened the door. "Collin, come on in. It's okay."

"I don't want to be stayin' where I ain't welcome," Collin said to the Dodges.

"You can stay if you keep out of the way and keep your hands to yourself," Howard explained.

"I ain't no thief," Collin said. "I pays me way. If I don't have the money, I go without. That is the way of it."

"Well, that is good to know," Howard said. He nodded his head toward Rosalie. "You can take a chair back by the wood stove. Jack, I have more boxes to bring out front. You come with me."

"Collin," Jack called out, "write your ABC's on your slate." Then he disappeared through a green floral curtain that hung over the door to the back.

When Jack returned, he found Collin sitting with the slate in his lap. He held the slate up for Jack to see. "I've written me ABC's twice, so I have," Collin said.

Mrs. Dodge had been dusting the countertop to the left of where Collin sat. She nodded her head and said, "He did indeed. I've been keeping my eye on the lad and he did just as he said."

"Well," Jack began, "Can you write them again in small letters?"

Collin frowned. "I ain't so good with the small letters," he said.

"I need you to climb up there and hand down those wooden boxes, Jack," Mr. Dodge said.

Jack looked up at the shelf and nodded his head, "Yes, Sir," he said. He began to climb the ladder. He glanced over his shoulder and saw Collin struggling with the assignment he had been given. At one point, he allowed the slate to fall into his lap and he rolled his eyes upward out of frustration.

"What is the problem?" Mrs. Dodge asked, walking around the counter to look down at the slate. She bent over and said, "Ah, I see. You have written the letter "n" backwards. It's supposed to be something like an "h". It's like this." Mrs. Dodge took the chalk from Collin's hand and marked on his slate. "You see?" she asked, smiling down at him.

As the morning went on, Collin worked hard at every instruction Jack gave him. Mrs. Dodge helped often when Jack was busy. When lunch time rolled around she asked Collin to stay and have lunch with them. "Thank you very much, Ma'am, but I have to run. I have to help me Ma fix somethin' for me brothers and sisters to eat," Collin said, with a smile. "I'll see you tomorrow, Jack," he said, before darting through the door and disappearing down the street.

"Does your friend know we are not open on Sundays?" Mrs. Dodge asked.

"I don't know," Jack replied.

"Well, come along, Jack," Mrs. Dodge said. "I've fresh baked bread and pork gravy in the back."

As they sat around the table in the back of the store where the Dodge's lived, Mr. Dodge said, "That boy, Collin, isn't a bad sort of lad. I think he would make a fine employee. I don't see what Mrs. Patrone's problem with the family is."

Jack swallowed and said, "Mrs. Patrone doesn't like Collin because he popped her son, Anthony, a good one in the school yard. Anthony is a bully, and Collin was defending someone."

"Oh, my," Mrs. Dodge said. "Is he a ruffian?"

"No, he keeps to himself. He just wants to get an education so he can help support his family. Anthony is the ruffian. Collin was only helping," Jack explained.

The Dodges looked across the table at each other. Jack hoped he hadn't said too much.

Judy Lennington

"I see," Mr. Dodge said. "Who was Collin helping?" he asked. Jack cleared his throat. He felt his face flushing. "Oh, I think I understand now," Mr. Dodge said.

"What?" Mrs. Dodge asked.

"Collin was defending me," Jack said, looking across the table at Mrs. Dodge. "Anthony Patrone and Melvin Riley lay waiting for me every day. They pull pranks on me and sometimes they get physical. Collin and I have an agreement. He keeps them off my back, and I will help him learn to read and write so he can get a job on the docks."

"Is Collin dangerous?" Mrs. Dodge asked looking from her husband to Jack.

"No Ma'am. Collin is a good boy. He works hard and he is trying to help support his family. I wouldn't listen to what Mrs. Patrone has to say about him, if I were you," Jack said. The Dodge's looked at each other in that secret way grownups did and remained quiet. Jack assumed he had said enough and ate his lunch quietly.

After lunch, Mr. Dodge and Jack returned to the store. Several customers stopped by and Jack was surprised to find that most of them didn't buy anything. They merely dropped by to talk about events of the day. Some had news from East Liverpool, and some had news from the docks. Jack kept busy, and before long it was time to go home for supper. Mr. Dodge stood holding the door open for Jack. "Thank you, Jack. You gave us an honest day's work equal to what any grown man would have done. Will we see you back here after school Monday?" he asked.

"Yes, Sir," Jack replied. "Is it alright if I continue to tutor Collin while I work?"

"I don't see why not. We may even find something for your friend to do while he's here. It won't pay much, but it may help his situation out some," Mr. Dodge said.

"Thank you, Sir," Jack said, smiling. "Collin will be very happy to hear that."

Jack skipped happily as he made his way home. He thought about the events of the day. The Dodge's understood Collin was a good boy and not someone they needed to fear. He had accomplished so much today. He had earned some money of his own, helped the Dodge's, helped Collin with his studies, and even helped get Collin a job. He felt very proud of himself as he continued along his way. He looked up and noticed the sun was dropping over the trees in the western sky. His father would be coming home from work shortly after he arrived home. He couldn't wait to tell his grandfather about his day. He climbed the steps to their porch just as a family was passing in the street. The adult couple nodded their heads just as Jack realized it was the Raines family. "Good afternoon, young man," the gentleman said.

Mrs. Raines was leading a young boy by the hand. The boy stared up at Jack. Leading him by the other hand was Lynette Raines. She wrinkled up her nose at Jack as they passed. Jack turned to look back at them. Lynette turned to stick her tongue out at Jack. He quickly looked away. He smiled as he continued to climb the steps. Not even Lynette Raines was going to get to him today. He took a deep breath and instantly smelled supper. He opened the door to find his grandmother smiling down at him. She took his hat and helped him out of his coat. "How was your day, Jack?" she asked.

"It was fine, Ma'am," Jack replied, looking over at his grandfather who sat near the fireplace.

Judy Lennington

"What do think of your new job?" Lester asked.

"I like it just fine," Jack said. "The Dodge's are fine people. They even let Collin do his studies while I worked. They were real nice."

"Are you sure that is wise?" his grandmother asked. "I mean, if anything comes up missing they are likely to blame both of you, Son."

"Collin isn't a thief, Grandmother. He would no sooner steal from the Dodge's as he would steal from us. You don't know him as I do," Jack replied, going to stand near the fire.

"Well, I hope you know what you are doing. All it takes is one time for something to come up missing," Delores said. "Maybe Collin isn't a thief, but should something come up missing I guarantee you, Collin McCauley is the first person that will be blamed for it." She turned and began stirring a pot that hung over the red embers of the fireplace.

Jack thought about what his grandmother had said. He knew her words were true. He felt sorry for Collin, being an Irishman and all. They had a reputation of being drunkards and unreliable workers. He heard the latch on the door and turned to see his father enter the room. Jack ran to greet him.

Sheldon laughed as Jack embraced him. "Well, how was your day, Jack Gideon?" Sheldon asked.

"It was great, Father. I got a job," Jack said, excitedly.

"What? Where?" Sheldon asked, stooping down to look Jack in the eye.

"I went with Grandfather to the mercantile this morning and Mr. Dodge asked me if I would like a job helping him around the store after school and for the summer. He pays five cents a week," Jack replied.

Sheldon looked over at Lester who nodded his head and smiled. "It appears Jack won't be spending so much time climbing trees this summer," Lester said.

"Well, what are you going to do with all that money?" Sheldon asked.

Jack noticed his grandmother taking a step closer to them so she could hear better. "I don't know yet, but I know I need some new clothes and maybe a pair of shoes. I also was looking at a catalogue Mr. Dodge keeps on the counter and I saw a real nice set of pottery dishes made right in East Liverpool. I was thinking maybe Grandmother might like real china dishes with matching saucers and cups."

Delores covered her mouth with her hand and gasped. Lester rose to his feet and said," Well, that is right nice of you, Jack. A boy your age usually thinks of foolish things he would rather have. Those are some mighty nice thoughts you have there," he said, making his way to the table. "I'm mighty proud of you."

Sheldon stood up and smiled down at Jack. "I'm proud of you as well, Son."

"Thank you," Jack replied. "If I have any left over, I was thinking of helping Collin's mother get to a doctor. I'm pretty worried about her. I wouldn't want to see anything happen to her. Collin doesn't have any other family to take them in, if she were to die."

Sheldon placed his hand upon Jack's shoulder. "You are too young for such a heavy weight upon your shoulders, Jack. Let the Lord in Heaven work his wonders upon Collin's family," he said, smiling down at Jack.

Delores took another step closer and said, "It appears as though our Jack is still tutoring the Irish boy. The McCauley boy went to the store and Jack tutored him while he worked for the Dodge's."

Sheldon looked down at Jack and frowned as he asked, "Did you ask for their permission to do that, Jack?"

"Oh, yes, Sir. I would never do such a thing without asking first, Sir. They were hesitant at first, but they are okay with it now. Mr. Dodge said he might find some work for Collin as well. I think he sees that Mrs. Patrone is a busy body and trying to make trouble for the McCauley's," Jack explained.

"Now it isn't very nice of you to be calling Mrs. Patrone names, Son," Sheldon cautioned.

"I know, Father. Normally, I wouldn't do such a thing, but when I got to the mercantile today, Mrs. Patrone was there trying to convince them to sign a petition to force the McCauley's out of their home and into the poor house," Jack said.

"How do you know that was why she was there?" Sheldon asked.

"Mr. and Mrs. Dodge pretty muchly confirmed it, Sir," Jack replied.

Sheldon glanced over at his Father and smiled. "Well, I think we should mind our own business. The more we get involved, the more responsible we are going to be if things go badly. Do you understand what I'm saying?" Sheldon asked, looking down at Jack.

Jack nodded his head, "Yes, Sir," he replied. "But Collin is my friend, Father. It's a might hard to sit back and keep quiet. I want to help him as best I can."

"I understand Jack, however, there is only so much you can do," Sheldon said. "I think you are doing plenty by tutoring Collin. That is the best anyone could do for that boy now."

Jack thought about what his father had said. Sheldon went to the basin and began to pour water into it. Jack stood stationary as he pondered over the conversation with his father. "You can begin to set the table, Jack," his grandmother said.

"Yes, Ma'am," Jack replied as he shook himself from his thoughts. As he lifted the stack of plates from the shelf he looked over at his grandfather who was staring into the flickering flames of the fireplace. "Grandfather, you never did finish telling me how old Limpy lost his leg."

Lester nodded his head and smiled. "Well now, as I recall the way Limpy told it, they were chasing after a cow. That is what they call a mother whale. They had just put their boats in the water and were climbing down into them when from out of nowhere a bull whale rammed their ship. He hit it hard and drove it straight into the lowering boats. He said men went flying in every direction into the water. The bull surfaced and churned up the water some and dove again. They were all scrambling to get into the boats. Before long, the whale rammed the ship again. This time he nearly split it in two. They knew it was going down. The men on board began tossing provisions down into the smaller boats. The whale made a third pass at them and this time he focused his attack upon the smaller boats. He smashed nearly every one of them until there were only small pieces of wood floating on the surface for the men to hang onto to. Men were crying and screaming all around. As darkness came upon them it got quiet. Limpy said when the sun came up there were only a few of them left clinging to debris."

"Is that when he lost his leg?" Jack asked.

Lester shook his head. "No, not at that time. He said there were about six of them bobbing around out there in the cold, icy, water. He said someone yelled that something had nipped him. Then one by one they started being drug under and surfacing again, screaming and shouting."

"What was it?" Jack asked. "Was it the bull whale?"

Lester shook his head again. "No, it wasn't a whale. It was sharks. They were attracted by the smell of blood in the water. He said that the men disappeared, one by one, until there was only him and the first mate, Joe, left. Joe was an older man and he had never been very kind to Limpy in the past. Limpy said he wasn't very kind to anyone, really. They huddled together as they clung to a large piece of debris. Limpy said they hung on to that wood taking turns sleeping, while they waited for a rescue ship. He said it was about two days after the sharks attacked that he felt something pull him under. He heard Joe screaming and he was sure he was a goner. He fought the shark off and managed to surface to the top. For some reason, he couldn't understand, the shark left him be. He assumed he must not have tasted very good. He said that Joe spent the last two days praying to God to save them and thought that may also have been why the shark let him live. Anyway, another whaling ship happened by and rescued them. They spent another ten months on board that ship before they were on dry land again. A member of the crew fashioned a wooden leg for Limpy out of the drifting debris they clung to in the ocean. Limpy said old Joe never did go to sea again. He moved in with his sister in Massachusetts and died in bed one night."

"Jack," Delores said, "Supper is ready. You need to finish setting the table so we can eat."

"Oh," Jack said, looking back at his grandmother. "I'm sorry, of course."

While Jack finished placing the dinner ware on the table, Sheldon carried his dirty water outside and tossed it over the side of the porch. He returned, wiped out the basin, and began to pull a clean shirt on. Soon, they were sitting around the table while Lester said grace.

Sheldon began explaining the events of his day and the gossip that was going around the plant. "We're working on something new at the plant. Some rich man in New York is building a new paddle boat. We've heard it is going to be really something." He took a bite and chewed his food, while everyone watched him, waiting for the rest of the story. "Apparently, this rich guy is putting a floating gambling casino on the rivers. We've heard he has the money to spend, and he's sparing no expense."

"Gambling!" Delores huffed. "I suppose there will be prostit...." She did not finish as her eyes fell upon Jack.

It grew quiet around the table. Jack looked over at his grandfather and said, "Limpy must have been in terrible pain, floating out there after that shark attacked him. He's lucky to have survived."

"That he was, Jack. He said his main concern was that his bleeding leg would attract other sharks. Maybe, one that wasn't so picky about the taste of human flesh," Lester said.

"I'll have no such talk at my table," Delores said. "There is enough pain and agony in the world. We don't need to call attention to it at the dinner table."

"But Grandmother, this was a long time ago," Jack protested. There was no need for Delores to comment. Her glare at Jack said it all. He looked down at his plate and resumed eating.

"I suppose you will be working late in the evenings," Lester said, looking over at Sheldon.

Judy Lennington

"I assume so. At least I hope so," Sheldon said. "There were rumors of a lay off last week. Now it looks like we will keep working."

"Do you think they will hire Mr. McCauley?" Jack asked, with a mouth full of food.

"Jack," Sheldon said, pointing toward Jack with his fork. "Mind your table manners. Empty your mouth before speaking."

"Yes, Sir," Jack said, swallowing hard.

Sheldon sighed as he watched Jack. After a long pause, Sheldon shook his head. "They are not going to hire Mr. McCauley, Jack."

"How can you be sure, Father? You said yourself that they will be busy. Why wouldn't they hire Mr. McCauley?" Jack asked, with an empty mouth.

"I've heard rumors about your friend, Collin's father, Jack," Sheldon said, lowering his gaze. "I didn't want to say anything, but I suppose you have a right to know, since you've taken on the responsibility of helping the family. I want you to know that I am very proud of you for that. However, Mr. McCauley, it seems, isn't much of a worker. From what I've heard, he only works until he earns his first pay and then he's off drinking it up some where's. I'm told he's only good for a day, or three at the most."

Jack felt a lump come up in his throat. He knew this to be true, but did not want to say it out loud. His grandmother may object to Jack's helping Collin if she knew the truth about Mr. McCauley. After a long pause, Jack said softly, "I don't see why the whole family should suffer because of their father."

Lester cleared his throat. "Jack, you don't understand. It's the drink. I am certain that Mr. McCauley is a good man. Once the drink gets a hold of a man, he has no control. He hates himself and would do anything to change what he has become, but he doesn't have the will power to take control of his life. The drink owns him and everything he does. It was the same way with old Limpy. I tried and tried to get him to leave the bottle alone. Once I came close. He was sober for a while, but just a whiff of the stuff, and he was helpless to abstain from its control over him. He fought the demons in the bottom of the jug until the day we buried him in the river."

"Maybe Mr. McCauley will be different. Hasn't anyone ever beat the demons? Maybe, if we pray real hard for him, God will hear us and help him," Jack pleaded.

"He has to want to be helped, Jack," Delores said. "I don't think he wants our help, or anyone else's for that matter."

Jack felt his chest tightening. Tears welled up in his eyes as he wiped at them with his sleeve. "There has to be something we can do to help the McCauley's. We can't let Mrs. Patrone send them to the poor house. I know if I had a mother and brothers and sisters, I wouldn't want to be separated from them. Collin is doing everything he can to keep his family together. Isn't there anything we can do to help?"

He noticed his grandmother's face reddening. She looked over at her husband and took a deep breath before lowering her gaze to her plate. Sheldon reached over and placed his hand upon Jack's arm. "Jack, I understand how you must feel. Unfortunately, we are not able to help every needy family that comes along. We are barely getting by as it is. You have my permission to continue tutoring the McCauley boy, and whatever you feel necessary to do to help them, is fine with me. However, if it turns out that what you do is not enough, I do not want you to feel that you have failed them. You are already doing more than anyone else. I am proud of you."

"I am proud of you as well," Lester said, nodding his head.

Jack could not bring himself to respond. His throat had constricted and he continued to wipe at the tears that refused to stop welling up in his eyes. He had lost his appetite and asked to be excused from the table. He stepped outside into the night air and sat on the steps to the porch. He looked upward at the milky way as it spread across the night sky. He said a silent prayer to God for help, not for himself, but for the McCauley's. Before long, his father stepped out and sat down beside him. Sheldon placed his arm around his son's shoulders and said, "Jack, you are so young for such a heavy burden. Perhaps you have taken on more than you can handle," Sheldon said, looking upward.

"Father, I know you think I am doing this because I want Collin to protect me from Melvin and Anthony," Jack began, "The truth is, that is exactly why I was doing it in the beginning. But not anymore. I went to the chair factory and saw Collin sweeping in all that dust. I could hardly breath. He told me his mother is sickly and I know it is because of breathing in all that dust. I know how I felt when my own mother laid in her bed trying to breath. I remember what it felt like to think she might die, and I remember what it felt like when she did. I still feel it every day. Collin is trying so hard. I think what you say about his father might be true, but I can't give up hope that somehow, we can help him. Somebody has to try. Why can't we try?"

Sheldon pulled Jack close and kissed the top of his head. "Oh Jack, what can we do? You don't seem to understand. You can't help someone if they don't want your help. We can't force them to accept our help. They will just think we are being busy bodies. People are strange in how they think sometimes. I think, from what I've heard you say about your friend Collin, that he is a proud young man. He is trying to do what is best for his family. He has taken on adult duties and he is just a boy himself. I hope he succeeds for all their sakes, I really do. But I don't want you to undertake such a burden at your age. You are young, and you should be doing things a young boy your age likes to do. I have no problem with you working at the mercantile. I think it is a valuable experience for you. But I would also like to see you climbing trees and exploring the hillside too."

Jack looked up at his father. "How did you find out about me exploring the hillside?" he asked.

Sheldon laughed and rubbed the top of Jack's head. "I was a boy here in Wellsville, once myself. I climbed trees and explored the hillside every chance I got. I wouldn't be afraid to bet that your grandfather did the very same thing. As I recall, the rocks break apart and form a shale that slides down the hillside and causes you to lose your footing occasionally. I also recall that the copperheads like to crawl out onto the rocks and warm themselves in the sun. You should be mindful of them. It's not only copperheads, as I recall. I recall seeing a timber rattler a few times up there. They are even more dangerous."

"I've never seen a rattler up there. I have seen a copperhead, but they are mostly afraid and try to avoid me," Jack said, smiling. "I do think about sliding into one when the shale gives way and I lose my footing. I keep to the trees mostly for something to hold on to."

Sheldon nodded his head. "I did the same thing. See? We aren't all that different after all." He squeezed Jack's shoulders and said, "Why don't you go inside and get ready for bed. Tomorrow morning comes early. After church, we will go fishing together."

Jack smiled up at his father. "I've been waiting all week to go fishing. I hope it don't rain," Jack said, climbing the steps. "Good night, Father," he called out, as he went inside.

Sheldon remained outside. It was a lovely evening. After some time, he was joined by his parents. Lester struggled carrying a chair in one hand, while leaning upon his cane. Sheldon jumped to his feet and took the chair from his father. His mother sat down on the chair as Sheldon went inside for a second chair for his father to sit upon. He returned to his spot on the steps where he could look up at the sky above them.

It was a quiet Saturday evening. To his left, he noticed a lantern glowing from Mrs. Cartwright's house. Beyond that was the Griffin's house. The houses that lined the street were basically all built the same. They were two room houses with lofts above. Some had ladders leading to the loft, some had stairs. Some had windows in the loft and some didn't. They were simple homes built to fulfill the needs of their occupants. They were homes of the working class of Wellsville. As Sheldon looked southward he saw larger, more elegant homes. They were the homes of the elite that lived on Water Street. Their view was that of the Ohio River and beyond its banks, Virginia.

Movement to his left, caught his attention. It was Mrs. Cartwright making her way toward them. "Good evening," she said, smiling up at them from the lawn.

"Good evening," Sheldon said. "Come on up, I'll get another chair."

Mrs. Cartwright waved her hand and shook her head as she said, "Oh, please, don't bother. I'm not staying. I saw you out here and I wanted to tell you what a fine young man Jack is. It is a pleasure to have him in my school. He has undertaken quite a large responsibility for one so young, as he has been tutoring the McCauley boy. He is doing an excellent job of it, too. I am quite surprised at how quickly the McCauley boy has caught on. He is progressing very well. I must say that I don't believe it likely that he would do as well on my teachings alone."

Sheldon smiled. "That is very kind of you to tell us. I'm afraid we have been a little hard on Jack recently for his taking on such an enormous challenge for one so young," he said.

"Well, I am not here to tell you how to raise your son, Mr. Gideon. However, I will say that it appears he is up for the challenge. He would make a fine school teacher someday," Mrs. Cartwright said. "Well, it is a lovely night, and I do have work to do. You folks enjoy your evening. I just thought you should know." She turned and began to walk away.

"Mrs. Cartwright," Sheldon called after her. "This McCauley boy, what do you think of him?"

Mrs. Cartwright turned and took a deep breath. She seemed to choose her words very carefully. "Collin McCauley is in a most unfortunate position. He is three grades behind the other children his age. I believe that to be the result of the family's constant relocating. He appears to have serious social disadvantages. However, his willingness to learn is the most intense I have ever seen in all my years of teaching. I can only imagine why. If you are asking me as to whether he is a bad influence upon your son, Jack, I can only tell you that since his association with Collin, Jack has also changed. He is not as timid and sad as he was before. Is that a good thing? I believe it to be. However, I am not his parents. I am only there to do one thing, and one thing only. It is my duty to see to it he gets an education. Have I answered your question, Mr. Gideon?" she asked, smiling.

Sheldon nodded his head. "I believe you have, Mrs. Cartwright. You have a good evening and rest assured that Jack and I will drop by tomorrow afternoon to split some wood for you."

"That is very kind of you, Mr. Gideon. Now I see where Jack gets it," she smiled, and turned to continue walking toward her own home.

Sheldon watched her as she went about making her way up the steps to her front porch. "It seems she never ages. She looked the same when she was my own teacher," he said.

Lester chuckled. "I'll bet she doesn't feel the same. We are all getting older. I remember her when I was a boy. She was younger than I, but she was quite the little lady. Nearly every boy in school wanted to walk her home, when she was young."

"Lester!" Delores said.

"Well, it's the truth," Lester said.

"Did she ever marry?" Sheldon asked.

"No, she did not. She was engaged to a young man who fought in the war. I believe he was killed in action. She never married," Lester replied.

"I remember hearing about that, but I had forgotten all about it," Delores said. "From as far back as I can remember, she has lived right there in that little house all by herself."

"What a pity. I hope she is happy," Sheldon said. "She was always good to me when I was in school."

"You were a good student," Delores said. "You never gave any of us any trouble."

"Except for that one time," Sheldon said laughing. "I seem to recall Father taking me out back and strapping my legs a good one."

"I can't remember what you did," Lester said, looking from Sheldon to Delores. "What did he do, again?"

Sheldon laughed. "I was hiding behind the mercantile with Rusty Kendall. Remember, we were peeking through a hole in the outhouse at Rosalie Dodge. I remember it was while her father was still living, and he caught us. He went to our parents and both, Rusty and I, got whacked for it."

Lester laughed. "Oh, I remember now."

"Shame on you, Sheldon," Delores said. "How can you look that poor woman in the eye after that?"

"As I recall, I had to sweep their floors and stock their shelves for a whole summer because of it," Sheldon said. "As I think of it, I imagine it is the same thing Jack is doing for them now. It wasn't so bad. I wonder if it brings back memories for Rosalie."

"Sheldon Gideon!" Delores barked. Lester and Sheldon were both laughing. Before long, Delores began to giggle as well. "Shame on you, Sheldon," she said, covering her mouth with her hand.

Jack woke to find his father snoring. He gathered his clothes quietly and carried them down the ladder. His grandfather had a roaring fire in the fireplace when he reached the ground floor. She seemed to be in an unusually good mood this morning. This Sunday morning, they were having eggs for breakfast. "I thought it would be a pleasant change from the boiled oats," Delores said, smiling down at Jack.

"I thought our chickens weren't laying. Where did the eggs come from?" Jack asked.

"Hermon and Hilda sent a basket over," Lester replied.

"Hilda?" Jack asked.

"Well, I doubt Hilda was aware of what was happening, but the eggs came from their chickens rightly enough. Even though

Judy Lennington

Hilda may not recall it, she babied those peeps until they growed up to be nice laying hens," Lester said, poking at the fire. "Is your Daddy still sleeping?"

"Yes, he was sleeping soundly. He was snoring when I came down," Jack said, pulling his trousers on. He pulled his suspenders up over his shoulders and slipped his feet into his shoes. The laces drug on the floor as he clomped toward the door.

"You need to tie those shoes, Jack Gideon, so they don't drag in the mud," Delores called out to Jack as he stepped outside. He was on his way to the privy. He looked around as he clomped toward the small wooden building out back. The birds were chirping this morning. The sky was clear. Jack was happy, for there were no dark clouds in the sky. All he had to do was make it through church without falling asleep and he would find himself sitting down by the river's edge with his father and their fishing poles.

When Jack returned inside, he could hear his father rustling about above them. "I smell eggs," Sheldon said, climbing down the ladder. "It smells good."

"You can thank old Hermon for that," Lester said, tapping his cane upon the floor.

"How does it look out there, Jack?" Sheldon asked.

"It looks like a fine day to go fishing, Father," Jack replied.

"Good then, fishing it is," Sheldon said, rustling Jack's hair. He turned and stepped outside. Before long he returned with his suspenders dangling at his hips.

"You boys sit down and eat your eggs," Delores said.

Everyone seemed to be in a good mood this morning. Jack looked from one face to another as they sat at the table talking about absolutely nothing of any significance. He wondered what had happened after he went to bed last night to cause them all to be so cheerful. Whatever it was, he was grateful for it. He helped his grandmother clear the table, and even helped to dry the dishes. Then he climbed the ladder once again and dressed in his finest clothes for church.

They walked to church together. They moved at a slow pace, so as not to leave Lester dragging behind. That was fine with Jack, as he would rather skip church and go straight to the river. However, he found he could day dream his way through the hour-long sermon, without being criticized, if he didn't fall asleep.

Jack sat in a pew with his father and grandparents. He looked around him as people began to file inside the small church. He felt prickly hairs on the back of his neck, standing on end. He turned around in his seat to see Milly Thompson sitting right behind him. As he expected she stuck her tongue out at him. This time, her mother saw her, and reached over to pinch her on the leg. "Ouch!" Milly cried out.

"Milly Thompson, shame on you. In church of all places. You'll be eating soap for dinner when we get home," Mrs. Thompson said. Jack turned around in his seat and covered his mouth as he grinned. For once, he didn't mind her sticking her tongue out at him. Jack wanted to turn around and look again, but refrained. He could hear Milly's sniffles behind him and knew she was crying. This was icing on the cake as far as Jack was concerned. He found himself smiling nearly the whole hour he sat, staring blankly, at the minister. He said a silent prayer to God, thanking him for punishing Milly for being so mean. Soon they were on their feet. The minister was praying. It was a long, winded, prayer this Sunday morning, and Jack found himself shifting from one leg to the other. At one point, his father reached over and placed his hand on Jack's shoulder to hold him still. "Amen," the congregation said.

Now Jack turned around and looked Milly Thompson square in the eye. Her eyes were red and puffy from crying. Jack smiled and waited for the Thompson's to step out into the aisle. Jack's family stepped out behind them and shuffled their way outside where the minister was waiting to greet them.

"Your son is a fine Christian young man, Sheldon," the Reverend said. "He sat listening to every word of the sermon this morning. You must be so proud to have such a fine young Christian boy in your household. Perhaps he will grow up to be a minister someday."

Sheldon shook the minister's hand and said, "He is a fine young man. We are proud of Jack. As for what he grows up to be, well, that is up to Jack."

Jack and his father walked ahead of Lester and Delores, who constantly stopped to talk to fellow parishioners. Jack looked up at the sky and smiled. "God has certainly blessed us with a fine day to go fishing," Jack said.

Sheldon chuckled and said, "He certainly has."

"I don't think I want to be a minister, Father," Jack said. "I hope you are not disappointed, but I don't think I could stand up there and talk that long."

Sheldon grinned and nodded his head. "I know what you mean. It's hard enough staying awake, isn't it?"

Jack looked up at his father and smiled. "Do you have trouble staying awake too?" he asked.

"Sometimes. Not so much now, but I recall being your age once. I often fell asleep in church. Of course, we had a different minister back then, but he was just as long winded as Reverend

Johnston," Sheldon said, smiling down at Jack. They were getting close to home now. "You hurry along and dig up some worms. I'll get changed and pack us a light snack."

"Okay, Father," Jack called out as he ran toward the house. As he was climbing the porch steps he looked off into the distance and saw the Thompson's turning the corner to make their way onto Water Street. He smiled again at the thought of Milly sitting on a stool with a bar of lye soap sticking out of her mouth. Maybe God was on his side.

Jack hummed as he walked alongside his father on their way to the river. They made their way southward along the dirt road that cut through Wellsville from the river docks, up over the hills, and on toward Niles, Ohio. Jack carried two fishing poles, while Sheldon carried the can of worms and a picnic basket. They turned right when they reached the docking area and followed the river bank until they came to a favorite spot. Jack baited the hooks while Sheldon drove sticks into the ground to rest their poles upon. Before long, they were sitting quietly, staring at the flowing current, as they waited and watched for something to bite.

Something caught Jack's attention and he looked to his left. A familiar figure was approaching from the docking area. He watched as it approached nearer and nearer. It was Collin McCauley. Jack's heart sank. He liked Collin, but this was a special time he and his father shared on Sundays. He swallowed the lump in his throat and said softly to his father, "Here comes Collin McCauley."

Sheldon looked to his left. He pushed his cap back on his head and said, "Well, at last I will have a chance to meet this infamous Collin McCauley."

Judy Lennington

Collin waved as he drew near. He walked up to Jack and squatted low in the hard dirt. Jack looked down at Collin's bare feet and said, "Hello Collin. What brings you down this way?"

"I remembered you said you go fishing with your Dah on Sundays. I'm in need of larnin' right bad, so I am. I was hopin' you could larn me some today. I brung me slate with me," Collin replied, nodding his head at Sheldon.

Jack forced himself to smile. He looked over at his father and said, "This is my father, Mr. Gideon."

Sheldon extended his hand to Collin. "It's a pleasure to make your acquaintance, Mr. McCauley. I've heard a lot about you from Jack."

"Thank you, sir," Collin said, nodding. He took his slate from inside his shirt and sat down next to Jack. "I've been workin' on me small letters. I thinks I knows them well enough. Now I need to larn how to sound them out and read the words they make when you put them all together. I don't know how to begin."

Jack thought a moment. He studied Collin's slate as he thought. "Let's start with a sentence in our reading books. Do you have a reading book?" Jack asked.

"I have one in me desk at school," Collin said.

Jack took the slate and began to write, "See Jack run. Run Jack run. See Jill run with Jack. See Spot run." He read the words as he wrote them.

Collin smiled and pointed to the slate. "Your name is in the reading book," he said.

"Yep," Jack said smiling. "This is how you spell my name." He began to sound out the letters that formed his name. He did not want to do this today, but did not want to risk alienating Collin. He would glance over at his father, occasionally, to find him smiling at the two of them.

Bend in The River

    As the afternoon wore on, Sheldon reeled in three big catfish. They shared their picnic lunch with Collin, who worked very hard on sounding out his letters. He was determined to learn as much as he could, as quickly as possible. Soon it was time to start walking the inclining road toward home. Sheldon invited Collin to join them for dinner. Collin declined as he had chores to do. Before parting, Sheldon gave Collin the largest of the three catfish to take home for dinner. As he walked away, Sheldon smiled down at Jack and said, "I am very proud of you, Jack, for taking on such a chore." In that instant, Jack felt ashamed for not wanting Collin to join them on the bank of the river.

    When they arrived at the house, Sheldon and Lester began to clean the fish. It was time for Jack to go off exploring on the hillside. He ran across the dirt streets, behind houses, and up the shale hillside until he could run no more. He clung to the trees and low-lying limbs for support, to keep himself from sliding down the hill. All the while, he watched for snakes. It was a perfect day for them to sun themselves on a warm rock. Jack crossed a dirt path that wound along the hillside, and continued his climb all the way to the top. He stood looking down at Wellsville below. He could see the rows of smaller homes, much like the one he shared with his father and grandparents. They lined the bottom of the hill on the back side of the primary business street. To the far right was Stevenson Company, where his father worked. He picked out the mercantile and the chair factory. Beyond the main street was Water Street and the row of larger, more elegant homes owned by the elite.

    Jack squatted low as his eyes followed the dirt road that led to the docks and the river. He could see across the bank to Virginia. He had never been across the river, but his father and grandfather

Judy Lennington

had. He wondered what it was like over there. He remembered Mrs. Cartwright telling them about the Indians that lived in the area long ago and how they raided the homes all up and down the river. He also remembered her telling them that settlers would buy wooden rafts and boats to float them and their belongings on until they found a place they wanted to build their homes on. They would dismantle their wooden boats and use the lumber for their homes. Jack tried to imagine what it would be like to float down the river and fight off the raiding Indians. It must have been an exciting time to live here in Wellsville.

Jack stood up as he looked at a large rock that was called "Chief Logan's Profile Rock". He tried to imagine what the chief really looked like. He terrorized the settlers along the river's bank with murderous raids in retaliation for the murder of his family members at the hands of white settlers. Jack imagined the chief standing on the top of the hill, in the very spot he now stood in, with a bow and arrow arched, ready to release upon an unsuspecting victim. This was Jack's favorite place. From up here, he could see everything. He climbed up here every chance he got. Not many children would brave the slippery loose slate and shale rock on the steep hillside. They also feared the snakes. Jack looked around, carefully inspecting every spot he imagined a snake to be lurking. Satisfied that he was safe, he once again looked down upon Wellsville again. It was time for his descent. He was getting hungry.

Jack carefully made his way from tree to tree as he worked his way down the hillside. It was normal to lose ones footing a time or two, but he always managed to recover his footing without getting hurt.

He had reached the dirt path that wound around the hillside. He paused to look below and noticed Milly and Lynette jumping rope in the yard between two of the larger homes on Water Street. Instantly he felt the hair on the back of his neck standing on end. Apparently, Milly's mother had forgiven her daughter for her unruly behavior in church earlier that day. Jack sighed and began to work his way on down the inclining hillside. As he neared the bottom, he noticed movement on the ground below. It was a snake, not a copperhead or rattler, just a corn snake. However, it was a snake and everyone knew that girls were terrified of snakes.

Jack hurried to catch the snake. He held it at arms-length and studied it for its ferociousness. It coiled around his arm and tried to bite him as he held it tightly behind the head. It was completely coiled around his arm by the time he reached the streets below. He had removed his coat earlier as he got warm climbing the hillside. He had it tied around his waist. Now Jack untied the knot, using one hand, and covered the arm with the coiled snake, so it could not be seen. He made his way toward the area he had seen the girls playing.

Jack pretended to be, nonchalantly, walking down Water Street. As he neared the girls took notice of him and quickly skipped toward him intending to taunt him. "Here comes Jack Spratt, he ate no fat," Milly began singing.

"Where do you think, you're going, Jack Spratt? You're on the wrong street," Lynette teased.

"I can go anywhere I want," Jack said, stopping to watch them dance around him.

"You have no business on this street," Milly said. "You are poor and almost a full-blown orphan." She began to skip around him, "Jack be nimble, Jack be quick."

Judy Lennington

Jack smiled. "Hey Milly, how did you like the taste of soap when you got home from church?" he asked, taunting them back.

"I didn't have to eat soap, smarty pants. My mother forgot all about it by the time we got home, so there!" Milly said, sticking her tongue out at Jack.

Lynette began to stick her tongue out at Jack too, and by this time they were dancing around him, getting closer and closer, while sticking their tongues out and taunting him.

Jack smiled and removed his coat from his arm, extending it straight out toward them. The girls squealed and began to scream, running toward the large house, "Momma, Momma, he's after us with a snake!" Jack watched them run inside the house, and began to walk, hurriedly, down the front street.

Soon the front door swung open and Mr. Thompson stepped out onto the porch with his hands upon his hips. "What have you got there, boy?" he called to Jack. Jack began to walk faster. He wanted to stop and put the snake down, but feared Mr. Thompson would catch him, so he began to run. As he ran, the snake curled a tighter grip on his arm. He feared if he slacked his grip it would bite him so he gripped it tighter. Now he was running between two houses. He paused to look behind him. Mr. Thompson was nowhere to be seen. He realized that the snake was not gripping his arm anymore. He looked down at it, as it hung limp from his grasp. Its tongue was hanging out of its mouth and its eyes bulged. It was dead. Jack dropped the snake and ran for home.

Jack stepped into the kitchen through the open door. His grandmother was cooking and the heat from the fireplace made the house too warm to close the door. "Where have you been?" Lester asked, chuckling.

"I was playing on the hill," Jack replied.

"You better go wash your face," his grandmother said. "You are sweaty and dirty. You look like you were running from someone."

Jack went to the basin and poured some cool water into it. He began to wash his face and neck with the cool water. It felt good upon his flushed face. "You mind what I said about them snakes, boy," Lester said, tapping his cane on the floor. "This is a troublesome time of year. Next to Dog Days, this is one of the worst times for them. They've been holed up in the ground all winter and they like to be out moving about now that it's getting warmer. They can't move too fast because they are still stiff, from the cold, so they strike at nearly everything, to defend themselves."

"Yes, Sir, I know," Jack said. He looked around the room. "Where is Father?"

"He went for a walk a while ago. I think he went to inspect the new railways they are building," Lester said. "He asked if I would like to go along, but my legs are bothering me today."

"Can I go find him?" Jack asked.

"I don't know if you can or not," His grandmother began, "however, if you mean; may you go find him, I suppose you may."

Jack smiled and nodded his head. "Yes, Ma'am, that is what I meant, all right. Thank you," he said, as he dried his hands. He carried the basin outside and tossed the dirty water off the side of the porch, before returning. He wiped out the basin and returned it to where he had found it. Now he grabbed his coat again and ran from the house to find his father.

Jack spotted his father standing on the hillside gazing toward the river. He tied his coat around his waist again, and ran toward him. He was breathing heavy when he reached the place where his father stood. Sheldon was smoking a pipe and he exhaled a plume of smoke upward as Jack reached him. "What have you been up to, Jack?"

"Not much, sir," Jack replied. "I was climbing the hillside and I went for a walk on Water Street before I went home. Grandfather told me where to find you." He looked in both directions at the area where talk of the new rail road tracks were going to be laid. "How far is it going to go?" he asked.

Sheldon looked eastward. "I suppose it will go all the way to the Pennsylvania state line, I reckon. Beings it is the Cleveland & Pittsburgh Railroad, I imagine it will go as far as Pittsburgh," he said, puffing on his pipe again.

"I heard they are putting a new bridge on Lisbon Street," Jack said, trying to mimic the way his father stood on the hillside.

"I heard something earlier too," Sheldon said. He looked down at Jack who was looking up at him, anxiously waiting for him to continue. "I ran into Mr. Thompson as I was walking along Water Street." Jack's face began to flush. He could not speak. "He said a boy that fit your description was chasing his daughter and the Raines girl with a snake. He said he frightened the dickens out of them. You wouldn't know anything about that would you, Jack?"

Jack swallowed the lump in his throat. He looked away from his father's gaze. He knew better than to lie. He tugged on the collar of his shirt, as he began to sweat. Unbuttoning the top button of his shirt, he nodded his head slightly and said, "I caught the snake up near the hillside. I was carrying it when they came out teasing me. They called me names and said we were poor and I was almost an orphan." Jack looked up at his father. "They tease me like that all the time. They are mean, nasty, girls, Father," he pleaded.

Sheldon puffed on his pipe and exhaled, watching the smoke drift above them as it disappeared into the air. "Well now, that certainly puts an interesting twist on things," he said.

"It's like that every day with them girls, Father," Jack said.

"Do you get teased often about being poor?" Sheldon asked.

Jack nodded his head. "And because Mother is in heaven. They tease me about being almost a full-blown orphan, too," he said, watching his father closely.

Sheldon was quiet for a moment. "Those are two issues you have no control over. I hardly see how a man can look the other way over issues that are out of his control." Sheldon looked down at Jack, and with a very serious look upon his face he said, "I think a man might be justified to scare off a couple of girls, under those circumstances. I'm not saying a man is justified to get physical, you understand. We never push or hit a girl. You do understand the difference, don't you, Jack?"

"I understand, Father," Jack said, with a sigh of relief. He looked up at his father and said, "I must say, it felt good watching Collin push ole Milly Thompson down in the dirt."

Sheldon fought back a smile as he puffed on his pipe. "I imagine it did at that, Son. However, we know better than that, don't we?"

"Oh, yes, Sir," Jack replied. "I would never lay a hand on a girl. But that don't mean I don't think about it. Sometimes I even picture it in my head. It helps sometimes. Not every time, but sometimes."

Sheldon smiled again. "I imagine it does," he said.

There was a long pause before Jack asked, "Am I in trouble because of the snake?"

Sheldon looked down at Jack and smiled as he reached out to squeeze his shoulder. "I don't think so. I think this time you may have been justified. However, that doesn't excuse what you did. I think this once we might let it slide, but I wouldn't do it again, if I were you."

"Oh, no, Sir," Jack said, shaking his head. "I won't do it again, Sir."

Sheldon looked down at the steep bank where he assumed the new railroad would pass through. "I don't think we should mention this in your grandmother's presence, Jack," he said. "Her being a female and all, I don't think she would understand."

"I won't say anything, Father. You don't have to worry about that," Jack said, looking up at his father. "Thank you for understanding, Sir."

"You are welcome, Jack," Sheldon said. "Now, what are we going to do about those girls taunting you at school?"

"I got it covered, Father. I have a secret weapon," Jack said, smiling up at his father.

"Are you referring to Collin McCauley?" Sheldon asked.

"Yes, sir," Jack said, nodding his head. "He hates them girls about as much as I do, I reckon. He doesn't take their teasing. He said he will keep them and the ruffians off my back if I continue to tutor him."

"I suppose he gets teased in school too," Sheldon said.

"Not so much," Jack said. "He did in the beginning, but now everyone leaves him alone. Collin can look out for himself pretty good."

"Well, you know it isn't right for Collin to get physical on your behalf, either. If he is doing it for you, it isn't much different than you doing it yourself," Sheldon explained.

Jack shuffled his feet. He felt uncomfortable now. "He's the only weapon I have against them girls, Father. And Melvin Riley and Anthony Patrone too. They are even meaner than the girls. They pick on me something terrible. They take my lunch from me and shove me around, even beating me up when they catch me off by myself. If it wasn't for Collin, I wouldn't have any defenses against them."

Sheldon pursed his lips as he thought about what Jack was saying. "I see," he said. "I suppose I must ponder this a while."

"Until you come up with a solution, Father, is it alright if I allow Collin to stand up on my behalf? It sure has been nicer at school since I started tutoring Collin," Jack said.

Sheldon smiled down at Jack. He rustled Jack's hair and said, "I suppose for now, it is alright. But remember one thing, Jack; if Collin is acting on your behalf, you are just as responsible as he is for his actions. You mind what I'm saying now."

"Yes, sir," Jack replied. He sighed a sigh of relief. As he stood staring down at the rushing Ohio River below, he thought about what his father had just said. It certainly was something to think about. He felt his palms sweating.

"Come along," Sheldon said turning. "Your grandparents will be wondering where we are."

Jack followed his father as they made their way home. The sun was going down. Soon Jack would be going to bed and shortly after that, his father would follow. Tomorrow was the start of another week. His father would go to work every morning and Jack would go to school. Their house came into view, and Jack noticed someone standing on the front porch talking to his grandparents. As they neared, Jack recognized Hermon Griffin, and he was alone, which was unusual. Hermon never left his wife, Hilda, alone.

As Lester noticed them approaching, he began to wave at them. They quickened their pace until they reached the porch. Hermon looked down at them from the porch and asked, "You didn't happen to see Hilda out there anywhere, did you?"

Sheldon shook his head, "No, sir, we didn't. Did she wonder off again?"

"Again?" Jack thought to himself. He was not aware of Hilda wondering off before. Surely, she knew how to find her home.

"I went to the privy and when I came back, she was gone," Hermon said, wiping his sweating forehead. "It will be dark soon, and I'm worried."

"Should we send Jack to fetch Wayne?" Sheldon asked.

Hermon nodded, "I suppose he has a right to know. Maybe he can help find her."

Sheldon looked down at Jack, placing his hand on Jack's shoulder, he asked, "Jack, do you remember where Mr. Griffin's son, Wayne, lives?" Jack looked up at his father and nodded his head. "You run over there and tell him that his mother has wondered off and we need his help in finding her." Jack nodded his head again and turned to run back toward Water Street.

Jack ran as fast as he could. He ran past the Thompson house, noticing Milly playing on the porch alone. "Jack Spratt, who are you running from?" she called down as he passed. Jack didn't even look in her direction. He continued running until he reached the Griffon house. He passed through the iron gate and ran up the porch steps of the grand brick house. He knocked on the door and then noticed a knocker in the center of the door. He was reaching for the knocker when the door swung open.

"What is it?" Gretchen Griffin asked, looking down at Jack. "What do you want?"

Gretchen Griffin was the third of four grown daughters born to Wayne Griffin and his wife, Louise. All the girls had married and moved away with the exception to Gretchen. It was said that Gretchen was betrothed once, and her fiancée' traveled to New York on business and never returned. Gretchen was what the folks called a spinster. She remained at home with her parents. She was a tall, thin, lady with a long slender neck. Her long hair was piled upon her head making her appear even taller. Her face was boney and her deep brown eyes were sunk deep into her head.

"I asked you a question, boy. Why are you pounding on our door?" Gretchen asked.

Jack struggled to catch his breath. He held his stomach, as he took deep breaths. "Mr. Griffin sent me," Jack gasped.

"What is it?" Gretchen asked, stooping low to make eye contact with Jack. "What has happened?"

Jack took a deep breath and closed his eyes as he said, "It's Mrs. Hilda Griffin, she has wondered off somewhere. Mr. Griffin asked me to fetch your father."

Gretchen turned and disappeared into the house, leaving Jack to stand on the porch alone. He could hear her calling out, "Daddy, Daddy, Grandmother has wondered off again."

Jack waited and soon Gretchen returned with both her parents. Mr. Wayne Griffin was pulling on his coat as he stepped out onto the porch. "Where was she last seen?" he asked Jack.

"At home, I suppose," Jack replied. "Mr. Griffin said he went to the privy and when he came back she was gone. That is all I know, Sir."

Judy Lennington

"You run along home, Son," Wayne said. "I'll saddle my horse and start looking for her."

Jack began to walk toward home. He heard Mrs. Louise Griffin calling out to her husband, "Should we start searching also, Wayne?"

"It couldn't hurt," Wayne called back.

Jack didn't turn around. Instead he locked his eyes on the Thompson house ahead as he walked Water Street. As he passed he noticed that Milly had gone inside. He breathed a sigh of relief. He was nearly passed when Mr. Thompson came rushing down the stone walk toward him. "Hold up right there, Son," he called to Jack who quickly began moving faster. "Stop right there!" Mr. Thompson called out. Jack closed his eyes tightly as he waited for Mr. Thompson to reach him. He feared he was about to be scolded for the incident with the corn snake. "What's happened? Where were you off to in such a hurry?" Mr. Thompson asked.

Jack felt his throat constrict in fear. "I was going to the Griffin's house, Sir," Jack replied looking up at the stout gentleman.

"Why were you in such a rush? Is there some kind of emergency?" Mr. Thompson asked.

"Mrs. Griffin has wondered off. Mr. Griffin asked me to fetch Mr. Wayne Griffin to help search for her," Jack said with a raspy voice.

Mr. Thompson looked around the area. He looked down at Jack and said, "You tell Mr. Griffin that I will be searching along the river. If they find her, have someone seek me out and notify me."

"Yes, Sir," Jack said, nodding his head. Mr. Thompson released his grip on Jack's shoulder and turned to walk back toward the house. Jack turned to begin his journey home again. As he went, he looked left and right, looking for any signs of Mrs. Griffin. As he was returning home, he noticed a horse and rider moving down the street to his right. He knew it was Wayne Griffin.

Jack climbed the porch steps and went inside to find his grandmother pacing the floor, wringing her hands. "May I help search for Mrs. Griffin?" he asked.

Delores shook her head. "No, it will be dark soon. I wouldn't want to have a search party out searching for you too."

"I can't get lost in Wellsville," Jack said.

"I know that, Jack, but anything could happen out there in the dark. Besides, you have school tomorrow. Now get yourself a slice of bread and then bathe and get ready for bed," his grandmother said, without looking at him.

Jack sighed and removed the cloth that covered the bread. His grandmother rose to her feet and took the bread from him. She placed it on a plate and poured coffee over it, from the pot on the stove. She returned the pot to the stove and began to sprinkle sugar over the soggy bread. Jack smiled up at his grandmother. "Thank you, Grandmother," he said.

"You are a good boy, Jack Gideon," she said, smiling and cupping his face in her hand. "You will grow up to be a fine young man."

"Thank you, Grandmother," Jack repeated before taking the first bite of the treat he knew as coffee soup.

"Mr. Griffin is searching for his mother on horseback," he said with a mouth full. "Mr. Thompson said to tell Mr. Griffin that he will search down by the river. He wants someone to find him and tell him if they find Mrs. Griffin."

Delores nodded her head. "That is good. I am certain they will find her." She smiled down at Jack and ran her hand over the top of his head. "You are a good boy, Jack Gideon. You will grow to be a fine young man someday," she repeated.

"Thank you, Grandmother," Jack said, taking another bite. He finished his meal and began to bathe near the fireplace. As the night moved in, it got colder. Soon he was in the loft listening for sounds of his father and grandfather returning. They had been searching for a long time. He said a silent prayer that Mrs. Griffin would be found soon and that she was safe and warm. His eyelids grew heavy. Somewhere, far off, there was the sound of voices, but Jack was too sleepy to hear them clearly. Then the night grew dark and quiet and he slept.

When Jack woke he immediately sat up. His father's bed was made up and Jack was in the loft alone. He quickly dressed and hurried down the ladder to find his grandparents sitting at the table. "Did they find Mrs. Griffin?" he asked.

Lester nodded his head. "They did, indeed. She is back home. She was pretty cold and very confused, but she is safe now."

"Good," Jack said, as he sat down at the table. "Where was she?" he asked.

"She was walking the hillside toward East Liverpool," his grandfather explained. "Wayne found her. He and Mr. Thompson both stumbled upon her about the same time. I believe Hermon is having the doctor look at her today."

"They need to take her out of that house," Delores said.

"Where would she go?" Jack asked. He looked at both of his grandparents and said, "They wouldn't send her to the poor house, would they?"

Delores reached over and patted Jack's hand. "No Jack, that isn't what I meant. I think she should go to live with her son and his family. Wayne's wife and daughter should be able to take

Bend in The River

better care of her than Hermon can. He can't watch her twenty-four hours a day all by himself. I just think between Louise and Gretchen, she will be looked after better."

"Now Delores," Lester said, "You know Hermon is not going to let that happen. They have been together far too many years for that."

"I just think that it would put everyone's mind at ease if there were more people looking after her. You know Hermon isn't in any condition to take on such a huge responsibility, Lester. Especially, at his age," Delores said.

Lester smiled over at Jack, "Well, it certainly isn't something you should be worried about, Jack. It will all work out."

"I suppose it will," Jack said taking a bite of his boiled oats.

"Are you going to work at the mercantile after school today?" Delores asked.

"Yes Ma'am, unless you need me here at home," Jack replied.

"No, I don't need you here, but I do like to know where you are going to be," Delores said, smiling over at her grandson.

"How many more days of school do you have, Jack?" his grandfather asked.

"Two more weeks, Grandfather. Just ten more days," Jack said, smiling across the table at his grandfather.

Jack began walking toward the school house. His mind was on the events of the night before, as he moved along. Paul Harris and his younger sister, Anna, had caught up with him as they moved toward the school house. Their father was the Wellsville policeman. Paul said, "Hey Jack, I heard you had some excitement out your way last night."

Jack nodded his head. "Yes, Mrs. Griffin wondered off. They found her though. She is alright and back at home," Jack said.

Judy Lennington

"Daddy said she was nearly froze to death," Anna said.

"Don't be silly, Anna," Paul said. "It didn't get that cold last night. She was chilled to the bone, but she wasn't frozen."

"Well Daddy said she was," Anna said, in defense.

"It was just a figure of speech, you knucklehead," Paul said.

"I'm telling Mommy, you're calling me names again. She said you were not to call me names," Anna said.

Jack remained quiet as he listened to the brother and sister arguing. "This is why I am glad I do not have a sister," he thought to himself. "I hate girls." The school house came into view. Some boys clustered around the air root that Jack claimed as his own. He did not see Collin McCauley among them. Jack felt his palms sweating. Paul Harris broke off running toward the group of boys, while Anna continued walking beside Jack.

"Hey Jackie Boy, I see you got a girlfriend," Melvin began to tease.

Anna began to run ahead of Jack. He watched her as she ran up the steps and into the building. Jack remained quiet, looking about for signs of Collin to come to his rescue. "What if he isn't here?" Jack asked himself, as he began to worry.

"Who ya lookin' for Jackie?" Melvin continued to taunt. "You lookin' for your watch dog?"

Mrs. Cartwright stepped out onto the porch with the school bell in her hand. She glared over at Melvin, who instantly became quiet. Jack climbed the steps and walked past her as he entered the building. Mrs. Cartwright began to ring the bell. Jack heard her say to Melvin as he passed her in the doorway. "Melvin Riley, I believe we need to work on our grammar after school today."

Jack smiled to himself as he made his way to his seat. He looked around the room for Collin, who was nowhere to be seen. He felt his heart sinking in his chest. Mrs. Cartwright tapped on her desk with her pointing stick and called for quiet as she began to read roll call. When Jack's name was called, he raised his hand and said, "Here," and she moved on to the next name. As she called out "Collin McCauley," there was dead silence. Jack allowed his eyes to drift to Melvin Riley and Anthony Patrone. They sneered back at him and he knew he was in for a thumping before this day was over. Roll call was complete and Mrs. Cartwright was placing her list of names into her desk drawer when the door opened and Collin hurried toward his desk.

"I am delighted to see that you were able to join us today, Mr. McCauley. However, I would appreciate it very much if you managed to be more punctual in the future," Mrs. Cartwright said.

"Yes Ma'am," Collin replied as he slid into the seat behind Jack.

Jack looked in the direction of Melvin and Anthony and smiled back at them. He felt better, now that his fears had been put to rest.

At first recess, Jack and Collin went to sit on the air root. Dark clouds were moving in and the smell of spring rain was in the air. Jack and Collin spoke softly as Jack coached Collin on his sounding out words. When Mrs. Cartwright rang the bell, the first drops of rain began to fall. As they returned to their seats the rumble of thunder could be heard overhead.

Mrs. Cartwright went to the first row where the Huffman twins sat. They were both dressed alike, with dark wavy hair and large dark eyes. Jack often stared at them in hopes of finding some little hint of a difference so he could tell them apart. Mrs. Cartwright made them tie colored twine upon their wrists so she could tell them apart. Jack wondered if their own parents could tell which was Donald and which was Dennis. He became so engrossed in the twins that he had not noticed Mrs. Cartwright moving to his row. "Jack Gideon!" she said sharply. Jack jumped and everyone began to laugh. Jack felt his face growing hot as he sat up straight in his seat. "It's so nice of you to join us this morning," Mrs. Cartwright said, walking up the aisle to stand near Jack. "I asked you a question, Jack," she said.

"I'm sorry," Jack said. He heard snickering from the other children. Mrs. Cartwright turned and glared at the offenders.

"I asked you to read paragraph one of page six, aloud, please," Mrs. Cartwright said, lowering her head and looking down at Jack.

"Yes, Ma'am," Jack said, sliding from his seat to stand tall. Holding his reading book in his hand, he began to read aloud. When finished, he sat down again and looked up at Mrs. Cartwright. He held his breath as she took a step closer to Collin's seat.

"Collin, would you read paragraph two please?" Mrs. Cartwright asked.

Jack heard snickering, and knew it was Melvin and Anthony. He glared in their direction, but they held their gaze upon Collin, with smiles spread across their evil faces. They were ready to burst into laughter, even knowing that it would bring a stern reaction from Mrs. Cartwright. Jack looked down at the paragraph and sighed. At least it was a short paragraph of only two sentences. Jack dared not turn around and look. He heard Collin slide from his seat. Looking down, Jack could only see the hem of Mrs. Cartwrights skirt dangling near the floor behind him. He closed his eyes and listened as Collin took his time and sounded each word out carefully. Melvin and Anthony snickered, and Mrs. Cartwright pointed her finger directly at them, shutting them up. It seemed to take forever for Collin to read those two sentences, but he completed them without any prompting from Mrs. Cartwright.

"Very good, Collin," Mrs. Cartwright said. "I see you have been working very hard." She stepped back and smiled down at Jack, before moving to Lewis Tully. "Lewis, would you mind reading paragraph three please?" she asked, moving on back the row.

There were four third graders in this row. Vivian Gardner usually sat in the first seat in front of Jack. Vivian had not been coming to school lately. Jack overheard the older children saying that Vivian had the mumps. She was quarantined. Jack's grandmother had explained that mumps was very contagious and a quarantine meant they were confined to their homes, with no contact with the outside world. Vivian was one of four children. They had all been taken out of school until the quarantine was lifted.

Mrs. Cartwright moved to the front of the third-grade row again and said, "You will take out your arithmetic books now and work on your multiplication tables. You will be quizzed on them tomorrow. Then she turned and moved to the fourth-grade row.

Jack looked down at his math book. He became aware of the rumbling thunder that was barely audible now. Perhaps the rain would move on too. Jack took his chalk in his hand and began to mark his numbers on his slate. He concentrated on the times table written in the arithmetic book. Suddenly, he became aware of movement to his left. Anthony Patrone was being sent to sit on the stool in the corner. Jack watched as Anthony placed the cone shaped hat upon his head and sat with his back to the class, his nose in the corner. Jack was disappointed that he did not see what offense Anthony was guilty of. He knew one thing, though, Anthony would be meaner than ever at lunch recess. Jack heard scraping of chalk on slate behind him. Collin was not taking notice of Anthony's punishment. He was working on his times tables.

Judy Lennington

As the day wore on, Jack became lost in his own studies. Occasionally, he would look up at Anthony Patrone's back as he sat squirming on the stool in the corner. From time to time, Mrs. Cartwright would instruct him to stop fidgeting. Giggles would erupt and she would call for order throughout the room. Soon it was lunch time and they were instructed to stay indoors as it was still raining outside. The seats were slid against the walls and the jump rope was brought out. As before, the two last students remaining in the high jump game was Harry Moser and Collin McCauley. This time, Collin managed to beat Harry, leaving Harry to sulk as Mrs. Cartwright announced it was time to put the seats back and prepare to resume class.

Anthony Patrone was back at his seat in the row of sixth graders. Melvin sat behind him, and often poked at Anthony's back. Mrs. Cartwright noticed this, and Melvin took a turn at sitting in the corner on the stool with the cone shaped hat on his head. Jack thought it was a perfect day despite the falling rain.

Jack worked on his studies as Mrs. Cartwright moved from row to row, giving instructions. Jack was always listening. He became aware of her lecturing the tenth graders. "Soon, Wellsville will have its very own telegraph office. There are plans to have it in place by the end of the year, and we will no longer rely upon the news from Pittsburgh's Gazette newspaper. We will hear of news from all over the eastern coast far north and south, shortly after the news occurs. This is very good for our community. As we speak, poles are being cut from Little Yellow Creek and Big Yellow Creek for the lines. It is estimated to be done by the end of the year," Mrs. Cartwright was saying. Jack sat quietly watching her as she spoke. He noticed that he was not the only one, for most of the students realized the significance of her lecture. She smiled at those listening intently and nodded her head. "You can rest assured, class, that Wellsville will very soon begin to grow significantly. The impact this telegraph line will have upon our town will no doubt be quite significant. Only time will tell how significant, but significant, none the less. Now please return to your assignments." Now, every head in the room dipped downward to their slates.

As the end of the school day neared, everyone became fidgety. Mrs. Cartwright rang the bell and the students hurried from the building, darting through the sprinkling rain. Harry Moser and Paul Harris were asked to bring in fire wood for the next day. Jack and Collin ran toward the mercantile. They reached the cover of the porch, laughing. As they entered, Mr. Dodge was on the ladder and Mrs. Dodge was behind the counter waiting on Mr. Garfield. Mr. Dodge smiled and called out, "I see my relief has arrived." Jack noticed Mr. Garfield studying Collin closely.

Mrs. Dodge leaned across the counter and said, "These young men are helping out around here. To be quite honest with you, Mr. Garfield, they have only worked one full day, and I don't know how we got along without them all these years."

Mr. Garfield spoke softly, "The red-haired boy, he looks to be a member of that Irish family living over the chair factory."

Mrs. Dodge nodded and replied, "That is Collin McCauley. I believe his family does live over the chair factory. He certainly works very hard."

Mr. Garfield gathered his wares in his arms and said, "That's not what I heard about his father." He nodded his head in Collin's direction and left the store.

Jack noticed Collin's face was flaming. Mrs. Dodge came from around the counter and Mr. Dodge began to hurry down the ladder. "Don't you pay no mind to what Mr. Garfield said, young man," she said to Collin. "Folks often criticize what they don't understand."

Collin lowered his head and said, "It's alright, Ma'am. What he said is true. Me Dah is not a workin' man. Truth is, he can't hold a job, no how. He works just long enough to get money in his pocket for a drink or two at the pub. He will stay at the pub until he is penniless. He comes home drunker than a skunk and beggin' me Ma for money to return to the pub. Me Ma has to hide every penny she makes from him, lest we starve." Collin looked up at Mr. Dodge who stood near his wife. "That is why I have to larn how to read and write whole words. I have to get me a job on the docks to support me family. Me Dah, has left to find work in Pittsburgh. He wanted to move us all out that way, but me Ma's health is too poorly to move on. He says he will come for us when he has something permanent and suitable. We knows he ain't gonna return. He will never give up the drink. They will find him dead in some gutter in Pittsburgh some night and we will not hear of it," Collin explained.

"Oh, how very sad for you and your family, young man," Mrs. Dodge said.

"It is what it is," Collin said. "Don't feel sad for us. The little ones don't understand, but me Ma and me, we know it is the best thing to happen to us." Collin looked at the two adults listening to his every word.

"Well," Mr. Dodge said, "You are welcome to work here, but I can't afford to pay you what you would make at the docks, Collin. If I could, I certainly would." He smiled at his wife and said, "But, I certainly can help you with your studies. I don't see how learning to read about a boy, girl, and a dog is going to help you read shipping manifests. I will teach you how to read inventory sheets and shipping logs. Rosalie here, can help you with the mathematics. I'm good, but she is better at math. We will do whatever we can to help."

Collin's face flamed. He smiled and said, "I be thankin' you folks."

"You come with me, Collin," Mr. Dodge said. "You can help me stock some shelves and I will show you how things come in here and how we keep track of everything. I'll help you with the paper work."

"And you, Jack Gideon," Mrs. Dodge said with a chuckle, "I have a special project for you." She giggled as she turned to walk back to the counter again. Jack followed her as they moved behind the counter. She bent over and pointed her finger as she said, "I found some mouse droppings under here this morning. I need you to get down there and pull everything out from under the counter. I need it all cleaned and swept up good. I have some traps set down there, so mind your fingers, boy." She smiled as she stood upright and looked down at Jack again. "We can't have mice running amuck in here and getting into the flour bin, now can we?" she asked.

"No Ma'am," Jack replied.

"That's a good boy," Mrs. Dodge said turning on her heel to move away.

Jack began his chore with reluctance at first. He was fearful of setting off a trap with his fingers. Carefully he pulled everything out from under the counter. He peered underneath carefully, each time, before reaching in. He was busy when he heard a familiar tapping noise. He knew it was the sound of his grandfather's cane. He popped his head up from under the counter and smiled at

Lester Gideon who stood waving a lunch tin held in his left hand while he gripped his cane with his right.

"Delores sent something over for the boys to eat," Lester said.

"Now Lester," Rosalie Dodge said hurrying toward Lester. "You tell Delores that I am not about to let these boys work all evening without feeding them. I figure a square meal as part of their payment," she said, taking the lunch tin from Lester's hand.

"I know, Rosalie, I know," Lester replied. "I tried to explain that to her, but you know Delores."

"Well, you might as well sit a spell and have a snack," Rosalie said pointing to a chair near the stove. "It's mighty damp outdoors this evening. Take some of the chill off before you head back home."

Lester looked around the room. "You working by yourself this evening, Jack?" he asked.

Jack shook his head. "No Sir," he replied. "Mr. Dodge and Collin are in the back."

Lester nodded his head as she lowered himself onto a chair. He peered into the lunch tin and winked at Jack. "I suppose I could use a little bite of something. You won't tell your grandmother will you, Jack?" he asked

"No, Sir," Jack replied.

"Are you learning anything in school these days?" Lester asked taking a bite of sugar bread.

"Oh, yes Sir," Jack said. "Mrs. Cartwright was saying today that the telegraph is coming to Wellsville. She said it will bring the latest news right to our doorstep. She said it should be up and running by the end of the year."

Lester nodded his head. "I did hear that. It will be very good for this community. That along with the railroad going right through here, should be very good for all of us." He looked around. "How is the tutoring coming along?" he asked.

"Collin is a fast learner, Grandfather. He read aloud in class today without any mistakes. It took him a while, and he had to sound out every word, but he managed to do it well enough. There are some that can't do any better, and have been going to school every day," Jack explained. He looked over at Mrs. Dodge who was watching him. "I better get back to work."

"Yes, you better indeed. I did not come here to hold you up," Lester said. "It looks like this rain is going to last all night, so you watch yourself coming home. We don't want you getting sick on us, now."

"I'll be careful Grandfather," Jack said.

"Well," Lester said, "nights like this is when old Limpy and me would sit under a porch and talk about his whaling days. He was full of some good stories, old Limpy was. I could listen to him talk all night."

"I'd like to hear some of those stories sometime, Grandfather," Jack said.

Lester nodded his head. "Of course, Jack. Some time when you aren't working." Lester stood up and pulled his coat collar up around his neck. "Well, I'll be on my way." He began to shuffle his way toward the door. Jack watched him until he was outside. He smiled over at Mrs. Dodge and stooped down to finish his cleaning from under the counter.

Collin and Jack joined the Dodge's at their table in the back of the store. It was a small table and Jack assumed they had another table in their living quarters above the store. Jack had never been upstairs, but imagined it to be small, but adequate. This evening they were having bacon and boiled potatoes. Collin didn't talk much during dinner, and Jack assumed he didn't get many meals like this one at home.

Soon they were back in the store, stocking shelves. For his final chore of the evening, Jack was instructed to fill the coal bucket and take out the ashes. Mrs. Dodge gave him a canvas cover to protect him from the drizzling rain. He returned to find Collin had already left for the evening. Mr. Dodge said he had to get to the chair factory and sweep up the floor before he could retire for the night. Jack thought about Collin's living conditions as he made his way home in the rain. He found his father and grandparents waiting for him in the kitchen.

"How was your day?" Sheldon asked.

"It was fine, Father," Jack replied.

"Do you have any studies to do before bed?" his grandmother asked.

"No, ma'am. Mrs. Cartwright gave us time to study in school. We are being tested tomorrow on our math skills," he said.

"Well, how about we go over your math while you bathe," Sheldon said.

Jack nodded his head as he began to remove his damp clothing. His grandmother hung them near the fireplace, for Jack would wear them again tomorrow. His father sat on a three-legged stool, smoking his pipe as Jack began reciting his multiplication tables. "One time one equals one. Two times one equals two." On he went, until he had recited his multiplication tables all the way through.

"Well, it looks like you are ready for your test. I expect you to pass without any problems," Sheldon said. "Now off to bed with you. I'll clean up your mess," Sheldon said rustling Jack's hair.

Bend in The River

Jack was restless tonight. Usually the sound of the tapping rain would sooth him into a deep sleep, but tonight he was restless. He heard his father come to bed as he laid quietly in the darkness of the loft. There were no windows up here, leaving only a faraway flickering light that came from the fireplace below. Jack woke with a start as his grandfather called up to him. He sat up and rubbed his eyes, as he had been awake for most of the night, and had just recently drifted into a deep sleep.

Jack sat quietly listening to his grandparent's conversation while he ate his boiled oats. Finally, he was dressed and pulling on his coat as he prepared to leave for school. "I'll see you tonight, Jack," his grandmother said, as he went out the door. Jack waved back at her and jumped off the porch, breaking into a dash for the school house.

He slowed down as the school house came into view. He studied the playground carefully, mindful of the whereabouts of Melvin and Anthony. He noticed Milly and Lynette watching him and braced himself for their taunting. "Jack Spratt, could eat no fat...," they began to sing together. Jack ignored them and climbed the steps to enter the building. He sighed; relieved to see Melvin and Anthony approaching from a distance. He would reach the safety of Mrs. Cartwrights desk before they could get to him.

Mrs. Cartwright smiled and nodded her head as he entered the building. Jack removed his coat and hung it on a peg. Mrs. Cartwright had been watching him and motioned for him to come to her desk. Jack felt his chest constrict as he approached, not knowing what to expect. "Jack, I wanted to congratulate you for the wonderful progress Collin has been making lately. You have done well, young man. I feel confident that should you decide to

Judy Lennington

become a teacher, one day, that you will make a fine one," she said, smiling across her desk at Jack.

Jack felt his face flushing. "Thank you, Mrs. Cartwright. It is mostly Collin's doings, ma'am. He wants to learn and he has been studying very hard."

"I figured as much," Mrs. Cartwright said. "I do fear that he wants to learn, so he can quit school and pursue a career somewhere. It would be such a waste of a good mind, for him to do so. He has enormous potential, Collin McCauley does."

"Yes, ma'am," Jack said. "I agree; however, I don't think you, or I, will ever persuade him to stay in school. He is convinced that he needs to find a suitable job to support his family."

"Well, what a shame that is," Mrs. Cartwright said shaking her head. "He is so young to take on such a responsibility. However, he would not be the first to do so." She smiled at Jack again. "You better take your seat now. I am about to ring the bell."

Jack was walking back to his seat when he noticed Collin entering the building. As he passed Jack, he asked, "I thought you weren't coming to school today," Collin said softly.

"I came inside to avoid the nasties," Jack said. Collin smiled and slid into his seat behind Jack.

"Take your seats, children," Mrs. Cartwright was saying. Jack turned around to face the front of the class and Mrs. Cartwright who stood patiently waiting for everyone to be seated. He tried not to make eye contact with the nasty girls or Melvin and Anthony. He folded his hands and waited for Mrs. Cartwright to clap her hands, indicating that roll call was about to begin.

Mrs. Cartwright made her way to the third-grade row. She instructed the three third graders to write their multiplication tables on their slates. They were being tested. Jack noticed that he was done before Lewis Tully who was moved to sit in front of him. He could hear Collin's chalk scraping across his slate and knew that he was not finished. Vivian Gardner was still out with the mumps. Jack folded his hands on the top of his desk and sat quietly waiting for Mrs. Cartwright to make her way back to his row again.

"Jack Gideon!" Mrs. Cartwright's voice broke the silence. Jack jumped as he brought his head upright. He had drifted off to sleep. A large lump formed in his throat making it difficult to breath. "I think you should take a seat up here," Mrs. Cartwright said, pointing to the stool in the corner.

Jack fought back tears as he made his way to the front of the class. He did not want the others to see him cry. He placed the cone shaped hat upon his head and climbed up onto the stool, facing the corner.

He listened while Mrs. Cartwright went from row to row with her instructions. He heard her congratulate Lewis Tully for getting all his multiplication problems correct. There was a long silence and he knew she was reviewing his tablet that sat on top of his desk. After a long time, he heard her say, "Collin McCauley, you have done very well. You have gotten all your times tables correct, however, you have written your number three backwards, therefore, I am compelled to mark it as a mistake. You are not to be discouraged, Collin. This is quite an accomplishment. I am very pleased with your progress."

Mrs. Cartwright made her way to the next row. Jack sat staring at the blank wooden corner. From time to time, he felt his head bobbing and his eye lids becoming very heavy. Twice he felt as if he was about to fall off the stool. The frightful results of such an occurrence brought panic up into his chest. At last Mrs. Cartwright rang the recess bell. Jack placed the cap on the stool and hurried to get his coat. He was anxious to get some fresh air to shake the sleepiness from his head. He knew he was about to be teased by nearly everyone on the playground, but he would have to endure it to get through the rest of the day without drifting off again.

To his relief, Collin was waiting for him on the large air root of the old Elm tree. As he made his way toward Collin, laughter and snickering from the children followed him. He tried to block it out of his mind, but felt his cheeks flaming as he crossed the playground. "Pay them no mind," Collin said, smiling as he approached. "They'll find entertainment somewhere else."

Jack nodded his head. He knew Collin spoke the truth. In fact, it was the very same advice Jack had given Collin several times in the past. Somehow it didn't seem the same when it was he, who was being teased this time. He sat down on the air root and looked down at the ground. "I didn't sleep well last night. I got so sleepy up front, I feared I might fall off the stool," Jack said, softly.

"That would have been a sight," Collin said, chuckling.

"It isn't funny Collin," Jack said looking over at Collin.

"I know exactly how you feel," Collin said. "You spent a couple of hours sitting in the corner. Imagine how many times I've sat there, sometimes half the day. Staring at that damn corner, trying to stay awake, bored out of my bloomin' mind."

Jack gasped and nudged Collin with his elbow. "Don't let anyone hear you swearing, Collin. You'll get a few good whacks for that, and the whole day in the corner. Mrs. Cartwright will make you sit there with a bar of soap in your mouth, and maybe make you stay after school to write on the board. You can't work for Mr. Dodge if you have to stay after school."

"It won't be much longer and I'll be gone from here, least ways. I'm aimin' to make this my last year in school, Jack. You need to find a way to stand up for yourself, cause I ain't gonna be here to help you this summer and next year," Collin said, looking over at Jack.

"But what about your studies?" Jack asked.

"I aim to work real hard and larn all I can by the time school is out. I aim to get me a job down on the docks. My family needs money, and we ain't got time for me to go all the way through school," Collin said. "I'm beholden to ya for all ya done for me, Jack. I ain't never gonna forget it, and I'm proud to call you a friend. But me Ma and kin are gonna be kicked out if I can't pay Mr. Armstrong some money right soon. He's been pretty good about lettin' us stay there, but I'm afraid his patience is wearin' mighty thin."

"I can give you my earnings at the store if that will help," Jack said.

Collin shook his head and looked down at his bare feet as he said, "I'm mighty grateful for the thought, Jack, but we McCauley's ain't a family to take charity from no man."

"Then call it a loan," Jack said.

"Thank ya, but no thank ya," Collin said. Mrs. Cartwright stepped out onto the porch and rang the bell. Recess was over. Collin stood up and waited for Jack to do the same. They walked across the playground together. Milly and Lynette stood back watching them pass. As they climbed the steps, Jack noticed Melvin and Anthony sneering from a few feet away. Collin looked directly at them and they lowered their gaze. Jack felt his heart sink. What was he going to do without Collin to protect him? They entered the building and took their seats. Mrs. Cartwright

Judy Lennington

stood at her desk waiting for everyone to be seated. She clapped her hands, indicating that the class was to be quiet. Then she approached the first row and began to issue instructions for the afternoon.

The day wore on, and soon the bell was rung to dismiss the class for the day. Collin and Jack ran together toward the mercantile. Jack noticed that Collin seemed to be happier when they were working at the mercantile with Mr. and Mrs. Dodge. He also noticed that Mr. Dodge seemed to enjoy taking Collin under his wing and teaching him to read and write inventory sheets and shipping documents. Mrs. Dodge seemed to enjoy having Jack there to get into the small places to clean and drive off the vermin that constantly looked for nesting places. Today, Jack was given the chore of washing the windows inside and out. It was a better day and Mrs. Dodge wanted to hang new signs in the windows. She wanted them clean and free of streaks. This required Jack to wash them and rewash them several times to get the dust from the coal stove off the glass.

Jack was standing on an overturned wooden barrel, buffing the dried soap from the inside of the large glass window. Reverend Johnson waved at Jack as he approached the front door. Jack returned the wave and smiled at the Reverend. He continued to work diligently as Mrs. Dodge came from the back, carrying a large silver spoon, and began to converse at the counter.

"What will it be today, Reverend?" Mrs. Dodge asked.

Jack could see their reflection in the glass as he continued to polish the streaks away. "I'll have some of that fine tobacco, Mr. Dodge keeps in the bin behind the counter, Rosalie. I'll also have a sack of finely ground wheat flour," the Reverend said.

"How is Mrs. Johnson?" Rosalie asked, bending down to open the bin behind the counter that contained the tobacco.

At that moment, Mr. Dodge stepped through the curtains that separated the main floor from the storage room. "Hello Reverend Johnson. It's rather late for you to be out and, about, isn't it?" Mr. Dodge asked.

"It is, indeed. I'm late for supper, Howard. I was just over at the Griffin house. Hilda passed away a few minutes ago, it seems she got too much exposure to the chilly night air," the Reverend said. Jack held his breath as he continued to listen. "Unfortunate thing, she seemed to be more alert in her last moments than she has been in years. I believe she knew she was dying, and the funny thing is, she wasn't a bit afraid. She smiled up at Wayne and asked him to look after his father for her. Poor Hermon is going to be lost without Hilda. He's been looking after her for so long, he likely will not know what to do with himself. As I left, Wayne was trying to persuade him to go stay with him and Louise over on Water Street."

"I don't see Hermon leaving that old house," Rosalie said. "It was his father's house. He and Hilda raised their children in that old house."

The Reverend was nodding his head. "I know, Hermon wasn't having any of it, but after everything has time to settle down and he finds himself all alone over there he may change his mind."

"Well, I for one, hope he does," Rosalie said. "He isn't getting any younger. Look at old Mrs. Cartwright who lives right next door to him. She has been alone for nearly her whole life. Never married, and never had any children. I think her teaching is what keeps her going. If it wasn't for that, she would likely fade away."

Judy Lennington

The Reverend began to pack tobacco into his pipe as he said, "That whole street is full of well-seasoned folks. The residents are nearly as old as those old houses are. I suppose the day will come when they are all gone and those old houses will be torn down and newer homes will pop up all over this town. It will be a welcomed sight for Wellsville, but a sad day for its citizens who are left behind without our older friends. This town was built on the backs of those old folks and their families. There is much to learn if one takes the time to listen."

"You are certainly right about that, Reverend," Mr. Dodge said.

At that moment, Collin passed through the curtains, carrying a sheet of paper. He stopped and waited for Mr. Dodge to acknowledge him before asking, "What is this word, Mr. Dodge?" Collin asked.

Mr. Dodge looked at the sheet of paper and smiled. "Well, let's sound it out, Collin."

Collin frowned and bit his bottom lip. "Pot, a, to, ess," Collin said, staring at the paper.

"Now put the sounds together like I told you and keep repeating them until they sound like a word," Mr. Dodge said. Jack noticed the Reverend and Mrs. Dodge standing very quietly watching Mr. Dodge and Collin.

"Pot, a, to, ess," Collin said. "Pot, a, to, ess." He smiled up at Mr. Dodge and asked, "Potatoes?"

Mr. Dodge nodded his head and smiled. "That is right Collin. Potatoes. We are selling seed potatoes this spring to help with the famine in Scotland and your home country, Ireland."

"What is a famine?" Collin asked.

"It means, a shortage of food. We are helping to feed the poor and hungry folks of those countries," Mr. Dodge explained.

Collin raised his eyebrows and said, "That is kind of ya to do such a thing for folks you never met afore,"

"Well, that is what Christians do, Collin," Mr. Dodge said smiling. He placed his hand on Collin's shoulder and said, "And it isn't afore, Lad, it is before."

"Yes sir, before," Collin said. "Thank you, sir." He then turned and passed through the curtains again, disappearing into the back.

"I hear there are plans in the works to move the potatoes on a steamer bound for Pittsburgh without charge for shipment or storage," the Reverend said.

"Folks can be awfully kind when they want to be," Rosalie said.

"Speaking of being kind, it is awfully kind of you and Howard to undertake what you're doing for that Irish lad. Not many folks would trust him back there by himself, you know," the Reverend said.

"Well, we were reluctant at first, but it was Jack over there, that brought him here. Young Jack Gideon was tutoring Collin after school. He asked permission to allow Collin to come to the store so Jack could tutor him while he worked," Mr. Dodge said nodding his head toward Jack.

Jack smiled at them through the glass. "What a fine Christian thing to do, young man," the Reverend said.

"Yes, sir. Thank you, sir," Jack replied as he began buffing the window again.

"That is exactly what I was talking about earlier," the Reverend said. "It's folks like the Gideon's that are the backbone of this community. Old Lester grew up in that old house, just as Hermon grew up in his. I believe they were friends growing up."

Rosalie chuckled. "As I recall, old Lester had a very unusual friend growing up. Now there was a young man with a fine

Judy Lennington

Christian heart. He befriended that old one legged drunk when no one else would have anything to do with him. They were an odd pair, the two of them were. That old man and young Lester. I recall seeing them here and there all over town. Old Limpy would be telling his tales of whaling, and who knew if they were even true or not, but Lester listened intently to every word. I recall the day they buried old Limpy on the river. Hermon Griffin's father rowed a boat out onto the river with Limpy's body all wrapped in linens. Hermon and Lester were mere lads at the time. Those two boys were inseparable until old Limpy came into Lester's life. Everyone joked that they were twins until old Limpy came along. I think nearly the whole town can tell you where they were the day they buried old Limpy in the river. I doubt anyone living in Wellsville at the time missed it. We all stood watching Mr. Griffin row out there and the three of them stood up in the boat with their heads bowed, saying a prayer I assume. Then they rolled the body over the side. They had placed rocks into old Limpy's pockets and inside his shirt before sewing and tying those linens around him. He sunk straight away. Then Mr. Griffin rowed his boat back to shore."

"I recall hearing folks talking about that, but I didn't live in these parts at that time," the Reverend said. He looked back at Jack and said, "I bet your grandfather is full of old whaling tales. That makes for a nice evening around the fire."

Jack nodded his head, but remained quiet. He continued to buff at the window. The evening sun was just low enough that it shone into his eyes. Mrs. Dodge went to stand near the window and said, "That looks pretty good to me, Jack. I think you can put your things away while I finish our supper."

"Yes, ma'am," Jack said. He climbed down from the barrel.

Bend in The River

Mrs. Dodge turned and walked back toward the counter. "I don't know how we got along before Jack and Collin came to help out. You'd think I would have more free time on my hands, but I don't. If you will excuse me Reverend, I have dinner in the pot," she said, nodding politely. The Reverend nodded his head as well and watched as she turned to leave, passing through the curtains and disappearing.

"I'll say it again, Howard, that boy back there is a lucky lad to have stumbled upon a couple like you and Rosalie," the Reverend said.

"Awe, this is only a temporary situation, I'm afraid. Collin is learning to read and write shipping manifests because he wants to go work on the docks. If I could afford to pay him what he'd make down there, I would. But, I can't and I'm happy to have him here for as long as he chooses to stay," Howard said.

"I best be on my way," the Reverend said. "My wife will be waiting dinner on me. She gets a might testy after too long." He smiled and placed his cap on his head. He turned and walked toward the door. "You keep up the good work Jack Gideon."

Jack smiled as the Reverend opened the door and left. Jack placed the barrel back where he found it and began gathering his cleaning supplies. He carried the dishpan of soapy water to the edge and tossed it over the boardwalk. Then he returned to find Mr. Dodge waiting for him. "You are doing an excellent job, Jack. You can be proud of yourself. You be sure to tell your grandparents that the Mrs. and I are right pleased with the way things are working out. We'd like to keep you on all summer if it's alright with them."

"I think they are agreeable with that, Sir," Jack replied.

Judy Lennington

"Well, good. Now let's go wash up and have a bite to eat, what do you say?" Mr. Dodge asked.

"Yes, Sir. That sounds mighty fine with me, Sir," Jack replied.

Jack passed through the curtains and began to roll up his sleeves. Mrs. Dodge was rummaging through the drawers of her china cupboard. "What are you looking for?" Mr. Dodge asked.

"I can't seem to find my big silver spoon," Mrs. Dodge said. "I am certain I had it earlier. I thought I left it on the table there."

"It'll turn up when you clean up after us," Mr. Dodge said, smiling over at her. "Where is Collin?" He turned and went to the storage room. "Collin, come wash up for dinner."

Collin was quiet at dinner. Mr. Dodge did most of the talking. Soon they had finished their meal and the boys went back to finish up for the day. The sun was barely visible over the tree tops when Collin and Jack said good evening to the Dodge's. As they parted ways, Jack broke into a run toward home. He would be arriving about the same time as his father. He looked over his shoulder just as Collin was climbing the stairs to the apartment over the chair factory.

"There he is," Delores said smiling over at Jack as he entered the house. "How was your day today?"

"It was fine ma'am," Jack said removing his coat. "It is a warm evening out there. I expect I won't need my coat much longer."

Lester hung his cane on the back of a chair and slowly lowered himself to sit upon it. "I expect so. How were the Dodge's this evening?"

"They are fine, Grandfather, but the Reverend was in earlier and he said Mrs. Griffin died this evening from exposure she suffered yesterday," Jack informed them.

Lester hung his head and sighed heavily. "I'm right sorry to hear that. Old Hermon isn't going to know what to do with himself without Hilda to care for."

Delores placed both hands upon the table and asked, "Do you suppose we should take something over there?"

"The Reverend said their son, Wayne, was trying to convince Mr. Griffon to go live with them over on Water Street," Jack said, as he began to wash for dinner. At that moment, the door opened and Sheldon entered the room. He looked around at the sad faces and shook his head.

"Mrs. Griffin passed away today," Delores said softly.

"Oh, I am very sorry to hear that," Sheldon said, placing his lunch tin on the floor near the door. He sighed and went to wash his hands in the same wash basin Jack had used only moments ago, "I'll have dinner later. I suppose someone should pay their respects."

"May I go with you, Father?" Jack asked.

"Did you eat with the Dodge's?" Sheldon asked.

Jack nodded his head. "I did."

"What did you have?" Delores asked.

"We had salt pork and boiled potatoes," Jack said. "Speaking of potatoes, Mr. Dodge said we are growing potatoes this summer and shipping them to Scotland and Ireland to feed the hungry over there. Did you know this, Grandfather?"

Lester shook his head. "No, I did not. I suppose there is a lot that is going on out there I am missing lately. These old knees are keeping me pretty close to home."

"I suppose it wouldn't hurt for you to tag along," Sheldon said.

Jack jumped to his feet and went to stand by the door. "Mind you take your coat, Jack," Delores said, nodding toward Jack's coat that hung on the peg near the door. "Now that the sun went down, it is likely to get a might chilly out there."

"Yes, ma'am," Jack said lifting his coat from the peg. Sheldon placed his hat on his head once again and draped his coat over his arm. He rustled Jack's hair and nodded toward the door. They stepped out into the night air. The sun was barely visible now. Jack jumped off the porch as Sheldon took the steps. They walked side by side.

As they passed Mrs. Cartwright's house, Sheldon asked, "Are you still tutoring that Irish boy?"

"No Sir," Jack replied. "Mr. Dodge has taken over. He said Collin can't learn to read manifests on the docks by reading about a boy, girl, and dog running up a hill."

Sheldon laughed. "I suppose he has a point."

Jack kicked at the dirt and said, "Collin has been working real hard. Mrs. Cartwright said she is very impressed with his progress. I don't think Collin will be going back to school next year." Jack kicked at the dirt again and said, "I don't know what I'm going to do when he starts working on the docks. He's been keeping Melvin and Anthony off my back."

"Well, by next year things might be different," Sheldon said as they neared the Griffin house. "You will be surprised at how much difference a full year makes." They climbed the steps to the Griffin porch. The door was standing open and Jack could see the main room was full of people from the town.

"Come on in," Hermon called out to them. "I'd offer you a chair, but they are all taken."

"That is alright, Hermon," Sheldon said. "We just wanted to check on you. Is there anything you need?"

Hermon shook his head. "Naw, I can't think of a thing. Mr. and Mrs. Gibson helped take Hilda out of here a little while ago. Her funeral is tomorrow. Wayne has asked me to go live with him and Louise. I said I might give it a trial run, but I don't want to clear the house out until I see how it's going to go. Ain't too crazy about leaving, but I figure it is going to seem pretty quiet here now that Hilda is gone. It's been just me and her for so long as I can remember." His voice trailed off.

"Hermon, you will be surprised at how much better you are going to feel after you get settled in with Wayne, Louise, and their daughter Gretchen," Mrs. Booth said.

"Maybe you're right, Ida, but I don't expect it to happen overnight," Hermon said. "Hilda kept me pretty busy around here. I'm going to be lost without her. I'm thinking I'm not going to know what to do with myself."

"Give it time, Hermon. Give it time, I say," Mr. Booth said.

"How's your Pa, Sheldon?" Mrs. Booth asked. "We haven't seen him around lately."

"Oh, his knees have been bothering him. You know it is that time of year with the weather changing and all. He's been staying close to home," Sheldon explained.

"I hear this young man here, has been working over at the mercantile with Mr. and Mrs. Dodge," Mr. Booth, said smiling down at Jack.

"Yes, Sir, he has," Sheldon said smiling at Jack.

"I also hear he has been hanging around with that Irish boy that lives over the chair factory with his no count father and a whole brood of kids," Mrs. Patrone said. "I'd be a bit pickier about who he associates with, if I were you."

Judy Lennington

Jack snapped his head to the left at Mrs. Patrone's remark. He had not seen her sitting there in the corner. Her bulky frame caused the chair she had been sitting on to disappear, leaving the impression that she was squatting in place. Jack glared at her with contempt, but remained quiet.

Sheldon coughed into his hand and said, "Well, it would not be very Christian of Jack not to befriend a fellow in need. I am very proud of him for taking on the responsibility of tutoring the young McCauley boy. Anyone in need should have the full support of this community," Sheldon said smiling back at Mrs. Patrone.

"Well, he's a ruffian, that McCauley boy is. He laid into my Anthony for no apparent reason. Bloodied him up, really bad, too," Mrs. Patrone said.

Jack sucked in air, and was about to say something when his father squeezed his shoulder, indicating that he was to remain silent.

"Well, if I recall what it was like being a boy in Wellsville, I would say there is something more to this story than we are aware of," Mr. Booth said. "You know what they say, there are three sides to every story. What he said, what she said, and what really happened." He smiled over at Mrs. Patrone. Jack shifted in place. He felt his face flaming. He felt like he should say something, but knew it was not his place. Therefore, he remained silent. He did, however, continue to glare at Mrs. Patrone who fidgeted in her seat, nervously, after being put into her place by Mr. Booth.

"Well," Sheldon said, "I suppose Jack and I should get back home. Our dinner will be waiting for us on the table." He reached out to shake hands with Hermon. "If you need anything at all,

Hermon, all you have to do is ask. We understand you would do the same should the tables be turned."

Jack shook hands with Hermon and followed his father outside. They began walking back to their house. Jack looked up at his father and said, "The Dodge's said they didn't think Mr. Griffin would move in with his son and his family. They said he would likely never leave that house because it was where he was raised."

"That's true, Jack," Sheldon said. "He was raised there. As far as I know, it is the only house Hermon has ever lived in. It's the same way with your grandfather. He was raised in the house we live in. Lots of times I have asked him why he doesn't tear that old house down and move into a bigger one. It isn't like he can't afford a bigger house. He claims he is happy right where he is."

"All of the houses on this street are old," Jack said.

"That is because they are the homes of the first settlers in Wellsville. The bigger homes were built way later. Someday these old houses will be torn down and newer, bigger, houses will go up." Sheldon smiled down at Jack as they reached the steps to their house. "But sometimes, it's the old things that are more valuable. I know that doesn't make much sense to you now, but someday you will understand."

Jack nodded his head. "Yes, Sir, you are right. It doesn't make sense to me, at the moment." Sheldon laughed and the two of them climbed the steps and entered the open door to find Jack's grandparents waiting for them.

Jack dressed into his night clothes while his father explained the events taking place at the Griffin house. His father did not mention the statement Mrs. Patrone made about Collin McCauley. Jack wanted to say something, but decided to keep it for another day. He sat staring at the flickering embers of the fireplace. Sheldon

Judy Lennington

placed another log on the fire, causing embers to drift upward and disappear. Jack looked over at his grandfather, who also stared into the fireplace. "Grandfather, do you remember any good stories about your friend Limpy?" Jack asked.

Lester's eyes seem to sparkle as he smiled down at Jack. "Why, as a matter of fact, I do recall a tale or two old Limpy told me." Lester tapped his cane upon the wooden plank floor and smiled as he looked down at Jack, who was scooting closer toward him. Lester shifted in his chair and took a deep breath as he began, "Limpy said he recalled his very first voyage. He said he wasn't older than fourteen when his father died. He recalled his grandfather being very gruff as he was very much against his mother marrying his father. He said his father was quite fond of the drink, and did not provide well for his family. Limpy had a younger brother, I can't recall his name now, but I do recall him as being quite sickly. They lived off whatever means they could find. Limpy's real name was Charles Woodward. I believe I told you that already."

Jack nodded his head. "Yes Sir, you did tell me that." His mind instantly went to Collin McCauley. It appears Collin and old Limpy had much in common.

Jack smiled up at his grandfather as Lester cleared his throat and continued. "Well, the boy died late in the fall. Limpy said his mother never quite got over the boy's death. He said his mother stood up to his father and they argued quite a lot after that. He said his mother often took a good thumping by his father's hand, and often Limpy would intervene on his mother's behalf, which usually ended in a good beating from his father. He said a stranger showed up one night to tell them that his father had been found face down in the street, dead by choking on his own vomit after a night of drinking. He said not he or his mother shed one tear over the loss."

"Lester," Delores said, "Are you certain this is the right story to be telling the lad?"

Lester nodded his head. "Jack is old enough to hear this. Besides, he needs to learn that there is a whole other world out there, and it isn't always a better one." He looked over at Sheldon who sat staring at the fire. He wore a frown upon his face, but did not say anything to deter Lester from continuing with the story.

"Well now, as I was saying," Lester began. "The next morning, Limpy set out to find work to support himself and his mother. As I said before, he was merely fourteen years old. He went to the pub where his father was well known by the proprietor. He obtained employment by washing the ale glasses, spittoons, and scrubbing the floors. He said it was not the most desirable of jobs, but it put money in his pocket at the end of every night. He hadn't been to school in over a year, so his education was not suffering for the likes of it."

Lester cleared his throat again and continued, "Limpy said it was late in the night when he returned home. He found a letter from his mother on the table saying she had gone back to live with her parents and he was to join her there. She was unaware of the whereabouts of her son all evening, and assumed he had ran away from home as so many boys his age had done. Limpy recalled that his grandfather had been very cruel to him and his brother in the past and had no desire to live under the same roof as the grumpy old fart."

"Lester Gideon!" Delores exclaimed.

"I apologize my dear. I was using Limpy's very words. I had forgotten that an old sailor's tongue may not be suitable for the ears of a lady, however, it is what he said." Lester winked at Jack and continued, "Limpy said that was the last night he spent in that house. The next night, while working at the Pub, he overheard some sailors talking about getting as many hands as they could round up for a winters voyage. He inquired as to what type of voyage they were talking about and was informed that they were whalers. He signed up and joined the crew that very night. He was given a hammock on board the ship to sleep in. He said they set sail two days later."

"Did he ever see his mother again?" Jack asked.

Lester shook his head. "No, Jack, he did not," Lester replied.

"I think it is time for you to go to bed, Jack," Sheldon said, snapping his fingers to get Jack's attention. "That sun will not hesitate to rise, just because you wanted to sit up and listen to a story. You have put in a full day and you will require a full night's sleep."

Jack recalled dozing off in class. He did not want to do that again. "Yes, Sir," Jack said, rising to his feet. "Will you tell me more tomorrow evening, Grandfather?" Jack asked.

Lester nodded his head. "I will indeed, Jack, my boy."

Jack embraced his grandfather, grandmother, and father. He climbed the ladder to the loft and crawled under the layers of blankets. He stared up at the reflecting lights coming from below until he could not hold his eyes open any longer. He heard his father climbing the ladder, and soon he crawled on his hands and knees to sit next to Jack as he laid in his bed. "Are things working out for you at the mercantile?" Sheldon asked.

"Yes Father, they are working out quite well. I will get paid on Friday. It will be my very first paycheck," Jack said, smiling up at his father.

Sheldon chuckled and said, "I remember my first paycheck. I recall I had it spent before I received it." He looked down at Jack and asked, "Do you have something special planned for your first paycheck, Jack?"

"I do," Jack replied. "There is a catalog on the counter and it has a picture of a beautiful set of china made at a pottery in East Liverpool. I was thinking of buying it for Grandmother. I think she would like a set of dishes where all the cups have handles and everything matches. What do you think, Father?"

Sheldon smiled. "I think your Grandmother would like that very much. That is very thoughtful of you to want to spend your first paycheck on someone else. Most boys your age would think of something for themselves."

"Perhaps my next paycheck, I could find something for myself. Grandmother works very hard and never asks for anything for herself. She cooks all my meals and washes my clothes. She complains when I get myself muddy, but she works very hard at keeping my clothes clean. I think she deserves something special for all she does," Jack said, blinking his tired eyes.

"Well," Sheldon began, "I am very proud of you, Jack." He leaned down and hugged Jack. "You get to sleep now. You have a full day of school tomorrow before you go to work."

"Thank you, Father," Jack said pulling the quilt up around his neck. He watched as his father disappeared down the ladder to the lower level, and out of sight. He slept soundly until the sound of his grandfather calling his name from below the next morning. It was a new day. Jack jumped from his bed and quickly smoothed the blankets. He dressed and hurried down the ladder to the kitchen. Something smelled very good this morning.

Judy Lennington

"Your grandmother obtained a few eggs this morning from the henhouse. It appears the chickens are laying again," Lester said smiling.

Jack looked down at the plate his grandmother placed before him on the table. Bacon and eggs covered the plate. It was the perfect Sunday morning breakfast and it was a week day. Jack smiled up at his grandmother who stood waiting for his approval. "Thank you, Grandmother. It looks divine."

Delores rustled Jack's hair and smiled. "I wanted to surprise you," she said.

"This is a wonderful surprise!" Jack said, taking a big bite of scrambled eggs.

"Did you sleep well enough?" Lester asked.

"Yes, Sir, I did. Thank you for asking," Jack said, with his mouth full.

"Jack," his grandmother said, looking over her shoulder at him.

Jack swallowed and said, "Yes Grandmother, I know. I apologize for talking with my mouth full. It's just too good. I'm sorry." He scooped up a big spoonful of scrambled eggs and shoved them into his mouth. His grandmother shook her head and turned to look away.

"Maybe we can finish my story when you get home tonight," Lester said. Jack took a bite of bacon and nodded his head as he rolled his eyes. Lester smiled and tapped his cane upon the floor. "Are you working at the mercantile this afternoon, after school?" he asked. Jack could only nod his head as he continued to chew. Finally, his meal was gone.

Jack stepped outside to go to the outhouse. Upon returning he said, "It smells like rain."

"My knee tells me it's going to rain all day," Lester announced. "You mind you take something to shield you in a downpour on your travels."

"Yes, Grandfather, I will. Thank you for the reminder," Jack said, taking his coat from the peg near the door. Delores waited patiently for him to put his coat on before handing him his lunch tin. "Goodbye Grandmother, Grandfather. I'll see you later," Jack called out as he turned and darted through the door into the early morning light. There was a heavy fog hanging over the river this morning. The mist was heavy on Jack's face as he hurried along toward the schoolhouse.

It was too foggy for anyone to be waiting outdoors in the morning air. As Mrs. Cartwright announced that class was about to commence, Jack became aware of students coughing. Mrs. Cartwright was aware of it as well, for he noticed her frowning as she looked around the room at the faces looking back at her. It often occurred, this time of year, for several of the children to come down with something or another. Jack remembered the story his grandfather was telling him the night before, about Limpy's little brother being sickly. He was very aware of what it was like to have someone sick in a home. His own mother had died in her bed. Mrs. Cartwright's tapping her desk with her pointer brought him back to the moment. "Class, if anyone here feels they need to go home, because they are ill, they may be excused at this particular time," Mrs. Cartwright announced. Jack watched as Melvin Riley and Anthony Patrone both rose from their seats. "Melvin, Anthony, are you both ill?" Mrs. Cartwright asked suspiciously.

"Yes, Ma'am," Melvin said, nodding his head and holding his stomach.

Judy Lennington

Jack could tell that Mrs. Cartwright was not convinced. She watched them very closely as they began to move toward the wall where their coats hung on pegs. "You tell your mother's that I will be by to check up on you after school today," Mrs. Cartwright called after them.

The boys looked at one another and clutched their stomachs as they moved toward the door. They closed the door behind them. Mrs. Cartwright went to the window and watched as they broke into a run into the morning mist. She shook her head as she turned back to the class. With a heavy sigh, she asked if anyone else was feeling poorly. When no one responded, she took her pointer and went to the first-grade row.

Jack tried to concentrate on his school work, but found it difficult as a storm closed in upon them. The thunder rattled the walls of the old-school house and the lightning flashed vibrantly, startling Mrs. Cartwright a few times. Jack smiled to himself as he thought about Melvin and Anthony picking such a lousy day to play hooky. A few other students coughed a couple of times, but it wasn't any more than usual. The fear of something contagious had passed. When lunch time came around it was pouring rain outside. The desks were slid to the outside walls and the jump rope was strung across the room. Collin pulled Jack to the side and asked him to help him with his writing skills instead of joining the others in the game.

Collin was learning very quickly. Jack was amazed at how much Mr. Dodge had taught Collin, for he was sounding out words as he wrote them on his slate. Some of the words were misspelled, but for the most part, they were readable and Jack feared that Collin would soon find himself working on the docks down at the river's edge. What was Jack to do?

Bend in The River

Class resumed and the storm moved on, leaving the rain to continue to fall. The day was long and gloomy, and finally the bell rang to dismiss the class. Collin and Jack ran together toward the mercantile. Upon arriving, they found Mrs. Dodge in a very strange mood. Mr. Dodge took Collin to the back and Jack did not see him again until they sat at the dinner table together at the end of the night. Business was slow, due to the falling rain, and there was much cleaning to be done. Jack found himself sneezing frequently as he crawled into the tight spaces he was instructed to clean for Mrs. Dodge. They dined upon bacon and boiled potatoes, however, Mrs. Dodge had baked the most fabulous bread pudding for desert.

Before leaving, Mrs. Dodge pulled the boys off to the side of the counter and asked, "Have either of you boys seen my large silver spoon?"

"No Ma'am," they both replied.

"I seem to have misplaced it somewhere and I really would like to find it," she explained. "You see, it was my mother's spoon, so you can see how important it is that I find it again. I know I had it yesterday, early in the evening. However, I seem to have misplaced it before you boys left for the night. That is why I thought perhaps you may have seen it lying about somewhere."

"No Ma'am, I don't recall seeing your spoon," Collin said, looking over at Jack.

"We will keep our eyes open for it," Jack said.

Mrs. Dodge took a deep breath and closed her eyes. "I can't ask anymore of you," she replied. She smiled and said, "You boys have a good night. Be careful out there for it is pouring hard. You're welcome to stay until it calms down if you've a might to."

Judy Lennington

"No thank you, Ma'am," Collin said. "I have to get to the chair factory and sweep up before I turn in for the night. "Me Ma is still under the weather, and Mr. Armstrong is expecting to find everything ship shape when he opens in the morning."

Mrs. Dodge reached out and placed her hand upon Collin's shoulder. She studied his face closely for a moment before smiling and bidding him a good night. Jack felt as if something was amiss, but was not quite certain what it was. Mr. Dodge stood quietly in the background watching them say their good nights and locked the door after them when they left. They paused on the porch, looking out at the pouring rain. "What do you suppose all of that was about?" Jack asked, looking up at Collin.

"I don't know," Collin replied. "She's awful attached to a spoon, if you ask me. Do you reckon she thinks one of us took it?"

"I didn't take it. I recall seeing it in her hand, but only the one time," Jack said.

Collin shrugged his shoulders and said, "I don't recall seeing it after that." They looked at one another again and Collin said, "I'll see you tomorrow." Then he darted out into the rain. Jack watched until he was out of sight, before he too, made a dash toward home in the pouring rain. He was drenched by the time he got home. As he stood on the porch, he heard the splashes of someone running toward him in the rain. He stood on the porch shivering as he watched his father come into view. Sheldon laughed as he climbed the steps to the porch. They were both shivering and soaked to the skin.

Delores had dinner on the table. Jack sat politely sipping a cup of hot tea while the others ate. His grandmother always asked him what he had for dinner at the Dodges. At Jack's reply, she usually raised her eyebrows. Jack wondered if she was concerned that he was eating well enough or if she was just being nosey.

Jack had changed into his nightshirt and sat near the fire while his grandmother cleared the table. His father was also dressed for bed and their clothes hung on hooks driven into the stone wall that surrounded the fireplace. They would hang there until morning. By that time, they would be dry enough to wear another day.

Jack watched his grandfather as he seemed to be deep in thought, staring at the fire blazing away in the fireplace. The rain continued to pelt at the windows and roof of the little house. "Grandfather, would you mind telling me more of the story about Limpy and his whaling experiences?" Jack asked.

This seemed to light a spark in Lester's eyes. A smile spread across his face as he nodded his head. He closed his eyes and began, "Let me see now, as I recall, I left off at Limpy's first voyage at sea. You remember my telling you that he was only on two trips to sea. Well, that might not seem like much, but what you must know is; a trip may take as long as two years."

"Two years?" Jack asked, scooting closer. "Why did it take so long?"

"Well, the whales don't get together and swim out to greet the ships you know. They had to go in search of the whales. Yes sir, that was quite an accomplishment. You see, there were lots of ships hunting and killing whales. There still are, I reckon. By this time the whales knew what they were up to, and they avoided being caught. The ships had to hunt them and then they had to chase them down," Lester explained. Jack noticed his father was moving closer now, for he too was interested in the story.

"Were the whales fast?" Jack asked.

"Yes, they were, but not as fast as you might think. However, they could dive deep. That was a danger to the whalers," Lester said. He paused a few moments as if he were trying to remember where he had left off. "Limpy said he slept in a nap sack. That is a hammock type of bed made from a linen sheet stretched to hang from post to post. He said all the ships hands slept in them and when the ship hit rough water, they swung back and forth. He said at first, he got very sea sick. Of course, he was not the only one. He said when the seas got rough the smell of puke was so strong, that even the most experienced sailor got sick. I recall he told me that they weren't at sea very long before he regretted his signing on, but out there on the ocean, it wasn't like you could just walk off the boat." Lester giggled.

"How long before they caught a whale?" Jack asked.

"Well now, as I said before, the whales don't come looking for the ships. They can hear for long distances under the water and they learned what a ship sounds like. They spend most of their time trying to avoid being discovered by the ships, don't you know. Also, their numbers were dropping as whaling was a growing business in those parts," Lester said. "Limpy said they spent many days just bobbing around out there on the water. He scrubbed the deck and dumped waste, I reckon he did whatever the mates needed done. He said he was the youngest of all the mates on ship, so he got the dirtiest of all the jobs. He said they bobbed around out there for months, and mind you, this was early winter, so that sea was a cold one. He said his hands nearly froze a time or two." Lester smiled as he watched Jack's face.

"He said he was swabbing the deck one afternoon. That means he was scrubbing the deck," Lester explained. "He said there was a man up in the stern, sort of perched up there, watching for a spray. That is when a whale blows the water out of its blow hole as it surfaces. You can see the spray from far off. Well, this particular man shouted, 'There she blows!', which means he spotted a spray. That's when things got active on the boat. The smaller boats were lowered into the water."

"How many?" Jack asked, scooting closer.

"I believe there were two or three of them, I'm not certain about the numbers, but I know there was more than one. Maybe three boats, as I seem to recall," Lester frowned and shook his head as he thought on the question.

"It doesn't matter, Grandfather. Go on with the story," Jack said.

"Well," Lester began, "As I said, the boats were lowered into the water and the men scrambled down into them. They began rowing as fast as they could, toward the whale.

"Couldn't the whale outrun them?" Jack asked.

"Well now, the whales are big and slow compared to the other fish in the ocean. I suppose the bigger you are the slower you are," Lester said. "The first mate was yelling, 'We'll get fast this rising!'."

"What does that mean?" Jack asked.

Lester took a deep breath and let it out slow. He closed his eyes and said, "As I recall, it is what they say every time the whale re-appears." He looked down at Jack and smiled. "Limpy said the old man was in the boat with him. The old man is what they call the ship's captain. He was yelling out orders and Limpy said he was very nervous, this being his first time and all. He said the whale was massive and he overheard someone say it was a young bull whale. He said it was huge for something that was supposed to be a juvenile. He said he hoped nobody found out that he was praying they never came up on a fully-grown whale, for this one frightened the whit's out of him."

"Did they kill it?" Jack asked.

"Well now," Lester began, "As I recall, Limpy said they got right up alongside this huge creature and Limpy said he looked him square in the eye. The old man hurled a harpoon as soon as the whale broke water. That means as soon as he surfaced."

"I figured as much," Jack said.

"Limpy said the young bull was a Sperm Whale. The first mate yelled out, 'You're buried to the hitches, Captain!'. That means it was a successful dart. They had managed to dart the whale and the harpoon was latched to a line. Limpy said they were hooked on, that meaning they were fast to the whale. He said the whale dove with the harpoon buried in his flesh and scared the dickens out of Limpy when he breached a full, which means he jumped clean up out of the water. Then he started to dive, and dive he did. A hand began calling out the lengths of line they were losing as the whale dove deeper. Limpy said it was getting near the end of the line and everyone began to get nervous. You see, if the line ran out the whale would likely pull the boat under. He said everyone was watching the line unravel as the whale dove. When it was nearly at its end, the old man ordered them to cut the line. It was the only thing they could do. So now they had a loose whale on their hands. The second boat made ready for the whale to surface. 'There she blows', someone shouted from the second boat. They rowed as fast as they could in the direction of the spray," Lester said.

"I thought they didn't have any more line," Jack said.

"They didn't, but they could assist the second boat, if need be," Lester explained.

"Oh, I see," Jack replied.

"Well, as it turned out, the second boat managed to harpoon the cachalot, which is what they call a Sperm Whale. And so, the entire process began again, only this time all the action was in the second boat. By this time, the young bull was getting tired and he had a harpoon in his lung, so he couldn't breathe very well. They were hooked on good this time. The bull would mill in one direction and then another, trying to dislodge the iron, that being the harpoon. A flurry commenced. That is what they call the struggle of a dying whale. The two small boats moved in to tackle the whale. He said by this time they were in white water. That is a foam caused by a thrashing whale. It comes usually right before the whale dies. Then it was over. They had taken the whale and latched on to it good. They towed it back to the ship and fastened it secure to the side where they could start carving it up until they could haul it aboard and barrel the oil for storage until they were land bound again," Lester smiled.

"How do you remember all of the words and what they mean?" Jack asked.

Lester threw his head back and laughed. "Oh, I spent many a day and night sitting with old Limpy, listening to his going on and on about his voyages. I know it all by heart now," Lester said.

"You best get to bed boy," his grandmother said running her hands through Jack's hair. "It is past your bedtime, and tomorrow is another school day. Hopefully, it won't be raining when you head out tomorrow."

"Are we having eggs for breakfast again tomorrow, Grandmother?" Jack asked.

She laughed and nodded her head. "I believe there are a couple more out there. Lord knows I may need you to fetch them for me. If this rain continues through the night, the mud will be knee deep."

"I can get them for you," Jack said, rising to hug his grandmother. "I would be happy to get them for you."

"That's a good lad," Delores said, smiling at Jack.

Jack hugged his grandfather and began to climb the ladder. His father climbed up behind him and announced that he too, was going to bed. Jack laid in his bed listening to the rain pelting the roof. Before long his father began to snore and Jack flipped onto his side, covering his ear with his pillow. He squeezed his eyes shut tightly and soon he too was asleep.

It was morning and the rain was still falling. He stretched as he rose from bed. He bent down to smooth out his covers and smiled as he looked down at the crumpled blankets. "'Twas a flurry in the night," he said. He smoothed out the layers of quilts and climbed down the ladder. Jack pulled on his grandfather's old shoes and clomped his way to the outhouse and then to the chicken coop where he gathered eight eggs for breakfast. As he entered the house again he felt the heat from the fireplace upon his face. "It's a humid morning out there with all of this rain," Lester said, poking at the fire as it blazed.

"Yes, Sir," Jack replied. "It smells like earth worms outside."

"That's a sure sign of spring, my boy," Lester said, smiling over at Jack.

Delores was busy preparing breakfast. "How many eggs would you like this morning, Jack?" she asked.

"I think I could eat three eggs this morning, Grandmother. That is, if you have them to spare," Jack replied.

"I believe I could spare three eggs, rightly enough, since it was you who waded through the mud to fetch them for me. Saves

Bend in The River

me from having to go out in this nasty weather this morning," Delores said.

Jack took note of the good mood his grandmother appeared to be in this morning, as she seemed awful chipper for the second day of rain. Usually that put her in an awful mood, however, this morning she was cheerful.

"It's Friday, boy," Lester said. "Are you working at the mercantile tomorrow all day?"

"I suppose so. That is, of course, if they need me. It's been kind of slow over there with all the rain. What are you going to do today, Grandfather?" Jack asked.

"If it stops raining, I may pay my respects to Hermon. "I've been meanin' to see how he is doing, but I can't get around very well in the mild weather, let alone go out in this ankle-deep mud and rain," Lester replied.

"If it rains all day today, Grandfather, you might try writing a little note to your friend Hermon. I could deliver it for you after I get home," Jack said.

"Now that is mighty kind of you Jack," Lester said. He tapped his cane on the floor and asked, "Isn't that mighty thoughtful of Jack to do that for me, Delores?"

"It surely is, Lester. We've been blessed to have good children and grandchildren," Delores said. "Although we don't see much of our other young'uns, we're lucky to have Sheldon and Jack here with us. You might want to mention that in your note to Hermon. He might want to take that into consideration seeing as his son has invited him to go live with him and all."

Jack was pulling on his warm school clothes that had hung near the fire all night to dry. He was buttoning his shirt when his grandmother placed his eggs on the table. She sliced a thick

Judy Lennington

slice of bread and placed a spoonful of lard on the top of it. "Eat up, Jack. I can't have you going off to the Dodges with a growling belly. Lord knows what Rosalie Dodge would be telling her customers about us."

Jack climbed onto his chair and looked up at his grandmother. "Thank you, Grandmother. I can't say as I've ever heard Mrs. Dodge gossiping about the folks here in Wellsville in my presence," He said. He bowed his head in prayer.

Delores waited until Jack raised his head again and said, "Of course she is too much a lady to say such things in your presence, Jack. But, folks do talk." She patted the top of Jack's head and said, "You might want to save some of that lard for your hair this morning, Jack. You look like you've seen a ghost." Lester began to laugh as he leaned his cane left to right from where he sat on a wooden chair near the fire. Jack reached up and smoothed his hair while smiling back at his grandfather.

"I reckon the rain will take care of it," he said. "I'm likely to be soaked by the time I get to school."

"Perhaps," Delores began, "Beings today is your first payday, perhaps, you should buy yourself one of them umbrellas or parasols."

Jack smiled. "I already know what I'm buying with my first paycheck," he said, taking a big mouthful of eggs.

"What would that be?" Delores asked.

The room grew quiet as Jack chewed the mouthful of breakfast. He swallowed and smiled, "It's a surprise," he replied. He finished his breakfast and began to prepare for his dash through the rain.

"You have a good day at school, Jack," his grandmother said, patting Jack's unruly hair.

Bend in The River

"You listen to Mrs. Cartwright and fill that head of yours full of useful knowledge so you will be somebody important one day," Lester called from across the room.

"I hope I can remember everything I learn as good as you remember what Limpy told you," Jack called back.

"I said useful knowledge, Jack, my boy," Lester called out again.

Jack turned to look back at his grandfather, "Who's to say what Limpy told you wasn't useful, Grandfather? I found it quite interesting. Perhaps you should write it all down into a book. It would make a fine book, maybe even a novel sold all over the country."

Lester laughed. "Wouldn't that be something? At my age, no less."

"You never know," Jack said. "You told me it was never too late to learn." Jack smiled, and darted from the doorway. His grandmother stood with the door open watching him run until he was no longer visible. He splashed in the mud, as he held his lunch tin over his head to protect himself from the downpour. He climbed the steps to the school and entered the building to find most of the children had obviously chosen to stay home today.

Mrs. Cartwright sat at her desk, scraping the mud from her shoes. The hem of her long skirt was soaked and muddy from dragging behind her as she made her way to the school house. The fire in the stove roared, and Jack hung his coat on a peg nearest to the stove. He had lots of spots to choose from today, as there were only a few students who showed up. Melvin Riley arrived, but Anthony Patrone was not with him. Jack wondered if their parents found out they had played hooky yesterday. Jack avoided Melvin as he watched for Collin to arrive. Soon Mrs. Cartwright rang the bell. Collin did not come to school today.

Judy Lennington

The rain continued to fall. It was the second day in a row that the class would remain inside for recess. Jack kept to himself, and avoided going anywhere near Melvin. Neither Milly or Lynnette were in school today. Lewis Tully and Jack were the only two in the row of third graders. During recess, Jack sat quietly near a window, watching the rain fall. The roof of the old schoolhouse was tin, so the pelting rain made a roaring sound. The day drug by slowly and finally it was time for the dismissal bell. Jack ran as fast as he could toward the mercantile. He did not want to be caught by Melvin.

He breathed a sigh of relief as he entered the mercantile. Mrs. Dodge was at the counter talking to Mr. Moser and one of his older sons. They smiled over at Jack as he entered. Jack got the distinct feeling they had been talking about him before he arrived. The words his grandmother spoke earlier that morning came rushing back at him.

Mrs. Dodge nodded her head at Jack and smiled. "Mr. Dodge is needing some assistance in the back, Jack. Are you alone this afternoon?" she asked.

"I believe so, Ma'am. Collin wasn't at school today," Jack replied, as he hung his coat on a peg. As he passed Mr. Moser and his son, he could hear Mrs. Dodge saying something too low that Jack could not hear.

Jack found Mr. Dodge standing on a wooden barrel as he moved things about on a shelf high over his head. He looked down at Jack and asked, "Are you alone today, Jack?"

"Yes Sir, I believe so, Sir. At least I think so, for Collin wasn't in school today. Mrs. Dodge said you needed help with something, Sir," Jack said.

Bend in The River

Mr. Dodge placed his hands upon his hips and said, "Well now, that is true, however, you won't be much help with what I need. You see, Jack, you are too small. I was hoping Collin could help me out with all that stuff up there on those high shelves. They've been up there so long, I don't even know what I have. I've begun taking inventory, and you, my friend, are too small to reach." He jumped from the barrel and placed his hand upon Jack's shoulder. "You wouldn't happen to know where Mrs. Dodge's silver spoon made off to, would you Jack?" he asked.

Jack shook his head. He had forgotten all about the silver spoon. "No Sir, I haven't seen it."

Mr. Dodge took a deep breath and stood up straight, placing his hands upon his hips once more. He looked around the room and said, "Where could it have made off to on its own?" He looked down at Jack and smiled, "You see, Jack, to strangers it's just an old silver spoon. It may not be worth much, except, of course, for the silver content. But to Mrs. Dodge, that spoon is priceless. You see, Lad, it was her mother's spoon. Beings as her mother died when Rosalie was quite young, she puts a lot of stock in things that belonged to her mother." Mr. Dodge bent down to look Jack square in the eye. "I don't think I have any cause not to believe you when you say you don't know where it is, Jack. But, if you know someone who might know where it is, I would be very pleased to know. I might go as far as pay a small reward for that information."

Jack raised his eyebrows. "A reward?"

"Yes, Son, that is right. I'd pay a reward. Of course, it wouldn't be much. It is just a spoon, after all," Mr. Dodge said.

"I could use the reward, Sir," Jack said. "I wish I knew where it was. I truly do. I'll mention the reward to Collin. He could use the money too."

Mr. Dodge smiled down at Jack as he stood up straight. "You do that, Son," he said, looking around the room. "Well now, let me see what I can find for you to do."

Mr. Dodge stood on the barrel and handed items from the shelf to Jack. Jack in turn, lined the items on the floor along the wall. Mr. Dodge gave Jack a rag to dust the items while he wrote in his ledger. Then Jack handed the items back up to Mr. Dodge as he replaced them on the shelves. They were eating dinner when Collin arrived.

They heard the bell over the door ring. As Mr. Dodge was rising from the table, Collin entered through the parted curtains. He was soaked through and held his dripping hat in his hands. "Pardon my intrusion, Mrs. Dodge, Mr. Dodge. I'm sorry for being so late. It's me Ma, you see, she's been feelin' poorly lately, and with this weather, well, she's sort of real bad today," he explained. "Me sister, Katherine, does a fine job of lookin' after her and all, but we had to call the doctor in today. We feared we were losin' her."

"Oh my," Mrs. Dodge said, rising from the table. "How is she now?"

"She's some better, but she is still in a bad way, Ma'am. Doc says she's critical. We don't have the money to pay for the medicine she needs, and without it, she might not make it through the night." Collin shifted from foot to foot. "I was wonderin' since I worked for nearly a full week and all, well, I was wonderin...."

Bend in The River

Mr. Dodge walked around the table and placed his hand upon Collin's shoulder. "Young man, how much do you need?" he asked.

"I need a dollar, Mr. Dodge. I know it is a lot of money, and I know I haven't done a dollars' worth of work yet, but the doctor said the medicine costs a dollar. Me Dah cleaned out our savings and lit off to drink it all up before he died in the streets. We're kind of on our own over there," Collin said, hanging his head.

"A whole dollar?" Mrs. Dodge asked.

"Yes, Ma'am. I know it's askin' a lot, but the doctor has been helping us for so long and we ain't been givin' him a penny. He says this medicine is expensive and he can't give it out like he has been. We're kind of in a bad way now, and I'm awful sorry to have to ask you good folks. You've been so good to me already," Collin said.

Mr. Dodge nodded his head. He looked over at his wife and said, "I suppose it wouldn't be very Christian of us to turn you away, Son, after all you've done around here. You come with me and I'll give you a dollar. Of course, I expect you to work this money off." They were disappearing through the curtains as he spoke. Jack hurried to follow as Mrs. Dodge was right behind them. "Now, you wouldn't recall seeing Mrs. Dodge's silver spoon lying about anywhere would you, Collin?" Mr. Dodge was asking, as he opened the cash register drawer.

Collin looked confused by the question. He shook his head and replied, "No Sir, I don't recall seeing it anywhere, except when she came out here carrying it in her hand. The last time I saw it, she had laid it on top of that counter over there. I swear, I didn't take it, Sir, if that is what you are asking."

Judy Lennington

"No, no," Mr. Dodge said, shaking his head. "It's just that we can't seem to find it anywhere, and it was something very special to my wife. It belonged to her mother who died when Rosalie was a young girl. It is sentimental to Rosalie. She doesn't have many things that belonged to her mother. You can understand that can't you, Collin?"

"Yes, Sir," Collin said, looking down into the open money drawer. Mr. Dodge noticed him looking, and quickly shut the drawer. "Well," he said with hesitation, before handing Collin a silver dollar. "Remember what I said, Collin. I expect you to work off this debt.

"Yes, Sir. I will remember. As soon as me Ma is out of danger, I will be back and work this dollar off for you, Sir. You can count on it. Thank you, Sir. I bid you good day," Collin said. He turned and quickly darted through the door, into the late afternoon and pouring rain.

"A whole dollar, Howard?" Mrs. Dodge asked.

"Now, Rosalie, we will speak of this later," Mr. Dodge replied. They turned and began to walk toward the curtains. Jack followed quietly. They resumed their seats at the table. Afterwards, while Mrs. Dodge cleared the table of dinner, Mr. Dodge and Jack went back to their inventory. Soon it was time to leave.

"Before you go, Jack, we need to settle with what we owe you," Mr. Dodge said going to the cash register drawer. "Now let's see, we agreed upon five cents a day, and you started on a Tuesday, so that is four days at five cents a day..." he looked over at Jack.

Jack nodded his head and said softly, "Twenty cents, Sir."

"Very good, Jack. Twenty cents it is," Mr. Dodge said.

Mrs. Dodge spoke up, "And two licorice sticks."

"And two licorice sticks," Mr. Dodge repeated.

"I do believe, he had his eye on a set of china for his grandmother, Howard," Mr. Dodge said.

"I did," Jack said, "But if you don't mind, Sir, I would like you to put my twenty cents toward what Collin owes you. That is, if you don't mind, Sir. I know it doesn't square things up, but it may take a whole month for him to pay off what he owes on his own. I'd like to help out a friend."

Mrs. Dodge covered her mouth with her hand. Just then the bell over the door rang and Mr. Garfield entered shaking the rain from his hat. "Good evening, Howard, Ma'am, I know it's late, but I need a small sack of lye. My wife will need to make some soap" he said.

"I'll get it," Mrs. Dodge said.

Jack stepped to the side so Mr. Dodge and Mr. Garfield could talk. Jack would wait for Mr. Garfield to leave before he and Mr. Dodge finished their conversation.

"We'll she won't have a shortage of water, if this rain keeps falling," Mr. Dodge said, with a smile.

Mr. Garfield nodded his head. "Yes, the river is getting pretty high. I hope it stops soon. The peepers have looked through glass three times now, so I don't expect it to freeze again. Yes, spring has sprung." He brushed the rain from his shoulder. "We are scrubbing the daylights out of everything, because that little Gardner girl died today from complications that came from the mumps. My wife is keeping the kids home from school and scrubbing the dickens out of everything under the roof."

"Vivian Gardner?" Jack asked.

Mr. Garfield looked down at Jack. "Why yes, I believe her name was Vivian. She would be about your age, young man," Mr. Garfield said.

"She was my age. She sat in the front seat of my row at school," Jack said.

"Well, she won't be sitting there anymore, Son. If I were you, I'd be checking myself for lumps under my chin. She was sick for a long time with the mumps. They are nasty enough on their own, but she was too weak to fight it off. You tell your mother to keep you home from school so you don't catch the mumps. My wife is keeping our children home until the danger is past." He looked over at Mr. Dodge and said, "It is a good thing there is only one more week of school left. They don't learn much that last week anyway."

Jack sighed as he thought of Vivian Gardner. Her hair was always braided into two long braids that hung down her back. He remembered the time Lewis Tully dipped the ends of her braids into the ink well on his desk. He got a good whooping and sat in the corner all day. Rumor was he got another good strapping when his father found out. Now Vivian was gone. She was in heaven with Jack's mother. Jack tried to picture the two of them sitting on a bench under a beautiful blossomed tree in bright sunlight. They both were wearing white robes. They looked well and happy where they sat, smiling down upon Jack. Mrs. Dodge entered the room and shook Jack from his daydream.

"Did I hear you say someone died?" she asked.

"He said the little Gardner girl died, Rosalie," Mr. Dodge said.

Rosalie covered her mouth. "How dreadful!"

"Well, what do I owe you for the lye, Howard?" Mr. Garfield asked.

"Four cents, George. You be sure to say hello to Ester and the kids for us," Mr. Dodge said.

"I will," George Garfield said shaking his head. "Folks are dropping like flies around here. First Hermon Griffin's wife, and now the Gardner girl. I understand some drunk died a week or so ago, too. They say he choked on his own vomit." He shook his head as he made his way toward the door. "What a waste of life," he said, opening the door. "Well, you folks take care and mind what I told you, boy, about those glands in your neck. You tell your mother what I said." Then he turned and left.

Jack looked up at Mr. Dodge. Howard smiled and said softly, "I doubt he recognized who you were, Jack."

"I understand, Mr. Dodge. If you don't mind, would you please put my twenty cents toward what Collin owes you?" Jack asked, swallowing the lump in his throat.

"I will do whatever you wish, Son," Mr. Dodge said, with a smile. "You be careful out there now. It's raining pretty hard. You hurry along and don't dawdle."

"Yes, Sir. Thank you, Sir." Jack turned and nodded his head toward Rosalie, "Good evening, Ma'am," he said, before turning and hurrying out the door. Jack thought about Vivian Gardner as he ran toward home. He arrived before his father, and found his grandfather waiting with a hand-written note to his friend Hermon Griffin. As Jack had promised, he ran out into the rain, again, toward the Griffin house. He noticed the candles burning on the table through the open door of Mrs. Cartwright's as he ran passed. He found Mr. Griffin sitting at the table holding his head in his hands as Jack reached the porch.

"Jack, my boy, come in. You're soaked to the skin, Lad," Mr. Griffin said, rising from his chair.

Jack handed the note to Hermon and waited for him to read it. Hermon's eyes welled up with tears as he read the note. He wiped at his eyes and said, "This is a nice note your grandfather has sent me." He shook the note in his hand as he said, "This means a lot to me. Thank you for bringing this over in this nasty weather." He looked around and asked, "Could I give you a cup of warm tea before you go back out there in the rain again?"

Jack looked around. He was hoping to get home and out of his wet clothes, but a cup of warm tea sounded good at the moment. Jack nodded his head and replied, "That would be very neighborly of you, Sir."

Mr. Griffin placed a few lose tea leaves into a cup and poured boiling water over them. He stirred the leaves until the water turned a dark color. He handed it to Jack and smiled. He reached for a jar full of golden honey and dipped a spoon into it. It streamed from the end of the spoon as he lifted it out of the jar. Mr. Griffin spun the spoon until the streaming honey wound around the spoon. Then he dipped it into the dark liquid. Jack sat sipping at the tea and staring at the fireplace. "They say the river is rising," Mr. Griffin said.

"I heard that today at the mercantile," Jack replied.

"Oh, that's right. You are working at the mercantile in the evenings after school. How do you like working for a living, Jack?" Mr. Griffin asked.

"I like it. The Dodges are good folks. It's hardly what I would call work. It is more like fun. I work on Saturday's too," Jack replied.

"Well now, a boy needs his Saturdays to go off on his imaginary adventures, as I recall," Mr. Griffin said, smiling across the table at Jack.

"Yes, Sir," Jack said. "I would rather work for the Dodges right now anyway. There isn't much adventure to be found in weather like this."

Mr. Griffin nodded his head. "That would be true," he said. He took a deep breath and said, "I recall the days when your grandfather and I were about your age. Your grandfather was about the same age as you when he became friends with old Limpy. We weren't good friends yet, but I recall the two of them well enough. You hardly saw one without the other. I was forbidden to associate with old Limpy, therefore, I didn't know your grandfather very well. As time went on, your grandfather sort of grew on old Limpy and he started cleaning himself up a little. Folks were a little more tolerable toward him about that time. I became friends with your grandfather right before old Limpy passed away. My own father was the one that rowed us out to the middle of the river to give Limpy the burial he asked for. Of course, it wasn't officially a burial at sea, but it was as close as we could give him. After that, your grandfather and I became the best of friends and still are."

"Yes, Sir. That is pretty much the way Grandfather tells it too," Jack replied. He finished his tea and said, "Well, if you don't mind, Sir, my father should be getting home from work about this time. I really should be going. I thank you for the tea, Sir."

"You are quite welcome, Jack. You drop by anytime you feel like it. I'll be right here," Mr. Griffin said.

"You aren't going to live with Wayne, Sir?" Jack asked.

Mr. Griffin shook his head. "I'm not going anywhere else until the good lord calls for me, Jack. You be sure to tell your Grandfather to come visit me right here in my home."

Judy Lennington

"Yes Sir, I will tell him, Sir," Jack replied. He placed his wet cap upon his head and took a deep breath before darting from the porch.

As Jack ran, he felt the warm tea in his belly working its way to his bladder. He ran harder, for the rain and splashing water puddles made his bladder feel heavier. He began to undo his trousers as he ran and reached the outhouse just in time. "Ah," he said allowing his head to fall back, and closing his eyes. He had made it. He buttoned his trousers and ran inside the house. His father was sitting at the table sipping a cup of hot tea.

"Get out of those wet clothes and have a cup of warm tea before you go to bed, Son," Sheldon said.

Jack began to remove his wet clothes. They clung to his skin as he peeled them off, leaving them inside out. His grandfather began to turn them right side out as he undressed. "Did you get your first paycheck today?" his grandmother asked.

"Oh, that is right. Today was payday for you. How did that feel?" Sheldon asked.

Jack frowned and continued to undress. He glanced at his grandfather quickly and said, "It was okay."

"What did you buy?" his grandmother asked.

"I didn't buy anything," Jack replied.

"So, you are saving to buy something then," his grandmother said, turning to look at him. Jack did not respond, so she turned and began to prepare a plate of food for her son, Sheldon. She placed it on the table in front of Jack's father and placed her hands upon her hips. "They did pay you didn't they, Jack?" she asked.

There was a long pause of silence before Jack replied. "Yes, Ma'am, they paid me alright. I told Mr. Dodge to put my pay toward a debt someone owed him."

"You told him what?" Delores asked, stepping closer.

"Delores, please," Lester said, straightening his arm and hand toward her. "Give the boy a chance to breath. He just got home. Good Lord in heaven!" Lester took a deep breath and glared at his wife, who turned quickly, placing her back to them. "Jack, finish undressing and have a seat at the table," Lester said.

Jack pulled his night shirt over his head. Delores placed a cup of warm tea on the table in front of him. He stared down into the dark liquid and took a deep breath. He knew if he drank this cup of tea he would be running to the privy all night. He placed his hands around the cup to warm them. He took another deep breath and said, "Grandfather, Mr. Griffin said he isn't going anywhere. He thanks you for the nice note and it means a lot to him that you took the time to write it. He asks that you drop by to visit when the weather is more accommodating."

Lester smiled and patted Jack's arm. "Thank you for delivering the note for me, Jack."

It grew quiet again. Sheldon leaned closer and asked, "Jack, is there something you need to tell us?"

Jack took another deep breath and said, "Collin wasn't at school today. His mother is poorly. He said they called for the doctor and he said she might not make it through the night without medicine that costs a whole dollar. He asked Mr. Dodge for an advance on his paycheck to pay for the medicine. I told Mr. Dodge to put my paycheck toward what Collin owes." Jack felt his eyes filling with tears as he looked up at his father. "I remember what it feels like to lose my mother, Papa. I don't want my friend Collin to go through what I went through. Besides, he doesn't have a father to raise him and his brothers and sisters. They would go to an orphanage." Jack wiped at his eyes.

Sheldon sat up straight and looked over at his mother. He swallowed the lump in his throat and wiped at his own eyes. "Well," he began, "I would say that was very Christian of you, Son. I am very proud of you."

"Is Collin going to pay you back?" Delores asked.

"Delores!" Lester said. Delores turned again and began mumbling to herself as she worked near the fireplace. It grew quiet again.

After a while, Jack said, "Mr. Garfield was in at the mercantile right before closing to buy some lye so his wife could make soap. He said Vivian Gardner died from the mumps this evening and you should check under my chin for lumps, or mumps."

"The Gardner girl died?" Delores asked, turning to look at him.

"That is what Mr. Garfield said. He said he isn't letting his children go back to school this year because of the mumps," Jack explained.

Delores sighed. She motioned for Jack to come to her, as she said, "Come here, let me have a look at you."

Jack spun around and rose from his chair. Delores began feeling the glands in his throat. She smiled down at him and said, "You are fine. You drink your tea and off to bed with you. You must go to work tomorrow and whatever you choose to do with your money is up to you." She winked at Jack.

Jack hugged her around the waist. "Thank you, Grandmother," he said. He said good night to his father and grandfather before climbing the ladder for bed. Tonight, he was chilled and huddled under the covers, holding them tightly around his neck. He thought about Vivian Gardner. She was the same age as Jack. She had an older brother who was in the seventh grade, but he kept pretty much to himself. It was well known that he was sweet on Georgia

Sweeney who was also in the seventh grade. Vivian was on the shy side. She kept to herself, mostly. He remembered a time when she tried to befriend Milly and Lynette, but for some reason it did not work out. As Jack laid there thinking back over the years he spent at school, he couldn't remember Milly or Lynette having any other friends. He certainly understood why. They were mean and nasty. They also thought they were better than most of the other children. They were two of the very few children who went to school with Jack, that lived on Water Street. However, the few that did live there weren't as mean and nasty as those two girls were. He wondered if Milly and Lynette felt sorrow over Vivian's passing. Then his thoughts went to Collin's mother. Jack flipped over on his side and pulled the covers tighter around his neck. Tears stung his eyes as he recalled his own mother's gasping for her last breathes. Poor Collin, how frightened he must be feeling tonight. Jack was too cold to get out from under the covers, but he said a prayer that Collin's mother would make it through the night and the medicine would help her to get better so Collin could go to school Monday. It was the last week of school, and Jack was certain that Collin would not be returning to school next year.

It was Saturday morning. Jack rose to find his father had already left for work, which was normal as he rose while it was still dark. Jack climbed down the ladder and hurried outside to the privy. To his surprise, it had stopped raining, but dark and threatening clouds loomed over Wellsville as if to say, "I'm not done with you yet." Jack could hear the river rushing as he made his way back to the house. The water was high from the rain. There would be no fishing on the banks tomorrow.

He entered the house to find his grandmother holding his clothes which hung near the fireplace all night. "They aren't dry yet, Jack. They were soaked and the humidity was too high. You must find something else to wear today," Delores said, hanging his clothes back where she had found them.

"Yes, Ma'am, I believe I have other clothes fit to wear," Jack replied.

"Well, don't wear your school clothes, Son. It's likely to rain again today, and you've been coming home soiled from all the cleaning you've been doing at the mercantile," Delores said. She turned and went to the iron skillet to flip the pancakes. "I can't believe Rosalie allowed it to get so dirty in there. What with her selling food products and all."

"Now Delores, don't go getting all uppity," Lester said. "Rosalie does well enough. That's a big place and it's packed with everything the Wellsville citizen's need. Just keeping the shelves stocked is work enough without you judging her like that. I'm surprised at you. Remember what the good book says. 'Judge and you shall be judged'."

"Hush now Lester, I wasn't judging Rosalie. I was merely thinking aloud," Delores said, placing a pancake on Jack's plate. She smiled down at Jack and said, "I know Mrs. Dodge does the best she can. I'm sure she appreciates you helping out the way you do." She turned and poured more batter into the iron skillet. "Of course, she pays you five cents a day. That isn't bad for a young boy your age."

"And two licorice sticks," Jack said. "Oh!" he looked up at his grandmother and said, "I forgot my licorice sticks yesterday."

"Well, it is probably just as well. As soaked as you were when you got home, they would have been a sticky mess in your pocket," Lester said, smiling over at Jack.

Bend in The River

"I suppose you are right, Grandfather," Jack said, taking a large bite of pancakes. "Thank you for this special breakfast, Grandmother." Delores turned and smiled down at Jack. "I reckon today will be Vivian Gardner's funeral," he said with his mouth full.

"Empty your mouth before speaking, Jack," his grandmother said.

Jack chewed the mouthful of food and swallowed. "I said," he began.

"I heard you," Delores said. "I suppose it will be. I reckon it will be a closed coffin, since she may still be contagious. I wonder if anyone else in the family has the mumps. I wonder if they will lift the quarantine for the funeral."

"You are putting too much thought into it, Delores," Lester said, lifting his cup to his lips. "I didn't know you knew the Gardner's that well. You talk like you were planning on going to the funeral or something."

"Lester Gideon, why shouldn't we consider going to the funeral. They are members of our community," Delores snapped back. "They live in a bigger house, and they have more money than we do, but they aren't any better than we are. They die the same as we do, and they grieve just the same. It is true they are Methodists, but as you, yourself, said, we shouldn't judge them."

Jack closed his eyes and tried to block out his grandparents arguing. He had heard enough. He was thinking about Collin and his predicament. He wondered if maybe he shouldn't leave a little early for the mercantile and check on his friend. Yes, that is exactly what he would do. He began to eat faster now. He heard his grandfather say, "Slow down there, boy. You eat like your starved to death, or something."

"I want to stop by Collin's place this morning as see how his mother is doing," Jack explained.

- 209 -

"Well then," Lester began, "You best get an early start. Mind you don't get caught in the rain. It appears as though it's going to start up again at any moment," he said, rubbing his knee. Delores sighed, but said nothing.

Jack ate the last of his pancake and finished dressing. He laced his shoes over his knee socks and lifted his coat from the peg. "Thank you for a fine breakfast, Grandmother," he said, as he went through the door. Jack was always mindful of his manners. He had been taught that manners were a sign of good breeding, and although they were not wealthy, his family was proud. People had remarked upon Jack's good manners. His grandparents had always told him that there was no excuse for rudeness. Jack had thought about that many times. He was aware of his own feelings being hurt when he felt bullied or criticized. His father had told him that if he took the time to make others feel good about themselves, they would return the favor. Jack knew that wasn't always the case. Milly and Lynette could care less if his feelings were hurt. In fact, they reveled in knowing they had managed to hurt his feelings. He assumed the same was true of Melvin and Anthony. The only thing was, they preferred a different kind of feelings being hurt. They were more into causing physical pain. He hurried along for the dark clouds were right over head and it looked as though the rain was about to fall at any moment. It had taken Jack all night to get warm. He didn't want to get soaked to the skin and he didn't want to work in his wet clothes all day long.

He was climbing the steps to the apartment over the chair factory. He put his ear to the door. He heard voices inside. The first drops of rain were falling as he tapped on the door and it flung open wide. A young girl stood in the door with long, curly, red hair and freckles covering her entire face. She had the bluest eyes Jack had ever seen. "Who is it Katherine Mary Margaret?" a weak voice called from deep inside.

"It's for Collin, Mama," the pretty young lady said, looking over her shoulder. She looked upward at the falling rain and stepped back, opening the door wide. "Please, come on in. I shouldn't keep the door open. We don't want Mother to catch a draft," she said.

Jack stepped inside and the young lady closed the door behind him. It was a gloomy day and the room was dimly lit. Jack squinted his eyes to look about him. In the corner, an older woman with hair like that of the young lady standing next to Jack, was propped up on two pillows. There were four children gathered around the woman, all staring right at Jack. He cleared his throat and said, "I'm Jack Gideon. Collin's friend."

"Oh, yes, Jack Gideon," the woman said in short breathless spurts. "It's a pleasure to finally meet you." She waved her hand in the air and forced herself to smile. "Forgive me for not getting up. I have not been well."

"I know," Jack said. "That is why I came by. I wanted to see how you were feeling and if there is anything you need."

"What a thoughtful young man you are, Jack Gideon. How very kind, too." The woman took a deep breath and coughed into her hand. "Forgive me, Jack. The doctor said I am through the worst of it, but I am still not well enough to get out of bed, yet," she said, forcing herself to smile.

"I'm very sorry you aren't well," Jack said.

"Well, I was much worse yesterday," the woman said. "I thought I was a goner for sure. But the doctor gave me some medicine last night and it made a world of a difference." She allowed her head to fall back upon the pillow. The conversation was draining her strength.

"You rest Mama," the girl said. She looked over at Jack and said, "You just missed Collin. He wanted to get an early start at the mercantile this morning. He left right after breakfast," she smiled at Jack and swayed side to side as she spoke. "I'm Katherine Mary Margaret McCauley. Collin is my younger brother. He is the second eldest." She pointed to the other children as she said their names, "That one there, is Grace Katherine Margaret, then Irene Coleen Mary, and the two little boys are Connor and Tristan."

"Why aren't you in school?" Jack asked.

"I'm needed here to look after the others and Mother," Katherine said.

"Shouldn't they be in school too?" Jack asked.

"We move around too much. Me mother teaches us here at home. Of course, Collin decided to go to school and larn to read and write, for the purpose of findin' gainful employment. He wants to work on the docks. We hear there is good wages paid to them that can read and write." She leaned close and whispered. "Me Dah died recently and me Ma isn't well enough to work. It falls upon Collin's shoulders to look after us now. He is the man of the house."

Jack watched her closely as she spoke. There was something about her that held his interest. She was very pretty, but she was a girl. No doubt she was cruel and nasty just like the rest of them. He cleared his throat and said, "Well, I better get to work too. I came to tell you that a girl in school died yesterday from the mumps. You might want to pay attention to anyone who may come down with a sore throat or become sick."

"Oh, now, that is a shame. We will heed your warnin' Jack Gideon. I thank ye for dropping by. Ye be careful out there in the rain now." Katherine said.

Jack nodded his head. "Thank you." He looked over at the woman lying in the bed watching them. "I'm happy to see you are feeling better Ma'am. Take care now."

The young lady opened the door and held it open for Jack to pass through. As he hurried down the steps he heard her call out, "Good bye now, Jack Gideon." Jack waved back at her and pulled his coat up around his neck as he dashed toward the mercantile. Soon he was under the roof that covered the board walk that passed in front of the main businesses. He had reached the mercantile. He entered and hung his coat on a peg. Mrs. Dodge must have heard the bell over the door, for she came hurrying through the curtains.

"Jack, you made it. It appears to have started raining again," Mrs. Dodge said.

"Yes, Ma'am, I don't know what we are going to do with all this mud," Jack said, as he removed his coat.

"I've been told the river is getting high too," Rosalie said. "I hope it stops raining soon, because business is very slow. Folks don't like coming out in this weather." She smoothed her hair and looked around the room. "I still haven't found that spoon. It upsets me so, not knowing where it is."

Jack hung his coat on a peg and turned to look back at her. "I'll keep my eyes open, it has to be here somewhere," he said, looking back at her.

She watched him a moment and turned. "Collin and Mr. Dodge are in the back. You may want to see if Mr. Dodge needs your help. If he hasn't anything for you to do, seek me out, for I could use help this morning."

"Yes, Ma'am," Jack replied, as he went through the curtains that led to the stock room and private quarters.

Jack found Collin sorting through a wooden barrel of different items. He appeared to be organizing its contents. "Where is Mr. Dodge?" Jack asked.

Collin shrugged his shoulders. "I believe he stepped out back to use the privy." He leaned close and lowered his voice. "Jack, he keeps bringing up that silver spoon. You didn't take it, did you?"

Jack shook his head. "No, Collin, I did not. I wouldn't do such a thing. Did you?" he asked.

Collin raised his eyebrows. "Do you think I would do such a thing to these people after they have been so good to me? I am not me Dah. I did not take it, I swear. I fear they may think I did. I fear they may send me away, and I need this job. I have to find that spoon."

"If you find it, they may believe you took it and brought it back," Jack whispered.

"I did not take the spoon," Collin repeated, sternly.

"I recall seeing it," Jack said. Collin raised his eyebrows and Jack leaned close. "I recall Mrs. Dodge was holding it in her hand when she was at the counter talking to a customer. That was the last and only time I recall seeing it."

Collin frowned and asked, "Who was the customer?"

"It was the Reverend," Jack said. They both shook their heads as they realized that the Reverend would not steal from the Dodges.

It grew quiet for a moment and Jack knelt to help Collin sort the items in the wooden barrel. "I see your mother got the medicine she needed."

Collin looked over at Jack. "How do you know this? Were you by the apartment?" he asked.

Jack nodded his head. "I stopped by to see if there was anything I could do to help."

Collin shook his head. "You shouldn't have done that. We are beholden to no one. We are very private."

"You are my friend, Collin. You can trust me. I trust you, and I would never betray your trust," Jack replied. It grew quiet again. After another moment, Jack said, "Your sister Katherine is a very beautiful young lady."

"She is too old for you, Jack. She is older than me," Collin said.

"I know that, Collin. I wasn't implying that I wanted to marry her. I was merely remarking how beautiful she was," Jack said.

At that moment, Mr. Dodge returned. "Jack, I see you didn't melt out there this morning," he said, laughing.

"No Sir, I didn't melt," Jack said.

"Well now, I don't think it requires all three of us to sort out this hardware. Perhaps you should find Rosalie and see if she needs a hand," Mr. Dodge said.

Jack rose to stand and said, "Yes, Sir. Thank you, Sir." Then he turned to walk away. The bell over the door rang and Mr. Dodge turned to pass through the curtain.

Jack went to the kitchen where Rosalie was weighing salt and placing it into bags to stock on the shelves. Mr. Dodge appeared and said, "Rosalie, would you come out front a moment. There is someone who wishes to speak with you."

Rosalie looked around the kitchen as she wiped her hands on her apron. "You better come with me, Jack," she said.

Jack got the impression that Mrs. Dodge did not trust him alone, and followed Mrs. Dodge through the curtains and into

Judy Lennington

the sales room. Reverend Johnston stood at the counter smiling at them. "Rosalie, I've been meaning to stop in, but with Mrs. Griffin's passing and now the Gardner child, I have been so busy," he said smiling. He reached inside his coat and pulled out the silver spoon, holding it up for her to see. "Was this meant to be a gift? I found it wrapped inside the wrappings of my purchases the other night."

Rosalie clapped her hands together and said, "Praise the Lord, my spoon." She hurried to retrieve the spoon from the Reverend. "I have been looking everywhere for this spoon. It was my mother's and it broke my heart to think that..." her voice trailed off.

"Well, you must have, inadvertently, wrapped it with my purchases without noticing it. We were involved in conversation about Mrs. Griffin's passing, as I recall," the Reverend said, smiling. "Well, now it is home where it belongs. My conscience is clear, for I feared you might suspect that I took it. I really couldn't see any purpose in you making a gift of a silver spoon," he said, chuckling.

Rosalie placed her hand over her heart. "You have no idea how much it means to me that you returned my spoon. I know it may not seem such a thing of value, but to me it is priceless," Rosalie said, holding the spoon close to her heart.

"Well, of course, as you said, it was your mother's," the Reverend said. He took a deep breath and said, "And now, I must return to my duties. We hope to bury the poor little Gardner girl today, although this weather isn't accommodating. The poor little girl has been sick, for so long, with the mumps. I have been forbidden to enter the house as it is still under quarantine. Poor Mrs. Gardner must make all the arrangements alone. They will be placing her coffin on the porch this morning. Friends and family will not be calling. How very sad for the poor woman. I'm afraid the family will mourn alone."

Rosalie nodded her head. "It is very sad indeed," she said, while clutching the spoon close to her bosom.

Jack stood back watching as the Reverend prepared to leave. Once he was gone, Rosalie turned to her husband and raised the spoon for him to see. She smiled and said, "I think this calls for celebration."

Mr. Dodge walked over to where she stood and leaned close. In a very low voice he spoke to her. She looked over at Jack and nodded her head. "I owe you and Collin an apology, Jack. Please forgive me, for suspecting one of you may have taken my spoon."

Jack felt uncomfortable. He was aware of her suspicions, for she was not good at hiding them. He smiled and nodded his head as he replied, "I understand, Mrs. Dodge." He could think of nothing else to say.

"I must apologize to Collin," she said, hurrying toward the curtained door. "Have yourself a licorice stick, and get one out of the jar for Collin," she said, before disappearing through the curtain again. Jack wanted to mention that they were already owed a licorice stick as part of their weekly payment, but decided against mentioning it.

The day got busy in spurts, as the rain stopped a few times, and once the sun even came out. Most of the people who ventured out would linger to gossip about the death of Vivian Gardner. Jack listened as he worked, making certain he wasn't noticed. Each time the rain started up again, those who were in the store quickly left, and no one else came until the rain stopped again. It seemed everyone was worried about the rising river and getting their gardens in late. To Jack's relief, the rain stopped for the last

Judy Lennington

time about an hour before it was time to close for the day. At that time, there was a rush of business, which made the time pass very quickly. Before he knew it, he and Collin were standing outside the mercantile and Mr. Dodge was turning the "OPEN" sign around to let the public know the store was closed until Monday morning.

"I'll be seeing you tomorrow, Jack," Collin said. "That is, providin' me ma is still on the mend."

"I'm glad she got that medicine, Collin. I was worried about her," Jack said.

"You are a good friend, Jack, but I must ask that you respect me and me family's privacy. We aren't the sociable kind, so we're not. Folks don't seem to like us much, and we tend to let them be," Collin explained.

"Collin, not all folks are the same. A good Christian wouldn't treat another human being cruelly, especially when they are down and out. My family is not like that. We care about our neighbors and friends," Jack sighed and smiled, "And, I am your friend. I'll be watching for you tomorrow, but Father and I won't be down at the river. It is not safe to fish down there right now. The water is too fast for a line, anyway," Jack said, laughing.

Collin nodded his head and smiled as he said, "I suppose I can find you well enough. Wellsville isn't that big a town." He nodded his head and darted from the wooden boardwalk. Jack watched Collin until he turned out of sight, then he jumped from the boardwalk into a puddle that splashed all over him. He instantly realized he was about to get a tongue thrashing from his grandmother when he got home. His shoulders slumped as he began dodging puddles while moving in that direction. He looked up at the sun glimmering through the clouded sky.

Jack entered the house to find his grandfather in his usual chair near the fire. He smiled up at Jack as he entered. "I just finished remarking it was about time for you to come in out of the rain," Lester said.

"It quit raining," Jack replied.

His grandmother turned and said, "Good Lord in Heaven! What did you do, jump right into a mud puddle?"

Jack felt his cheeks begin to flush. "It's kind of hard to avoid the mud, Grandmother."

"Let him be, Delores," Lester said, waving his hand. "He's a boy, through and through. Have you forgotten what it was like raising Dallas and Sheldon?" He winked over at Jack who had begun removing his coat.

Delores turned and began to mumble to herself, like she always did when she was angry. Jack went to stand by the fire. "Anything going on down at the mercantile?" Lester asked.

"The Reverend was in, he was telling us about Vivian Gardner dying from the mumps. He said the family had to grieve on their own because of the quarantine," Jack said. "And, oh, yes, Mrs. Dodge got her spoon back."

"What spoon?" Delores asked, turning to look at Jack.

"She had this big silver spoon that was her mother's. It came up missing and she has been asking Collin and me about it for a couple of days," Jack explained.

Delores looked over at Lester and nodded her head. "What did I tell you? Didn't I say the boys would be suspected the first time something came up missing?" She looked back at Jack. "Normally, you would be above suspicion, her knowing us the way she does. However, you're lollygagging around with that Irish boy makes you a suspect as well. Now do you understand what

I was trying to tell you? That boy is trouble, and if you don't cut him loose, he will likely drag you down with him. We have the reputation of being respectable in this town. You will drag us all down with you," she said, shaking her finger at Jack.

"Delores, stop," Lester said, closing his eyes. "Just stop and let Jack finish what he was telling us." He smiled over at Jack just as the door opened and Sheldon entered the room.

"The rain has finally stopped," Sheldon said, as he hung up his hat and coat. He turned to look at them, and instantly realized he had walked in on something. "What's going on?" he asked.

"Rosalie Dodge had something come up missing. She has been questioning Jack and that Irish boy about it for days. Obviously, she suspects one, or both, took it," Delores said, placing her hands upon her hips.

Jack shook his head as he looked up at his father and said, "I didn't take anything, Father, and neither did Collin. It was all a mistake. A misunderstanding."

Lester tapped his cane on the floor and said, "Jack was trying to explain, but Delores went off on one of her rants, interrupting the boy."

"Well, perhaps you should start over, Jack," Sheldon began, sitting down at the table. "I would like to hear it from the beginning."

"What I would like to know, is why this is the first we have heard of it," Delores said.

"Delores, please," Lester said, shaking his head. "Let the boy talk." He smiled over at Jack and nodded his head. "Go on, Jack."

"Well, Mrs. Dodge was fixing dinner and she carried this large silver spoon out into the salesroom with her the other night. She said she left it lying on the counter, and it came up missing. She has been questioning Collin and me about it ever since. Mr. Dodge has been asking about it too. She said it was her mother's silver spoon. Her mother died when she was a girl, and she said she doesn't have many things that belonged to her mother. That is why it was so important that she get it back," Jack explained, looking at each face watching him and waiting for him to continue. "Collin asked me if I took it, so I was pretty certain that he didn't take it, but I had no idea where it could have gone." He took a breath and continued. "The Reverend was in today and apparently, Mrs. Dodge had wrapped the spoon in with his purchases the other night without realizing it. He said he had been meaning to return it, but with Mrs. Griffin dying and then Vivian Gardner, he was too busy to get away," Jack shrugged his shoulders. "That's about it. He was in today and returned her spoon."

"Did she apologize for suspecting you and the Irish boy?" Delores asked.

"His name is Collin, Grandmother. Collin McCauley, and yes, she did apologize. She even gave us each a free licorice stick," Jack said, smiling. "I already ate mine."

"Well, that is the least she could have done," Delores said, turning back to her boiling pot.

Lester rolled his eyes and smiled over at Jack. "It was all a misunderstanding. No harm done, Jack."

"No harm done?" Delores asked, looking over her shoulder.

"Delores, stop it. There was no harm done. If anything, the boys are more creditable now. She will likely feel more confident about them being there," Lester said.

Sheldon cleared his throat and said, "I see you wasn't as lucky as I was at dodging mud puddles on your way home."

Jack felt his face flush as he looked down at his muddy stockings. "I was just about to change for dinner, Sir," he said, looking up at his father.

"Well, be about getting it done," Delores said. Sheldon rolled his eyes again and shook his head. Jack began to remove his vest and suspenders. Sheldon began to pour a pan of warm water for them to wash in. Soon Jack and his father were stripped down to their underwear and pulling on clean clothes for dinner.

"What did Rosalie serve for dinner?" Delores asked, as Jack sat sipping a cup of warm milk.

"We had potatoes and onion stew with bacon," Jack said.

"Was it any good?" Delores asked.

"It was okay. I ate it to be polite," Jack said. He had learned by now, that his grandmother was very competitive when it came to her cooking. Any suggestion that Rosalie Dodge may have prepared something better than her, was taken as an insult. Jack prayed to God every night that he be forgiven for lying to his grandmother.

That night Jack lay in his bed thinking about the events of the day. He was grateful that the silver spoon had been found, and even more grateful that Collin had not taken it. His mind went to Collin and how hard he had been working to learn how to read and write. He knew Collin was already educated enough for the position he desired on the docks. This worried Jack, for if Collin were not available, Melvin and Anthony would quickly learn of it, and move in for an attack upon Jack. He felt himself begin to sweat. He grew more agitated as he could not get the threat out of his mind. He tried to think of other things. As he closed his eyes, the first vision that came to mind was that of Collin's older sister, Katherine. He found it strange that the McCauley girls had four names. "Katherine Mary Margaret McCauley," Jack whispered, under his breath. He envisioned her fair complexion, dotted with freckles, and her powder blue eyes, all framed by an array of red curls that outlined her beautiful face. Jack knew she was older than he, but he thought she was the most beautiful girl he had ever seen. It was a shame that she kept herself cooped up in that apartment all day, every day. The thought of Katherine Mary Margaret McCauley relaxed Jack, and soon he was breathing steady as he drifted off to sleep.

Jack woke to the sound of laughter below him. He rolled over to look at the bed where his father slept. It was empty and the quilts were neatly smoothed out. Jack sat up and stretched before crawling out from under his own quilts. He smoothed his bed and pulled on his everyday clothes. He would not wear them long, for it was Sunday. After breakfast, they would all dress for church. It was Jack's favorite day of the week, for it was the day he spent with his father. There would be no fishing today, but they would spend the day together doing something. He climbed down the ladder to join his family for the biggest and best breakfast of the week. This morning it was pancakes, which was Jack's favorite of all.

After breakfast, they all walked toward the church together. There was no rain this morning, but the streets were muddy and it sucked at one's shoes as they made their way toward the church. Reverend Johnston greeted them at the door as they formed a single row of people waiting to get inside. All the women's long skirts were caked with mud and there was a line of drying mud down the center of the aisle where they had walked to their seats. Jack sat on a bench between his grandfather and father. The doors were closed and the singing commenced. In an hour, they would be excused for the day. The Reverend and his family would dine with one of the parishioner families. Usually it was a family that lived on Water Street. It was seldom that the Reverend and his wife dined with a family that lived on Jack's end of town, as they struggled to put food on their tables enough to feed themselves.

Jack allowed his young mind to drift off into a day dream, paying attention to stand with the others for prayer when necessary. He was conscious of when the final hymn was sung, and a prayer was said, before it was time to step out into the mud again, and go home. Rosalie Dodge made a point of speaking with Jack's grandparents. She remarked at how helpful and polite Jack was. The subject of the spoon did not come up, but the look on Jack's grandmother's face told him it was on her mind.

It was a sunny morning this morning in Wellsville, Ohio. It would have been a perfect day to go fishing, but the river was too high and too fast from the recent rains. The mud was also an issue. Jack dressed in old clothes and pulled his boots on. There were places he would have to avoid for the mud was deeper than his boots were high. His father also pulled on old boots and the two of them set off toward Water Street. From there they could see the river below. They heard it long before it came into view, for it roared like a mad beast as the water made its way rapidly washing away at the bank. From the hill top they could see Virginia on the other side of the river. A house here and there speckled the wooded area. Smoke plumed from the chimneys. Leaves were sprouting from the trees, leaving a hint of green dangling in the air. The earth was coming to life again. Jack felt excited just looking at Mother Nature's promise for a warm summer season.

Jack looked up at his father who stood gazing across the river, drawing on his pipe. "What are we going to do today, Daddy?" he asked.

"It looks like a fine day to sit on the front porch and whittle," Sheldon said.

Jack felt disappointed. He was looking forward to doing something special with his father. Sitting on the front porch meant that at some point, a neighbor or two would join them and the conversation would go to adult subjects. He might as well go off on his own. He would like to climb the hillside, but it was far too muddy and slippery for that today. It would be a couple more days before he could venture the steep slope of sliding shale and mud. His disappointment must have shown on his face, for his father smiled down at him and said, "There will be many days to fish in this old river, Jack. It's always rushing, but never going anywhere." Jack smiled up at his father and nodded his head.

They walked the path toward East Liverpool. This would take them right past Water Street and the larger homes where Milly and Lynette lived. Jack kept his eyes upon the path as he moved behind his father. "When the railroad comes, it is going all the way to Pittsburgh, Pennsylvania, Jack," Sheldon said. "You've never been that far from home, have you?"

"No Sir, I have not. Have you ever been to Pittsburgh, Father?" Jack asked, looking up at Sheldon.

"Once," Sheldon replied, removing his pipe to exhale. He placed it into his mouth and bit down on it as he said, "It was shortly after your momma passed away. I was looking for work. Do you remember that?"

Jack thought a moment. "I do recall staying here with Grandma and Grandpa while you went somewhere, but I didn't know where you were. At least, I don't recall hearing of it," he said.

"Well, I was between jobs at the time, and I thought perhaps a new life in a new town, like Pittsburgh, would be good for you. So, I went to Pittsburgh. It didn't take me long to realize that it was not a place for us to start over. I came to realize that you needed family who cared for you and would look after you. Your grandmother wasn't about to let you go off to some big city and be raised by strangers either, so we agreed that it was best for all of us if you and I moved in with your grandparents," Sheldon explained.

"I never heard this before," Jack said jumping across the puddles that collected here and there. "I'm glad we didn't go to live in Pittsburgh," he said, looking up at his father.

He looked ahead and instantly saw Milly Thompson playing on her front porch. She had not noticed them approaching and Jack could hear her calling through the screen door, "Can't I go play with Lynette? Why can't I go play with Lynette? I want to go play with Lynette!" She stomped her foot as she yelled into the screen door. The door opened and Mrs. Thompson stepped through it. She swung at Milly's back side causing the girl to cry out. Mrs. Thompson drew her hand back for a second swing when she noticed them approaching. She gripped Milly by the arm and forced her through the door. Mrs. Thompson nodded her head and smiled, before disappearing inside. Jack tried not to smile, for it gave him such pleasure to see Milly Thompson thrashed a good one by her mother.

"Do the girls give you a good go at school?" Sheldon asked, looking down at Jack as they continued along the tracks.

Jack sighed and nodded his head. "Yes, they do. I try to avoid them, and I never, ever, hit them, but I sure would like to give them a good wallop every now and then."

"Well, if it is any comfort to you, I had the same problem when I was your age. I had Dallas to look out for me, but he wasn't always around," Sheldon said, chuckling. "I reckon you rely upon your friend Collin to look out for you."

Jack looked up at his father and nodded his head. "I don't know what I'm going to do when Collin goes to work at the docks. That Melvin Riley and Anthony Patrone are going to beat me to a pulp."

"I doubt they really hurt you, Jack. They want you to think they will, because it makes them feel big and bad. But if you fight back, and they know there is a chance that you may hurt them, they won't do much more than give you a shove now and again," Sheldon said.

"That's enough, Father. I don't like being picked on. It seems like they come at me every day, except when Collin is there to keep them at bay," Jack said.

"Well, Collin can't be there all the time. You have to stand up for yourself, sometime," Sheldon said, biting down on his pipe.

"But there is two of them on one, father," Jack looked up at Sheldon. "They seldom do anything when it is one on one. Of Course, Collin pounds both of them at the same time. He ain't afraid of them."

"I believe you mean to say," Sheldon began, removing his pipe, "He isn't afraid of them."

Jack nodded his head. "Yes, Sir, that's what I meant."

"Well, I can promise you one thing, Jack," Sheldon said, smiling down at Jack, "Time will change all of your problems. Ten years from now, this will only be a memory. I guarantee it."

"I hope you are right," Jack said. "I hope I'm still alive ten years from now."

Sheldon laughed and puffed on his pipe. "It will all work out." They stopped to look at the area where they heard the railroad would pass through town. "This right here, is going to change all our lives, Jack. This is the beginning of a new life for everyone in Wellsville."

"What's that?" Jack asked, looking up at his father.

"The railroad, son. I'm talking about when the railroad comes through town," Sheldon replied.

They stood quietly for a moment, before turning to walk back toward home. They made their way through the mud to the front porch where Jack's grandfather was sitting in the warm sunshine, rubbing his knees. Sheldon went inside and came out with two chairs. "Thank you, Father," Jack said, politely as he sat down on one of the chairs.

Jack sat swinging his legs and listening to his father and grandfather talking. Movement caught his eye, to his left. It was Collin McCauley smiling up at him. "Good afternoon, Jack," Collin said, politely. Jack smiled down at his friend. He normally would feel offended that Collin had interrupted his Sunday and his time with his father, however, today was different. Jack was bored, and he knew that his father would spend the day sitting on the front porch talking with adults. Jack was happy that Collin came by when he did.

"Come on up," Jack said, waving at Collin.

"Hello, Collin, how are you this fine sunny afternoon?" Lester asked.

"I'm fine, Sir," Collin said. Jack could tell he was uncomfortable by the way he swayed from side to side, nervously.

"Want to go exploring with me?" Jack asked.

"Sure," Collin said, smiling.

"Jack, try to avoid the mud as best you can, and mind dinner time," Sheldon said. He smiled over at Collin and added, "Collin, you are welcome to have dinner with us, if you want."

Collin smiled and replied, "Thank you Mr. Gideon, but I can't stay for dinner. Me Ma is still poorly, and I need to get back for dinner. Me sister, Kate, will be expectin' me."

Sheldon nodded and said, "I'm sorry to hear that your mother is still ill."

"She's much better, but still bed-bound," Collin replied. "Doc says she's comin' along right well enough. He said it will take a few days, maybe a week before she's on her feet again."

"Well that is good to hear," Sheldon said.

Jack nudged Collin and began to descend the steps. "I'll be back in an hour or so," he said. Then he motioned for Collin to follow him as he made his way around the back of the house. "I'm glad your mother is feeling better. That medicine must have been exactly what she needed," Jack said.

Collin nodded his head. "Yes, that is what the doc says. He said she shouldn't be in a big hurry to get back to working. She is still so weak. I got to get me a job on the docks, Jack. I need to make more money fast. Mr. Armstrong is asking for rent money."

Jack felt his chest tighten. He knew Collin's situation was not a good one, and the only way to help him was for him to go to work on the docks. He also knew that when Collin went to work on the docks, he would be defenseless, when it came to Melvin and Anthony. He was in a no-win situation. Collin was his friend, and he was bound to help him in any way he could. He would help Collin with his lessons. They went to sit on a felled tree. Collin used a stick to write in the muddy earth. The sun was warm and there was a pleasant breeze blowing at the foliage around them. Jack yearned to explore. Collin breezed through his lessons. He was ready, but unsure of himself. The thought of taking on such responsibility was weighing heavily on his mind. Jack sensed that Collin needed encouragement. He patted him on the back and said, "I think that by the time school is out this week, you will be ready to go to work on the docks. You know enough, Collin. You are ready."

"I want to thank you, Jack," Collin squirmed as he sat on the log. "I've never had a real friend before, and you are exactly what I expect a friend to be like. I will forever be in your debt for what you've done for me and my family."

"I'd like to remain your friend, Collin. Even after you go to work on the docks, I would like us to be friends," Jack said.

"If I'm around, Jack, I won't let them bums get at you," Collin said.

"Well," Jack began, "I thank you for that. I must admit that I do worry about what they will do to me once you are not around to protect me."

Collin watched Jack for a moment. He smiled and said, "I'll tell you what, you've helped me with larnin', I'll help you larn to fight. I'll teach you all I know to defend yourself."

"Really?" Jack asked.

"Yep, the first thing you have to remember is aim to hurt them as bad as you can right off," Collin said, standing up. "Once they feel pain, they usually back off. That's when you go at em again. Afore ya know it, they'll be backing up and then they turn tail and run." He lifted his fists in the air and began circling Jack. "See this fist a cuffs style?" he asked. "Forget that stuff. That's for gentlemen and those blokes ain't gentlemen, by a long shot." Collin pulled Jack to his feet. "You tuck your head down and charge right at em. If there is two of them, you aim for the biggest of the two, and get him off his feet if you can. Remember to hurt him as bad as you can, right off."

Jack frowned and blinked his eyes. "I don't feel comfortable hurting someone bad," he said. "I just want them to run away."

"Well, that's the only way those two hooligans are going to run. You got to hurt them, Jack. Bite em if ya hafta. Picture in your mind a way to make em bleed. Once one starts sqealin' like a hurt pig, the other will get scared. They'll run from ya the first time, but that won't be the end of it. They'll be shamed and thinkin' of a way to get back at you. They'll likely be plottin' to jump ya when ya ain't expectin' it. Then ya got to get down and dirty, for you're likely to come out of it bleedin' yourself. Just remember, aim to hurt them the worst ya can," Collin said, with a nod of his head.

"I don't know," Jack said, unsure.

"Look, think of me as one of them blokes," Collin said, raising his fists in the air. "You come at me with all ya got, and we will start from there."

Jack shook his head. "I can't hurt you, Collin. I just said you was my friend."

"You ain't gonna hurt me, Jack," Collin said. "Come on, now, give it a go."

Jack shook his head again and looked over at Collin who was dancing around him with his fists in a tight ball. Jack took a deep breath and lowered his head. He closed his eyes and charged at Collin, pushing with all his weight to get Collin on the ground. It took everything he had, but at last Collin went down on the ground, laughing. He climbed to his feet and said, "Well, ya got me down right enough, but ya didn't hurt me none. Ya got to try to hurt me, Jack."

"I can't hurt you, Collin," Jack whined.

Collin laughed. "You won't hurt me, Jack." Collin reached his hand out to Jack, and pulled him to his feet. He watched Jack a moment and nodded his head. "You can do this."

Jack rolled his eyes. He did not want to do this. He wouldn't want to do it, even if it were Anthony and Melvin. It just wasn't who Jack was. He rolled his eyes again and took another deep breath. He charged Collin with every ounce of strength he had. He hit him hard and pushed with all his might. As Collin went over backwards, Jack grabbed at his face. His thumbs went for Collin's eyes. Collin grabbed his hands and pulled them away. "That's enough, Jack," he called out. Jack dropped back to sit on the ground, looking up at Collin, as he rose to his feet. Collin looked down at Jack and wiped at his eyes. "I think that is exactly what I was hoping for. That should work against those hooligans," Collin said, smiling down at Jack. Jack stood up and brushed the muddy dirt from his clothing. "Just remember, there may be two of them, so give them a good go at it," Collin said, smiling over at Jack.

Jack nodded his head. He was sweating and his face stung as he wiped at the droplets of sweat. "I'm sorry, Collin. I didn't mean to be so rough. I only meant to show you what I could do," Jack said.

Collin laughed. "You did fine, Jack. I am proud of you. Just remember to do the same thing when you come across them blokes. It may be best if you have a go at them right off, to let them know you mean business. Don't wait for them to make the first move."

"I'll try," Jack replied, feeling embarrassed.

"Well now, it is time for me to get back to me home. Me ma will be wondering where I'm off to," Collin said, slapping Jack on the back. "I'll walk you home and then I'll be on me way."

"Thank you, Collin. I appreciate your showing me how to take care of myself. I only hope I am able to fight Melvin and Anthony off, if I have to," Jack said.

"Just remember," Collin began, "Don't wait for them to make the first move. Pound them right off. Let them know you ain't afraid of em, and they'll think twice before they mess with ya."

Jack nodded his head. They walked together as they made their way toward Jack's house. Once the house was in sight, Collin slapped Jack on the back and turned to make his way home. Jack could see his father, grandfather, and Hermon Griffin sitting on the front porch. He climbed the steps and sat down on the porch floor.

"Where have you been, Jack?" Sheldon asked.

"I was with Collin. I was helping him with his studies," Jack explained.

"You look like you were sliding down the hillside, with all that mud on your backside," Sheldon said.

Jack's grandmother stepped through the open door and huffed. "Good Lord in Heaven, I'll be soaking those clothes for days, trying to get them stains out," she said.

Judy Lennington

"Delores, don't start on the boy. It's nearly impossible to avoid the mud with the weather we've been having," Lester said. "You go back inside and finish up what you were doing, and leave us men to our own business." Jack watched as his grandmother turned on her heel and went back inside.

Jack listened as the men talked about things going on in the community. None of it really interested Jack. He allowed his mind to wander, and soon he became aware of the silence. He looked around at the faces as they stared off across the yard. "Grandfather," Jack began, "Would you mind telling more of the story about Limpy's first voyage?"

Lester's eyes seem to sparkle. "Why certainly, Jack, my boy. Let me see now," Lester began. "Oh yes, he found himself living on the whaling vessel. He said he slept in a nap sack and the smell of vomit was everywhere. He was given the task of scrubbing the deck. He said all the scrubbing in the world couldn't get rid of the stench. They set sail and the days were endless as they bobbed around out on that freezing water. I think I told you it was early winter. They would raise a whale every now and again, but never caught one. Raise a whale means they would discover them. Then they got lucky. Limpy was in one of the small boats and they lost their rope to a whale that dove too deep. They had to cut the rope to keep the whale from pulling them under. So, the whale took their line, and the second small boat took chase. The boat Limpy was in had to stern all. That is what Limpy called it. It means to back away and let the other boat take charge," Lester was smiling as he went on. "Now the old man, that being what they called the Captain, was in the second boat. He stuck that whale good with a second harpoon. Once again, the whale dove. They began calling out as the rope disappeared into the deep ocean. Limpy said he feared the whale was going to dive deep once again. The whale surfaced and they were wood to black skin. That was a term they used when the stern of the small boat came up against the whale. They were that close. Now that old whale began to thrash and churn the white water. Blood was oozing out of both harpoons and she was getting mighty tired. Limpy said they moved their boat closer to help with the kill and she was just floating there, looking right up at them as she fought to breath. Finally, she gave in to the blackness of death and they had their whale, and Limpy saw his first kill." Lester rubbed his knees as he went on. "They latched on to the old girl and towed her back to the ship. Limpy said they tied her to the side of the big boat, and began cutting the thick chunks of blubber off her. He said the water was full of sharks that came to feed off the carcass."

"How did they get the sharks off her?" Jack asked.

"Oh, Limpy said that was normal for most kills. You work as fast as you can to limit what the sharks get, and try not to lose a man over the side in the process, because the sharks will eat a man before they realize it isn't the whale. Whaling is a dangerous business." Lester said. "Once they get most of the blubber off, they hoist the whale on deck where they finish it off. Limpy said they have fires and large pots where they cook the blubber down until it liquefies and they pour it into barrels and stash it below deck to haul back. He said the real money was deep inside the whale and it had to be scooped out by hand and separated from the cooked down blubber. When it got to where they couldn't reach it, they had to crawl inside the whale and finish scooping it out until every drop was removed. He said it was like liquid gold and they couldn't waste a drop of it. One of the older hands, Limpy called Old Red, because of his red hair, teased Limpy that they needed a small person to go down inside the whale to get the liquid gold. Limpy was the youngest of the crew, but lucky for him, he was not the smallest. There was a short skinny hand they called Skinny Mike, who always did this job. Of course, they hung Limpy by his feet and lowered him down into the stinking carcass for a good laugh before Skinny Mike went down to get the rest of the oil. Limpy said he wouldn't forget the smell of the insides of that whale until the day he died. It must have been pretty bad, I reckon. Limpy said they got about four whales on his first voyage and they sailed inland with a profitable voyage. When they cast off on Limpy's first voyage he was called a Greenie, as it was his first time. Now he was an experienced whaler and he was about to get his very first lay. That being, his first share of the profits." Lester said quickly, looking over at Sheldon. He was smiling as he explained the terminology used by the whalers. He was proud of himself for remembering, and Jack was enjoying the story immensely. Even Sheldon and Mr. Griffin sat quietly listening to Lester as he talked.

"Were four whales a good run?" Sheldon asked.

Lester smiled over at Sheldon and nodded his head. "I think they could have gotten more, but as I understand it, they were out there just short of a year and a half getting the four of them. They were hoping to get a Bowhead or two, for they had the most oil. Limpy said all four of these were Cash a Lot, which were Sperm Whales. He said the pickings were getting thin, about this time, as the waters had been fished out, with Whaling being such a big money-making industry at that particular time. Then, the seasons had a lot to do with when and where the whales were. They were always on the move, searching for whales, which were always on the move as well."

Bend in The River

"Did Limpy help with all four kills?" Jack asked.

Lester nodded his head as he said, "Yep, at least that is what he told me."

"Did he get to harpoon any, himself?" Jack asked.

Lester laughed and shook his head. "There was too much at stake for a greenhorn to be in control of the harpoon, son."

"But you said he wasn't a greenhorn anymore, after the first kill," Jack interjected.

"Naw, he wasn't, however, he wasn't exactly what you might call the most experienced whaler either, Jack. There were men in them boats that had been doing this for many years. For some, it was their only way of life. Limpy had a long way to go before he would be given that particular position. It was usually the first mate or someone up in rank. Why the captain, himself, didn't always take the old harpoon in hand. There were times when he did, and times when he didn't," Lester said, smiling down at Jack.

"I get it," Jack said, smiling back at his grandfather. He looked out across the yard. "I wish I could see a whale someday. I'll bet they are enormous."

"They're a big fish right enough," Lester agreed. "One thing is certain, you aren't likely to see one in that old river down there."

"Speaking of the river," Sheldon began, "Have you noticed the amount of wagon's moving toward Niles lately? Things are really picking up down at the docks."

Jack looked over at his father and frowned. "I suppose Collin will get a job down there after school lets out this next week. He's ready, I suppose. He reads and writes well enough, and Mr. Dodge has been helping him with the paper work at the mercantile. I'm going to miss him."

Judy Lennington

Hermon Griffon was lighting his pipe. He paused and said, "We had such a mild winter that the river traffic has been heavier than normal for this time of year. The docks have been busy all winter. You can walk up on the trail that follows the hillside and look down any time of day to see a steady stream of wagons coming and going down at the docks. I reckon they could use a strong back to help out." He puffed on the pipe and exhaled. "Of course, knowing how to read and write, would make a young man like your Irish friend pretty valuable to have helping out down there. I'm told they don't pay very good for the young ones until they've been there a while."

Jack watched the old man puffing on his pipe. He turned to look out over the front yard again, as he said, "It probably wouldn't matter, as Collin needs the money to support his family."

"Oh yeah, I recall hearing they found his Papa dead in the streets. I heard he drank himself to death," Mr. Harmon said, gripping the pipe between his teeth. He looked over at Lester and shrugged his shoulders. "Ain't that the same way old Limpy's pappy passed away?"

Lester nodded his head. "It is, indeed," Lester said.

"Was Limpy's father an Irishman?" Hermon asked.

Lester shrugged his shoulders and began to tap the cold tobacco out of his pipe. "I don't recall as Limpy ever said. His last name being, Woodward, I don't expect he was. That doesn't sound much like an Irish name to me, but I am not knowledgeable on such matters," Lester said, as he packed fresh tobacco in his pipe.

"So, Grandfather, tell me more about Limpy's whaling expeditions," Jack coaxed.

Lester drew a long breath and closed his eyes. "I recall every one of them, as Limpy told them to me over and over. He said they caught four sperm whales on his first expedition and they were at sea from early winter until late summer of the next year. A full year and a half they bobbed around out there. He said there were nights when that old nap sack swung like a flag in the wind, while they fought their way through rough seas and storms. They went months without so much as sighting a spray from a whale. Then there were times when they took chase and the whales got away. It was a bona fide experience for a young man of Limpy's age, it being the first time he left home an all. He said his mother went to live with his grandfather, and he was a gruff sort of fellow. Limpy recalled meeting the man only once and remembered he was not kind. He had no intentions of living with the old man. He traveled to Massachusetts in hopes of making a home there where he could send for his mother. He reckoned her life with that mean old man couldn't have been that delightful. Of course, that never happened. Old Limpy died not knowing whatever became of his mother."

"That is sad." Jack said, looking over his shoulder at his grandfather.

"Which part?" Lester asked. "Not knowing what happened to his mother, or her living with her father, him being mean and all?"

"All of it, I reckon," Jack replied, looking back across the yard. He was thinking how very lucky he was to have grandparents who loved him and cared for him. Then he thought about Collin and his five siblings. He had three sisters and two brothers. Jack had always wished he had brothers and sisters to play with, growing up. Now he wasn't so crazy about having any sisters, but he certainly would enjoy having a brother or two to play with. He didn't care much if they were older or younger. Just someone to share his adventures with. Then he thought of Melvin and Anthony. An older brother would be nice. Someone who would watch over Jack and protect him after his friend Collin went to work on the docks. Of course, if his brothers were younger, it would fall upon Jack to protect them. This caused Jack to think about the training, earlier in the day, with Collin. He clutched his fists tightly as he recalled Collin telling him to charge his enemies and aim to do the worst damage right off. He didn't want a confrontation with either Melvin or Anthony, but if it had to happen, Jack preferred it be one on one and not two against one.

It was a long day. The conversation turned to events of the past week and plans for the weeks to come. Jack sat quietly as he listened to the adult conversation. He felt as though he was invisible. The sun continued to shine, and the mud thickened as the day wore on and the water began to evaporate. It was late in the day when Mr. Griffin announced it was time for him to leave. Jack watched as he trudged his way through the thick muck toward his house. It was about that same time that Mrs. Cartwright stepped out onto her porch, with a chair, to soak up the late afternoon warmth. She smiled over at Jack. He looked over his shoulder at his father and grandfather, who were talking about the price of a sack of salt. He jumped from the porch and went to visit with his teacher.

"Hello, Jack. What a beautiful afternoon," Mrs. Cartwright said.

"Yes, I suppose," Jack replied. He climbed the steps to her porch and sat down at the top. "There sure is a lot of mud."

Mrs. Cartwright laughed. "There certainly is, however, that is what happens when you get as much rain as we've gotten lately. There is nowhere for the water to go and we are surrounded by hillsides." She smoothed out her skirt. "Is your friend, Collin, still studying?" she asked.

"Yep," Jack said, with a nod of his head. "I mean, yes Ma'am he is."

"Well, you have done an excellent job with tutoring him, Jack. I am quite amazed at his progress," Mrs. Cartwright said.

"Oh, that wasn't all me," Jack replied. "Most of it was Collin. He wanted to learn really badly, and he wanted to learn as much as he could as fast as he could, so he could get a job down at the docks to help support his family."

"Oh, I see," Mrs. Cartwright said, frowning. "I suppose that means he won't be coming back next year."

Jack shook his head. "No Ma'am. I don't reckon he will. Of course, I suppose it is a possibility that he won't get a job down at the docks." Jack sighed. "I don't know what he would do in that case."

"Well, we can't control what another human being does. It's a different point of view when you walk in someone else's shoes. People often do things that seem strange to us, but there are reasons why they do such things. Often, we would do the exact same thing if we were in their shoes," Mrs. Cartwright said, smiling down at Jack. She watched Jack intently as he seemed to think about what she had just said to him. Jack was thinking about Melvin and Anthony. Whatever made them as mean as they were? He also thought of Milly and Lynette. They seemed to have everything, and they were also mean to him and others who didn't have as much. Jack wanted to ask Mrs. Cartwright about that, but decided not to bring it up.

"I understand you and Collin have been working at the mercantile. I'm told you both are quite helpful to Mr. and Mrs. Dodge. By the way, they both speak very highly of you and Collin," Mrs. Cartwright said, with a smile.

"That is very kind of them," Jack said, thinking about the incident with the silver spoon. "Mr. Dodge has also been helping with Collin's studies. I suppose, you might say, he has taught him far more than I ever did. He has taught Collin how to read all the papers that go with items from the dock and the store. That is going to be very helpful to Collin."

"I suppose so," Mrs. Cartwright said. "I'm told Collin has siblings that don't come to school."

Jack nodded his head and began to speak when he remembered Collin telling him that they liked their privacy and didn't want everyone knowing their business. He realized that Collin may not approve of this conversation. Jack nodded again, and said, "I don't know anything about them. He doesn't talk about his family much."

"I see," Mrs. Cartwright said. "Mrs. Patrone has a petition going around regarding them, as I understand."

"You need to have that talk about walking in other people's shoes with Mrs. Patrone," Jack said.

Mrs. Cartwright laughed. "I suppose someone should, indeed."

"Well," Jack said standing erect. "I suppose I should be getting back home. It was nice visiting with you, Mrs. Cartwright. If ever you need any wood brought in or anything I may be able to help you with, just give a yell out to me when you see me over there this summer."

"That is very thoughtful of you Jack," Mrs. Cartwright said. "I will remember that." She watched as Jack jumped from the porch onto a large stone at the foot of the porch steps. From the stone, he managed to avoid the mud until he reached his own porch. His grandfather was still sitting on the chair, but his father was gone.

"Where is Father?" Jack asked.

"He took a stroll," Lester replied. "I think he is feeling restless. He doesn't sit still much. That will change when he reaches my age."

"Which way did he go?" Jack asked.

Lester pointed eastward. Jack jumped from the porch once again, and began searching for signs of his father. He spotted him, making his way down the street. Jack hurried to catch up with him.

"There you are, Jack," Sheldon said. "Did you have a nice visit with Mrs. Cartwright?"

"Yes, Sir. I didn't stay too long," Jack replied. "I offered to help her with chores this summer."

"That is kind of you, Son," Sheldon said, rustling Jack's hair. "You're a good boy and I am right proud of you. I think you may grow up to be a fine young man."

"I hope so, Sir," Jack said, looking down at the ground as they walked along. He was avoiding the mud as best he could. "Where are we going?" Jack asked.

"It's far too nice a day to sit around," Sheldon replied. "I get restless. I would rather be fishing, how about you?" Sheldon looked down at his son as they continued along.

"Yes Sir," Jack said, smiling. "I would rather be fishing too."

"Well, perhaps next Sunday the river will be more accommodating," Sheldon said, as he looked ahead.

Jack realized they were on the street where Collin lived. He looked up at his father, who did not seem to take note of it. Jack fixed his eyes upon the apartment over the chair factory and looked for movement inside the windows. The sound of laughter caught his attention and he noticed two red haired figures moving about between the broken boards of a fence that went around the grounds of the shop.

"Looks like your friends are having a good time back there," Sheldon said. "Would you like to go say hello?"

Jack looked up at his father and shook his head. "I don't think they like strangers much," he said.

"We are hardly strangers, Jack," Sheldon said. "Collin is your friend, and he has spent time with me as well, down by the river. I don't think he would mind. Besides, it wouldn't be very neighborly of us to pass by without saying hello."

Jack swallowed the lump that was forming in his throat. His father was already making his way in that direction. There was nothing Jack could do now, but follow behind, and pray that Collin would understand. As they neared, Jack recalled Mrs. Cartwright's comment about walking in another person's shoes. Too bad Collin hadn't been there for that conversation.

"Hello, how are you all this fine afternoon?" Sheldon called out, as they approached the fence.

Two little girls had been playing a game in the scrap yard of the chair factory. Both had red curls that seemed to adorn their heads like a bonnet, hanging down their backs. Their porcelain complexions were dotted with freckles and they both had the same Smokey blue eyes with dark blue circles around their iris'. The older one, Jack remembered, was called Grace. She was around Jack's age. The younger one, wasn't much younger. Her name was Irene. As Jack's father spoke, they both froze in place. They noticed Jack and smiled, but remained quiet.

"Is Collin around?" Jack asked, to break the silence.

Bend in The River

Grace shook her head. "He is working in the factory. He cleans up every day for Mr. Armstrong as mother still isn't well enough to be exposed to the dust."

"Oh, I'm sorry to hear your mother still isn't well," Sheldon said. "Is there anything we can do to help?"

Both girls shook their heads. Grace looked down at her younger sister and said, "In fact, we should be checking on her. She may be needing something."

Jack knew they were uncomfortable with the interruption. He felt a tightness gripping his chest as he feared Collin would be angry with him. Collin was likely to think that Jack had brought his father over here to interrupt their Sunday. He tugged on his father's elbow and said, "Father, perhaps we should move along." He smiled back at the girls who were in the process of backing further away from them. "It was nice meeting you again. We were just going for a walk and happened to see you over here. We thought we would say hello as we passed by." Jack called out to them as he tugged on his father's arm again. "You have a good afternoon, now."

Sheldon looked down and Jack and smiled. "Forgive us, ladies, for the interruption. Please tell your mother we said hello, and hope she is feeling better soon." He stepped back and watched as the two girls ran for the stairs that led to the apartment over the chair factory.

"What was that all about?" Sheldon asked, when they were a safe distance away from the fence.

"They don't like strangers, Father," Jack explained. "Collin has made it very clear that he doesn't want anyone coming around."

"Even you?" Sheldon asked. Jack nodded his head. "I thought you and Collin were good friends."

"We are. We are practically best friends. That is why I must do as Collin asks. I don't want to make him mad at me. What if he decides not to speak to me again, because I was hanging around his place?" Jack asked.

"We were hardly hanging around his place, Jack," Sheldon said. "We were walking by and stopped to bid them a good day. That is a kindness. A polite kindness. I would hope that Collin would do the same if the situation was reversed."

"All I know is, Collin has asked me to stay away, and I said I would." Jack felt his face flaming in the late afternoon sun. He tugged upon his collar.

"Alright," Sheldon said. "I apologize if I have placed you in an uncomfortable situation with your friend. If he becomes angry with you, tell me and I will gladly explain it to him on your behalf."

"Thank you, Father," Jack said, with a sigh.

"Well, let's swing by Third Street and see how the construction on that bridge is coming along," Sheldon said, smiling down at Jack.

They walked along Third Street, standing a few minutes to look down at the work being done on the bridge. There were others who ventured to stop by as well. Sheldon knew most of them and conversations about the work would commence leaving Jack to stand patiently by. Finally, they were moving toward home again. This time they took another route that did not go by the chair factory. Jack was relieved, for he feared Collin would have learned about their visit by now and would be watching for them to return.

The sun was just above the tree line when they arrived back at Jack's grandparents' house. His grandmother told them to remove their muddy shoes before entering her kitchen, and Jack and Sheldon both did as they were instructed. Jack's grandmother pinched Jack's sleeve where a little mud had soaked through and huffed, but did not complain. Sheldon winked at Jack as they both began to wash in the basin. Jack pulled his night shirt over his head for the sun was completely down now and he would be going to bed soon. Tomorrow would start a whole new week, and it was the last week of school. Jack climbed the ladder to the loft and laid staring up at the ceiling as he thought about what he was going to say to Collin tomorrow at school.

Jack sat at his desk, waiting for Mrs. Cartwright to get to his row. She had instructed Harry Moser to work with the Huffman twins on their writing skills. Jack stared at the empty desk where Vivian Gardner used to sit. He wondered about her last moments in this life and prayed that she was with his mother in Heaven. Before he knew it, Mrs. Cartwright was standing near Lewis Tully's desk. "Today will be your last spelling test. I want you to take your time and make certain you have spelled each word correctly for it will determine your final grade. Later you will also have your last arithmetic test, so be alert, and no cheating or peeking," she instructed. "Now wipe your slates and prepare, for we are about to begin."

Jack felt Collin's leg bouncing nervously behind him. "Administration," Mrs. Cartwright said clearly. She paused and repeated the word slowly, looking at each of the students in the third-grade row. "Administration."

Jack sounded the word out as he wrote it on the slate. He listened for the sound of Collin's chalk on his slate. He closed his eyes and prayed that Collin was spelling the words correctly. "Worship," Mrs. Cartwright said next. After another pause, she repeated, "Worship." She went on until she had recited the ten words. "Please put your chalk and slates down," she instructed.

She approached Lewis Tully's desk and lifted his slate. Jack noticed her mark a check on one word, before returning the slate. She wrote her determination upon her own slate that hung around her neck. Now she was inspecting Jack's slate. She smiled down at Jack as she handed him his slate back with an "A" marked on it. "Very good Jack," she said, smiling. Now she moved back to Collin McCauley. Jack continued to stare straight ahead. He could hear her marking on the slate. He strained his ears to hear how many marks Collin got. He only heard two marks on the slate. Mrs. Cartwright wrote her determination upon her own slate and moved toward the front. As she moved away with her back to them, Jack quickly turned to look back at Collin. He lifted his slate to show he had two wrong marks. Jack sighed for he had hoped Collin would get an "A" also, but two wrong words weren't too bad.

Mrs. Cartwright instructed them the study for their arithmetic test and moved on to the fifth and sixth grade row. Jack felt his palms growing sweaty as he wrote his times tables upon his slate. He erased them with his sleeve and wrote his division tables next. He continued, on and on until the recess bell was rung. He met Collin on the large air root of the old Elm tree. There was still a lot of mud on the playground, so they remained standing. "Are you ready for your math test?" Jack asked.

"I've memorized it backwards and forwards so many times, I see numbers in my sleep," Collin said. "I have to pass my arithmetic test, Jack. I just have to," Collin said, nervously.

"I don't think you're going to fail, Collin," Jack said. "You've been doing so well."

"I don't care if I pass or fail, Jack. It makes no difference to me, as I don't have any intentions of coming back to school. I do need to larn my readin' and cypherin' to get that job on the docks. A good report card mark will go a long way when I apply for the position," Collin explained.

"Well, I'm confident that you will do well. I know how hard you've been working on your studies. Even Mrs. Cartwright has said how far you've come," Jack replied.

"Yes, but me marks in the beginning will go against me, I'm thinkin'," Collin said. "I failed nearly every test in the beginning."

"That is true, Collin, they will go against you," Jack said. "But what do you care? You aren't coming back. If the report card gives you a bad mark, don't use it. You could always just read something, and do some addition for whomever you talk to about a job."

"I suppose that would work," Collin said, smiling. "Thank you for the suggestion, Jack, me boy. I'm beholden to you once again." He kicked at the air root and added, "I suppose I'm going to miss you. I wouldn't want you tellin' anyone I said that, but it be true enough."

"Thank you, Collin. I'm going to miss you too," Jack said.

Collin took a deep breath and said, "Grace told me you and your Pa was talking to her."

Jack nodded his head. "Yes, I am sorry. I know I said I wouldn't pry into your personal life. You must believe me, Collin, I had no idea my father was going to stop by."

Collin nodded his head. "I suppose there was no harm done. Mrs. Patrone hasn't been by lately, poking her nose about into our business. Me Ma is doing much better; thanks to the medicine the doctor gave us. She's up and about again. She still has her bouts of coughing, though."

Judy Lennington

"Well, maybe the warmer weather will be what she needs to shake it," Jack said.

Collin nodded his head. He was about to speak when Mrs. Cartwright stepped out onto the porch and rang the bell. Without a word, the two of them walked toward the schoolhouse. The next time they spoke, would be after school and on their way to the mercantile.

Mrs. Cartwright instructed them to write their times tables onto their slates. She quickly came back and graded them before instructing them to write their division tables. Jack got every one of them right. To his amazement, so did Collin McCauley. He didn't have to turn in his seat to look, for Mrs. Cartwrights smiled broadly and told Collin out loud how proud she was of him that he got them all right. Soon the class was excused for the day and the two of them were making their way toward the mercantile. Collin couldn't stop smiling. Jack was happy for his friend. As they entered the store, Mr. Dodge was waiting for them and Collin proudly announced his test results.

"I am so proud of you Collin. You've been working very hard," Mrs. Dodge said, placing her hand upon his shoulder.

"We are going to miss this young man," Mr. Dodge said to the Reverend, who stood near the register. "We have relied most earnestly upon both these young men, lately," he said.

The Reverend left and Mr. Dodge announced that he was leaving Collin to work alone. Mr. Dodge was going to hitch a wagon and pick up a delivery at the docks. Mr. Greenly usually made deliveries, but he was down with rheumatism. Collin offered to go along and help, but Mr. Dodge insisted that he was needed at the mercantile.

Bend in The River

It seemed, as though Mr. Dodge had been gone a long while this evening. The traffic coming and going along Mud Road was heavy today. They assumed he was sitting somewhere near the docks waiting his turn to be loaded.

Jack was taking the ashes out of the potbellied stove when Mr. Moser and his son, Harry entered the store. Harry nodded his head at Jack, as he stood near his father, who was having a conversation with Mrs. Dodge. As Jack finished dumping the ashes into the metal bucket, the door opened and Katherine McCauley entered the mercantile. She was looking around, and Jack assumed she was looking for Collin. "Do you want to see Collin?" he asked her.

She nodded her head and replied, "Yes, please, Jack."

As Jack turned to go through the curtains to the back, he noticed Harry Moser staring at Katherine. Jack called out to Collin, who hurried out front where his sister waited. "Kate, is me Ma alright?" he asked.

Katherine nodded her head and said, "She asked you to bring this home with you." She handed Collin a crumpled piece of paper. Collin frowned as he silently sounded out the words on the paper. He looked up at his sister and nodded his head again. Katherine smiled and hurried out the door. Collin stuffed the note into his pocket and went to the back again.

Jack was sweeping up the ashes that had missed the bucket and scattered about the floor. Harry Moser approached him and asked, "Who was that girl?"

Jack smiled. "That is Collin's sister, Katherine," he said. He could read Harry's mind, for he hadn't taken his eyes off her since she entered the store.

"Why doesn't she come to school?" Harry asked.

Judy Lennington

"She stays home and cares for her mother and siblings," Jack replied.

Harry nodded and as he stretched his neck to watch Katherine as she disappeared. Mr. Moser announced that they would be getting along and Jack followed them outside as he carried the bucket of ashes to be dumped. He noticed a horse approaching at a gallop. It was Delbert Grimly. He jumped from the horse and handed Jack the reigns. "Hold him for me, Son," Delbert said. Jack watched as Mr. Grimly dashed inside the mercantile.

Almost immediately, Mrs. Dodge emerged with Mr. Grimly. "Jack, you and Collin look out for things until I get back. Mr. Dodge has had an accident," she called out to Jack as Mr. Grimly climbed into the saddle and reached down to take her arm, hoisting her up to stride behind him. He turned the horse and they galloped off. Collin came outside to stand on the porch, watching them, as they rode off.

Jack looked up at Collin and asked, "I wonder what happened to Mr. Dodge?"

Collin looked down at Jack and said, "I heard that man telling her that Mr. Dodge had been kicked in the head by a mule down at the docks. He said they sent for the doctor, but thought she should come right away."

Jack looked back at the horse and riders as they turned onto Mud Road and went over the hill toward the docks. Wagons were coming up the hill as if nothing had happened. Jack reached down for the bucket and said, "Mrs. Dodge has left us in charge. We must see to it that she doesn't regret it."

Collin nodded and said, "I hope Mr. Dodge is alright."

It was past closing time. Jack and Collin both stood near the window watching outside. Jack saw a figure making its way toward the mercantile and instantly recognized the silhouette of his father. Jack held the door open for him as he entered. "Why are you lingering, Jack? Has something happened?" Sheldon asked, as he entered through the front door, looking around for signs of the Dodge's.

Jack nodded his head. "Mr. Grimly came for Mrs. Dodge earlier. Mr. Dodge has been kicked in the head by a mule. She left us in charge until she returns," he explained.

"Oh my, that is dreadful," Sheldon replied, removing his cap. He looked out the window and said, as the glass fogged up, "I hope everything is alright." He looked over at the door and reached out to turn the open sign so that it read closed.

"We shouldn't leave the place unattended until she returns," Jack said, stepping close to the window to stand next to his father.

"No, I suppose you shouldn't," Sheldon said. "I suppose I could go investigate. Where, exactly, did this happen?"

"At the docks, I think," Jack said. "Mr. Dodge went to get some supplies. For some reason, Mr. Greenly wasn't available to make the run, as he usually does."

Sheldon nodded his head as he looked around. He sighed and said, "I'll hike down that way after I carry in enough wood to keep the fire going all night. You can help me, Jack. Collin, you fetch us if they come back before we return," he said, with a nod of his head. Jack followed his father through the curtains and out the back door where the wood pile was. They carried several arm loads of wood and kindling inside and stacked it near the fireplace in the back of the store. They passed through the curtain again to find Collin standing at the window.

"Someone is coming," Collin said, going to the door. They went outside just as a wagon was approaching with several men on horseback riding behind it.

"Oh, you boys are still here," Mrs. Dodge said, from the back of the wagon. She had been holding her husband's wrapped head in her lap. Sheldon helped the doctor and another man get Mr. Dodge out of the wagon. Collin held the mercantile door open as they carried the limp Mr. Dodge inside, and through the curtains, to the back. They placed him in the bed and the men left, while the doctor examined him.

Sheldon stood back with his hands upon Collin and Jack's shoulders as they watched. "I believe he has fainted," the doctor said. He looked up at Sheldon and said, "He took a good wallop along the side of the head. I believe it cracked his skull some, but I've seen others come through it well enough with plenty of bed rest. Of course, only time will tell how bad it really is." He glanced over at Rosalie and back at Sheldon quickly.

Rosalie sat down on the side of the bed and said, "Thank you boys for staying. You can go home now. I'll see you both tomorrow after school."

Jack and Collin went through the curtain and waited for Sheldon to speak privately with the doctor and Rosalie. He joined them and walked outside with the boys. "Collin, how is your mother?" Sheldon asked.

"Oh my, I forgot to get the salt and flour," Collin said, covering his eyes. He shrugged his shoulders and said, "I'll come by early in the morning before school." He smiled at Jack and Sheldon as he replied, "Me ma is doin' right well enough. She's up and about some during the day. Thank you for askin' Mr. Gideon."

"Well, I am glad to hear she is doing better," Sheldon said. "You be sure to give her our regards. Remember, we are here if you have need of us, Son."

"Thank you, Mr. Gideon," Collin said. "I best be on my way now. Me family will be wonderin' where I am."

Sheldon nodded his head and placed his hand upon Jack's shoulder, guiding him in the direction of home. They moved slowly along in silence for a while. The sun had dropped below the tree line and it was dark by the time they reached the house. With Rosalie being gone, Jack had not eaten, and by this time, dinner was over at home.

"Where have you been?" his grandmother asked, as he entered the front door.

"There was an accident and Mrs. Dodge asked us to mind the store until she got back," Jack said, climbing onto a chair to unlace his shoes.

"What kind of accident?" Lester asked, tapping his cane nervously.

"Mother," Sheldon began, "Jack has not had anything to eat. Would it be possible to rustle up some leftovers?"

Delores nodded her head, but remained standing firmly awaiting a response to the question her husband had asked. "What kind of accident?" Lester repeated.

Sheldon pulled out a chair and began to explain. "Howard took the wagon to the docks for a shipment of supplies. Doc said one of the wagons was loading and the doubletree got lodged on a root. He said Howard stepped behind a mule to release it and the mule kicked, hitting Howard on the side of the head. He's hurt bad. Doc says he won't know how bad it really is until he's had a couple of day's rest. Apparently, it cracked his skull."

Judy Lennington

"My oh my," Delores began. "I recollect old Sam Benson getting kicked in the head when I was a girl. He never was right after that."

Sheldon shook his head slightly and frowned as he looked over at Jack. Delores quickly covered her mouth. Jack looked up at his father and asked, "Is Mr. Dodge going to be alright?"

"We don't rightly know Son. Like Doc said, we will give it a couple of days." Sheldon sighed, and began to drum his fingers on the table. He looked up at his mother and asked, "Is there anything for the boy to eat, Mother?"

"Oh yes," Delores said nervously. She turned and scooped a tin cup into an iron pot hanging over the coals of the fireplace. She poured it into a tin bowl and placed it on the table. She stared at it a few moments, before getting a spoon from an old metal pan sitting on the side board.

"Thank you, Grandmother," Jack said, taking a bite. "This is very good stew. I am so hungry."

Delores smiled and watched as Jack ate every bite of his stew. He scraped the bowl and rose from his chair to carry it to the wash pan. Delores took the bowl from him and said, "You have had a full day, Jack. You best be off to bed."

Jack hugged her and went to embrace his grandfather. He hugged his father last, and climbed the ladder to the loft. He was exhausted, but somehow, he knew it would be hours before he would be able to sleep.

Jack spent half the night tossing and turning. His father's snoring seemed much louder than usual. Sometime before dawn he dropped off into a deep sleep, and his grandfather had to yell at him several times before he got up. He sat staring at his bowl of boiled oats. He thought about pretending to be sick so his grandmother would allow him to stay home from school, but decided that she would also expect him to stay home from working at the mercantile, and he wouldn't miss that for the world.

He ate his breakfast and began trudging along on his way to school. Most of the mud had dried up by now, except for places where springs and soft places in the soil seemed to hold the water the longest. He was following a path that cut across the back yards of houses and made its way to the school. It was a path often traveled by the students on this side of town. As he reached a line of Maple Trees he heard giggling. He stopped to listen, and it grew very still. He began walking again, only half paying attention, for he was still very tired from his previous night of sleeplessness.

"Jack be nimble, Jack be quick," someone was singing softly. It was a boy's voice. It was a familiar voice. He paused to listen. "Jack jumped over a candle stick," it sang again. He knew this voice. It was Melvin Riley. Jack stopped when Melvin stepped out from behind a tree to block his path. Jack looked around for Anthony Patrone, who was usually close by. They seemed to hunt in packs like wild dogs. Jack saw no signs of Anthony. He stood frozen as Melvin stepped closer. "How high can old Jack jump, I wonder," Melvin said, with a slur. "I think I'm about to find out."

Jack recalled the words of instruction that Collin had left with him. "Don't wait for them to make the first move. Surprise is the best attack. It will catch them off guard and they will be slow to respond." Jack took a deep breath and dropped his lunch tin upon the ground. He lowered his head and charged at Melvin with every ounce of strength he had. His last recollection was that of Melvin's eyes opening wide with surprise. Jack's head hit Melvin square in the chest and Melvin stumbled backwards. He did not drop to the ground, but caught himself as he stumbled back. As he

Judy Lennington

straightened up, Jack charged him again, and this time Melvin went down hard. Jack straddled him and began plummeting him with both fists about the face and head. Jack lost track of everything that was happening. All he could think about was to keep hitting Melvin as hard as he could, for as long as he could, until Melvin got the dickens beat out of him. Finally, Melvin began squealing like a pig, and Jack stopped with both fists in the air.

"Do you yield?" Jack asked.

Melvin was crying like a girl as he begged, "Don't hit me anymore. Don't hurt me."

"Do you yield?" Jack repeated.

"Yes, yes," Melvin whimpered.

Jack climbed off Melvin and stood up with both fists in front of him as if he was about to resume his attack. "Get up!" Jack shouted.

"I'm telling," Melvin said.

Jack took a step closer and began rotating his fists in the air as if he was about to unleash another attack. "Okay, okay. I won't say a word," Melvin whined.

Melvin began to brush the dirt from himself while Jack stood watching. "Are you going to tell?" Jack asked.

Melvin shook his head. "I won't tell anyone," Melvin said. He turned and ran toward the school house.

Jack stood watching until Melvin was completely gone from view. He felt his knees trembling. A smile crept across his lips as he began to realize what had just happened. Melvin was a good head taller than Jack and three whole years older, yet Jack had just taken him down. He felt proud of himself. Suddenly, he felt revitalized. He smiled as he took up his tin and began skipping to school.

Jack stopped near the air root to brush himself off. Milly Thompson and Lynette Raines were giggling, and he assumed they were laughing at him. He narrowed his gaze and took a step toward them. They grew quiet, as they stared back at him with wide, frightened, eyes. Finally, they ran inside the school house. He smiled to himself and climbed the steps to enter the school. He was sorry about Mr. Dodge's accident and he hoped he would be alright, but today was the best day of his life, and no one was going to ruin this moment for him.

Collin was late to arrive at school this morning. Jack assumed he had went to the mercantile, as he said he would. He looked at Jack as he walked passed his desk, and frowned, for he instantly sensed something was different this morning.

Jack could hardly wait for the first recess bell to ring. He met Collin outside at the big air root of the Elm tree and told him all about his run in with Melvin Riley earlier that morning. "That's good, Jack. You've turned the tables on them. I'm proud of you, standing up for yourself that way," Collin said. "Now you need to be weary, for they are likely to come at you in pairs next time."

"What?" Jack asked. "What do you mean?"

Collin began to explain. "You've showed them that one on one doesn't work out to their advantage, don't you see. They'll be layin' for you and they will likely do it together, you know, the two of them."

"But, I put the fear of God in old Melvin Riley. Why would he come at me again?" Jack asked.

"Because he knows there is safety in numbers. If he and Anthony both come after you, they are likely to have the advantage. I'm just tellin' you to be on guard for an ambush," Collin said.

Judy Lennington

Jack began to sweat. "The two of them together will beat the crap out of me Collin. I got lucky and caught Melvin off guard this morning. Normally, I wouldn't have a chance against him. Now you're telling me they are both coming after me. You didn't tell me that before. I would not have taken Melvin on if I had known that," Jack protested.

"Calm down, me friend. You have proved you can hold your own in a fight. They might not try anything at all, but if they do, I'm just warnin' ya, that it will likely be the two of them jumpin' ya in private somewhere," Collin explained.

"Oh, no, what have I done?" Jack moaned. The bell rang and he followed Collin inside. The rest of the day was a blur. Finally, Mrs. Cartwright rang the dismissal bell and Collin and Jack walked together to the mercantile. Jack looked about to see where Melvin and Anthony were. He saw them moving in the opposite direction and he sighed with relief. He was safe for now.

Mrs. Dodge was waiting for them when they arrived. She clapped her hands with excitement, and hugged them both. "Mr. Dodge was awake earlier. He is alert, but he sleeps a lot. The doctor has been by twice today and feels that he is going to be fine. He just needs his head to heal." She was wringing her hands as she looked directly at Collin. "Collin, he asked me to ask you to stay on full time, to help with the store until he is back on his feet." She bit her lip as she waited for Collin to respond.

Collin frowned as he pondered over what she had just asked of him. "Me? Are you certain that is what he was askin' ya, Mrs. Dodge?"

She nodded her head. "Yes, I am certain. He said you are familiar with how things are done around here." She gripped him by the shoulders. "I know this is not what you were hoping for,

Collin. I can't pay you what you would make at the docks, and I know that was what you've been working for. It would be just until Mr. Dodge is on his feet again. The doctor says it should be a few weeks before he is up and moving around again." She let go of his shoulders and stood up tall.

"But, Mrs. Dodge," he began, "I am not very good at cypherin' numbers yet. I can't say I may not make a mistake now and then. You need someone who can tally up accounts and what not."

"I will work with you on your numbers, Collin," she said. "When Mr. Dodge is better and you want to go to work on the docks, you will be better prepared. It will only be a few more weeks," she said.

Collin sighed as he watched her. Finally, he nodded his head. "Alright, Ma'am, I'll stay until Mr. Dodge is on his feet again."

Mrs. Dodge clapped her hands again. "Oh, thank you, Collin. I have been praying all day that you would agree to stay on. I don't know what I would have done if you had refused."

Collin shook his head and said, "I don't see how I could refuse, Ma'am. You and Mr. Dodge have done so much for me, already. I owe you so much."

Rosalie waved her hand and replied, "Oh, you don't owe us anything, Collin. We are happy to help in any way we can. Now… let me see, I have so much to do, I hardly know where to start." She turned and looked about. The bell over the door rang and Harry Moser entered. He smiled over at them and looked around.

"May I help you, Harry?" Mrs. Dodge asked.

"I need one of them licorice sticks, Mrs. Dodge," Harry replied.

"Certainly," Mrs. Dodge said. She went to the jar and began to fish out a licorice stick.

Harry made his way over to Collin. "I see you are still here," he said.

"Oh, Collin is going to be working here full time until Mr. Dodge is on his feet again," Mrs. Dodge said, smiling.

Harry seemed to be nervous about something. Jack watched from near the wood stove. "Is your sister going to go to school next year?" he asked.

"My sister?" Collin asked. "Are you referring to Katherine? Naw, she won't be goin' to school. She'll stay home and look after the younger ones. Me ma still ain't well enough to look after them herself." Collin looked Harry up and down. "Why are you so interested in Katherine?" he asked.

"Oh, I was just curious," Harry replied. "I didn't know you had any brother's and sister's until she came into the store."

Collin narrowed his gaze and said, "Well, you don't need to be thinkin' about me kin. You just forget you saw Katherine, and you don't need to be sportin' any ideas about courtin' me sister, either."

"Awe, Collin, I meant no harm," Harry replied. "Your sister is the most beautiful girl I've ever laid eyes on."

"Like I said," Collin said, shaking his fist at Harry, "You don't need to be thinkin' about me sister."

Harry was five years older than Collin. He was not much more than skin on bone, but he was a strong farm boy who would be a formidable opponent in a brawl. Jack felt his chest burning and realized he had been holding his breath as he watched and listened to them. Mrs. Dodge came around the counter and placed her hand upon Collin's shoulder. "Now boys, let us not have any shenanigans going on in here. Collin, you and I must have a talk in the back room." She handed Harry a licorice stick and said,

Bend in The River

"Harry, this one is on me. You take it and hurry along now." She watched as Harry walked to the door.

Before leaving, Harry turned and said, "Collin, I meant no disrespect toward you or your family. I would like to be your friend."

Collin opened his mouth to speak and Mrs. Dodge instantly placed her hand over his mouth. "That is very nice of you, Harry," she said, smiling. "You hurry along home now." Harry left and Mrs. Dodge removed her hand and looked down at Collin. "Now Collin, we can't have you arguing with the customers. That is something we must straighten out right from the beginning. You must put your personal feelings aside when working with the public. In fact, you must remember that the customer is always, and I mean always, right."

"Always?" Collin asked.

Mrs. Dodge nodded her head. "Always. You must never do or say anything to upset a customer. They are always to be treated with the utmost respect. That is the way it is and always has been when dealing with the public. You are no longer a stock boy, working in the back. You will be right out front, dealing with everyone," she said.

"I don't know, Mrs. Dodge," Collin said, shaking his head. "Folks don't warm up to me the way they do you and Mr. Dodge. I'm referring to me being Irish and all. For some reason, folks don't take kindly to us Irish."

"Nonsense, Collin," Mrs. Dodge said. "An Irishman practically founded this town. In 1803, the first settlers were from Scotland. They were neighbors to the Irish."

"The Scotts and the Irish are not the same, Mrs. Dodge," Collin said, shaking his head.

"Well, maybe not, but I need you to put my mind at ease. Please tell me that you will not be disagreeable with the customers. No matter what the circumstances. I can't tell you how important this is," Mrs. Dodge said.

Collin swallowed hard as he thought about it a moment. Finally, he nodded his head and said, "I'll try, that's the best I kin do."

"Well," Mrs. Dodge said. "I suppose I can't ask anymore of you." She was still wringing her hands. She looked around and spotted Jack standing near the stove. She took a deep breath and said, "There you are, Jack. I believe I could use your help this morning. I have some canned goods that need arranging over here." She went to the far wall and began to explain that she needed the jars and small crocks arranged neatly on the shelf. Jack sensed that she was still nervous. The bell over the door rang and she hurried to the counter. It was Mr. Thompson, and Milly was with him.

Jack kept his back to them. He knew if he looked their way, Milly would likely stick her tongue out at him. He kept himself busy, but listened to the conversation.

"How is Howard this morning?" Mr. Thompson asked.

"Oh, he is much better this morning," Rosalie began. "The doctor was by early and he said he thinks we got lucky. Howard was talking some, and it appears he will recover completely with a little bed rest."

"Well, that is good to know," Mr. Thompson said. There was a pause and then he said, "I see your help is still here. I suppose you will be needing them until Howard is on his feet again."

"Oh yes, I don't know what I would do without Jack and Collin," Rosalie said.

"You are aware that that Irish boy pushed my Milly to the ground on the school yard. I'd keep an eye on him if I were you. He's a ruffian and likely a thief as well," Mr. Thompson said.

"Mr. Thompson," Rosalie began, "Collin McCauley is not a thief. In fact, we have asked him to stay on until my Howard is back on his feet. I can assure you that you are mistaken. What happened at the school yard, I cannot attest to as I was not there, however, I have come to know Collin and I feel quite comfortable with his presence."

There was a long pause in the conversation and Jack couldn't help but glance over his shoulder. Milly was standing with her back to him, clutching her father's hand. It appears she was looking at Collin, who had been avoiding eye contact up until this moment. Now he turned and stared her straight in the eye. Mrs. Dodge looked his way and said, "Collin, would you mind giving Jack a hand with those bigger crocks over there. I fear they may be too heavy for him to lift above his head." Collin nodded his head and walked toward Jack. The corners of his mouth curled only slightly as he approached Jack. They worked without speaking, both listening to the conversation going on behind them.

"Are you coming to the church social next Sunday?" Mr. Thompson asked.

"Oh, I do not know," Rosalie said, smoothing her apron. "I cannot leave Howard, and I don't know how he is going to feel then. I hope he is well enough that both of us may attend," she said politely.

"I hope so, too, Rosalie. We will pray for his recovery," Mr. Thompson said. He smiled down at his daughter and said, "Well, come along Milly, we should be getting home." He smiled at Rosalie and tugged on his hat, before turning to lead his daughter toward the door. As they neared the door, Milly looked back at Jack and stuck her tongue out at him. Rosalie had been watching and quickly covered her mouth with her hand as she loudly cleared her throat. Milly's face flushed as she realized that Mrs. Dodge had seen what she had done. Mr. Thompson did not look back. He continued to pull Milly along by the hand as they made their way outside and along the porch toward the front street.

Rosalie went to stand near the boys. "What a nasty little girl, that Miss Thompson is," she said, shaking her head. "You boys go to school with her, don't you?"

"Yes Ma'am," Collin replied, lifting a large crock from the floor and placing it on a shelf over Jack's head.

"Well, it seems to me that she certainly could use someone to teach her some manners. I don't see how a parent could possibly tolerate their child being so rude in public and not do something about it. Perhaps Mr. Thompson will deal with her when they get home. I certainly would hope so. He had to have seen what she did." Rosalie was shaking her head as she looked down at the floor.

"Yes Ma'am," Collin said, without looking away from his chores.

"Well, I suppose I have been gone from Mr. Dodge long enough. Will you boys be alright on your own for a while?" she asked.

"Yes, Ma'am, we will be fine," Collin replied.

Mrs. Dodge smiled at them and turned to go through the curtains to the back of the store. Jack and Collin worked in silence for a brief time before Jack said, "I hope she falls on her face and bites that nasty tongue off." There was a pause, and then Collin burst into laughter. Soon both boys were laughing at the thought of Milly Thompson without a tongue.

Customers came and went and Collin served each of them as if he had been doing it for years. It seemed to come naturally to him. Jack remarked upon it when they were alone again and Collin blushed. "Seriously Collin, you should consider having a store of your own someday," Jack remarked.

"I'll never have the money to buy such a business as this," Collin replied. "I am the type more suited for labor. I have a strong back and shoulders. I am not afraid to get me hands dirty, and I will work hard. The Dodge's are fine people. I will forever be beholden' to them for giving me this opportunity. But, the way I sees it, you got to work with what God gives ya."

"My father always said we are what we make of ourselves," Jack said. "If you want to be a laborer, that is fine. However, should you decide you want to be something more, there is nothing but you, stopping you."

Collin chuckled and they continued until the shelf was neatly lined with the crocks and heavy jars. They ate with Mrs. Dodge in the back and finished out the night sweeping the floors and cleaning up for the next day. The boys carried in several armloads of wood for the stove and fireplace, out front and in the back. Mrs. Dodge stood at the door and watched as the boys parted ways and went home for the evening. In four more days, school would be out for the summer. Jack skipped all the way home.

The last days of school passed without incident for Jack. He and Collin were becoming close friends now, and Jack dreaded the thought of them going their separate ways. He knew that as soon as Mr. Dodge was on his feet again, Collin would go to work on the docks and Jack would likely see him only in passing. Mrs.

Dodge had asked Jack to remain on at the store for the first two weeks of his summer break. Jack agreed, not so much for the money, but for the opportunity to spend more time with Collin.

Mr. Dodge was up and moving about, unsteadily, with the aid of a cane. It was odd to see him making his way about holding on to objects. He didn't spend much time in the store, as he napped often and complained of bad headaches. He did, however, manage to make an appearance every day to tell the boys what an outstanding job they were doing and how much he appreciated they're helping.

It was Tuesday when a wooden box was delivered to the store with Jack's name on it. He was excited, for he knew the content was the set of china he ordered for his grandmother. Collin helped him open the box. Inside the china was neatly placed, surrounded by fine slivers of shaved wood to protect the delicate, thinly sculptured, handles of the cups. Mrs. Dodge agreed to allow Collin the use of her horse and wagon to deliver the box after hours that evening.

The day seemed to drag by. Finally, Collin went out back to hitch up the horse and wagon. He and Jack carried the wooden box out the back door and lifted it into the wagon. Jack rode in the wagon, holding on to the box as they made their way down the street toward Jack's house. Sheldon greeted them on the porch. "What have we here?" he asked.

Jack jumped down from the wagon and smiled up at his father. His grandparents were stepping out onto the porch as Jack said, "It is a present for Grandmother."

Delores clapped her hands. "My china," she said, just above a whisper. Collin slid the box to the edge of the wagon. Sheldon

Bend in The River

jumped off the porch and helped to lift the large wooden crate. The two of them carried it inside.

Sheldon began prying the top off the crate. Collin backed up to stand in the doorway. He watched their faces until the crate was open and Delores lifted a cup into the air to marvel over it. Collin smiled over at Jack and said softly, "I should be going, Jack. Me own family will be wondering where I am by now and I have to return the horse and wagon to the Dodge's before I start for home." He looked over at Jack's grandmother and said, "It is a good thing you done here. You've made your grandmother very happy. You take care of your family and hold them close. Family is the most important thing in life. I only wish me Dah had done better by his family."

Jack placed his hand upon Collin's shoulder and said, "Collin, my family is your family. Don't ever forget that. You will always be welcome in our home."

Tears welled up into Collin's eyes as he wiped at them with his sleeve. "Thank ye Jack. I've never had a real friend before I met you. If you ever find you have need of me, you seek me out." Collin slapped Jack on the back before turning to leave. Jack watched until the wagon disappeared into the dark night.

Jack helped his grandmother unpack the set of china. She marveled at each piece as it was carefully removed from the wooden crate and inspected for chips. She carefully wiped each piece and placed it on a wooden shelf where it was in plain sight for all to see. She stood marveling at the display with flushed cheeks.

"It is the finest gift anyone has ever given me, Jack." She hugged him tightly and kissed his cheek. "I am so proud to have such a delightful grandson." She kissed him again and smiled down at him as she cupped his face in her hands.

As Jack laid in his bed that night, staring up at the plank ceiling, he felt a heaviness in his chest. He was happy that he had given his grandmother the set of china. However, he dreamed of someday living in a big house on Water Street. Perhaps one day he would have saved up enough money to buy or build such a house for his grandparents. It was with these thoughts upon his mind, that he drifted off to sleep that night.

Jack was to start work at the mercantile right after lunch. Collin worked all day for the Dodge's, but he did go home for lunch as he needed to check on his family. As Jack was making his way to the mercantile, he noticed Collin coming from down the street, toward him. Jack waved and hurried down the street to meet his friend. Once they met, they walked together.

As they neared the mercantile, they saw a familiar figure walking toward them. It was Mrs. Cartwright. She waved at them and hurried her pace as they grew closer. She was out of breath when they finally met.

"Collin my boy, do you mind if I walk with you? I want to speak with you for a moment." She said, huffing and puffing.

"Of course, Mrs. Cartwright," Collin said, with a look of puzzlement upon his face. Jack listened as he walked along.

"I want to explain something to you, Collin," Mrs. Cartwright was saying. She clutched her throat and took a deep breath. "Oh my, I am winded." She took a few deep breaths and continued. "It's about your report card, Collin," she said.

Collin frowned and his face flushed, but he remained silent. "You see, I had to fail you, Collin, because your average grade was not high enough to pass. However, I want you to know that

Bend in The River

it is because you were so late in starting school. If you had started with the rest of the students, you would have passed with flying colors. You are an excellent student. It would be a shame for you not to continue your education, Collin, my boy." Mrs. Cartwright paused to breathe again. She smiled and went on. "I was thinking that if you continued your tutoring with young Jack Gideon here, all summer long, I could test you before school started again. If your grades improve, I am certainly willing to give you a passing report card so you may move on to fourth grade with Jack."

Collin began to shake his head. "That is right kind of you Mrs. Cartwright, and I certainly do appreciate the thought, but I'm not going back to school next year. I hope to get a job on the docks to support me family," Collin explained.

"Oh dear, what a shame," Mrs. Cartwright said. She looked down at the ground and asked, "What of your siblings? I understand they have not gone to school either."

Collin nodded his head. "That be true, Mrs. Cartwright. I larn me sister Kate, and she works with the younger ones. I repeat everything Jack here teaches me after school with Kate. Me Ma kin read and cypher some, but she is larnin too," Collin said.

"Oh my, I had no idea," Mrs. Cartwright said. Jack had no idea either. "Well, if you should change your mind, Collin, please come by my house and we will work something out. I have never had a student progress as quickly as you have in this past few months. I feel you have enormous potential, and I would love to see you go as far as you can with your education. I see no reason why you couldn't become a lawyer or even a doctor as bright and willing to learn as you are."

"Me, Collin McCauley, a doctor?" Collin asked, smiling.

"You certainly are capable if that is what you want to become. There isn't anyone stopping you," Mrs. Cartwright said.

"Thank you, Mrs. Cartwright, for the kind words. No one has ever been this kind to me before. No one ceptin' Jack here, and his kin, and of course, the Dodges. I'm beholden to you for takin the time to tell me," Collin said, growing even redder than before. Jack wondered if anyone had truly been this kind to Collin before, and why not.

Mrs. Cartwright smiled and patted Collin on the shoulder. "Well, I must get back home. You think about what I said, Collin. My door is always open, should you change your mind." She winked at Jack. "And you Jack Gideon, you know you are always welcome as well. You have done an outstanding job with Collin here. I think you would make an excellent school teacher yourself, someday." She smiled again and began to walk away. She waved her hand in the air as she moved toward home.

"What do you know about that?" Collin asked, looking down at Jack. "Can you see it, Jack, me boy? Me, Collin McCauley, a lawyer or a doctor, no doubt."

"I can see it Collin. You would be a good doctor or lawyer," Jack replied.

"Well," Collin said, pushing his cap back on his head. "I better get to work or Mrs. Dodge is going to find someone else to help her this afternoon."

Collin helped Mrs. Dodge in the back most of the morning. Each time the bell over the door rang, Mrs. Dodge would emerge through the curtains, patting the bun in her hair neatly in place and smiling. When dinner time arrived, she was certain to prepare a light meal for Jack and Collin. It was then that Jack learned that Collin was helping her with Mr. Dodge. By the end of the day,

Collin was nowhere to be found. Mrs. Dodge bid Jack a good night, and he left without seeing his best friend again that day.

Jack walked toward home with his head hanging. The sun was low over the pine trees off in the distant toward Yellow Creek. He heard a whistle and looked up to see Melvin and Anthony standing near a picket fence at the Nelson's house. They were smiling as Jack stopped, standing motionless, and watching them closely. Immediately, he remembered Collin's advice, that he was not to wait for them to make the first move. Jack lowered his head and charged the two of them. Before he made contact, he saw Melvin's eye's open wide with surprise. He gripped Anthony by the shirt and Melvin by the ear as the three of them went tumbling to the ground.

Melvin was squealing as Jack tightened his grip on his ear. Anthony was trying to wiggle free of Jack's grip and climb to his feet. Jack reached out to push on Anthony's knees, causing him to tumble to the ground again. This time the fence caught onto the back of his shirt and Jack heard a ripping. Melvin managed to get free of Jack's grip and scrambled to his feet. Once he was up he tried to kick at Jack, who grabbed Melvin's foot and twisted it. Anthony was hung up on the fence, and could not reach behind him to free himself. He was calling out to Melvin for help, but now Melvin was limping off in tears, while holding his ear.

Jack stood to his feet and laughed as Anthony continued to squirm, while hooked onto the picket fence by the back of his torn shirt. "I'm gonna kill you, Jack Gideon. My Mom is gonna make you buy me a new shirt for this," Anthony yelled.

Jack laughed out loud and turned to walk away. He said over his shoulder as he was leaving, "It's worth the price of a new shirt, seeing you squeal like a girl, Anthony Patrone." Anthony was still shouting at him as he turned onto his street. He heard Mr. Nelson asking, "What's going on out here? What are you trying to do to my fence?" Jack began to skip happily as he neared his house. He entered the house smiling.

"What happened to you?" Sheldon asked looking at Jack's soiled clothing.

"Melvin and Anthony were waiting for me at the Nelson's place. They thought they were going to beat on me, but I showed them that they were no match for me," Jack said, proudly.

"You took on two older boys by yourself?" Sheldon asked, rising from his chair.

Jack nodded his head, as his grandmother began to pull his suspenders off. Normally, she would be complaining about his soiled clothing, but since he gave her the set of china, she was more tolerable.

"What happened, Son?" Lester asked.

"They were waiting for me at the Nelson place. They must have been waiting for Collin and me to part ways. They were waiting for Collin to be far enough away, so he wouldn't hear the scuffle, but Collin stayed behind at the store. I didn't give them the chance though. Collin told me a long time ago, not to wait for them to pounce on me. He said surprise was in my favor. It certainly was in my favor this time. I let them have it good. Melvin ran off crying, and as far as I know, Anthony is still hanging on Mr. Nelson's picket fence," Jack said, laughing.

"You hung Anthony upon the fence?" Lester asked, tapping his cane on the floor.

Jack was mighty proud of himself now. He smiled and nodded his head. "Honestly, it just happened. I didn't hang him on the fence on purpose, but it worked out in my favor. I may not have been able to handle them both at once had not it been for Anthony getting stuck on the fence." Jack climbed onto the chair and folded his hands on the table in front of him. "He said I owed him a new shirt. I suppose I should start saving my money. It will be worth the price of a new shirt," he said, smiling.

Lester allowed his head to drop and Jack thought he saw his grandfather smiling. Lester raised his head and said, "I'm mighty proud of my grandson for taking on two boys the way he done."

"Well, isn't anyone aware that Mrs. Anthony is going to come calling tomorrow, seeking retribution for tonight's activities?" Delores asked, placing her hands upon her hips.

Lester waved his hand in the air. "Oh, pooh on Mrs. Anthony. Her son got what he deserved. If he had been successful at beating the daylights out of Jack, here, she would claim she knew nothing about it."

"You are probably right, Lester, I am just saying," Delores said, running her finger along the shelf where the china sat. "You know how she is."

"Oh, I know how she is, alright," Lester said, tapping his cane upon the floor nervously. "She pokes her nose into everybody's business, but when it comes to her own business, that is another story altogether. That boy of hers is trouble. He has always been trouble and the bigger he gets the more trouble he becomes." Lester was becoming flushed now.

Sheldon cleared his throat and said, "Well now, a torn shirt isn't that big of a deal. We will buy him a new one if she insists, but lying in wait to pounce upon our Jack is something I think we should address. I don't rightly care whose son it is."

"I agree with Sheldon," Lester said, still tapping his cane. "Why, I recall being Jack's age once. I know what it's like to have older boys pouncing upon you, Jack. It happened to me, once. It was only the one time, but I recall it well."

"What happened, Grandfather?" Jack asked.

"It was Greenie Jackson and his sidekick, Larry. I was only ten years old at the time. They were thirteen, and big enough to be working on the docks, much like your friend Collin McCauley. I don't recall what sparked their enthusiasm, at that moment. I just remember Greenie poking me in the chest with that stubby finger of his, and pushing me to the ground. They kicked me a few times and Larry held my arms while Greenie punched me in the stomach. They thought they were mighty big when they were together. It didn't get them anywhere. Old Greenie dropped dead at an early age, while pulling on a stubborn mule and Larry was hung, so I heard, for stealing a horse and wagon up north near Niles somewhere."

"Wow, I never heard this before," Jack said. His grandfather was staring at the hot embers in the fireplace as he recalled the incident. "It wasn't nothing compared to the beatings old Limpy took from the hooligans in town. He got it right regular from Greenie and Larry, as well as others. It seemed he was a prime target in those days. Of course, old Limpy was no child, mind you. He was a fully-grown man. But at the time, he was nearly always drunk, too drunk to stand on his own, what with having a wooden peg leg and all."

"Why did they beat on him, Grandfather?" Jack asked.

"Because it was easier than beating on someone who could stand up to them and possibly fight back," Lester said, looking over at Jack. "That is the way of it, with bullies. They never pick on someone who is likely to get back at them. The advice your friend Collin McCauley gave you was good advice, Jack. I wouldn't be afraid to bet that you surprised those two boys by giving them a good go right at the start. They weren't expecting that, I am certain of it."

"No, they weren't. Old Melvin sure squealed like a pig when I grabbed his ear and held on for dear life. It had to hurt, and I made certain I didn't let go, because I knew if I did, he would likely have me. As long as I held onto Melvin's ear, I only had to worry about Anthony. But the fence took care of Anthony for me," Jack said.

Sheldon had been standing by silently, watching and listening. He rubbed his chin and took a deep breath as he glanced over at his mother who was shaking her head. "I expect we will be receiving company tomorrow," Delores said. "Old Mrs. Patrone is going to be huffing and puffing all the way over here from the other side of town."

"Let her come," Lester said, narrowing his gaze, as he looked up at his wife. "I will stand up to her if she comes around here bad-mouthing Jack on account of her son's getting his shirt hung up on a fence while trying to attack our grandson. I'll have none of it from her or anyone else."

"I'm not certain we should get involved, Dad," Sheldon said. "Kids will be kids and there was no harm done. I know what those two boys plotted to do was wrong, but kids have a way of working things out for themselves. If we get involved we are likely to make enemies of the Patrone family. I'm thinking we should wait and see what happens." He looked over at Jack, who sat staring up at him with his mouth hanging open. "I'm not saying you did anything wrong, Jack. I'm not saying I'm taking sides against you either. I'm just saying we should let the chips fall where they may and wait to see what happens without making a big deal of the whole situation. There is a chance that as you get older, you and those boys may be able to work things out and become friends. If we get involved, that is likely never to happen."

"Are you saying I might become friends with the likes of Melvin Riley and Anthony Patrone? Is that what you are saying, Father?" Jack was shaking his head. "I could never be friends with those two hooligans."

"I understand that you feel that way now, but things change, and you may not feel that way in the future. What if one of them boys grows up to be a doctor in this town and you, or someone you love, need medical help? How are you going to feel about asking them to help you? Maybe it is one of your children, or your wife who need their help. You need to think about those things," Sheldon explained.

Jack lowered his head as he pondered over what his father was trying to explain. He could see how something of that nature could indeed happen. He nodded his head and asked, "What should I do?"

"I'm not telling you what to do, Son. You need to figure this out for yourself. I'm merely trying to make you see how your actions could have a long-term affect. You go on up to bed, now, and think about what I said. If you want to talk about it some more, I am here for you," Sheldon said.

Jack nodded his head again and turned to walk toward the ladder which led to the loft. He looked over his shoulder to see everyone watching him. He sighed and began to climb the ladder. Once he reached the top, he undressed and crawled under the quilt. He ran his hands over it. He recalled it to be the same quilt that covered his mother as she laid in her bed struggling for every breath before she died. He looked toward the ceiling and prayed that she would guide him to do what was right. Tears stung at his

Bend in The River

eyes as he thought about his actions. Collin's advice had been right, as his quick actions certainly were unexpected by Melvin and Anthony. Could his father be right as well? Was it wrong of him to attack them? If he had waited for them to make the first move, they would have beaten him to a pulp. He had no doubt about that. It was with these thoughts rumbling through his mind that he tossed and turned until the early morning hours, at which time he drifted off to sleep out of sheer exhaustion.

Jack ate his breakfast while staring into his bowl of oats. His grandfather was coming in from the privy. Jack could hear his cane upon the wooden plank porch outside. It was a breezy morning and the door was closed. As Lester entered the door blew against the wall with a loud bang, causing Jack to jump. "Whew! Its blowing up something out there. I wouldn't be surprised if it isn't raining by noon," Lester said.

"More rain is the last thing we need," Delores began, "They laid logs up the turnpike because the wagons were having a time getting up the hill. The dirt and mud washed over the logs and now you can't even see them. We need a spell to dry some of this mud up before we get any more rain."

"How are you doing this morning, Jack, my boy?" Lester asked.

"I'm fine, Grandfather. I didn't get much sleep last night," Jack replied.

"Oh, I'm sorry to hear that," Lester said, lowering himself into his favorite chair near the fire place. He instantly began tapping his cane, as was his fashion, while staring into the brilliant embers of a dwindling fire. "A breezy morning, such as this, reminds me of the times I spent with old Limpy. We would sit on a wall or porch somewhere and he would tell me tales of drifting at sea with the wind whipping away at the sails. He said the sea squalls would toss the ship and sometimes heave it so high it would hit bottom hard, throwing a full-grown man completely off his feet."

"It's hard to imagine such an experience," Jack said. "You said he was only out to sea on two occasions. How did you get so much information from two occasions, Grandfather?" Jack asked.

"Well, my boy, you need to understand that each time they went to sea it would last for months and sometimes even years," Lester began to explain. "The whole idea was to stay out there until they were loaded full of whale oil. It made no sense to come home from a broken voyage."

"What is a broken voyage, Grandfather?" Jack asked.

"That is what they called an unprofitable voyage, Son. You know," Lester winked, "a voyage with no oil or very little thereof."

"You sure know a lot of terms the whalers used, Grandfather," Jack said, rising to his feet and carrying his empty bowl to the sideboard.

"Well now, that would be because I spent many an hour listening to Limpy talking about his experiences," Lester explained.

"I'd like to hear more about how he lost his leg and about the wooden leg he used," Jack said, pulling on his sweater.

Lester nodded his head and sighed. "Yes, I suppose I wanted the same thing when I was your age." He tapped his cane and smiled. "Perhaps some other time when you don't have to rush off to work." Lester chuckled slightly.

Jack hugged his grandparents and hurried off toward the mercantile. The wind whipped at him, making it necessary for him to hold onto his cap. He was conscious of his surroundings, as he did not want another encounter with Melvin and Anthony.

Rosalie Dodge was waiting for him at the door when he arrived. She smiled at him and closed the door behind him. "I don't expect us to be very busy this morning because this wind," she said. Jack could only nod his head as he removed his sweater and cap. Jack was placing a piece of wood in the stove when Collin came in.

"It's blowing up a storm off in the west," Collin said, looking over at Rosalie. "How is Mr. Dodge this morning?"

Rosalie nodded and smiled as she replied, "He is eating his breakfast. It takes him a spell longer, since his accident, but he manages all by himself. I let him be while he eats. He says I make him nervous and he feels like he needs to hurry along when I'm around." She went behind the counter and turned to look out the window behind her. "We certainly don't need any more rain," she said, softly.

"It's still pretty muddy out there," Collin said. He looked over at Jack who stood quietly listening to their conversation. "How are you this morning, Jack Gideon?" Collin asked, smiling.

"I'm fine, Collin. I didn't get much sleep last night," Jack said, frowning. "I had a problem on my way home, last evening."

Collin looked over at Mrs. Dodge who was listening. She sighed and said, "Well, Jack, if you will sweep the floor for me, I would appreciate it very much. Collin, you tidy up on the shelves out here while I attend to Mr. Dodge. When you have finished, I may need your assistance in the back for a spell." She nodded her head and patted the bun on the top of her head, before hurrying through the green floral curtains.

"What happened?" Collin asked.

"Melvin and Anthony were waiting for me out by the Nelson's place. I recalled what you told me about surprising them and being the first one to make a move," Jack began. "I surprised them alright. I latched onto old Melvin's ear and held on for dear life.

He screamed like Milly Thompson." Jack couldn't help but smile before taking a deep breath and continuing with his account of events that occurred last evening. "Anthony got his shirt hung up on Mr. Nelson's fence and he was waving his arms about trying to free himself. It's a good thing, too, for if he got free, I have no doubt that I would have been a goner."

"What happened?" Collin asked, stepping close to Jack.

"Melvin ran off, leaving Anthony," Jack laughed, feeling quite proud of himself. "He screamed all the way home, I suppose. I left then, and Anthony was still hung up on Mr. Nelson's fence. He was yelling and cursing at me, when Mr. Nelson came out to see what all the commotion was about."

Collin slapped Jack on the back and smiled. "You done good, Jack, me boy." He frowned and said, "Of course ya know this means war a tween you and them, on account of you humiliating them the way ya done."

Jack took a deep breath and held it. He thought his chest was going to explode. He let the air out and said, "I reckon I have a good thumping coming because of it. My father thinks I should apologize, I guess."

"Apologize? For what?" Collin asked.

"He thinks I made a mistake by jumping them the way I done. He thinks violence only begets violence. I see his point, in a way, but I must tell you Collin, I don't want to apologize to them rascals for doing what I done. They were aiming to hurt me, and I think if the tables were turned, they wouldn't apologize to me," Jack said.

"Darn right they wouldn't," Collin said. "I'm mighty proud of you for standin' your ground, Jack. I only wish I would have been there to give them a good poundin', myself."

Jack sighed and said, "If you had been there, it is likely that nothing would have happened. We both know they are afraid of you, Collin."

Collin smiled proudly and replied, "Yeah, because they know I'm not afraid of them. Now they know you ain't afraid either, and they will be more careful in the future." Collin slapped Jack on the back again and said, "I ain't your father, Jack, and I don't mean to go against his teachins' and all, but, I think you done the right thing. They'll be more careful about layin' and waitin' on you in the future. You can be sure of that. They don't want word to get around that you beat the two of them. Especially you bein' a third grader and all."

"I'm a fourth grader now, Collin," Jack corrected.

"Right, a fourth grader," Collin said, smiling. He turned and walked through the curtain, leaving Jack alone. Jack took the broom and began to sweep. The wind continued to howl outside, drowning out the sound of footsteps on the boardwalk out front. The bell rang over the door, announcing someone had entered the mercantile. Jack turned to find a very red-faced Mrs. Anthony. She was panting as she brushed her clothing and proceeded to tuck her fly away hair under her bonnet that was tightly tied in a bow, that was barely visible under her double chin. She looked over at Jack and took a deep breath, holding it to give her the appearance of being even larger than she already was. She began to shake her finger as she said, "There you are, you, nasty little boy. How dare you show your face publicly after what you did to my son last evening. Well, had it not been for Mr. Nelson hearing his screams…"

It was at that moment, Mrs. Dodge entered through the parted curtain and asked, "Mrs. Anthony, what brings you out in this weather today?"

"Rosalie Dodge," Mrs. Patrone said, gasping for air. "I am quite certain that you are unaware of what type of help you have working for you." She began shaking her finger at Jack again, as she went on. "This young man here, only last evening, attacked my son over at Mr. Nelson's place. Why he hung him upon Mr. Nelson's fence by his shirt and had it not been for Mr. Nelson hearing him calling out for help, Lord in Heaven only knows what would have become of my Anthony." Mrs. Patrone took a step closer to Rosalie and placed her hands upon her hips. Her rather large middle moved up and down with each word, as she said, "I think it would be in your best interest to let this Gideon boy go, before anyone else gets hurt, possibly on your premises."

"Now Mrs. Anthony, I find Jack Gideon to be an excellent worker and see no reason to let him go. I also have to question how your Anthony, who is how old now?" Rosalie tipped her head to the right as she waited for the gasping Mrs. Patrone to respond.

"Anthony is about to turn thirteen, next month," she said, stiffening.

Mrs. Dodge smiled. "Thirteen, you say." She looked over at Jack. "How old are you, Jack?"

"I'm ten, Mrs. Dodge," Jack said, with a flushed face. "I'll be in fourth grade next year."

"Fourth grade," Mrs. Dodge repeated. She smiled over at Mrs. Patrone. "I hardly see how a ten-year-old could possibly hang a thirteen-year-old on a fence by his shirt, all by himself. As you can see," she waved her hand toward Jack. "Jack, here, isn't even as big as most other boys his own age. Now how is this possible?"

Mrs. Patrone was not going to be deterred. She narrowed her gaze and leaned forward to look Mrs. Dodge square in the eye, as she said, "Rosalie Dodge, I'll have you know I am not in the habit of lying and neither is my son. If he says, Jack Gideon here, did what he said, then I believe him." She began to shake her finger at Rosalie again, "I'll remind you that I am a paid-up patron of this mercantile, and as such, I expect you to take my words into consideration. I will not do business with any business that keeps this type of riffraff on hand. That also goes for the McCauley boy you have working for you. Why, his father died in the streets, drunk, choking on his own vomit, and with soiled pants, I heard. Wellsville is a respectable community and we don't take kindly to this type of behavior. It is my opinion that they should be forced to leave this community. However, I do not have the authority to throw them out. I will, however, speak of this at the next town meeting. I will also mention this conversation if you choose not to do anything about it."

Mrs. Dodge forced a smile and sighed. "You do what you feel you must, Maybelle. I cannot let Jack, or Collin, go. Neither of them have given me any reason to do so. They have always been an excellent addition to our establishment, and they will remain employed here until one, or both, gives me cause to think otherwise. As for your son, I think you would be best inclined to investigate the incident closer. Now if there is nothing else I can help you with, I bid you good day. Mind the wind, on your journey home."

Mrs. Patrone huffed. "Well, I declare! I'll be doing my shopping in East Liverpool after today. Good day to you Mrs. Dodge!" She opened the door and stepped into the wind. A gust grabbed her long skirt and blew it up over her face and head. She squealed and fought to get it off her face and covering her under garments. Jack began to snicker and noticed Mrs. Dodge shaking her head. He

Judy Lennington

instantly turned and began to resume sweeping the blown debris that had entered during Maybell Patrone's visit.

Jack's face was hot and flushed with embarrassment, however, as Mrs. Dodge turned to go through the curtains, he couldn't help but smile to himself. Now he understood what his father was trying to explain the previous night. Because of his actions, the Dodge's had lost a patron. His smile faded at the realization. He felt ashamed. He hoped he wouldn't have to apologize to Anthony Patrone, for no matter how ashamed he felt, he refused to submit to such a suggestion, no matter who suggested he do so. As far as he was concerned, they got what was coming to them.

Jack busied himself with his chores. He applied himself whole heartedly at doing the best he could. He would not give the Dodge's any cause to regret hiring him on to help.

The day finally ended and Jack and Collin were about to go home. They stood on the board walk in front of the mercantile, staring out into the dusk. "Are you going to the church social after services this Sunday?" Jack asked.

"I doubt it," Collin said. "You saw by Mrs. Patrone's attitude how folks feel about us Irish here in town. I think it best if we kept to ourselves. We've been doin' it long enough and gettin' by just fine."

Jack shook his head. "You shouldn't let that old Mrs. Patrone get under your skin, Collin. You've proved to everyone else that you are respectable and trustworthy. Folks in these parts take notice of you working here with the Dodge's. I don't think you need to worry about that, and I don't think Mrs. Patrone is a good judge of character, either," he said, looking up at Collin.

Collin shrugged his shoulders. "Me family has no friends in this town, nor no other, for that matter. We hardly know a soul, ceptin' for Mr. Armstrong and you, Jack."

"Then come along to church with my family, Collin. We would be happy to walk to church with your family. In fact, we would be right proud to do so. Perhaps it will give the folks here in Wellsville a chance to get to know you better. It may do your mother good to get out into the fresh air and enjoy herself, instead of being cooped up in that apartment day after day, with all that dust underneath her," Jack said. "I recall a time when my grandfather told me I needed to get outside and breathe some fresh air because the air inside the house gets stale. It's possible that your mother has been breathing stale air for too long a time."

Collin frowned at Jack's words. He took a deep breath and said, "I'll mention it to me family tonight. I'll let you know tomorrow, Jack, me boy, but don't be countin' on it."

"I can't ask any more than that, Collin. I'll see you here tomorrow," Jack said, smiling. They smiled at one another and jumped from the elevated wooden boardwalk at the same time, walking in different directions. Jack looked from left to right, as he moved along, expecting another run in with Melvin and Anthony, but they did not show themselves. He arrived home with slumped shoulders for he wasn't certain how his grandmother was going to take the news about Mrs. Anthony's visit to the mercantile today.

"What brings about this long face, I see?" Lester asked, as Jack entered through the open door. Jack's grandmother turned from the side board to look back at him, but remained quiet.

Jack shook his head and climbed upon a chair. He looked through the open door behind him. "I'll wait for Daddy to get

Judy Lennington

home before I explain. That way I'll only have to tell it once," he said, with a sigh.

Delores said, without turning around, "It's probably that bossy Mrs. Patrone, no doubt. She must have stopped by the mercantile today. She was here as well."

"She came here?" Jack asked.

His grandmother was nodding her head. "She was here, as I said." She turned and winked at Jack. "Have no fear, Jack, we sent her on her way."

"Oh, Grandmother, I am sorry to be the cause of so much grief," Jack said, covering his eyes with his hands. "I thought I was doing the right thing. Melvin and Anthony have been trying to get their hands on me for months now. I suppose I've really made a mess of things."

"What did you do?" Sheldon asked, from behind Jack as he entered the house. Jack turned to look back at him and covered his eyes again, as he moaned.

"I'm sorry, Daddy. I thought real hard about what you said last night, and I can't bring myself to feel sorrowful for my actions. Those boys are bullies, and they've been picking on me all year. I just can't take it any longer," Jack whined.

"You shouldn't have to," his grandmother said.

Jack uncovered his eyes and look over at his grandmother who stood watching him. He couldn't believe what he had just heard her say. "You think I did the right thing?" he asked.

Delores nodded her head. "I didn't in the beginning, mind you," she said. "But when that nosey Maybell Patrone traipsed into my kitchen, uninvited, and began poking her stubby finger in my direction, I wanted to flatten her good. I thought about how you must have felt when those two boys started on you."

Lester began to laugh. "You sure missed a historic moment, Jack, my boy. It was one I will never forget. Your grandmother leaned close and told her to stick her finger up her nose. Then she let a few words slip that I haven't ever heard her say before." He was laughing out loud and swaying his cane from left to right in a rapid motion as he spoke. "I was a might proud of her, too."

"Oh, hush now, Lester, the boy didn't need to hear all of that," Delores said, with a red face. She looked back at Jack and said, "I have a feeling that Anthony Patrone gets his orneriness from his parents. Maybell Patrone has been bullying folks in this town long enough."

"Mother, she will not let this lie," Sheldon warned. "She'll be complaining at the town council and she will speak with Reverend Johnston."

"Let her complain all she wants," Delores said, placing her hands upon her hips. "I've a mind to say a few things myself. Like I said before, folks have been putting up with her being a busy body long enough in this town. I think it's high time someone did something about it. It will be worth the price of a new shirt, just to see her squirm for a change. Mind you, we are not rushing out to buy that shirt in no hurry, either. Not without a fight, that is."

Sheldon sighed heavily, and pulled out a chair. As he slid onto it he asked, "Jack, what exactly transpired at the mercantile today?"

Jack allowed his arms to drop onto the table top. He swallowed hard and began, "Well, Mrs. Patrone came into the store and told Mrs. Dodge she expected her to fire me and Collin. Mrs. Dodge defended us. She said we were both good workers. Mrs. Patrone said she was going to take her business to East Liverpool if Mrs. Dodge didn't fire us. That Mrs. Dodge stood right up to her and said Collin and me, I mean I, hadn't given her any cause to fire us. She told Mrs. Patrone to do whatever she wanted, but we were staying. That Mrs. Patrone left in a huff."

"She won't take her business to East Liverpool. It's out of her way, and she's too lazy for that," Delores smirked.

Sheldon frowned in her direction. He looked back at Jack and asked, "Did Mrs. Dodge say anything to you after Mrs. Patrone left?"

Jack shook his head. "No Sir, she kind of gave me a warning look because I sort of snickered when the wind blew Mrs. Patrone's dress up over her face when she stepped outside. But she didn't say anything about it. She just gave me that look, you know which one I'm talking about, and went through the curtains to the back."

Sheldon pursed his lips and smiled over at Jack. "Well," he said with a sigh. "I suppose we should wait and see what happens next."

"Oh, I can tell you exactly what is happening next," Delores said, as she turned to go back to her pot that was sitting on the side board.

"Mother, not in front of Jack," Sheldon said. The room grew quiet as each of them drifted deep into thought.

"Father, I've invited Collin and his family to the church social this Sunday. Collin said they don't socialize much with strangers and I told him they were welcome to go to church with us and sit with us. I hope that is okay," Jack said.

Delores turned to look back at Jack with a frown upon her face. Sheldon looked from his mother, back at his son and smiled. "I think that is very neighborly of you, Jack. It's very Christian of you too. I'd be a might proud to have them accompany us to church."

Delores took a deep breath and turned back to her chores. "I think you should start washing up for bed, now," Sheldon said, smiling over at his son. "After the day you've had, you could use a good night's sleep."

"Yes Sir," Jack replied.

The talk went to people and events that occurred where Sheldon worked. Jack washed in the basin and pulled his night shirt over his head. He carried the basin outside and tossed the dirty water off the side of the porch. After returning the basin to its rightful place he kissed everyone and prepared for bed. As he kissed his grandmother, she smiled down at him, cupping his face in her hands and said, "You don't fret yourself over the events of the day, Jack, my boy." She winked and said, "I certainly am fond of my beautiful set of china." She patted him on the back and he climbed the ladder to the loft. He lingered close to the opening and listened to the conversation taking place below. Their words were spoken softly. However, he could make out a sentence here and there.

"Honestly, Sheldon, what were you thinking by encouraging the boy to introduce that Irish family to the community?" his grandmother asked.

"Mother, if we are going to war with the Patrone's, we might as well stick our neck all the way out there and get this over with. Reverend Johnston can't preach love thy neighbor and encourage his flock to turn their backs on a needy family because they were born on another continent. Jack's inviting the McCauley's to the church social was the right thing to do and I support his decision to do it. I'm very proud of him for his convictions, and you should be too," Sheldon said.

"I am proud of our Jack, Sheldon. You know I am very proud of him. He is a very good boy and he doesn't deserve to be treated the way that braggart, Mrs. Patrone is treating him," Delores said.

"Now let's not stoop to name calling, Mother," Sheldon said. "I recall telling Jack not to sit back and take it, so I suppose I am as guilty as he is."

"He did the right thing, Sheldon. The shirt is irrelevant," Lester said. Jack could picture him swaying his cane as he spoke. "We will buy the Patrone boy a dozen shirts if it would end this torment our Jack is going through. And, yes, your mother was right not to take any guff from Maybelle Patrone. We are not the ones in the wrong here. It is her boy who came after our Jack, and it was Maybelle who came here looking for a fight as well. And, by God, we gave it to them. I say we don't back down. If it is a war they want, they came to the right place."

Jack covered his mouth so as not to be heard gasping. "You are right, Dad. I just think there must be a smarter way of going about this thing, than a feud with the Patrones. We all have to live in this town together," Sheldon said softly. "I need to think on it. I better get washed up for bed, dawn comes pretty early."

Jack scrambled as quickly and quietly as he could to get under his covers. He rolled to face the wall so his father would think he was sleeping. He said a silent prayer that God would intervene and make the whole issue with the Patrone's disappear. Jack smiled to himself as he thought how wonderful it would be to wake in the morning to find that the Patrone's themselves had disappeared. He fell asleep before his father came to bed. When he woke, his father had already gone to work for the day.

Jack climbed down the ladder to find only his grandmother in the kitchen. He concluded that his grandfather must be outside, in the privy. It was not long before Lester entered the kitchen. He smiled when he saw Jack sitting at the table eating his morning boiled oats. "Good morning to you Jack," Lester said. "It looks to be the makings of a fine day out there. The nights have been getting warmer and soon summer will be upon us."

Jack smiled as he ate his breakfast. When his mouth was empty, he said, "I hope Mrs. Dodge allows me to work all summer at the mercantile. Collin will be leaving soon, and I'm hoping she can use me full time, with Mr. Dodge being on the mend and all."

"Rosalie Dodge is lucky to have the likes of you working for her," his grandmother said, without turning to look back at him.

Lester winked at Jack. The subject of Anthony or Maybelle Patrone did not come up. Jack went out to the privy and returned to wash his face and hands before leaving for the mercantile. The sun was up over the tree line, and it looked to be a beautiful day. He looked to his left at the hillside where he liked to climb trees and play. He longed to run in that direction, but continued along his way toward the mercantile. The hillside was not going anywhere, and neither were the trees that called his name in the breeze.

Jack entered the mercantile. The store front was empty. He heard voices in the back, but did not venture through the curtains. That was the private living quarters of the Dodge's. He began to remove the ashes from the potbellied stove. There were not many ashes this morning as the warming temperatures resulted in the stove being used less. Jack assumed that within the next week, the stove would likely not be used again until the fall brought colder temperatures in the night and early morning hours. The curtains parted and Collin stepped out into the sales room. Jack was surprised to see him there.

"You are early this morning," Jack said.

"I am indeed. I needed to speak with the Dodge's straight away," Collin replied.

"Did you speak with your Mom about going to church with us Sunday?" Jack asked.

Collin nodded his head. "She is going to think on it, some. She said she doesn't want to appear rude, but fears your kindness may cause you embarrassment by us being with you," Collin explained. "You, yourself, saw how Mrs. Anthony acted yesterday. She is not the only one in this town that feels that way toward me family, Jack. We don't want no trouble."

"Awe, Collin, don't you be fretting about that old goat," Jack said. "She dropped by our house yesterday too. She was looking for trouble and my grandmother sent her on her way. As I understand, there were strong words spoken, and my grandmother stood her ground. You forget that I had a fight with her son. You are not the only one she is out to get right now, so it ain't, I mean it isn't, like you are the only one she is mad at. We are prepared for what comes, and we are ready for her."

Collin looked down at the floor and nodded his head. "I will mention it to me Ma again this evenin'."

"Okay, that will have to do for now." Jack said smiling.

Collin remained in the back for most of the day. When the bell over the door rang, he sometimes appeared to stand behind the register. Jack remained close, in case he needed help. To Jack's surprise, Collin handled every transaction carefully and without any complaint from the customers. Jack watched the customer's closely. He studied their faces as they spoke with Collin. To his relief, they were friendly, for the most part. Some even stood by after their purchases and talked with Collin as if they had known him for years. Willis Harris, the town's constable, talked with Collin for quite some time. Jack could tell that Collin was uncomfortable, as he shifted from foot to foot and wiped at his forehead several times during the conversation. Mr. Harris asked about Collin's family and how they were getting along since his father's passing. He asked Collin what their plans were for the future, and if they were staying on in Wellsville, or moving on. Jack wondered if the basis for the questioning had anything to do with Mrs. Anthony's going door to door with a petition to run the McCauley's out of town. The conversation ended with Mr. Harris telling Collin that he had been hearing good things about them and what hard workers they were. He guaranteed Collin that he would make himself available if ever he felt he needed a grown man to talk to. Mr. Harris left then and Collin stood shivering a moment before he disappeared behind the curtains again.

Jack was proud of the way Collin was conducting himself at the mercantile. As he watched him standing behind the counter, Jack thought how grown up Collin appeared. He was larger than most boys his age. He looked older than he was, and although his English needed some working on, he was polite and courteous to everyone. Mr. Dodge had trained him well.

Rosalie boiled a stew bone with cabbage, carrots, and potatoes for dinner. Jack cleaned his bowl and was relieved when he was offered a second helping. He was full by the time the meal was concluded. While Collin helped with clearing the table and getting Mr. Dodge settled down for the night, Jack carried in fire wood to the back and front for the next day. He stacked it high to ensure that they would have enough to get them through the night and for cooking the morning meal. He and Collin stood on the wooden walk outside, staring off at the setting sun, to the right of the Yellow Creek area.

"You handled yourself quite well today, Collin," Jack said, looking ahead. "I watched you closely. You're ready for that job on the docks."

"I've got some decidin' to do Jack," Collin said, looking over at Jack. "Mr. Dodge has asked me to stay on at the mercantile. He doesn't feel he will ever be able to do like he done before, and he says Mrs. Dodge can't do it all on her own." He sighed and looked down at the wooden floorboards. "He can't pay me what I would make at the docks, but he said he would help me with furtherin' me education, and possibly let me Ma work a couple days now and again to help with rearin' the family. He thinks maybe me brothers and sisters could go to school and larn some too. I told him what Mrs. Cartwright said about me being a doctor or lawyer and he thinks I should go back to school in the fall."

Jack smiled. "That would be great, Collin! What are you going to do?" he asked.

"I'm gonna talk with me Ma on it. She'll know what is best for the family. She's always had a good head on her shoulders. I told Mr. Dodge I would give him an answer in the morrow," Collin said, looking off into the distance. "I worry about how folks are going to feel about us settling here, for good, you know."

"Awe, don't worry about that, Collin," Jack said. "You saw how the Constable Harris treated you. Why, as I see it, if he wasn't put off with you being here, the rest should be a piece of cake."

"What about Mrs. Anthony and that petition?" Collin asked.

"I wouldn't worry none about her. She's just an old wind bag. Let's see how things go. You can't give up without a try," Jack replied.

"Well, the way I sees it, it will be up to me Ma to decide. She is still head of the family and it will be up to her," Collin said with a nod of the head. He looked over at Jack and placed his hand upon his shoulder. "I'll see you tomorrow, Jack me friend,"

Jack nodded his head and they both jumped from the wooden boardwalk at the same time, walking in different directions. Jack noticed Mrs. Cartwright climbing the steps to her porch as he arrived home. She was carrying three pieces of wood in her arms. He hurried over to her and took the wood from her arms. "Let me bring in some wood for you Mrs. Cartwright," he said, smiling up at her.

"I don't have much split back there, Jack. I appreciate your help though. These old legs can't walk and carry much of a load at the same time anymore," she said, leaning upon the porch post.

Sheldon was arriving home from work. He overheard the conversation and said, "I'll split the wood and Jack, here, can carry it in for you, Mrs. Cartwright." And so, it went, for the next hour, Sheldon splitting wood and Jack carrying it by the arm loads inside Mrs. Cartwright's cabin. When they left, she had enough wood inside to last her a couple of days. Sheldon crossed the yard and began splitting wood for their own fireplace, and once again, Jack carried it to the wood box on the porch. Lester sat on his wooden chair near the fireplace, leaning upon his cane, as Jack stacked a few armloads inside. His grandmother prepared a plate for Sheldon and soon Jack was washing up for bed while his father ate.

"What did you have for supper, Jack?" his grandmother asked.

Jack sighed and replied, "boiled potatoes with carrots and cabbage."

Judy Lennington

"What, with no meat? What kind of stew is that. Cabbage and potatoes with no meat, why, I never heard of such a thing," Delores huffed.

Jack tried not to smile as he said, "There was a meat bone in the pot for flavoring."

Delores stiffened and grew red in the face. "Oh, well, that is more like it." She turned away so he could not see her face. "It gives me comfort to know you had a wholesome meal." Jack's grandfather winked and smiled over at him. Jack carried his dirty wash water outside and tossed it over the side of the porch. A breeze blew gently, promising a cooler evening in the loft.

Jack was dressed for bed. His father had finished his dinner and Jack climbed onto a chair at the table. "Father, I spoke with Collin again about going to church with us Sunday. He is going to speak with his mother on it again tonight. Mr. Dodge asked him to stay on at the mercantile instead of going to work on the docks. He wants Collin to stay in school and further his education. He thinks Collin has promise," Jack said.

Delores turned quickly to look back at Jack. Lester put his left hand in the air, signifying that she was to remain silent. Sheldon smiled down at Jack and said, "That is very kind of Howard Dodge. I am quite certain he would not make such an offer unless he was sure Collin was qualified. As for Sunday, you and I have already discussed this, and I said it wouldn't be Christian, not to welcome that family into the church." He looked up at his mother, who stood nearby. He smiled and looked back at Jack, saying, "I would be proud to have the McCauley family accompany us to church Sunday. I hope they will consider staying for the church social picnic afterwards, as well."

Bend in The River

    Jack smiled up at his father. He did not have to turn to look back at his grandmother to see the expression she had on her face. He was well-aware that she did not share in his father's attitude toward the Irish immigrant family. He could only hope that she warmed up to the idea before Sunday. Jack slid off the chair and embraced his father. Then he embraced his grandmother and grandfather before climbing the ladder to the loft. He was tired after working all day and carrying wood for Mrs. Cartwright. He found sleep crept upon him shortly after reclining under the covers. The next morning, he woke to find his father had already gone off to work.

    Jack went down the ladder to face his grandmother. He expected her to be in a gruff mood this morning. He knew she did not want the citizens of Wellsville to see her going to church Sunday, accompanied by the McCauley's. He forced himself to smile at her as he slid onto his chair at the table. "Good morning," he said, smiling.

    His grandfather sat near the fire, smiling over at him. He swayed his cane from left to right. His grandmother smiled down at him and placed a plate of eggs on the table in front of him. "Good morning to you, too, Jack," she said.

    Jack raised his eyebrows, as he looked up at her. "Thank you, Grandmother," he said, slowly. He was not sure what to make of her attitude this morning. He expected her to be gruff and unfavorable, instead, she seemed accommodating.

    While Jack ate his breakfast, his grandfather announced he was going to the privy. Delores waited until she and Jack were alone, at which time, she pulled out a chair and leaned close, saying softly, "Jack, my boy, don't you fret none about the incident with the Patrone boy. I know your head is full of what everyone is telling you, right now. Just don't be fretting yourself over it. Things have a way of working themselves out. All the advice you've been getting is correct. Yes, you were right to let those two boys have it, and yes, you were right not waiting for them to make the first move. Your father is also right when he said we shouldn't get involved. I don't want you to get it into your head that because we don't get involved we are not supporting you, because, we are. We support you entirely. Just give it some time. Don't go off all riled up and start digging yourself in deeper." She patted Jack's arm and winked. "Just keep your head about you, and keep silent. Let them wonder what you're thinking. If you don't throw fuel onto the fire, it will burn itself out." Jack was about to ask her what she meant by that when his grandfather returned and she jumped to her feet to stand at the side board with her back to him.

Jack did not get another opportunity to speak with his grandmother on the subject that morning. As he walked toward the mercantile, the wind blew making it necessary to hold onto his cap. By the time he reached the mercantile, it was sprinkling rain. He sighed as he looked at the hill in the distance. He longed to climb it. It was the best part of summer recess. Now he regretted accepting the position at the mercantile. He removed his cap and entered the mercantile to find Mrs. and Mr. Dodge standing at the counter and Collin with his entire family gathered around.

"Jack, there you are," Rosalie Dodge called out to him as he entered. Collin and his siblings all turned to look back at him.

"Good morning," Jack said, somewhat confused.

"Good morning," the entire group called back to him. Jack hung his hat on a peg and took the broom from the corner.

"Wait a moment, Jack," Rosalie said, hurrying around the counter toward him. She took the broom from Jack and placed her hand upon his shoulder as she smiled down at him and said, "Why don't you come over here a moment. We were just having a conversation, and I think you should be involved." She guided him toward the counter, with her hand upon his shoulder.

Jack was bewildered. He stood looking at the faces staring back at him. Even his best friend, Collin, stared in silence. He took a deep breath and waited patiently for someone to tell him what was going on.

It was Mr. Dodge who broke the silence. "Jack, we were just having a discussion with Collin and his mother about a position here at the mercantile. We offered Collin a permanent position here, and yesterday, we asked him if his mother might be interested in working a few days a week. Rosalie has her hands full taking care of me, and she can't do it all by herself. Collin has been kind enough to help, but we need him on the floor. Now we appreciate all you do for us, Jack, and we certainly don't want you to get the impression that we are replacing you. In fact, we don't know what we would do without your help." Mr. Dodge laughed and said, "I never thought of myself as being irreplaceable. I didn't realize how much work Rosalie and I put into this place. Why it's taking three of you to replace me." He continued to laugh out loud. Jack smiled, but remained silent.

"Mrs. McCauley is going to help me in the back a few days a week until Howard is able to do more on his own. You will continue, as usual, only we won't need you every day as we have recently. We can't afford to pay you full time. I do hope that isn't going to be a problem, Jack," Rosalie said, patting the bun in her hair.

Jack smiled. He couldn't believe what he was hearing. He was, only moments ago, wishing he had more time to climb the trees on the hillside, and now he was getting his wish. He would still work a few days a week, and make some money to boot. He smiled wider as he thought of it. He nodded his head and cleared his throat before saying, "Yes Ma'am, that is fine with me."

"Good," Mrs. Dodge said, looking back at the others. "When can you start?" she asked Mrs. McCauley.

"I will be here whenever you need me," Mrs. McCauley replied.

Rosalie took a deep breath before saying, "Saturday's are our busiest day of the week. I could use you on Saturdays. On Tuesdays, Mr. Grimley makes a run to the docks for us. The boys are an immense help with that. Monday's is cleaning the shelves and preparing for Tuesdays delivery, I suppose I could use you on Monday's and Tuesday's as well. Some of it may prove to be heavy, but Collin has a strong back, and he doesn't seem to mind the lifting. He's been an enormous help in that regard," she said, smiling over at Collin.

"I'm happy to help," Collin said, with a nod of his head.

"Let's see now," Rosalie looked over at her husband. "What do you think, maybe Mondays, Tuesdays, Fridays, and Saturday's?" she asked."

Mr. Dodge leaned upon the counter and took a deep breath, before nodding his head, and saying, "That's a good start. We can always make adjustments as we go."

"That's it, then," Rosalie said, looking over at Mrs. McCauley. You can start Friday of this week. You will have to excuse us for now, for I really must get Mr. Dodge down for a nap. The doctor said he wasn't to get too much activity. The more rest, the faster the recovery," Rosalie took her husband's arm. "Collin, would you mind helping me get Mr. Dodge to his bed?"

"Yes Ma'am," Collin said, taking hold of Mr. Dodge's elbow and guiding him toward the back.

Jack suddenly found himself alone with Collin's family staring at him. He smiled and cleared his throat. "It's blowing in more rain," he said.

"Aye, rain that we don't be needin', I'm afraid," Mrs. McCauley said.

"I hope it's nice for the church social, Sunday," Jack said, smiling. "I hope you and the family can make it. You are very welcome to accompany me and my family to church. My grandparents said you are very welcome, and we would be proud to have you."

"Aye, that is very kind of them. I will be discussin' it further with me children, and Collin will let you know what we decide," Mrs. McCauley said, tugging at her bonnet. Jack could tell that she was nervous and decided not to pursue it any further. It wasn't long before Collin arrived through the curtains, just as the bell over the door rang. It was Doctor, Ernest Cope.

"Good day everyone," Doctor Cope said, removing his hat. "It looks like we are in for more rain. We certainly could use the sunshine to dry things up before the church social this Sunday." He smiled over at Mrs. McCauley. "Mrs. McCauley, it certainly is good to see you out and about. You are looking so much better than the last time I saw you." He placed his hat on the counter and took her hands in his. "You mind this damp weather now," he said. "I certainly don't want you having a relapse."

"Yes Sir, Doctor. I'll be mindin' what you told me, alright," Mrs. McCauley said. Collin stepped through the curtains then.

"That's a good girl," the doctor said. "Now," he said, smiling over at Collin. "I'm here to see how Mr. Dodge is coming along."

"The missus just put him down for a nap," Collin explained.

"Well, if you will excuse me, perhaps I can have a look at him before he drifts off to sleep," Doctor Cope said. He moved toward the curtains, and said, "Please excuse me," before he disappeared, leaving Jack alone with the McCauley's once again.

"Collin, me boy," Mrs. McCauley began, "I think I should get the children back to the apartment. We will be seeing you for dinner." She dipped in what Jack assumed to be a curtsy before guiding the smaller ones toward the door. Now Jack was alone with Collin.

"I hope you don't mind givin' up some of your days so as me Ma kin work for the Dodge's, Jack." Collin said.

Jack smiled and shook his head. "I don't mind at all. I don't want to spend my whole summer working inside, Collin. I was just thinking that on my way here this morning. I miss climbing the hills and trees. It's my favorite thing about the summer."

Collin smiled. "Good," he said.

"I asked your Mom about the church social. She couldn't give me a definite answer, but I do hope you all can make it Sunday. We would be proud to have you accompany us to church and stay for the picnic afterwards," Jack said.

Collin nodded his head and replied, "I kin promise we will discuss it. More than that, I kin not promise."

"I can't ask for more than that," Jack said.

"We best be getting' busy," Collin said, with a nod of his head. Jack began to sweep around the wood stove. He found himself humming as he worked. He was anxious to get up high in a tree somewhere and look down over Wellsville. It was summer, his favorite time of year. Soon he and his father would be fishing along the banks of the river again and eating fish for supper on Sunday evenings. He smiled to himself at the thought. The rain did not last long, and the sun began to shine. Jack couldn't help but think how much better his day was as it wore on. Soon it was time for dinner.

Rosalie had prepared bacon and eggs for dinner. Collin ate quickly, and Jack felt as though he was being rushed. Soon he and Collin were standing on the wooden boardwalk, preparing to leave for the evening.

"I'll speak with the family about Sunday when I get home, Jack," Collin announced.

"Thank you, Collin," Jack began, "I'll tell my family you might have an answer for us by tomorrow."

Collin nodded his head and paused only a moment, before jumping from the boardwalk and darting in the direction of his apartment. Jack began walking slowly, scanning the area for signs of Melvin and Anthony as he made his way toward home. Once he was sure the coast was clear, he began to run in that direction.

Jack arrived home just as his father was climbing the porch steps. "Why Jack, how was your day?" Sheldon asked.

"It was fine," Jack replied. "The Dodge's hired Collin's mother to work for them, so they won't be needing me every day." They were entering the kitchen now and Jack was aware of his grandparents listening to their conversation.

"How do you feel about that?" Sheldon asked.

"It's okay," Jack said. "I don't want to work every day of the summer, anyway."

"What do you mean?" his grandmother asked, pulling out a chair for him to sit on. "Why aren't you working every day?"

"Delores," Lester said, tapping his cane upon the floor. "Give the Lad a break. He is only a boy."

"Hush now, Lester. I'm talking to the boy," Delores replied, frowning over at his grandfather. She placed her hand upon Jack's shoulder and asked, "Jack, my boy, what happened?"

"Oh, nothing happened, Grandmother. I didn't do anything wrong or anything like that. Mrs. Dodge is having Mrs. McCauley come in a few days a week and she can't keep both of us on her payroll, so I won't be needed as many days," Jack explained.

"What is she going to be doing?" Delores asked.

"Well, mostly she is helping with Mr. Dodge, I think," Jack replied.

"Do you often help with Mr. Dodge?" his grandmother asked.

Jack shook his head. "No, Collin does most of that kind of stuff. I mostly sweep and clean."

His grandmother straightened herself up and placed her hands upon her hips. His grandfather cleared his throat and said, "I reckon there is just so much cleaning one person can do. He's probably got the placed pretty well cleaned up by now and they don't need him as often. That is probably it." He was watching Delores as she turned her back on them. "He isn't big enough to handle the heavy stuff, Delores. I can certainly see Rosalie's thinking on the matter."

"It doesn't matter," Sheldon said, placing his hand on Jack's arm. "It was only a part time job anyway. A boy Jack's age should be outside playing during his summer break from school. He shouldn't have to worry about a job. There will be plenty of time to worry about that when he gets older," he said, winking at Jack.

Jack looked over at his father and smiled. "Thank you, Daddy. I'm anxious to get outside and play."

"How many days is Mrs. McCauley working for Rosalie?" Delores asked.

"She's working Monday, Tuesday, Friday, and Saturday," Jack replied.

Delores turned quickly and asked, "You are only working Wednesday and Thursday?"

"Delores," Lester said.

"I'm only asking," Delores said, sharply.

"Yep. I mean, yes Ma'am. That's okay with me," Jack said, squirming on his chair.

"I think two days a week is plenty," Sheldon said, looking up at his mother.

Delores turned quickly and busied herself at the sideboard. "Are you working tomorrow?" she asked, without turning around.

"I forgot to ask," Jack replied. "I suppose so. They didn't tell me not to come in. I suppose I will go to work and if they don't need me, they can send me home."

"What did you have for dinner?" his grandmother asked.

Jack smiled over at his father. "We had bacon and eggs. Doctor Cope was there to check on Mr. Dodge." It grew quiet then. Jack assumed his grandmother was satisfied with what he had eaten for dinner. Before climbing the ladder to bed that evening, Jack told them that Collin should have an answer about the church social by tomorrow. Jack fell asleep and dreamed of eating his picnic lunch under one of the large Maple trees outside the church. He was sitting on the quilt that covered his bed and Katherine Mary Margaret McCauley sat across from him, smiling, with her red curls blowing in the breeze.

"Jack Gideon!" his grandfather called, from below. "Daylight's wasting. Are you going to get up this morning?"

Jack sat straight up. He had been dreaming. Morning had arrived so quickly and it was time to get up, already. How he longed to close his eyes and drift back into the dream, but he knew it would not happen. He rolled from his bed and smoothed out the covers. He pulled on his clothes and climbed down the ladder. His grandparents were both smiling at him as he reached the bottom. He pulled on his shoes and hurried out to the privy. The sun was shining and it was already a warm day. It would be a perfect day to climb the hillside and explore the high ground.

Jack ate his breakfast and hurried toward the mercantile. Folks were out early this morning, moving about in the warm sunshine. He heard the wagons bouncing their way up the turnpike toward their northern destinations. He climbed the steps to the mercantile to find Mrs. Dodge at the counter going through a catalog. She smiled as he entered and said, "Good morning Jack. Isn't it a beautiful day out there?"

"It is Mrs. Dodge. How is Mr. Dodge this morning?" he asked.

"Oh, Dr. Cope said he has been rushing things and needs to spend more time resting. I'm afraid we won't be seeing much of him for a few days. How are your grandparents?" she asked.

"Everyone is well. I forgot to ask you if you needed me to come in today," he said.

"Oh yes, well, let me see now," she said, pushing a loose strand of hair from her face. "I think we should start our new schedule next week. Do you mind working the rest of the week?"

Jack shook his head. "Not at all, Ma'am. It's still too wet to play outdoors anyway. Grandmother gets huffy about me getting too muddy."

Rosalie laughed out loud. "I understand."

Jack took the broom, as was his usual custom, and began sweeping wood splinters into a pile. Then he shook the ashes from the bottom of the wood stove and dumped them into a bucket that sat nearby. He swept up the wooden splinters and dumped them in the bucket before he carried it outside. As he was returning, he saw Collin arriving.

"Mornin' Jack me boy," Collin said, with a smile.

"Good morning, Collin," Jack replied.

"I'll have you know that me family had a long discussion last night about the church social. They are reluctant, but we decided to give it a go. Folks are either going to warm up to us or not. As we sees it, we aim to stay in Wellsville, what with me Ma working here at the mercantile and all. Folks might as well get used to seein' us around," Collin explained, as they entered the mercantile together.

"Oh, I think folks will take to you and your family well enough," Jack said.

"Whatever do you mean?" Rosalie asked, as they entered.

Jack smiled and said, "Collin and his family have agreed to accompany my family to church Sunday, and stay for the church social."

"Oh, how wonderful," Rosalie replied clapping her hands together. She smiled over at Collin. "Now don't you be fretting yourself over how folks are going to react to your family. Some will scoff, but for the most part, they will be friendly. Remember, they will be in the house of God. They will be on their best behavior." The bell over the door rang and Sherriff Harris entered.

"Good morning, everyone," the Sherriff said.

"Good morning, Sherriff," Rosalie said, walking around the counter. "What can I do for you this morning?"

"Oh, I need some chewing tobacco, Rosalie," he said.

"Of course," Rosalie replied hurrying toward the small bin of dried, loose tobacco.

"We had our town council meeting last night," the Sherriff said.

"Oh, anything worth talking about?" Rosalie asked, without turning around.

"Not much," the Sherriff replied. "Mrs. Anthony was stirring trouble up for this young man here and his family," the Sherriff said, pointing to Collin.

Collin's face flushed and he began to fidget. Rosalie turned with a white sack of tobacco, which she held out for the Sherriff to inspect. He peered into the sack and nodded his head in approval.

"Sherriff, I know I don't have to tell you that Maybell Patrone has had it in for the McCauley family ever since they arrived here. They have done nothing wrong. I certainly hope her complaints fell upon deaf ears," Rosalie said, placing her hands upon her hips.

"Oh, don't you worry about Maybell Patrone, none, Rosalie. She was given the floor and she said her piece. After that, it was business as usual. She tried to bring it up again, more than once, but it didn't do her any good. Before closing the meeting, she was told in no uncertain terms that the matter had no merit, and she was to drop it," the Sherriff laughed. "She left in a huff, but she normally leaves in a huff anyway." He turned to Collin and said, "Young man, I'm only going to say this once, you and your family are as welcome as anyone else in this town. You have been working hard, and Mavis Cartwright said that you've been working real hard on your lessons at school too. There were a lot of folks who spoke up on your behalf at the meeting last night. Now as long as you keep your nose clean and continue to contribute to this community, the way you've been, we will continue to stand up for you and yours. But mind my words, now, if you go off halfcocked and get yourself involved in shenanigans, we will have a problem, you and me. Do you understand what I'm saying?" he asked, narrowing his eyes as he looked over at Collin.

"Yes Sir," Collin replied, swallowing hard.

Sherriff Harris nodded his head and turned to Rosalie. "It seems folks around town have been paying attention to what you've done here with this boy. Some aren't on board yet, but most of them agree that they deserve a chance. Because the boy's father was a no count, doesn't necessarily mean the whole lot of them are bad. That was pretty much the consensus last evening. As for Maybelle, hell, everyone knows how she is. There wasn't one person present last evening that hasn't had a run in with old Maybelle Patrone at one time or another. That boy of hers is going to be a problem, too, if she doesn't reign him in. Don't think I didn't tell her so, too." Sherriff Harris turned to Collin again and smiled, "You keep your nose clean, as I said, and get yourself an education, Son. Mavis Cartwright spoke up for you at the meeting last night. She said how hard you been working on your studies so you can get a job on the docks and support your family. That's a lot for a lad your age to take on. That also speaks for your character."

Rosalie cleared her throat. "He isn't going to work on the docks just yet, Sherriff. He is going to help out here for a spell. Now that Howard is unable to work, we rely on Collin for all the lifting and heavy work. His mother is going to help four days a week too. We will be seeing more of them for a while," she said.

Sherriff Harris nodded and pushed his hat back on his head. "You remember what these kind folks have done for you, boy. You are beholding to them now. It's a good thing you are doing, helping the way you are. Not many lads in your shoes get breaks like the one you're getting."

"Yes Sir," Collin said, straightening himself to stand erect. "I will remember."

Sherriff Harris tipped his hat to Rosalie and smiled, "Ma'am, you have a lovely day."

"Oh, Sherriff," Rosalie called out to him as he turned to go. She smiled and folded her hands in front of her. "The tobacco, Sherriff. You forgot to pay for it."

"Oh, pardon me, Mrs. Dodge," the Sherriff said, walking toward her. "I got so distracted by that young man over there, that I plum forgot to pay for my tobacco." He reached into his pocket and pulled out a coin. He smiled and tipped his hat again as he placed the coin on the counter and turned to leave.

"Well," Rosalie began, "I suppose I should look in on Howard. You boys carry on out here until I return." With that, she turned and went through the curtains to the back.

Jack smiled over at Collin. "See, I told you folks around here weren't that bad," he said, smiling.

Collin's face was red, and he snickered at Jack's remarks. "I suppose so," he said.

"You will see this Sunday for yourself," Jack said.

Collin did not reply on the matter. He busied himself and it grew quiet. The bell over the door rang several more times, and Collin handled every transaction as if the store belonged to him. It appeared to Jack that they were busier than usual, and he assumed that it was possible that folks were curious to meet this Irish boy that was spoken so highly of at the meeting the night before. The day wore on, and soon Collin was going home for lunch and to check on his family. Jack sat at the table in the back alone, while Mrs. Dodge fed Howard, who was in bed.

Mrs. Dodge entered the kitchen and began to clear the table. "Mr. Dodge has a bad headache today. I haven't seen him in this much pain since right after the accident." She looked over at Jack and paused, as if she were in deep thought. "Jack, would you mind running out to fetch the doctor? I'm a might worried," she asked.

"Yes Ma'am, right away," Jack replied, as he jumped from the table and ran through the curtains, and out the front door. He ran all the way across two blocks, cutting across back yards, until he reached the doctor's house. He knocked on the door rapidly and hard.

"What is it?" Mrs. Cope asked, as she swung the door open wide.

"Mr. Dodge is feeling poorly. He has a bad headache, and Mrs. Dodge asked me to fetch Dr. Cope for him," Jack said, between pants as he gasped to catch his breath.

"Well, step inside," Mrs. Cope said, holding the door open for Jack to pass through. "He's with a patient, now, but I'll tell him you are here," Mrs. Cope said. She pointed to a chair in the hall. "Have a seat right there until he's finished." Jack sat down and began to swing his legs nervously. Time seemed to stand still. He listened to the second hand on the large floor clock as the seconds ticked away. He wrung his sweating hands, and stared at his feet as he continued to swing them back and forth. Soon the door opened and he jumped as it startled him. Dr. Cope smiled at him and stepped back to hold the door open for Mrs. Gardner and three small children.

As the Gardner's passed Jack, he stepped back, flattening himself against the wall to ensure none of them brushed against him. Dr. Cope laughed and said, "It's alright Jack, they are not quarantined anymore. The mumps have passed and they are all as healthy as you are."

"Yes Sir, I'm happy to hear that, Sir," Jack said.

"Now what can I do for you?" Dr. Cope asked.

"It's Mr. Dodge, Sir. Mrs. Dodge sent me to fetch you. He has a bad headache and she is worried," Jack replied, wringing his hands in front of him.

"Well then, I suppose I should get right over there and have a look at him," Dr. Cope said. "Would you like to ride along in my carriage?"

Jack nodded his head. "Yes Sir, if you don't mind," he replied.

Jack normally would run back the way he came, but the thought of possibly running into Melvin or Anthony, or worse yet, both, caused him to accept Dr. Cope's invitation.

"Come along, Jack. You can help me harness up old Dotty," Dr. Cope said. Jack followed him out a back door. "Grab that black bag on the floor there, next to the door, Jack," Dr. Cope said. Jack did as he was instructed. They hitched a black mare to the surrey and soon they were moving along at a trot towards the mercantile. Neither of them spoke, as the ride didn't take long. Jack tied the black mare to the hitching post, as the doctor disappeared inside. When Jack entered, he found Collin waiting for him.

"Is Mr. Dodge alright?" Jack asked.

"I'm not sure," Collin replied. "I'm glad the doctor is here. Mrs. Dodge is a might worried, so she is."

They both turned when they heard the bell over the door ring. It was Mrs. Cartwright. She smiled and said, "Good morning, boys. How are you this morning?"

"We're a might worried about Mr. Dodge, Ma'am," Collin replied. "Mrs. Dodge sent for the doctor because he has a bad headache. We are hopin' it's nothin' serious."

"Oh, my, my," Mrs. Cartwright said, shaking her head. "I was under the impression that Mr. Dodge was healing nicely and making a quick recovery."

"I think we all thought that," Jack said.

"Is there something I can get for you?" Collin asked.

"I'm in need of a sack of flour and a slab of bacon," Mrs. Cartwright said. She smiled over at Jack and looked back toward Collin as he began to scoop out a measure of flour. "I've been hearing such good things about you, Collin," she said. "I heard you might be staying on here to help Rosalie until Howard is back on his feet."

"Yes Ma'am," Collin replied without turning around.

"I'm so very proud of you, Son. Are you still planning on taking a job down at the docks?" she asked.

"I don't know, Mrs. Cartwright," Collin said, placing the sack of flour on the counter. "I owe these folks so much. I reckon I'll be stayin' on as long as they need me."

"I hear your mother is going to work a few days a week as well," Mrs. Cartwright said.

"Yes, Ma'am, she is," Collin replied, with a frown. Jack watched Collin closely, taking note of his facial expressions. Jack knew Collin was uncomfortable, as he did not like folks knowing his personal business.

"Well, I want you to know that offer I made you, a few days ago, still stands. I'm willing to help you pass to the next grade. I would also like to see your brothers and sisters in school next year. Nothing would give me greater pleasure," Mrs. Cartwright said.

"I'll think on it, Ma'am," Collin said. He cut on a large piece of salted pork that hung behind the counter. He wrapped it in gauze wrapping and tied a string around it. He smiled across the counter at his teacher and said, "I heard you spoke up for me and mine at the town meeting a fortnight. I be thankin' ya for what ya done."

"It wasn't anything, Collin. I didn't say anything that wasn't true. You're a fine boy and I'm honored to have had you for one of my students. I honestly believe that we are going to hear wonderful things about you some day. I feel it in my heart, and I want to do everything in my power to help you," Mrs. Cartwright said, smiling.

"Well, thank you just the same, Ma'am," Collin replied. "That will be seven cents, Ma'am."

Mrs. Cartwright wore a silk purse pinned to her shawl. She counted out seven cents and handed it to Collin. She watched as he counted the coins and placed them in the register. "Thank you, Ma'am. We appreciate your business," he said, politely.

Mrs. Cartwright smiled again and turned to look at Jack. Once more, she nodded her head and said, "Good day, Jack," as she turned to leave.

"Are you really going to think about going back to school, Collin?" Jack asked.

"I said I would," Collin replied. "The way I sees it, I might keep me foot in the door, a spell, until I see how things play out here. I kin always go down to the docks if it doesn't work out in my favor. Least ways, me Ma has a job now. It's a lot better than sweeping that dusty chair factory, what with her lungs bein' poorly, and all."

The bell over the door rang again. This time it was Mrs. Raines, and she had Lynette and Milly Thompson with her. Mrs. Raines smiled politely as they approached the counter where Collin stood waiting. Lynette and Milly were holding hands as they marched behind Lynette's mother. Mrs. Raines cleared her throat and looked around the mercantile. "Good afternoon, young man. Is Rosalie around?" she asked.

Jack stood near the wood stove watching Collin. The girls and Mrs. Raines had their backs to him. Collin didn't flinch once. He cleared his throat and stood erect. "No Ma'am, Mrs. Dodge is pre-disposed at the present time. Is there something I can do for you?" he asked.

Mrs. Raines appeared nervous. "Well, it's just that Rosalie or Howard usually take care of our business, and it's not that I don't trust you, young man, it's just that I have a personal issue that requires I do business with them, you see," she said, tugging on her bonnet.

"Are you referring to a personal bill with the mercantile?" Collin asked, looking her straight in the eye.

"Why, ah, yes, I suppose you might call it that," she rolled her eyes and took a deep breath before blurting, "I really would prefer to speak with Rosalie. I know Howard is under the weather these days, but if I might speak with Rosalie I would appreciate it, if you please, young man." She appeared to be rambling on, nervously.

"Mrs. Dodge cannot be disturbed right now, Ma'am," Collin said. "If it would put your mind to ease, she has explained how I am to handle accounts with credit balances. I assure you I am qualified, Ma'am."

Mrs. Raines turned white. "Credit?" she asked. "Young man, I'll have you know that I am Mrs. Raines. My husband is a prominent citizen of Wellsville and we do not need credit here or anywhere else for that matter." Lynette turned to look back at Jack. She nudged Milly who also turned to look back at him. Jack quickly turned his back on them, so as not to give them the chance to stick their tongues out at him.

Judy Lennington

"Pardon me, Ma'am. I meant no disrespect," he heard Collin saying. "It's just that Mr. Dodge has gone over the bookkeeping with me and explained everything. I recognize your name, for I see it in the books often enough." There was a long pause. The suspense was killing Jack. He couldn't help himself, so, he turned to look back at them. Lynette was looking at Collin, but Milly was looking straight at Jack and she stuck her tongue out at him. Jack quickly looked down at the floor. He felt his face growing hot.

"Young man, are you going to get Rosalie, or should I come back at another date?" Mrs. Raines asked.

"I suppose it would be best if you came back at another time when Mrs. Dodge isn't so busy," Collin said.

"Well!" Mrs. Raines huffed. "Come along girls." Jack heard their shoes clicking on the plank floor, but he did not look at them. He would not give them the satisfaction of allowing them to stick their tongues out at him again. He heard the door slam and turned to look at Collin.

"I hope I done right," Collin said.

"I think you did just fine," Jack said, taking a deep breath.

Collin wiped at his sweating forehead. "It's just that Mrs. Dodge told me I was to be more hospitable toward the customers. I recollect her saying the customer is always right. I could have gotten Mrs. Dodge, I suppose, but I know she is busy with Mr. Dodge and all."

"You did right, Collin. Mrs. Dodge won't be upset, if that is what you are worried about. Besides, there was no harm done. Mrs. Raines will come back and Mrs. Dodge will take care of her problem and that will be the end of it," Jack explained. "I think she was embarrassed to hear that you knew she had a bill at the mercantile."

"That ain't nothin'," Collin said. "Nearly everyone in Wellsville has a bill here. I don't know what makes her so riled up over it. It ain't nothin' to me or mine."

"Some folks are funny, I suppose," Jack said.

They had two more customers come and go before they saw the doctor again. He came through the curtains, carrying his black bag. He smiled at the boys and said, "You boys are doing an excellent job, so I hear. Keep up the good work. Keep your fingers out of your mouths and wash your hands often." He smiled again and left. Collin and Jack stood quietly looking at one another in amazement. Soon Mrs. Dodge came through the curtains.

"Well, thank you boys for looking after things for me." She took a deep breath and let it out slowly, closing her eyes tight. "Doc says Howard is going to have some bad headaches from time to time. He gave me some Laudanum to help him sleep when they come on. I suppose he'll sleep all day and night, which is a good thing. Hopefully tomorrow he will feel better." She smiled over at Collin and said, "Thank you for being here when I needed you."

"Mrs. Raines was here. She didn't want to do dealins' with me. She said she wanted to talk to only you about her account. I told her she should probably come back. She left in a bit of a huff, I'm afraid," Collin explained.

Rosalie Dodge snickered. "I can only imagine." She covered her mouth and looked away a moment. When she looked back at Collin she was composed. "Don't pay her no mind, Collin. Some folks like to put on airs and the Raines are some of those folks. She'll be back and I'll talk to her."

"Yes, Ma'am," Collin replied.

"Oh, my, where has the time gone? You boys must be terribly hungry as it is past dinner time," Mrs. Dodge said.

Judy Lennington

Collin looked over at Jack. "I'm not hungry, Ma'am. If it's alright with you, I would just the same prefer to go home and eat with my family," he said.

"Me too, Ma'am," Jack called across the room. "I will bring in some fire wood and be home in time to eat with Daddy."

Rosalie patted the bun in her hair. "Well, I suppose if you don't mind. I've been so busy with Howard that I forgot to put anything on the fire," she said, with a sigh.

"We'll be fine, Ma'am. We will do like Jack said and bring in some fire wood. I'll close up for you. You go check on Mr. Dodge. We will be out of here in no time. I'll lock up and we will see you in the morrow," Collin said.

"Yes Ma'am," Jack said, hurrying toward the back where the firewood was kept. They carried in enough wood for the night and the next morning. Mrs. Dodge reminded Jack that Mrs. McCauley was coming in tomorrow and he needn't come to work until Wednesday. He would work on Wednesday and Thursday. Jack smiled and nodded his head. He hoped he didn't appear too happy about his new schedule. He didn't want Mrs. Dodge to think he was ungrateful. Collin turned the sign around to indicate that the mercantile was closed for the day, then they parted ways and went home.

Jack arrived home only moments before his father. "How was your day, Jack?" Sheldon asked, as he removed his boots.

"It was okay," Jack said. "I didn't eat dinner at the Dodge's. I was hoping to eat with you this evening." He looked up at his grandmother who had turned to look at him. "That is if you don't mind."

"Why didn't you eat at the Dodge's?" Delores asked.

"Well," Jack thought carefully as he spoke. "Mr. Dodge had a bad headache, and I had to fetch Dr. Cope for Mrs. Dodge. The doctor was there a long time and Collin and I had to mind the store. Mrs. Dodge really didn't have much time to prepare anything, and she offered, but I suggested that I come home and eat with you all." He took a breath and watched his grandmother, waiting for her response.

"A bad headache you say," Lester said. "Is he alright?"

"Doc says it is normal and it is going to happen from time to time. Mrs. Dodge was awful worried though," Jack replied.

"I'm sorry to hear that," Sheldon said leaning his elbows upon his knees. He smiled and stood up. "Well, I suppose you are hungry."

"Yes Sir, I am very hungry," Jack said, smiling up at his father.

"She could have given you a slice of bread or something to keep your stomach calmed down until supper," Delores said, turning back to the pot she was stirring.

Lester sighed heavily and pushed himself up to a standing position. "I'll set another plate on the table," he said.

"Never mind, Dad," Sheldon said. "I'm right here. I'll get it."

"What are we having, grandmother?" Jack asked.

Delores turned and frowned at Jack as he sat at the table. "You aren't having anything until you wash those grubby hands of yours, Jack Gideon."

Jack smiled up at his father and slid from his chair as he went to the wash basin. He poured water into it and began to wash his hands. He was joined by his father who continued to smile down at him until they were scrubbed for dinner. Then the family sat down to eat together. Jack's grandmother seemed quite pleased with herself this evening. Jack suspected it had something to do with his eating at home with the family.

The conversation around the table was cheerful this evening. It appeared Jack did most of the talking. It wasn't that he had so much to say, but mostly because he was asked so many questions. When dinner was over, Jack's grandfather began to reminisce about the time he was a boy living in Wellsville. Jack's grandfather's parents were among the settlers who bought a boat and traveled down the river to settle here where the river crooked sharply. They dismantled their wooden boat and used the lumber to build this house they were living in. There were other settlers in the area at the time, and there were some conflicts with the Indians back then, but they survived as many others did, and the settlement continued to grow. More and more buildings went up and soon streets were laid out, until it turned into a small town. Now it was a lot bigger than it was when Lester was a boy. It wasn't as big as East Liverpool, but it was just as busy on the docks.

Lester talked about his brothers growing up and how they went off to work. He talked about life after their mother died. Lester's sister married and moved away as well. Lester stayed on and inherited the house. He married Delores and they raised their family. Jack had heard this story many times, and never grew tired of it. He could close his eyes at night and picture himself, in his grandfather's place, hanging out with Limpy, running the streets of Wellsville, and listening to the sailing stories Limpy told, time after time.

Now he laid in his bed with his hands behind his head, staring up at the ceiling. Tomorrow was Friday and it was the first day for Mrs. McCauley to work at the mercantile. Jack would remain home tomorrow. He smiled at the thought. The trees on the hillside had been calling to him. They were in full leaf now and the ground was drying up nicely. He couldn't wait to go outside to play. He was so anxious that he found it hard to fall asleep. He was awaking when his father came to bed, and awake when his father rose for work.

Jack found his grandmother was still in a good mood this morning. He went to the privy and gathered a few eggs from the henhouse for his breakfast upon his return. Lester sat near the fireplace, patiently waiting for breakfast. Before long, they were gathered around the table eating scrambled eggs and sugar bread. The front door stood wide open, as it was going to be a warm day outside. Jack was happy. It was a perfect day for exploring the hillside.

Jack climbed the loose shale bank until he reached the path that traveled east along the hillside. He crossed it and began to climb again. The terrain here was steeper and slippery as the morning sun had not dried the dew from the foliage. He watched out for signs of snakes and other vermin as he went. He noticed a timber rattler basking in the morning sun far to his left. He kept his distance as the snake flicked its tongue rapidly, sensing Jack's presence. He knew these snakes were also plentiful this time of year and usually in a foul mood, so he was careful not to disturb it.

Soon Jack was climbing a Maple tree with low limbs. He climbed high and wrapped his arms around the trunk of the tree as he peered down upon Wellsville. Wagons were lined as far as he could see coming from the east toward the docks. More wagons were lined as they moved up the hill headed north toward Youngstown, Niles, and all the way to the Great Lakes. Jack had never seen the Great Lakes except for on the maps Mrs. Cartwright displayed hanging over the chalk board at school. He lingered in the tree watching the dock activity and thinking of Collin. He could see small figures working on the docks, unloading wagons, and loading wagons. Boats docked and boats pushed off all the while not realizing they were being watched from high up above them.

Jack allowed his eyes to scan the area near his small house of two and a half rooms. It wasn't hard to find, as it stood nestled amongst other houses much like it to his right. Larger houses seem to loom over them and surround them as if to protect them from Mother Nature's harshness. Then there were the mansions that lined Water Street. Jack saw people coming and going about their daily lives. He continued to watch as he pulled a sugar bread snack from his pocket and bit into it. He closed his eyes and allowed the breeze that swayed the leaves to blow upon his face. He could smell the new leaves of the maple tree. He inched his way out onto a limb and sat down to eat the rest of his sugar bread. It was a perfect day.

Jack lost track of time. His sugar bread was long gone and the sun was straight above him, as it shone down upon the earth. It was lunch time. Jack inched his way from the limb and down the tree until he was on the ground. He patted the tree as he began to move down the bank, careful not to start slipping.

He skipped as he moved toward home. His stomach rumbled, pressing him to move faster. He saw movement to this left and he instinctively ducked behind a building. Was it Melvin, Anthony, or both? He remained motionless until he felt the danger was passed. As he cautiously peered around the corner, he saw Mrs. Garfield gathering laundry from her clothes line. It was a false alarm. He stepped into the opening and called out, "Good afternoon, Mrs. Garfield."

"Good afternoon, Jack. Aren't you working at the mercantile today?" Mrs. Garfield asked.

"No Ma'am, Mrs. McCauley works there today," he explained.

"Oh?" she seemed surprised. "I didn't realize she was working for the Dodge's."

"Yes, Ma'am. Well, you have a wonderful day, Mrs. Garfield," Jack called out as he began running toward home.

Jack found his grandparents waiting for him. "Where have you been, boy?" his grandmother asked.

"I'm sorry Grandmother. I lost track of time," Jack explained.

"I suppose you were up on the hill, high up in some tree, somewhere," she said, placing a plate in front of him.

"Yes, Ma'am," Jack said. He noticed her frown and instantly slid from his chair to wash his hands.

"That's a boy for you," Lester said, winking over at Jack. "Why, I mind the time when I was his age. I didn't spend as much time in trees, for I spent nearly every spare moment listening to Limpy's tales of the sea."

Delores huffed. "No one wants to hear about that old drunk's tales. Why, you don't even know if they were true. He may have been just making it up as he went to entertain a lad that wouldn't let him be," she said.

"Oh, they were true well enough," Lester said, nodding his head.

"I'd like to hear more of Limpy's tales, Grandfather," Jack said, sliding onto his chair again. He folded his hands and bowed his head while his Grandfather said grace.

After reciting the prayer, Lester said, "Jack, I'd be beholding to you, if you would give me a hand with weeding the garden after dinner."

Judy Lennington

"Certainly, Grandfather. You can tell me some more about Limpy while we work," Jack replied. They ate their meal then. Jack listened while his grandmother talked about mending some of Jack's clothes before the church social and darning Lester's socks. Soon Jack and his grandfather were making their way toward the garden.

Lester began to hoe the weeds growing in the rows between the plants while Jack crouched upon his knees pulling weeds around the plants that blossomed and promised to yield vegetables that would eventually sustain them for the winter months.

"Tell me more about Limpy, Grandfather," Jack said, looking up at his grandfather.

Lester leaned upon the hoe for a moment, before looking toward the sky and saying, "Limpy was young when he began his career as a whaler. Back then, an experienced whaler wore a pin on their shirts to signify that they had experience. Limpy told me that his goal was to earn such a pin. He never got the chance, however." Lester looked down at Jack. "His days as a whaler were cut short when that bull whale sunk their ship and put him and the crew in the ocean." He wiped at his forehead. "The ocean is big, Jack. Limpy said you could look in every direction and see nothing but water and sky for days and days. Occasionally, they would spot a ship off in the distance, but they avoided close contact. It was a code the whalers went by. You honored another ships space. It wouldn't be right to take a whale that another ship had harpooned. For the most part, the days he spent at sea were uneventful. He spent most of his days and nights listening to tales the other whalers told. He said most of them were tall tales, which meant there was little or no truth to them, but they were entertaining and helped to pass the time. Of course, when there was a breach or raise, by a whale, things moved pretty darn fast."

"I can't imagine what it must have been like out on the sea for days and days, with no trees to climb," Jack said, with a sigh.

"You certainly do like climbing trees, don't you Jack?" his grandfather chuckled. "I suppose everyone is different for a reason. Then, again, it was different times, when Limpy was a lad. I can remember listening to his tales and wishing I could go to sea. Then one day he was feeling low. It was the lowest I had ever seen him. It was that day that he told me about the shark attack that took his leg. He seemed to drift off into a dark place and explained every detail to me. Of course, me being a mere boy at the time, it scared the daylights out of me. I never yearned for a life at sea after that. I don't recall ever swimming in the river again after that day either," Lester laughed. He looked down at Jack, as he crouched upon his knees, looking up at him with wide eyes. "I know there aren't any sharks in that old river, Jack."

Jack turned back to his task of pulling weeds and said without looking up, "There are some mighty big catfish out there in that old river, Grandfather."

"They'd make some mighty fine eating, wouldn't they Jack?" Lester asked.

"Yes, and Daddy and I hope to catch them some Sunday. Just not this Sunday because it is the church social," Jack said. He looked up at his grandfather and asked, "Do you mind the McCauley's going to church with us on Sunday, Grandfather?"

"Oh, not at all, Jack," Lester replied. "Why would you ask me such a question? I thought you knew me better than that."

"I kind of thought you might not mind, but I think Grandmother is a might put off by it," Jack said, going back to work.

Judy Lennington

"She'll be alright, Jack. Don't pay her no mind. Sometimes she gets worried about what folks think or say, but I think in her heart she knows better. She'll come around," Lester said.

"These cabbage heads look like they could use some of that white lime Howard sells at the mercantile," Lester said. "Maybe we could take a walk later and see if they will sell some of it to us."

"Oh, he will sell it to us if they have it, Grandfather," Jack said. He looked up to see his grandfather smiling down at him. Jack smiled and said, "I'd like to see how Mr. Dodge is feeling, anyway."

"That's a good lad," Lester said. They worked until they had finished the garden. Lester put the hoe away and told Jack to brush his clothes off and wash up before they went to the mercantile. Soon they were making their way down the street in that direction. Jack walked slowly, to keep pace with his grandfather who moved along with the aid of his cane. The sun was hot today, and Lester wore a straw hat to shield his face from the sun. Jack did not wear a hat and he constantly wiped at the sweat running down his face, and stinging his eyes. He had rolled his long sleeves up to his elbows. Occasionally, he glanced toward the hillside. He couldn't help but think that the shade of the old Maple trees would feel delightful right now. Perhaps there would be time for that before dinner.

They arrived at the mercantile to find Harry Moser standing at the counter. Collin stood near the register, and Mrs. McCauley stood to the right of Harry. Apparently, they had walked in on a conversation that Collin was not in favor of.

"I mean no harm, Collin. I understand that you are head of the household, and thought it was only fitting that I asked your permission," Harry was saying.

Bend in The River

Collin was shaking his head. Mrs. McCauley smiled at them as they entered the store. "We will be right with you," she said, politely. She placed her hand on the counter and said, "Now Collin, hold up a moment. Mr. Moser meant no harm, as he said. I find it to be honorable of him to approach you in this manner. After all, you are the eldest son, you are the head of the household, and it is the proper thing to do. Now as for Katherine Mary Margaret, I think it is for her to decide. She is certainly old enough." She smiled over at Harry and turned to Collin once more. "Collin, it isn't fair to Kate. She can't stay cooped up in that apartment day after day, working and caring for the rest of us without some kind of life of her own. Besides, Harry here, is only asking your permission to ask her to accompany him to the church social. The decision should be Kate's."

Collin glanced over at Jack and his grandfather only briefly. His face was flushed. Jack knew that Collin was not in favor of their listening in on this conversation. He was a private person. Jack looked down at the floor. He felt embarrassed for his friend. "Maybe we should wait outside," Lester said, placing his hand upon Jack's shoulder. Jack nodded his head, and they walked outside together. They remained on the wooden boardwalk, looking out over the street. There was a roof over them that shielded them from the sun.

As they stood there, Melvin Riley came running toward them. Jack felt his back and neck stiffen as he watched him approaching. Melvin gave Jack an evil, hurtful look, and ran faster as he passed them by. Jack sighed with relief as he watched Melvin disappear between the buildings that lined the street. A wagon was coming up the street and Mr. Nelson called out to Lester. "It's a hot one today, Lester."

Judy Lennington

"It certainly is, Percy," Lester called back. "You better get in out of that sun."

"I'm headed home now, Lester. Take care of yourself," Mr. Nelson called out as he passed by. Jack recalled the night Anthony Patrone got his shirt hung up on Mr. Nelson's picket fence. He watched as the wagon moved along, bouncing about on the rutted dirt street, until it was no longer visible.

The door opened behind them and both Jack and his grandfather turned to look at Harry Moser as he exited the mercantile. He smiled over at Jack as he jumped off the wooden boardwalk and walked to their left. Jack assumed he was headed for the McCauley apartment to ask Katherine to accompany him to the church social. Jack felt disappointment, and wasn't sure why. "Come along, Jack," his grandfather said, nudging him with his elbow. They turned and went back inside.

"Mr. Gideon, what a pleasure it is to finally meet you, Sir," Mrs. McCauley said, extending her hand to Lester. "My son speaks so highly of you, Sir."

"Well, now, that is nice of Collin," Lester said, smiling over at Collin. "That's a good boy you have there, Mrs. McCauley."

"Thank you, Sir. I am so looking forward to meeting your wife. Collin said she is very kind as well," Mrs. McCauley replied. "What can I do for you this afternoon?" she asked. Jack couldn't help but think she acted as though she had been working here for many years. It seemed to come so naturally to her.

"Well, I was wondering if young Collin, here, might fetch me some of that lime from the back, for my garden. My cabbage plants are looking poorly," Lester said.

"Yes Sir," Collin said, coming around the counter.

Jack looked up at his grandfather and said, "I'm going to help Collin, Grandfather."

"That is fine, Jack. Mind you give Mrs. Dodge my regards should you see her now," Lester instructed.

"Yes Sir," Jack said, as he followed Collin through the curtains and to the stock room. "How is Mr. Dodge getting along?" he asked Collin.

"He sleeps a lot," Collin began, "Mrs. Dodge said it is what the doctor wants him to do and that is what the medicine is for." They went to the furthest wall of the stock room where a wooden barrel sat near the back door. A white dust had collected around the outside rim of the wooden cover of the barrel.

"I'm sorry we interrupted your conversation with Harry Moser, Collin," Jack said. "We couldn't help but overhear what you were talking about."

"Aye," Collin said, with a nod of his head. "He wants to court me sister, Kate. I know he was only askin' permission to ask her to go to the church social with him, but I ain't no dummy. He's been watchin' her close like. He's sweet on her rightly enough."

"Is she sweet on him?" Jack asked.

"I think she might be," Collin said. "She talks about him a lot. She says she hasn't been alone with him, but she sure talks about him a lot."

Jack sighed. "Katherine is a very beautiful young lady, Collin. A young man would be stupid not to notice it," he said. It grew quiet as Collin scooped out the white dusty powder into a tin can and placed a lid on it. He covered the wooden barrel again. "You know Harry Moser is going off to college. He won't be around long. I don't think he is a threat to Katherine or your family. He's going to be a lawyer. Lawyers are well to do folks that live in the big houses along Water Street. Maybe it wouldn't be such a terrible thing if he and Katherine got married. She would want for nothing." He couldn't believe he was saying this.

Collin scratched his head before wiping his hands on the white apron he wore over his best clothes. "I understand what ya are tellin' me, Jack, me boy. I can't explain why I object to Katherine Mary Margaret and Harry Moser. It ain't like he's such a bad guy and all," he said.

"Well, maybe you should trust your sister's instincts. Like I said, Harry is going off to college in the fall. What could happen?" Jack asked.

Collin looked over at Jack and raised his eyebrows. "You're too young to know, Jack, me boy. But I'm willin' to see what happens. It's just a church social, and Katherine is only fourteen years old." Collin smiled and carried the metal pail through the curtains again to find his mother and Jack's grandfather deep in conversation.

"Collin, I was just telling your mother, here, that I'm glad to see her getting on so well. Why, one would never know she was sick at all," Lester said.

"Yes, Sir," Collin said. "Doc Cope saved her life for sure."

"Well, Dr. Cope should know what he is doing, as he has been doing it for folks in Wellsville long enough," Lester said.

Collin placed the metal pail on the counter and asked, "Is there anything else, Mr. Gideon?"

"No, Son, I reckon not. If you would be so kind as to put this on my bill, I'll settle up with you later," Lester said. Jack felt his face growing hot as he recalled the conversation Collin had with Mrs. Raines. "You tell Rosalie and Howard I said hello and hope Howard gets well soon. Are they going to the church social?" Lester asked.

Bend in The River

Collin shook his head. "I'm afraid not, Sir. Mr. Dodge isn't well enough to go and Mrs. Dodge won't leave his side," Collin explained.

"Well now, you tell them they will be missed," Lester said, taking the pail by the handle and handing it to Jack to carry for him. "You folks come on by the house Sunday morning and we will all walk to church together."

"Yes Sir, Mr. Gideon, Sir," Collin said.

Mrs. McCauley nodded her head and smiled. "I look forward to meeting your wife, Mr. Gideon."

"We will be seeing you all come Sunday morning," Lester called out, as he waved his hand in the air.

"See you Sunday, Collin," Jack called out as he held the door for his grandfather.

Lester moved along slowly in the warm sun. He paused once under a large Oak tree that grew near the street. "Wait a moment, Jack, my boy. I need to catch my breath," Lester said, removing his hat and wiping at the sweat that run into his filmy eyes. "Whew! It's a hot one today." Jack stood patiently waiting for his grandfather to compose himself. Lester smiled down at Jack and nodded his head. "I'm fine, Jack. I could use a cold cloth from the water of that old pump over there," Lester said, handing Jack his handkerchief. Jack ran to the pump and began working the handle.

Mr. Herald Stevens heard his pump screeching and stepped out onto his porch. "Who is that at my pump?" he called out.

"It's me, Sir. Jack Gideon," Jack called out. "My grandfather needs some cool water for his face, Sir."

Mr. Stevens looked over at Lester leaning on the Oak tree. "Well, you got to prime that old pump Jack," Mr. Stevens said. "Here, I keep a bucket of water just for that purpose here next to the porch." He lifted the bucket of water and carried it to the pump. "You work the handle, Son, and I'll pour the water," he said. He raised the bucket and began to pour some of the water into the top of the pump. Water splashed onto Jack. It was cold and refreshing. Jack held the handkerchief under the spigot and allowed it to become saturated with the cold well water. Mr. Stevens placed the bucket under the spigot to fill it with more water for the next use.

Jack ran over to his grandfather and handed him the wet cloth. Lester removed his hat again and wiped his face and neck.

"Come over here and sit a spell, Lester," Mr. Stevens called out. I'll get you a tin cup of cold water to help cool you down."

Lester nodded his head and walked slowly toward Mr. Stevens porch. Mr. Stevens went inside and returned with a tin cup of cold well water for Jack's grandfather, who sat down on the porch steps, which were still under the shade of the old Oak tree. Jack sat on the steps next to his grandfather, watching him closely.

"I'll be fine in a minute, Jack, my boy," Lester said, wiping his face again. "I think I got too much sun today with working in the garden and walking to the mercantile."

"You aren't as young as you used to be, Lester. Hell, none of us are," Mr. Stevens said. He looked down at Jack and said, "Pardon my French, Son." Jack did not respond. He was concerned about his grandfather.

Jack sat quietly on the steps near Lester. Mr. Stevens stood nearby, patiently waiting to get more water, should it be necessary. Lester handed him the tin cup and smiled, "Thank you, Herald. I believe I'm feeling more like my old self again." He pushed himself up to a standing position, and looked down at Jack. "Are you ready to go home now, Jack?" he asked.

"Yes, Sir, if you feel up to it," Jack replied.

Lester leaned heavily upon his cane as he began walking toward the front street again. He waved to Mr. Stevens, and called back to him. "I'm in your debt Herald."

"You take care, Lester," Mr. Stevens called out to them as they moved on.

Jack turned and waved at Mr. Stevens. He picked up the tin of lime and walked close to his grandfather. Lester sensed Jack's concern. He patted Jack on top of the head as they moved along. "I'm fine now, Jack. You needn't worry about me and we needn't mention this to your grandmother. She'll just worry and it's in the past. There is no need to worry her about something that's over and done with."

"Yes, Sir," Jack said. They reached the house and Lester climbed the steps to sit down on a chair near the open door.

Delores came out onto the porch with a drying cloth in her hand. "What took you so long?" she asked. "I was beginning to worry."

Lester winked over at Jack. He looked up at his wife and said, "Oh, I was talking to that nice Mrs. McCauley at the mercantile. We had to wait while they dealt with another customer, and then when our turn came, we began talking and the time just flew by. Doc gave Howard some medicine that makes him sleep. The Dodge's won't be at the social Sunday. Rosalie won't leave Howard, and he is in no shape to be socializing." He sighed and asked, "You got any cool water, Delores? I'm a might parched."

Jack's grandmother went inside and returned with a dipper of water from the water bucket. "Did you get too much sun, Lester?" she asked.

"Maybe, but I'll be alright in a minute. It's just a hot one today," Lester said, smiling at Jack. He drank from the white dipper, then handed it back to his wife. "I told Mrs. McCauley to come here Sunday morning and we would all walk to church together."

Delores moaned under her breath and turned to carry the dipper back inside. She did not come back outside. Jack wanted to go to the hillside and climb high where the trees grew thick and lush. It would be cool there and he felt the need to climb a tall tree again. However, he was afraid to leave his grandfather. "What if something happened while I was gone? What if God called Grandfather to heaven and I wasn't here?" he thought to himself. He decided to stay nearby.

Delores stepped out of the kitchen with two wet cloths. "Put these around your necks, both of you," she said.

Lester sighed as he wrapped the cloth around his neck. "Now, Delores, we don't need you fussing over us. You'd think we never experienced a muggy day before."

"You keep forgetting," Delores said, as she placed a cloth around Jack's neck, "You ain't as young as you used to be. I keep telling you, and you keep shrugging me off." She smiled down at Jack. "He's as hard headed as that mule that kicked Howard Dodge in the head. You mind, now, don't you be like that."

Jack smiled up at his grandmother. He did not speak. He thought it may be in his best interest to keep silent. She turned and went back inside the house, leaving Jack and his grandfather alone on the porch.

"Don't pay her no mind, Jack. What would a woman know about what goes on in a man's head?" Lester asked, shaking his head and wiping at his neck with the wet cloth.

"Yes, Sir," Jack said, as he sat down on the top step of the porch. "It sure is hot. It's a good thing we got the garden hoed early."

"It sure is, and I thank you for helping me. Your grandmother is right when she said I'm not as young as I used to be. I rely upon you a great deal, Jack. I'm grateful you are here to help me." Lester paused while he wiped at his mouth and face. "I'm afraid as time goes by, I'm going to need your help more and more. Your father can't help much, what with him working six days a week, from sun up till sun down. We rely on him a great deal too, as he pays for almost everything around here."

"We are beholding to you and Grandma for taking us in the way you did," Jack said.

"As you should be," Lester said, smiling down at Jack from where he sat on the porch. "You should be grateful to all those who help. You never want to be expecting more than you got coming to you. In fact, you are better off not to expect anything at all." Lester laughed out loud. "That way every kindness is like a gift someone gives you, and you come to appreciate it more."

"Yes, Sir," Jack replied.

"Old Limpy told me that once," Lester said, looking off toward the treetops. "I often wondered why folks was so mean to Limpy. If they only took the time to get to know him the way I did. He was wiser than anyone I ever knew. Of course, my father died, and it fell upon my mother to rear us young ones on her own. My mother had her wits about her, well enough, but she hadn't seen and done the things old Limpy had. Now it is true, that she and my father came down the river on a boat and settled here. They lived through the Indian raids and what not. Those were tough times. You ain't never seen anything like that, Jack. We've tried to protect you."

"Did you see Chief Logan, Grandpa?" Jack asked.

Judy Lennington

"I saw Indians a few times, when I was young," Lester said. "I can't say any of them was Chief Logan. I can't say as I would know him if I saw him. Why, I expect they are still out there somewhere in the thickets, hiding and watching what we are doing to their land."

Jack looked toward the tree line. He imagined and Indian hiding behind a tree, watching them at that very moment. Lester laughed and Jack looked up at him. "Don't fret none, Jack. Those Indians have moved deeper into the forests. They aren't much for our way of life. They go where the hunting is plentiful. They aren't around here anymore, excepting for a few that married white men and settled here," Lester said.

"Are there any in Wellsville?" Jack asked.

Lester shook his head. "I don't think so. There may be some in East Liverpool, but not many. I can't think of a one to tell you the truth. I was only assuming so."

Jack looked toward the hillside off behind them. He wondered if he had ever been watched by an Indian as he climbed the trees and played among the rocky terrain.

"I'm thinking I could use a bite of something," Lester said. He narrowed his gaze, as he looked down at Jack. "I'm also thinking it would be best if you stay close to the house for a spell. It's too hot for you to be out there climbing trees. A nap wouldn't hurt you none, you know," Lester said, pushing himself to his feet.

"I'm not tired, Sir," Jack replied.

"I know, Son. It was only a suggestion," Lester said, before he disappeared inside the house, leaving Jack alone on the porch.

Jack went to the well and pushed the bucket off the side to drop down into the well. He watched as the rope that was tied to the bucket unraveled and he thought about the line attached to the harpoon in Limpy's tales. He cranked the handle and the bucket rose to the top. He pulled it off to the side and dipped the wet cloth into the water. The water was cold as he held the cloth in the water. He cupped his hands and drank the water he collected in them. Then he wrapped the cold cloth around his neck again. His shirt was wet and cool, which felt good. He went back to the porch and sat down on the steps again, scanning the tree line for anything that moved between the foliage. Were there still Indians out there? He hoped so, and he hoped he got to see one sometime. Jack wiped at his face and neck with the cold, wet, cloth. He heard movement next door and noticed Mrs. Cartwright coming out to sit on her porch. Jack jumped to his feet and hurried over to sit on her steps.

"Good afternoon, Jack," she said.

"Good afternoon, Mrs. Cartwright," Jack replied. "It's a hot one today, isn't it?"

"It certainly is," she said, patting her hair in place. "I wouldn't want to be working out there in this heat, today." She quickly realized that Jack's father was working in the steamboat factory. "Oh, forgive me, Jack. I wasn't thinking," she said, shaking her head. "How thoughtless of me,"

"That's okay, Mrs. Cartwright. I was thinking about the same thing. I know Daddy is used to working on days like today. I expect I will do the same thing someday."

"Oh, I hope not, Jack," Mrs. Cartwright said. Jack quickly looked up at her. She smiled and said, "I have higher hopes for you, Jack. I was hoping you would be a teacher someday. I think you would make a fine teacher."

Jack bit his lip as he thought over what she had just said. "I might like to be a teacher, but I really like to be outside, Mrs.

Cartwright. Even in the winter when it is cold outside. Why, I'd rather be outside than anywhere else. I don't mind working in the cold. I don't like working too hard in this kind of weather, but if I had to, I would do it right enough."

Mrs. Cartwright smiled and said, "I suppose you may change your mind as you get older."

"I might, I suppose," Jack said. "I know I want to live in one of the big houses on Water Street. I'd like to have a cook and maid so my grandmother doesn't have to work so hard. And a rocking chair in every room for Grandfather. I think he would like that. He sits on an old hard chair right now. Maybe Daddy wouldn't have to work at Steven's Company anymore and we could go fishing every day."

Mrs. Cartwright smiled. "It sounds like you have thought this through," she said. "I have no doubt that it won't happen, just as you have pictured it, Jack."

"Really?" Jack asked. "Wow! I certainly hope so, Mrs. Cartwright." He sat staring off toward the river, daydreaming. After a moment, he looked back at Mrs. Cartwright and asked, "Would you like me to bring in some wood for your fireplace?"

"No, Jack," she replied. "It is too hot to cook inside today. I suspect it will be a hot night as well. You may bring some wood out to the fire pit, if you don't mind. I'll be doing my cooking outdoors this evening."

"I'll do it now," Jack said, jumping to his feet.

Mrs. Cartwright was about to object to his doing it in the hottest part of the day, but it was too late. Jack had already disappeared around to the back of the house. She sat watching as Jack carried three armloads of wood to the fire pit, where a tripod with a cooking pot dangled over the cold coals. Jack wiped the sweat from his brow and asked, "Can I get you anything else?"

"No Jack, you've done plenty, and I thank you very much," Mrs. Cartwright said.

"I can bring out your vegetables for the pot, if you want," Jack suggested.

Mrs. Cartwright laughed. "Jack Gideon, you are something else. It is too hot, and I don't feel much like eating, right now. I do appreciate the offer, but it's too early. Thank you."

"You don't need the wood for a fire?" Jack asked.

"Oh yes, but not for a while. I certainly do appreciate you carrying the wood around for me," she said.

"Okay, if you don't need me I'll be going home now," he said.

"Thank you again," Mrs. Cartwright said. She watched Jack as he turned and walked next door to where his grandfather had returned to sit on the porch.

Lester was wiping his brow as Jack climbed the steps. "What have you been up to in this heat, Jack?" he asked.

"I was carrying wood out to the fire pit for Mrs. Cartwright, Sir. She is cooking outside this evening because of the heat." Jack replied.

"I believe we will be doing the same," Lester said. "It's too hot to have a fire in the house. We won't get a wink of sleep tonight."

Jack frowned as he looked out at their fire pit and then next door to where Mrs. Cartwright sat with her back to them under the fading shade of the large tree. He looked over at his grandfather and said, "It seems a might queer that Mrs. Cartwright will be over there cooking and we will be over here cooking, when we should be building just one fire and eating together."

Lester laughed. "You have something there," he said. He turned his head to face the open door. "Delores!" he called out. "Delores, come out here a moment."

Jack's grandmother stepped into the open doorway and asked, "What is it?"

"Jack, here, mentioned that it was a might queer that we build a fire and cook outside, while Mavis Cartwright eats all alone next door. He suggested we invite her to join us this evening." Jack wanted to protest that those were not his exact words, but remained silent.

"Well, invite her over, Jack," his grandmother said. "I'll peel another potato. Lord knows I could certainly use the feminine conversation for a change."

Jack jumped off the porch and ran toward Mrs. Cartwright again. She looked up at him, somewhat confused. "Jack Gideon, what is the hurry? It's far too hot for you to be exerting yourself so."

"My grandparents wanted me to invite you to join us for dinner this evening, Mrs. Cartwright," Jack said.

"Well, that is awful nice of them," she replied.

"It don't make no sense to build two fires when it's this hot," Jack said.

Mrs. Cartwright raised her eyebrows. "What's that you say? I believe you need to re-phrase that question, Jack Gideon. I certainly taught you better than that."

Jack thought for a moment and smiled before saying, "It doesn't make any sense to build two fires, Ma'am."

Mavis Cartwright smiled and nodded her head. "That's a boy. You tell your grandparents I would be happy to join your family for dinner. I could use the feminine conversation as well."

"Yes, Ma'am," Jack said, turning to run back to the porch where his grandfather was still sitting.

"She said yes," Jack said, as he reached the top of the stairs. He went inside where his grandmother stood peeling potatoes, "She said yes," he repeated. His grandmother smiled and nodded her head. Jack turned and went out to sit on the porch with his grandfather again.

Jack helped his grandmother carry everything to the outside fire pit. Lester remained on the porch with the wet cloth around his neck. The afternoon seemed to drag along as Jack constantly watched the sun move toward the tree line. He was anxious for his father to come home from work. He wanted to climb the hill again, but knew it was pointless to bring it up. He had been told to stay close to the house, and he was expected to obey.

Jack was sitting on a block of split wood when Mavis Cartwright walked across the yard to join them. She carried a basket of biscuits she had made the day before. Jack carried a chair from the kitchen for her. She smiled over at him as she sat down.

"Whew! It sure is a warm one today," she said, to Lester, as she sat.

"I can't take the heat like I used to," Lester replied.

Jack sat quietly listening to the conversation as it went back and forth about the heat and the affects it had on the elderly. Before long his grandmother had joined them, and the food was placed in the pot over the fire.

"Poor Sheldon, working in this heat," Mrs. Cartwright said.

"Yes, I imagine it gets mighty hot in that factory," Delores added.

"He was always such a good boy," Mrs. Cartwright said.

Jack's head perked up and he asked, "Did you teach my Daddy, also, Mrs. Cartwright?"

Mrs. Cartwright nodded her head, as she replied, "Yes, I did, Jack."

"How long have you been teaching here in Wellsville?" he asked.

Mrs. Cartwright raised her eyebrows and replied, "For a very long time, Jack. Wellsville was where I started teaching way back when I was in my early twenties. I've been teaching ever since."

"How old are you?" Jack asked.

"Jack!" both his grandmother and Mrs. Cartwright said, together. Jack felt his face growing hot with embarrassment.

Lester chuckled and said, "You may as well learn early, Jack, that a gentleman never asks a woman her age. It just isn't proper."

"I'm sorry," Jack replied, as he squeezed his knees together and stared into the flickering flames that licked at the dangling pot.

"Jack," his grandmother began, "A lady is sensitive about personal information such as her age and what not."

Jack decided not to respond. He got the impression that anything he might think to say would be of the sensitive nature. The sun continued to drop behind the tree line and soon a familiar figure came walking toward them. "Daddy," Jack yelled, as he jumped to his feet and ran to greet his father.

Sheldon rustled Jack's hair. "How was your day, Son?" Sheldon asked.

"It was fine. I played on the hillside this morning. Grandfather said it was too hot to climb trees this afternoon. He walked to the mercantile with me and had a little trouble with the heat on the way back. He's alright now, but he isn't moving around much," Jack explained.

Sheldon frowned as Jack explained their stopping to rest at Herald Steven's house. He paused looking down at his father who sat on a chair in the evening air. "Are you alright, Father?" he asked.

"I'm fine now," Lester said. "I just overdid it in the hottest part of the day."

Sheldon stood quietly a moment and then greeted Mrs. Cartwright. He excused himself and went inside to clean up before dinner. Jack followed him inside, talking about his day as they went.

Sheldon pulled his suspenders from his shoulders and removed his shirt. Jack filled the basin with cool water from the bucket. Sheldon took the bar of lye soap from the dish on the side board and began to scrub his face and neck. Soon he was climbing the ladder to change into clean clothes, while Jack emptied the dirty water over the side of the porch. Jack noticed the difference in the temperature as he stepped outside and re-entered the house. Sheldon was coming down the ladder as Jack entered and he said, "It's pretty warm in here, isn't it?"

"It sure is," Jack replied.

"It's a lot warmer up there in the loft," Sheldon said, raising his eyebrows. "I think maybe we should sleep out on the porch tonight."

"Can we?" Jack asked.

Sheldon nodded his head. "I think it would be a good idea. We aren't going to get much sleep up there tonight. It will be much cooler out on the porch."

"Oh goody, goody," Jack said, smiling. He skipped off to join his grandparents and Mrs. Cartwright, while Sheldon followed close behind.

Jack spent most of the night staring up into the star lit sky. The Milky Way spread across the sky illuminating the clouds so that they appeared to have silver outlines around each one of them. The tree line created a dark silhouette that looked like Indians dancing in a line with their arms reaching toward the Heavens. Jack thought of Old Chief Logan and what he may have looked like. A large rock formation nearby was said to be Chief Logan's head. Of course, Jack knew it couldn't be his actual head, but many folks attest to its likeness of the old chief. It never occurred to Jack before that they couldn't possibly know, as Chief Logan died long ago.

It was a still night. Jack could feel the foggy mist from the river in the air. It felt good on his face as he laid upon a quilt, spread over the hard porch floor. He could hear his father's snoring, which kept him awake. He sat up, at one point and stared off into the back yards of the houses closest to his. As he had done so many times before, he thought of what it might be like to live in one of the well-manicured mansions on Water Street. Mrs. Cartwright had hopes that Jack would become a school teacher. Jack appreciated her kind words of encouragement, but Jack had bigger plans. If school teachers were successful, why did she live in a little two room house on the back streets of town? No, Jack needed to become something more than a school teacher. Harry Moser was going to be a lawyer. Jack nodded his head at the thought. A lawyer would be someone who lived in a big house along Water Street. Perhaps Jack should become a lawyer as well. He found his eyelids growing heavy, and finally laid down on the quilt.

Jack woke to the sounds of his father's boots on the wooden porch. Sheldon was walking off the porch, making his way to work. Jack watched his father's strong back as he moved away

Bend in The River

from him. Soon he was out of sight, and Jack could hear his grandparents talking inside the kitchen.

"Jack, how was your night?" Lester asked, as Jack carried the quilt over his shoulder.

"It was fine, Sir," Jack replied.

"Come sit down and have a bit of breakfast," his grandmother said, waving a wooden spoon in his direction.

"I'm not hungry, Ma'am," Jack replied wiping at his eyes. "I think I'll sit a spell, until I'm fully awake."

"You do that, Son," Lester said, smiling. "It's going to be another hot one out there today. I have no plans to leave the house today."

"That's good to hear," Delores said, turning back to the pot that hung over the fireplace. "You might not want to wait too long, Jack. I'm cooking this morning, but then I'm letting the fire go out. We will be eating cold vittles today." She looked over at Lester and shook her head. "You complain about being so hot. How would you like it if you had to stand over hot coals preparing the meals everyone around here takes for granted?"

"Now, Delores, no one takes them for granted," Lester said, with a whining voice. "We all appreciate everything you do around here. We just don't want to embarrass you by bringing it up all the time," he said, as he winked at Jack. Jack covered his mouth, as he knew his grandmother was not in the least amused by the comments.

After some time, Jack thought he better eat his breakfast. He was sure to compliment his grandmother on how well it tasted. She mumbled something about Rosalie Dodge's cooking, and Jack assumed that she must be in a sour mood this morning. He hurried to finish his breakfast and dress for his day. It was Saturday, and tomorrow was the Church Social.

Jack carried his quilt to the loft and spread it evenly. It was early in the day, yet the heat up there was stifling. Jack knew it was going to be exceptionally hot. He also knew that his grandmother would balk at his playing in the hills. She would want him to stay close to the house. Jack would have to find a way to get up there early on. He scurried down the ladder and ran toward the open door, calling over his shoulder as he went, "I'll be back around dinner, Grandmother."

Jack jumped off the porch and ran toward the hill and trees. He darted through back yards and jumped over ruts in the dirt streets. He felt safe in the thought that Melvin and Anthony would not be lurking about the streets this early in the day. He carefully climbed the loose shale hillside, looking about for snakes. He used the same path he had taken hundreds of times before. He crossed the walking trail that cut around the middle of the hill toward the turnpike and over toward East Liverpool. Then he was climbing an even steeper grade toward the rocky top of the hillside. Jack did not see any snakes this morning. He assumed it was too early for them to be moving about. A stray dog moved along the path beneath him, and he paused to watch it until it moved into the higher weeds and disappeared. Jack found his favorite Maple Tree with the heavy limb that allowed him to settle and watch the activities of the community below.

There was a slight breeze and the leaves made a rustling sound. Jack closed his eyes and allowed the breeze to kiss his face. His hair was damp with sweat and he wiped at the moisture that was running down his forehead toward his eyes, leaving dirty streaks on his face. "I wish I could live in a tree house right here," he said aloud. It was his favorite place in all the world to be.

Bend in The River

He saw movement below and noticed the same dog, he had seen earlier, making its way up the steep bank. "Where are you going?" he asked, out loud. The dog seemed to pause and look around searching for where the voice was coming from. Jack began to scurry down the tree. "Hey, boy," he said. The dog began to wag its tail as it jumped on the tree anxious for Jack to reach the bottom. "Good boy," Jack said, rubbing the dog about the head and neck. "Where did you come from, and who do you belong to?" he asked. The ribs of the dog were protruding, and it appeared to be nearly starved. Jack lowered himself to a squatting position and the dog began to lick at his face. Jack chuckled and hugged the dog about the neck. "I'm going to call you Limpy," Jack said, hugging the dog again. Hours passed as Jack and his new friend played. Jack decided it was time to make his way home. The dog followed, jumping upon Jack with excitement. As Jack reached the house he pointed to the porch and said, "Stay! Limpy, stay!" The dog looked up at Jack, confused, and continued to follow him inside.

"What have you got there, Jack?" his grandfather asked.

His grandmother turned and yelled, "Get that stinky flea bag out of my house!"

"I can't make him stay outside grandmother, unless I shut the door," Jack explained.

Delores grabbed the broom and began to chase the hound from her kitchen. The spotted hound tucked its back end under itself and yipped as his darted around the kitchen. Jack began to cry, "No please don't hurt him Grandmother. He is just hungry and he is my friend."

"Delores, stop it!" Lester called out pushing himself up onto his feet. He limped, with the aid of his cane until he reached his wife, at which time, he grabbed the broom from her. "That will be enough," he said.

"I don't want that dog in my house!" Delores said, placing her hands upon her hips and standing nose to nose with Lester. "I won't have that dirty animal around my table."

"I'll teach him to stay outside, Grandmother," Jack cried. "It might take me some time, but he is smart and he will learn."

Delores turned toward Jack. "Do you mean to tell me that you aim to keep that animal for yourself? Without so much as asking permission from those that provide a roof over your head?" she asked, angrily.

"Delores, we will talk to Sheldon about it tonight. It will be his decision," Lester said.

"Sheldon will decide? Why on earth should Sheldon decide what goes on in this house. It is our house. It has always been our house. We allowed Sheldon and this boy to move in with us, but we did not give them our home. The last I checked it was still ours. Sheldon should be grateful we provided him and the boy with a roof over their heads and food in their bellies." Delores was mad. She was glaring up at Lester in an angry rage.

"That is enough, I said!" Lester shouted. "Tend to what you were doing and stop yapping about it!"

Tears welled up in Delores' eyes as she released her grip on the broom and allowed Lester to take it from her. She took a deep breath and turned her back to them, standing in the center of the kitchen trembling.

Jack was also crying. "I'm sorry, Grandmother," he said, placing his hand upon the hound's head as it sat next to where he stood.

"Never mind, Jack," Lester said, nodding his head toward the door. "Let's step outside for a while and let your Grandmother be." Jack began to walk toward the open door. The dog followed, moving at Jack's side. Jack could hear Lester's cane on the wooden plank floor as he walked behind them.

Jack looked up at his grandfather, "I'll let him go, Grandfather, but he's awfully hungry. It looks like he hasn't eaten in days."

Lester nodded his head and reached down to pat the dog on the top of the head. "He looks like someone's old coon hound, that maybe got lost in the woods. I expect there is someone looking for him," he said. He smiled down at the dog. "He looks like a mighty fine hound to me."

"How would we ever find who he belongs to?" Jack asked.

Lester rubbed his chin. "I suppose you could mention it at the mercantile in case anyone is looking for a lost hound. We could bring it up at the Church Social tomorrow, as well."

"I'll go over to the mercantile now, and maybe someone has already been in asking about him," Jack said. "I'd like to give him something to eat, but I'm afraid to ask Grandmother. She's so upset."

Lester nodded his head, "She is a might upset, that is true." Lester took a deep breath and reached down to pat the dog. He smiled over at Jack and said, "You don't worry yourself, Jack, and pay no mind to what your grandmother said in there. She's not herself today, because of the heat. She didn't mean the things she said."

Jack wiped at his running nose with the rolled-up sleeve of his shirt. He had no words, so he merely nodded his head. Lester rustled his hair and took a deep breath. He looked from the dog to Jack and finally said, "You run along to the mercantile. Take your new friend with you. I'll have a talk with your Grandmother, and everything will be alright."

Jack began to skip along in the direction of the mercantile. The hound roamed ahead of Jack, sniffing and lifting his leg to leave his scent behind. The hound seemed to have found something that smelled interesting, and disappeared under a porch. Jack turned his head to call out to it and ran smack dab into someone. When he turned his head to look, he was staring into the throat of Melvin Riley.

The smell of sweat and body odor was overwhelming. Jack wrinkled up his nose and turned his head. That was when he noticed Anthony Patrone smiling at him.

"Well, if it isn't Jack Spratt," Anthony sneered.

"Jack Spratt is about to become Jack Splat," Melvin chuckled.

"You ain't got any picket fence to help you now Jack Splat," Anthony said, through clenched teeth.

Jack couldn't speak, in fact, he couldn't move. It was as if he was trapped inside his own body. He wanted to run, but his legs wouldn't move, outside of the trembling of his knees. How he remained standing was a mystery to him. In fact, why he was thinking about his useless extremities, was a mystery to him. He should have been thinking about fleeing as fast as he could.

Melvin grabbed him by the shirt and pushed him hard. Jack felt himself going backwards. His arms flailed wildly as he landed on the hard ground. It was as if he were moving in slow motion. He noticed a dark cloud in the sky, as he went down, and a flash of lightning. It was about to storm, in more ways than one. Jack rolled over and began to push himself up. That was when Melvin kicked him in the stomach. Jack let out a yelp and wrapped both arms around his stomach, as he rolled on the ground moaning. All the while, Melvin continued kicking at his body, once kicking him in the corner of his mouth.

Bend in The River

Jack tasted blood. His vision was cloudy from the flying dust and dirt that made its way into his eyes. He closed his eyes tightly and tried to protect himself with his arms. Both, Melvin and Anthony were kicking him now. Jack did not see what happened next, but he heard it. There was a low growl before a snarl, as the hound attacked the two hooligans who were kicking Jack. There was squealing and screaming as the boys tried to run, and the dog bit at their legs. Jack wiped at his eyes, but could not see clearly. He could discern by the sound that Melvin and Anthony were running away and the hound was close on their heels.

Jack sat up and called out to the dog. "Here Limpy, come back here," he called.

There were no signs of the hound and the noises had stopped. Jack didn't know if they were out of hearing range or if the dog ran off. He rose to his feet and wiped at the blood dripping from his chin. His nose was bleeding. He touched his lip and it was cut. The taste of salty blood ran down the back of his throat. Jack spit and squeezed his nose shut as he tilted his head backwards. He looked around for the hound, and when he did not see it, he began walking toward the mercantile again.

Jack was about to climb the steps to the mercantile when the hound came bounding toward him with his tail wagging. "Who's your friend there," Howard Dodge asked. He had been sitting on a chair on the porch, enjoying the breeze. "Whoa, what happened to you?" he asked, when he got a good look at Jack.

"Oh, nothing," Jack replied.

"Nothing?" Howard asked. He called out, "Rosalie, come out here and tend to this boy."

Rosalie Dodge stepped through the open door and gasped at the sight of Jack. "What happened to you?" she asked.

Judy Lennington

Collin's mother stood in the doorway. "He's been in a scrap, haven't you Jack, me boy?" she asked.

"Yes, Ma'am," Jack replied.

At that moment Collin came hurrying outside. He lifted Jack's chin and narrowed his eyes as he asked, "It was Melvin Riley and Anthony Patrone, wasn't it?"

Jack nodded his head. "I'm not hurt bad," Jack said.

"What's that you got with ya?" Mrs. McCauley asked.

"It's a stray hound dog I found up on the hill," Jack said. "If it hadn't been for him, it would have been much worse. He tore into them when they were both coming at me all at once. I couldn't fight off the two of them together."

"Well, bring that hound inside and let's give him something to eat," Rosalie said. "He looks like he hasn't eaten in a while."

"Yes Ma'am, he sure could use something to eat, alright," Jack said, following them inside. "I was wondering if anyone mentioned losing a hound dog."

"No one has mentioned it," Rosalie said, dipping a cloth into a basin of water. "We can ask around at the church social tomorrow." She dabbed at Jack's lip. He winced in pain and she waited until he nodded to continue again. When she finished, she rinsed the cloth and gave it to Jack so he could wash his face. "I think you are going to have a shiner, young man."

"Yes Ma'am," Jack replied.

"We haven't heard anything about a stray dog, Jack, but we will ask around," Rosalie said. "Are you keeping him at your house?"

Jack frowned and said, "I'd certainly like to, but my Grandmother isn't fond of the idea. I don't know what is going to happen to him."

"Well, we can keep him out back for a couple of days," Mrs. Dodge said, "But I have my hands full, and doubt I have time to care for him the way I should. This is a nice hound dog and I think he should be with someone who has time to spend with him."

"Yes, Ma'am," Jack replied.

Rosalie turned to Collin and asked, "Collin, would you mind walking Jack home, just in case those boys are still out there somewhere?" A rumble of thunder rattled the glass panes of the windows. "You boys better get going so Collin can get back here before it starts pouring down."

"Yes, Ma'am," Collin said with a nod of his head. He looked over at Jack and made a waving motion with his hand, indicating that Jack should follow him. Jack placed the wet cloth on the side of the basin and followed Collin out the front door. Mr. Dodge was still sitting on the chair.

"You alright, Jack?" he asked, as they began to step off the wooden boardwalk.

"Yes, Sir, I'll be fine. I'm just scraped up some," Jack replied.

"Collin seeing you home, is he?" he asked.

"Yes, Mr. Dodge. Mrs. Dodge suggested I see him home in case those boys are layin' in wait for him somewhere out there," Collin said.

"That's a good boy Collin. You're a good friend to be standing up for Jack the way you do. Be careful and watch your back," Mr. Dodge said.

The boys began to walk down the dirt street toward Jack's house. The hound dog followed along, sniffing everything along the way. "Your dog, there, did right by you, Jack," Collin said.

"He isn't my dog, Collin. I would sure like to keep him, but my grandmother won't hear of it. I don't know what's going to become of him if nobody claims him," Jack said. "You make sure he follows you back to the mercantile, because my grandmother was chasing him with a broom and I wouldn't want anything to happen to him after what he did for me."

Collin nodded his head. "I'll make sure he follows me." He looked about as they moved along. "Now, what are we going to do about Melvin and Anthony?"

"I don't know Collin. I thought I taught them a lesson when I gave them a go, but I'm afraid I may have just made things worse. They got me good, and I'm afraid they aren't done with me yet," Jack said, as he lightly touched his lip. "How bad does it look?" he asked.

"They got you pretty good. You're gonna have a shiner and your nose is going to be pretty sore," Collin said.

"Not as sore as my ribs," Jack said, rubbing his ribs. "They were both kicking me in the ribs over and over and I thought they were going to break them at one point."

Collin raised his fists in the air and said, "They'll pay for that, Jack, me friend."

"Maybe we should let it go Collin," Jack said, still rubbing his ribs. "They get me, we get them, and then they come at me again. It goes on and on. When does it end?"

"It ends when they give it up," Collin said, looking down at Jack. "Jack, me boy, we can't let them get away with this. They beat on everyone smaller than them. They won't fight someone their own size. I say we give em another go."

"I don't know, Collin. I just want it to stop," Jack said, shaking his head.

They had reached Jack's house. "You better get back, Collin," Jack said. "Make sure Limpy goes with you."

"Limpy?" Collin asked.

Jack smiled and nodded his head, as he said, "I named him Limpy, because he is poorly looking, and he's my friend."

"Come on, Limpy," Collin called, as he turned to leave. The first drops of rain began to fall and Collin began to run. Limpy ran alongside him, barking and jumping at him playfully.

Jack climbed the porch steps and stood watching them until they were no longer visible. He turned to go inside the house. Something caught his attention and he glanced to his left, just in time to see Maybelle Patrone marching down the center of the street. Her arms were swinging with every step. She wore a frown and he could see the anger in her eyes from far off. Jack hurried inside.

"What happened to you?" Lester asked.

"Ah," Jack looked back at the open door and froze. Maybelle Patrone was climbing the steps and then she was standing in the open door with both hands upon her hips.

"You!" she shouted, pointing a shaking finger at Jack.

"Whoa there, Maybelle," Lester said, standing up. "What's going on?"

Jack was aware of his grandmother stepping closer. "You owe my son a new shirt and a new pair of pants. Not to mention that I will not be leaving here today without witnessing you getting a good strapping for what you done to my Anthony and the Riley boy," she said. Jack noticed that when she spoke her belly moved up and down with every word.

"Jack? What happened?" Lester asked.

Jack gulped and said, "Melvin and Anthony were waiting for me. They jumped me on my way over to the mercantile."

Lester raised his head and looked down his nose at Jack's face. "You gave them a good go again, did you?" he asked.

Jack shook his head, "No Sir, I wasn't able to handle the two of them. They surprised me and they got me pretty good this time."

"They did no such thing!" Maybelle Patrone huffed. "My Anthony is all tore up from that darn animal, of yours. It attacked him."

"I didn't tell him to attack them, Grandfather," Jack said, looking up at Lester. "He was trying to protect me. Anthony and Melvin had me on the ground and they were both kicking me. Limpy thought he was protecting me, and he tore into them and chased them off."

"My Anthony wouldn't do such a thing, unless provoked," Mrs. Patrone said, with narrowing eyes.

"Your Anthony is a bully, and a hooligan. He is trouble, just like his mother!" Jack's grandmother said, stepping closer.

"I demand a new shirt, a pair of pants, and this boy, here, get a good wailing before I leave here tonight," Maybelle said, pointing her finger at Jack again.

"This is the second time those two boys have jumped Jack, Maybelle," Lester said.

"Oh, no you don't, Lester Gideon. I'll not be put off this time," Maybelle demanded.

"You may not be put off, but if you don't leave on your own accord, you'll be thrown off," Delores said, stepping nose to nose with Maybelle Patrone, who was a whole head taller.

Maybelle gasped. "Well, I never..." she said. She turned and walked to the door where she turned and said, "This will be talked about with the minister tomorrow morning. He will have something to say about it to the entire congregation. And that dog, well, that dog will have to be put down!"

Jack gasped, "No, Grandfather," he looked over at Lester, who placed his hand upon Jack's shoulder. "He was trying to protect me, Grandfather."

"You know how folks around here feel about vicious animals, Lester Gideon. You know how it works. If a dog attacks a child, it is put down," Maybelle said, smiling cruelly.

"Too bad the same doesn't go for some of the citizens in Wellsville. It sure would make for a nicer neighborhood," Lester said, pointing to the door.

"Well!" Maybelle said, turning and marching toward the door. She called over her shoulder, "We shall see what Reverend Johnston has to say about all of this violence." They watched her back as she made her way off the porch taking one step at a time. She carried no umbrella, and it was sprinkling.

Jack turned to his Grandfather and said, "I am so sorry, Grandfather. I swear, I did not attack those boys. They came at me. They knocked me down on the ground and they were kicking me hard. Limpy was under a porch and when he heard me crying out, he went after them. He chased them off and came back to see if I was alright." Jack began to sob.

"Let's have a look at you," Lester said. He pulled down Jack's suspenders and lifted his shirt. He winced at the sight of Jack's ribs. He glanced over at his wife and sighed. "They could have broken the boy's ribs," he said. He looked back at Jack and smiled. "Limpy you say?" he asked.

"I named him Limpy," Jack said. "Of course, he probably has another name, but I call him Limpy and he comes when I call him by that name, too. I think he likes it."

Judy Lennington

"Where is the dog now?" Delores asked.

"Mrs. Dodge is going to feed him. She said he can stay there a couple of days until we can figure out where he belongs," Jack replied. His grandmother nodded her head and handed him a cold, wet cloth to put on his ribs.

At that time, Sheldon appeared. "It looks like the storm is blowing over already," he said, hanging his hat on the peg near the door. He looked over at Jack and asked, "What happened to you?"

"That nasty Patrone boy and his friend jumped Jack earlier. They beat him up pretty good. Took to kicking him in the ribs and darn near broke them. He's a mess," Lester said.

"If it hadn't been for Limpy they might have broken them good," Jack said.

"Limpy?" Sheldon asked. He looked over at his grandfather and shrugged. "Limpy?" he asked, again.

"Jack, here, found a stray hound. He has taken to calling him Limpy," Lester said.

Sheldon looked around the room. He looked back at his father and shrugged his shoulders again, confused.

"Jack found a stray hound, as I said," Lester began, "He was on his way over to the mercantile to see if anyone had been asking about a lost dog. The Riley and Patrone boys jumped Jack on the way over there."

Delores spoke up, "They had the boy on the ground and the two of them were kicking him in the face, head, and ribs. You should see the boy's ribs, Sheldon. It's a wonder they weren't broken." She lifted Jack shirt.

Sheldon went to inspect Jack's bruised ribs. "That looks like it really hurt," he said, looking down at Jack. Jack could only nod

Bend in The River

his head, as a lump came up into his throat. Sheldon sighed and asked, "What happened to the two boys who attacked you?"

"Limpy was under a porch," Jack began, "When he heard me yelling, he came running, and attacked them. He put them on the run and he chased them all the way home. He bit them in the legs, but I don't think it was that bad because, they sure ran fast enough." Jack began to cry then. Between sobs he said, "Now Mrs. Patrone said she wants Limpy put down because he bit Anthony."

Sheldon placed his arm carefully, around Jack's shoulders. He patted Jack on the back to console him. Sheldon looked around the room. "Where is this dog?" he asked.

"Mrs. Dodge is keeping him tied out back until someone claims him," Jack sobbed.

"Well, maybe he belongs to someone," Sheldon began. "If he does, we have no say over his fate. That will be up to his owner to decide. I understand how you feel, but for the moment, our concern is not for the dog. He is safe and in good hands. We need to tend to your wounds."

"I'll tend to him," Delores said. "You wash up for dinner."

Sheldon nodded his head and filled the basin with cool water. Delores sat Jack on a chair at the table and began to dab at his lip. "I'm sorry, Grandmother," Jack said, between sobs. Delores shook her head and patted Jack on the shoulder.

Jack's father helped him dress for bed. Once again, they slept on the front porch. Jack found it hard to get comfortable as his ribs hurt terribly. His father snored loudly. Jack laid looking at the night sky. Dark clouds hid the stars and made the night even darker. It was a humid night. When Jack woke in the morning, the dark clouds had moved out and the morning sun was shining. It was Sunday morning, the day of the church social. Normally, Jack would be excited about going to church, but today Mrs. Patrone was speaking with the preacher and others about having Limpy put down. It was not a joyful day for Jack. He wanted to climb the ladder to the loft and hide. He did not want to see or speak to anyone. His heart ached and there was no consoling him.

It was quiet as they sat at the breakfast table. "May I be excused from church today?" Jack asked.

"You may not!" Sheldon said. "You will go to church and you will hold your head up high. You said those boys attacked you. If that is so, it is not you who should be ashamed."

Jack nodded. "I spoke the truth, Father. But I don't want anything to happen to Limpy, on account of me."

"Well, nothing will happen to Limpy today. He will remain tied up at the Dodge's back door until tomorrow, or until everyone has a say in the matter," Sheldon said.

Sheldon helped Jack to dress in his finer clothes for church. They were stepping out onto the porch when they saw the McCauley's making their way toward them. Mrs. McCauley held the hands of the two youngest, Connor, who was seven, and Tristan, who was five. They were scrubbed and although their clothes were patched here and there, they were clean and neat.

"Good morning, Mrs. McCauley," Sheldon called out to them.

"Good morning Mr. Gideon. Thank you again for inviting us to accompany you and your family to church this morning," Mrs. McCauley said, smiling. She looked over at Jack and asked, "And how are you feeling this morning Jack Gideon, me boy?"

Jack nodded his head. It hurt to move and it even hurt to speak, but he forced a half smile, for fear of causing his lip to bleed again. Collin nodded his head at Jack. "You have a brave young man there, Mr. Gideon. You can be proud of that one, so you can," Mrs. McCauley said.

Sheldon looked down at Jack and placed his hand upon his head. "I am very proud of Jack," he said.

"We are all proud of Jack," Delores said. Jack looked back to see her standing with her chin in the air, yet she managed to smile at Mrs. McCauley in a manner that Jack had come to know as friendly.

"Shall we be on our way?" Lester asked. "I'm sorry to rush you along, but I don't move very fast and I'm usually one of the last to arrive. I wouldn't want us all to be late on my account." And so, they were all moving along down the street toward the church.

As they moved along they would occasionally encounter another neighbor going the same direction. Some raised their eyebrows at the sight of the Irish woman and six children. Mrs. McCauley managed to smile at everyone, but Jack could tell by the color of her cheeks that she was very uncomfortable. How brave she was to be here this morning. Jack knew that Mrs. Patrone would make her day miserable if she could. It was then that Jack decided to be as brave as Mrs. McCauley when he faced Mrs. Patrone and her son. Melvin's family never came to church. They had not been to the church socials in the past, either. Jack did not know if they went to another church or didn't go to church at all. That was fine with him. He would find it difficult enough facing Anthony and his mother. Mr. Patrone would be here today, but he was quiet and seldom said anything. Mrs. Patrone did all the talking in that family.

They were arriving at the church now. Lester spoke to everyone he passed along the way as he moved toward the steps that led up into the church. As they entered they moved toward the front of the church. Every head turned to watch them as they moved in a single file down the aisle toward the front. Jack wanted to turn and look back at Collin and Mrs. McCauley, but felt he should not. His father had a firm grip on Jack's shoulder, guiding him along. Jack wanted to complain about his father's grip causing him pain on his sore muscles, but decided against it.

The McCauley's took nearly a full bench all to themselves. Jack and his family sat on a bench right behind them.

Reverend Johnston approached the pulpit and raised his hands in the air. Everyone stood up. They sang together, and then he led them in prayer, after which time they all sat down again. The sermon today was on love for thy neighbor. Several times it appeared the Reverend was looking right at Jack. Had Mrs. Patrone already spoken to him about the events of the previous day? After a while he noticed Tristan McCauley had fallen asleep. Mrs. McCauley held him upon her lap. Jack could see the dampness of his hair as it was so warm in the building. This was the one time a year when the church was full and the heat was nearly unbearable. Reverend Johnston usually kept his sermons short on this occasion for that very reason.

They were standing again. Jack's father took Tristan in his arms and held him for Mrs. McCauley while the closing prayer was recited. Then he carried him outside and placed him on a quilt under the shade of an Oak tree that grew near the church.

Jack sat down on the quilt next to his father and Collin, while Sheldon and Jack's grandmother introduced Mrs. McCauley to some of their friends. Lester sat on a stump nearby, wiping the sweat from his forehead. Several folks commented on Jack's face and asked what happened. Jack knew it was bad to lie, especially on holy ground. He just shook his head and said, "It was nothing

Bend in The River

but a misunderstanding." Some folks would chuckle as they walked away.

Jack noticed Mrs. Patrone pulling Anthony by the arm and marching in what Jack assumed to be military style toward Reverend Johnston. The Reverend was talking to Mr. and Mrs. Huffman, as the twins stood patiently by, waiting to be released to play with the other children. Jack stiffened as he watched her march right up to them and clear her throat loudly. The Huffman's turned and walked away. Jack watched as the twins broke off in a run toward where the other children had gathered to play games.

Mrs. Patrone was shaking her finger at the Reverend. Her mouth seemed to be moving on and on and with every word her protruding belly moved up and down. Collin said, "Don't you be worrying about that old wind bag, Jack." But Jack could not take his eyes from her. His palms were sweating as he wrung his hands. Mrs. Patrone pulled up Anthony's knickers to show the Reverend where Limpy had bitten him. Then she looked directly over at Jack and pointed her finger at him. Jack felt fear rise in his throat. His cheeks were flaming. Still he could not look away.

As he sat on the quilt watching, his grandmother began to stride straight for where Mrs. Patrone and the Reverend were standing. "Oh no," Jack said, under his breath.

Collin sat up straight. "Should you go over there?" he asked.

Jack shook his head. "I'm not going over there," he said, with a quivering voice.

"You didn't do anythin' wrong, my friend," Collin said.

"I don't want to go over there," Jack replied.

Whatever Delores had to say, she said it and turned walking straight toward Jack. He watched her approaching with wide eyes. He knew he should rise to his feet, but didn't because he was afraid his legs would not support him. Delores reached her hand out to Jack and said, "Jack, come with me,"

"Please, Grandmother," Jack begged. "I don't want to start any trouble here, today."

"You do as I say," Delores commanded. "You get on your feet and come with me, right now!"

Jack looked over at Collin. His friend was as white with fear as Jack was. Collin shrugged and shook his head. He couldn't help Jack this time. Jack raised to his feet. His grandmother grabbed hold of his hand and began pulling him along in the direction of where the Reverend Johnston, Anthony, and Maybelle Patron stood. He winced with pain as his muscles ached terribly. As his grandmother pulled him along, he noticed Gretchen Griffin, standing nearly a head taller than all the other women, and she was looking right at them. Her mother, Louise was talking to her, but Gretchen had fixed her eyes upon Delores Gideon who was dragging her grandson, Jack, along by the hand and back of the collar. Gretchen knew something was amiss and she was curious. Jack felt as if everyone was watching him. He squeezed his eyes tightly shut and kept his feet moving, for fear of falling. He wondered if his grandmother would stop if he lost his footing. He had his doubts, so he kept moving. He just wanted to disappear.

"There he is," Mrs. Patrone was saying. Delores finally stopped pulling on Jack, but she did not turn loose of his collar.

"Hello, Jack," Reverend Johnston said. "I hear you got yourself a dog." The Reverend reached out, taking Jack's face in his hands. He turned Jack's face to the right, and back to the left. "What happened to your face?" he asked.

Jack stared up at the Reverend. Jack knew he dared not lie to the Reverend for that would be like lying to God himself. He swallowed the lump in his throat and said, "Well, I found this hound dog in the hill up north. He was friendly, but he was nearly starved. I played with him a while and when I went home, he followed me. He was friendly, like I said," Jack explained. "Grandfather suggested I ask at the mercantile if anyone had lost a hound. He thought he looked like someone's coon hound, and they may be missing him. He went right along with me, because he was friendly and all, like I said."

"And what happened to your face?" the Reverend asked, again.

"His face? His face, you ask," Maybelle Patrone interrupted. "Look at my boy, Anthony's leg!"

"Maybelle, you had your say," Reverend Johnston began, "Now I suggest you let the boy tell his side of the story. I've been around long enough to know every story has two sides."

Mrs. Patrone huffed, "Well, I declare!"

"No," the Reverend said, "You did declare, and now it is Jack's turn." He smiled over at Jack. "What happened to your face, Jack?" he asked, for the third time.

"Well, Sir," Jack began. He looked over at his grandmother who was nodding her head. It was at that time she let go of his collar. Jack tugged on his shirt and said, "Well, Anthony, here, and Melvin Riley began taunting me, Sir. The two of them together got me down on the ground and began kicking me."

"You should see the boy's ribs," Delores said.

"May I lift your shirt to see your ribs?" Reverend Johnston asked.

"Why would you want to see his ribs?" Mrs. Patrone asked, shifting her weight upon the other leg. "You didn't ask to see Anthony's legs. I had to show them to you. Why would you be interested in seeing his ribs? What does that have to do with anything?"

Jack was aware of eyes watching them. His grandmother began to pull his shirt from his knickers. She only exposed a small portion of Jack's back and ribs, but he could tell by the wincing look in the Reverend's eyes that it wasn't necessary to see anymore. The Reverend looked over at Anthony and asked, "Did you do that to this boy?"

"Of course, he didn't. The boy is lying!" Mrs. Patrone said.

"I didn't ask you, Maybelle!" The Reverend barked. He looked over at Anthony again and asked, "Do you know where you are, Son? You are on the grounds of God's house. Do you know what happens to those who lie?"

Anthony turned white. He began to cry. "Look what you have done to my son!" Maybelle Patrone exclaimed, looking over at Jack's grandmother. "How dare you, after what he went through with that vicious hound."

The Reverend looked back at Jack. "Tell me the rest of the story, Jack. What happened?"

"Well, Sir," Jack began. He feared Anthony would make him pay for this regardless of the outcome, so he might as well get it all out there. "As I said, they had me on the ground and they were both kicking me, when Limpy heard me yelling and came after them. He did bite them, Sir, but he was protecting me. It wasn't his fault. He would have been friendly towards them if they hadn't gone after me."

"See, what did I tell you?" Mrs. Patrone said. "Even this boy admits that the dog attacked my son and the Riley boy. He should be put down immediately."

Bend in The River

The Reverend took a deep breath and folded his hands in front of him. "Reverend," Jack's grandmother said, "If we put down every vicious being God put on this earth," she paused to take a deep breath. "There would be some folks, I won't mention names, but they would require being put down too. Not everything is black and white."

"I most heartedly agree, Delores," the Reverend said, nodding his head.

"I demand that animal be put down!" Maybelle stomped her foot. "And I also demand that these people buy my son a new pair of pants and a shirt that was torn on Mr. Nelson's fence a while back."

"Oh, I see the problem now," the Reverend said. "It appears to me that this is an ongoing problem your son seems to be having with this Gideon boy. Let me see if I have this right," the Reverend began, looking over at Anthony. This little boy, here, has been bullying you and the Riley boy. He has been roughing you up some, hasn't he? Maybe beating the tar out of you a time or two?"

Jack was aware that his father had stepped close now. He looked up at his father who winked down at Jack. Anthony Patrone was shaking his head. "No, Sir, that scrawny punk can't beat me up." He raised his fist in the air, "I gave it to him good, and I'll give it to him again!"

"Now I see," the Reverend said. He smiled over at Jack, placing his hand upon Jack's shoulder he said, "You run along now and play. Don't you worry about your friend, Limpy. I do believe he is a hero and should be treated as such."

"What?" Mrs. Patrone asked.

"Maybelle Patrone!" the Reverend said. "You should take that boy of yours and march him straight inside the church and kneel

- 369 -

before God and ask for his forgiveness. You have been stirring up a lot of mean gossip about a certain family who settled here recently, and I believe God is not happy about your actions. You owe that family an apology, as well as the Gideon family. Your son needs some restraint, and so do you." The Reverend looked around at all the faces watching and listening. "This is a special day for fellowship. We should not be harboring any ill thoughts toward our neighbors on this day or any other, for that matter." He waved his arms in the air to indicate that they were to go back to visiting one another. Maybelle Patrone grumbled to herself and grabbed Anthony by the arm. She pulled him along in the direction of their home. Jack could not look, although, he wanted to watch until they were out of sight.

Reverend Johnston smiled down at Jack. "I hear you have been tutoring a certain young man, and from what I hear, you are quite good at it. I also hear that you have been carrying firewood for Mrs. Cartwright and helping out at the mercantile." He patted Jack on the back. "You are exactly what today's sermon was all about, Jack. Wellsville could certainly use more young people such as yourself."

Jack frowned, for now he was wishing he had paid more attention to the sermon of the day. He smiled up at the Reverend. "What is to become of Limpy?" he asked.

"Limpy?" the Reverend asked, as he looked over in the direction of where Lester sat on the stump. "Now I wonder where you heard that name from," he smiled again. "I don't think he deserves to be put down after such a heroic deed. Where is he now?"

"He's at the mercantile," Jack replied. "Mrs. Dodge said he could stay there a few days, but she can't take on caring for him with all she has to do right now."

"If no one claims the dog, he is yours," the Reverend said.

"But...," he looked up at his grandmother.

"You heard what the Reverend said," Delores said. Jack's mouth dropped open. "Thank you for listening, Reverend," Delores said. She smiled down at Jack and said, "Come along, Jack. It isn't polite to invite guests to a party and leave them to fend for themselves." She tugged on Jack's sleeve and they walked away together.

"Thank you, Grandmother," Jack said.

"Now don't you go getting too attached to that hound dog, Jack Gideon. I don't want to listen to you crying your eyes out because his owner showed up and claimed him," Delores said, as they walked toward the quilt where Collin sat watching his sleeping brother.

"Yes Ma'am," Jack said. He said a silent prayer that no one would claim Limpy.

They reached the quilt and Delores told Lester to remain in the shade while she got a plate of food for him. Jack waited for her to walk away before he announced his exciting news to Collin and his grandfather. "Grandmother said I could keep Limpy if no one claims him."

"That's good news, Jack," Lester said. "Every boy should have a dog."

Jack sat next to Collin on the quilt. Folks walked past them and nodded or expressed some sort of greeting. Most of them were patrons at the mercantile who had come to know Collin. Tristan remained oblivious to all the goings on as he continued to sleep under the shade of the tree. His hair was damp with sweat and the thick red curls caressed his face like a bonnet.

Jack looked around the crowd of neighbors and friends. He noticed his father talking to Hermon Griffin and his son Wayne.

Judy Lennington

He was introducing Mrs. McCauley to them. Jack noticed his father seemed very pleased with himself today. Jack was happy to see his father in such a good mood. Sunday was the only day of the week that he did not work. How Jack wished it wasn't so necessary for his father to work such long hours in all types of weather. Jack missed him while he was at work.

Sheldon placed his hand on Mrs. McCauley's elbow and led her on to meet more of their neighbors. Jack looked over at Collin, who had seen it too. He did not seem pleased. He looked over at Jack and frowned. Jack shrugged, for he did not know how to respond. He wasn't exactly certain how he felt about it himself. Did it mean anything at all? Jack did not want to read more into the action than necessary, however, he had never seen his father do anything like that before. As his father and Mrs. McCauley moved along, Irene, Grace, and Connor stayed nearby. Jack couldn't help but wonder if someday they may be his brother and sisters. Irene was about the same age as Jack.

Jack's grandmother arrived carrying a plate for herself and one for Lester. She sat down on the quilt next to Jack. "Jack, you and Collin go get yourself something to eat. I will watch over this little one," she said.

"No, Ma'am," Collin said. "I will watch over my brother, Tristan, until me mother comes back. It is me duty as eldest son."

"Well, even the eldest son must eat at some point," Delores said, sternly. "Now go fetch yourself a plate. I will stay here with your brother until you return."

Collin took a deep breath. He appeared as though he was about to object, then had second thoughts. He nodded his head and said, "Come along Jack, me boy." He nodded his head at Delores and said, "I will be back straight away, Ma'am."

Jack walked next to Collin as they made their way toward a make shift table covered with food spread all along its length. "Why do you think me mother is hanging around your father, like some sort of lost puppy or somethin'?" Collin asked.

"I think my father is merely introducing her to everyone to make her feel more comfortable," Jack replied. "Does it bother you that she is spending time with my father?"

Collin looked down at Jack through narrow slits in his eyes. "She should be tending to her baby boy sleeping on a blanket with strangers, so she should," Collin said.

"My grandparents aren't strangers, Collin," Jack said.

"They are to Tristan," Collin barked. "if he wakes he will be scared. He's never been around so many strangers in his life."

"Well, hopefully, after today, none of these people will be strangers," Jack said.

"Well, none of these people have ever been what you call, neighborly before. In fact," Collin began putting food on a plate. "As I recall, some of these very folks tried to run us out of town."

"That's because they don't know you and your family. That is why my father is introducing your mother to everyone. After today, folks will have a different attitude toward your family," Jack said, as he heaped food upon his plate. They were walking back to the quilt.

Tristan had awakened and Delores was holding him on her lap. He smiled when he saw Collin and Jack approaching. "Here is your brother," Delores was saying. "See, I told you he was coming back." Tristan was wiping at his eyes. He went to sit near Collin and Collin shared his food with his baby brother.

"What's it like, having so many brothers and sisters?" Jack asked.

Collin spoke with his mouth full, "I have three sisters and two brothers. Both me brothers are younger. They aren't too much help, you understand. Me sisters are all younger as well, except for Kate. Kate, Grace, and Irene pretty muchly take care of the little ones. Kate and me, mostly everything falls upon our shoulders when me mother is down with the cough. However, she is good now and working at the mercantile. She said she thinks the good Lord in Heaven is looking out for us and someday it will all be better. It is her hope that all her children will be schoolin' soon. She thinks it is the proper thing to do, you see."

Jack looked up to see Constable Harris and a very tall, lean, dark haired man standing over them. "Jack," Constable Harris began, "This here is Mr. Pernell from over the hill, out Clarkson way. We understand you came upon a stray hound up in the hills."

Jack felt his heart pounding. He had a mouth full of food and could only nod his head. "Well, Mr. Pernell lost a dog on a coon's trail the other night. He says his hound is black and white spotted with a brown spot over each eye. Would that be the dog you found?" Again, Jack could only nod. He did not want anyone to see him crying, so he prayed to God that he was able to hold back the tears. "Would that be the same hound that bit the Patrone boy yesterday?" the Constable asked. Jack nodded again, and swallowed the mouthful of food.

The Constable looked over at Mr. Pernell. "It's pretty much like I said, the dog was protecting Jack, here. It was decided that Jack could keep the dog if no one claimed him."

Mr. Pernell sighed. "Would you like to keep that there hound dog, boy?" he asked.

"Yes Sir," Jack said, glancing over at his grandmother who was listening intently.

"Well boy, my family and I are about to move further north in a week or so. That there hound dog is a mighty fine animal and a good hunter, but we ain't got the room to take him with us. If you want him, and you promise to treat him well enough, I'd be in the mind to let you have him. Of course, that is, if your family is abiding by it," Mr. Pernell said, looking over at Lester and Delores who were nodding their heads.

Mr. Pernell reached his hand out to Jack, who stood up and shook hands with the man. Mr. Pernell and the Constable walked away and Jack turned to his grandmother and said, "Thank you Grandmother."

Delores smiled. "You are welcome, Jack Gideon. But the hound sleeps out on the porch. I'll not have him sleeping under my supper table."

"I'll train him to sleep on the porch, Grandmother," Jack said.

Jack and Collin took Tristan for a walk. At one point, Collin insisted they join his mother and siblings, who were talking to a small group of people near the food tables. Tristan ran to his mother, who lifted him into her arms. "This is my youngest, Tristan. He is five." Mrs. McCauley said, to Louise Griffon, her daughter Gretchen, and Mr. and Mrs. George Garfield.

"What beautiful hair your children have," Ester Garfield said. "What I wouldn't give for those curls."

Mrs. McCauley laughed. "You might change your mind if you had them. They have a mind of their own and can be quite unruly at times."

Mrs. Garfield reached up to touch Tristan's damp hair and he instantly turned his head to place it on his mother's shoulder. "He doesn't like to be touched by strangers," Collin said.

"Collin McCauley, that was not nice," Mrs. McCauley said. "Mrs. Garfield was being kind. Now I insist that you apologize to Mrs. Garfield right this minute."

Collin's face was flaming and Jack felt sorry for his friend's embarrassment. Collin lowered his gaze and said, "I apologize, Mrs. Garfield. I did not mean to sound impolite."

"Oh, that's quite alright, Collin," Mrs. Garfield said.

"Collin," Jack began, "Would you like to go down by the river to watch the boats?"

Collin nodded his head. Jack knew he wanted to run away, and Jack was happy to provide an escape. "Jack, mind you stay away from the water," Sheldon warned.

"Yes Father, I know," Jack said, nodding his head. He nodded his head again toward Collin's mother before the two of them turned to walk away.

As they neared the river bank, Jack noticed Katherine and Harry walking hand in hand along the bank ahead of them. Jack sensed the tightness in Collin's neck muscles. Jack began to talk about the times he and his father sat on the bank fishing on Sunday mornings and how it was his favorite day of the week. He noticed that Collin was not listening. Jack turned to his friend and said, "Look, Collin, you are my friend, and I feel I can talk about anything to you. I don't want you to get mad at me, but I think Kate and Harry make a fine couple. I know you feel responsible for your family, and right now you must be feeling like you are losing control, but think about what kind of future Kate will have if she marries Harry Moser. He's going to be a lawyer and possibly live in a big house on Water Street. Isn't that something you would want for your sister?"

"She's not old enough to get married," Collin said.

Bend in The River

"Maybe not right now, but Harry is going off to college soon. He isn't going to be ready to get married right away anyhow." Jack watched the couple moving along as if they were the only two people in the world.

"Who is going to help when me mother gets down again, if Kate is off somewhere on her own?" Collin asked. "I can't do it all, Jack."

"Well, Grace is only a year younger than you are," Jack said. "It seems to me that she is capable of taking on some responsibility with the younger ones. Besides, don't you have any plans of your own? Are you going to spend your whole life looking out for your siblings? Someday, they will be all grown up and off somewhere else. What are you going to do then?"

Collin took a deep breath and let it out slowly. His shoulders seem to slump as he stood looking across the river. "You are a good friend Jack Gideon, and wise for your years. If you don't mind, I would like to check in on Mrs. Dodge and see if she needs my help."

Jack nodded his head. "I understand, but I can't leave my family. They would worry about me, so, I guess I'll see you later." Collin did not say anything. He merely turned and walked away. Jack watched until he had crested the hill and was out of sight. He looked back at Katherine and Harry one more time before he, too, walked away.

Jack sought out his father. He was still in the company of Mrs. McCauley and four of her children. "Jack, there you are," Sheldon said, smiling down at Jack. Jack noticed that he seemed to have a gleam in his eye as he spoke. He could not explain it, but this bothered him. "Where is Collin?" his father asked.

"He thought he should check on the Dodges," Jack replied.

"Well, that is certainly very nice of him. Did you boys eat?" Sheldon asked.

"Yes, Sir," Jack said. "We ate with Grandmother and Grandfather." He looked up at Mrs. McCauley. She stood smiling down at Jack while holding Tristan on one hip.

Jack's father cleared his throat and asked, "Why don't you spend some time with us? We were just socializing with some of our neighbors."

"Yes, Sir," Jack replied. He looked down at Grace and Irene who stood smiling at him. He felt his cheeks growing hot. "Grandmother said I could keep Limpy," he said, to ease his own discomfort.

"That's what you said earlier," his father said, patting the top of his head. Sheldon looked over at Mrs. McCauley and asked, "Would you like me to carry Tristan for a while? He must be getting heavy."

Tristan quickly turned and embraced his mother around the neck. Mrs. McCauley smiled and said, "Perhaps after he's had more time to get used to you." Jack watched as his father played with Tristan. He felt his heart pounding. He had spent so much time convincing this family that they were welcomed as friends, and now he just wanted his father all to himself again. He had been trying to make Collin more receptive to Katherine Mary Margaret's relationship with Harry Moser. He was wondering if he should, perhaps, heed his own advice at this very moment. He smiled and looked away. He did not want his father to see his face, for he had never been successful at deceiving Sheldon Gideon.

"Hello, there Sheldon," Mr. Huffman called out. He walked with his wife on his arm and the twins, Donald and Dennis, trailing close behind. "Who is this lovely lady you have with you?"

Now it was Sheldon who was blushing. He swallowed hard and forced himself to smile. "This is Mrs. Margaret McCauley," Sheldon replied.

"Mrs. McCauley," Mr. Huffman said, extending his hand. "What a pleasure it is to meet your acquaintance. May I introduce my wife, Paulette. Paulette Huffman of course, and these are our sons, Dennis and Donald."

Jack sensed that Mr. Huffman was putting a lot of emphasis on the word Mrs., when referring to Mrs. McCauley. He noticed that it seemed his father was uncomfortable with the conversation.

Mrs. McCauley cleared her throat and asked, "My, my, how do you tell your son's apart?"

Mrs. Huffman smiled politely and straightened her back, as she said, "Oh, Mr. Huffman and I have no problems telling them apart. They are after all, our children. We place different colored twine on their wrists so that others can tell them apart. The red is Dennis and the yellow is Donald," she said boastfully.

Jack noticed the twins glancing at one another with an ornery gleam in their eye. He wondered if they had ever switched the twine from time to time. They smiled over at him and he smiled back. They were dressed in white knee socks with shiny black shoes that had a button strap across the top. They both wore royal blue velvet knickers and a matching vest. Under the vest they wore a white shirt with a large white ruffle in the front. Their dark hair was damp from sweating in the heat. Jack had never seen the twins dirty or even smudged. They always walked, holding hands and often spoke together when conversing with others. He thought them to be strange, but they were younger than he. Assuming they had passed to the next grade, they would go back

Judy Lennington

to school in the second grade. They had been the only first graders last year. Jack wondered what changes next year would bring.

The Huffman's were better off than Jack's family, but not well off enough to live in one of the new mansions on Water street. They lived in a two-story house with two full rooms downstairs and two full rooms upstairs. Jack overheard the twins telling another student that they each slept in a bed of their own with feather mattresses. Jack wondered what a feather mattress felt like. He and his family slept on homemade matts filled with straw. At times they were jaggy, but better than the wooden floor. Twice a year the straw was removed and fresh straw was stuffed inside the mattress. Grandmother would sew the mattress shut by hand. It was usually a full day's work, re-stuffing every mattress. He looked over at these two boys and wondered if they had ever slept on a straw mattress before. Once again, Jack thought of a day when he would live in one of the mansions on Water Street, and enjoy the luxuries that came with residing there. Mrs. Huffman had an air of elegance about her and she flaunted it. Jack vowed that someday, she would feel inadequate in their presence and his father would not feel embarrassed when conversing with them or anyone else in Wellsville. He stood by as the grownups talked about the social event and Mrs. McCauley working at the mercantile. Jack noted that not once did the Huffman's inquire about Howard Dodge's health.

Now the Huffman's were moving on. Sheldon smiled down at Jack and asked, "Can you tell those twins apart, Jack?"

Jack shook his head, "No, Sir," he replied.

"They certainly look identical," Sheldon laughed. "I suppose that is why they call them identical twins."

Bend in The River

Mrs. McCauley shook her head and said, "I don't know how I would have handled twins. My children were born close together exceptin' for Katherine Mary Margaret and Collin. Right after Kate was born, Thomas came to America to find work. Collin was born nine months after we arrived from Ireland. Then I was having babies one right after another."

"Where did you start out at?" Sheldon asked.

"We first arrived in New York. It was hard there. We shared a place with three other families until Thomas found work on the rail road. We lived in tents after that. I couldn't keep track of how many of us families shared the tents. We lived in one spot for a few days and then packed everythin' up, moving along to another spot. Every time we put the tent up, we shared it with different families. Winters were the worst. Then Thomas found work on the river and we moved from one river town to another. That was when he started hitting the pubs and bars every night before he came home. After a spell, he wasn't coming home at all, until he ran out of money. We've been fending for ourselves for a long time. Of course, you can tell every time he came home, another wee one would be born nine months later."

Sheldon took a deep breath. "I am so sorry to hear of your misfortune. I hope things will be better for you now."

Mrs. McCauley smiled and patted Sheldon's hand as she said, "We will be fine. The good Lord always provides. We may not be rich, but we always manage to find enough to eat when we are hungry and a dry roof over our heads when we bed down at night. I worry so about poor Collin. He is so young to take on such a big responsibility. I wish he would continue with his schoolin' and make somethin' better of himself. I don't want him to end up like his father."

"Collin is very smart. I doubt he will end up like his father." Sheldon said.

Jack stayed close and listened as they talked. He remained quiet as he listened to Collin's mother talking about their past.

"Mrs. Cartwright, the school teacher, stopped by the mercantile and said Collin was a fast learner. She said he had promise to become anythin' he wanted to be. I am so proud of my son, Collin. I want all my children to go to school and larn somethin' useful. I don't want them to grow up livin' in squalor. They are good children, every one of them." Mrs. McCauley said, as she walked along beside Sheldon.

"I believe this community is a good place to start," Sheldon said. "Wellsville is full of good people. Kind, responsible, people. Don't judge us by the Maybelle Patrones. If you took a poll, you might find that she is not liked or trusted here in Wellsville."

Mrs. McCauley laughed. "I suppose I guessed as much, but I lacked the courage to speak the words." They both snickered. Jack covered his mouth to keep his father from seeing his smile. Soon Sheldon had picked the shade of a large tree to sit under. The neighbors took turns stopping to introduce themselves to Mrs. McCauley and her family. They were still sitting under the tree when Collin found them. Jack could tell by the look on his face, that he was not pleased to find Sheldon was still with his mother. Jack grew fearful that this might be a turning point in he and Collin's friendship. How should he approach his father on the subject?

The day wore on, and Collin remained quiet. He was courteous to those who knew him from the mercantile and took the time to converse with him. Finally, they were packed up and walking toward home. As they reached the Gideon home, Sheldon said,

Bend in The River

"Perhaps I should make certain that Mrs. McCauley gets home safely."

Collin spoke up, "I'll see me family gets home safely, Mr. Gideon. They are my responsibility."

Sheldon smiled and extended his hand to Collin. Collin paused, but in the end, he did shake hands with Sheldon. "You are doing an excellent job of taking care of them, Collin. It's a huge undertaking of one so young, yet, you accomplish it with all the makings of a fine man. You should be proud of yourself." Collin merely nodded his head. Jack took note that his cheeks were flushed as he turned to guide his family toward the furniture factory and the apartment above.

It was several days before Jack saw Collin again. He had been preoccupied with his new friend and companion, Limpy. Limpy followed Jack into the hills and barked as Jack climbed the trees. They ran home, Limpy running ahead and circling back to jump and bark at Jack. Sometimes, Limpy would knock Jack off his feet and Jack would giggle as Limpy nuzzled him while he laid rolling from side to side.

Wednesday came, and Jack was to work at the mercantile. He had to tie Limpy to the porch while he was gone. Jack arrived at the mercantile before Collin arrived. "Jack Gideon, how are you?" Mrs. Dodge asked.

"I'm fine, Ma'am," Jack replied. "How is Mr. Dodge coming along?"

"Oh, Jack, he is doing so much better. He still gets terrible headaches, but Dr. Cope said he will probably always get headaches. But other than that, he is doing very well. He still walks with the aid of a cane, but his balance is getting better and

Judy Lennington

that is merely a precaution," Mrs. Dodge said. "Are you enjoying your summer?" she asked.

"Oh, yes, Ma'am," Jack replied.

"I suppose it is more fun with your new companion, Limpy, as I recall?" she asked.

"Yes, Ma'am. Limpy is his name, alright," he said, with a smile.

"Did you name him after your grandfather's old friend from when he was a boy?" Mrs. Dodge asked.

"Yes, Ma'am," Jack nodded his head.

"Has your grandfather been telling you stories about Limpy?" she asked.

Jack thought she certainly seemed to be asking a lot of questions this morning, however, he continued to nod his head and reply, "Yes, Ma'am." When the questions finally stopped he asked, "Did you know Limpy?"

She smiled over at Jack and now it was her turn to nod her head. "I vaguely remember him. Of course, no one knew him as well as your grandfather. They were such good friends. I don't rightly recall how that came to be as Limpy was so much older than your grandfather. Your grandfather wasn't as old as you are, I don't believe."

"He was the same age, Ma'am," Jack replied.

"Oh really? I didn't think so, but your grandfather would know. They seemed to hit it off right away. Before your grandfather and Limpy became friends, Limpy was no more than a smelly old drunk who slept in the doorways. After his association with your grandfather, he cleaned up and stopped drinking all together. Yes, Sir, it was a good thing too, for Limpy probably would have drank himself to death had it not been for your grandfather," she said. Jack looked around. He was relieved that Collin had not arrived yet, for it would certainly remind him of his own father's death at the hands of a bottle. "Well, Collin should be along soon," she said. She smiled down at Jack again and sighed. "Mrs. McCauley is working out very well. I do hope it doesn't offend you or your family that I cut back on your hours. I was trying to help a family in need."

"Yes, Ma'am," Jack said. "It doesn't offend me or my family. I think Mrs. McCauley needs the work and if everything works out, Collin may go back to school in the fall."

"Yes, I've spoken to him about that. Mr. Dodge has talked to him also. I believe he may do just that. Mrs. McCauley talks as though she may send her other children as well. All except for the youngest one, of course. I believe Tristan is his name, is that correct?" Mrs. Dodge asked, as she went to the door and peered out the window to watch for Collin.

"Yes, that's his name," Jack said.

"Here comes Collin now," Mrs. Dodge said smiling. "He is right on time."

Jack wondered if she noted that he had been on time as well. As he began to busy himself with the ashes, Collin stepped through the open door. "Mornin' Mrs. Dodge. Is Mr. Dodge up and about today?" Collin asked.

"He is, and as usual, he is waiting to see you in the kitchen," Mrs. Dodge said, smiling.

As Collin passed Jack he nodded his head and said, "Mornin' to ya Jack, me boy."

"Good morning, Collin," Jack said. As Collin disappeared through the curtained door way, Jack said softly, "Me boy." He noticed Mrs. Dodge looking at him in the most peculiar way. He busied himself with taking the ashes out.

Judy Lennington

As Jack was re-appearing, Mrs. Dodge said, "Jack, come over here and look at this."

Jack sat the bucket down and went to the counter where Mrs. Dodge kept the book open that folks often browsed through to order certain merchandise. "Look at this," she said, pointing to something in the book. "Have you ever seen anything like it?"

"What is it?" Jack asked, staring down at the odd iron looking dresser.

"It's a cook stove, Jack," Mrs. Dodge said, giggling. "See, you put wood in here and build a fire. It heats up the stove and you can cook on top, and it even has a compartment called an oven that you can bake in." Mrs. Dodge straightened up and looked down at Jack. "Isn't that the most remarkable thing? It's something someone came up with and it's marvelous. I've already ordered three of them. I hope to have one for myself one day soon," she said.

"How much do they cost?" Jack asked.

"Oh, they are expensive, but some of the folks on Water Street have ordered them. Well, three certain individuals have each ordered one. Mr. Dodge said they must be enormously heavy to move. They will come in boxes, in pieces and they will require some putting together, I imagine, but hopefully by the time we are ready for another order we will know how to install them well enough. What do you think of that?" Mrs. Dodge appeared to be waiting for him to respond.

"Maybe I can save up enough to buy one for my grandmother," Jack said.

"You will have to save for a while, but I think you can do it. You saved up for that nice set of china. And with your help, Collin's debt is nearly paid in full," she said. "Well, I just wanted

Bend in The River

to show you the latest thing. I really must get back to Mr. Dodge. You sweep up and do your normal chores. I'll be back soon." She disappeared behind the curtain leaving Jack alone out front.

It was a lovely day and a busy day for the mercantile. Jack couldn't help but notice how mature Collin appeared today. With Jack spending a few days off on his own, it appeared Collin had been learning without Jack's help. It was possible that the Dodges were helping him. Finally, they were all sitting at the dinner table. Jack couldn't help but think it felt like old times. He helped Mrs. Dodge clear the table after dinner while Collin accompanied Mr. Dodge to their private quarters to settle him down for the night. Then it was time to go home.

Jack and Collin stood on the front porch of the mercantile together. "How does your mother like working here?" Jack asked.

"She likes it fine. She seemed to catch on right quick enough, but she can't work the register yet. Mrs. Dodge said she would help her larn how to cypher once me mother gets used to workin' here." Collin looked out toward the tree line at the dropping sun. "Have you had any trouble with Anthony or Melvin lately, Jack?" he asked.

"No, I have not," Jack replied. "In fact, Collin, I haven't seen either of them around."

"Mr. Grimly said the Riley's moved away," Collin said. "I heard him tellin' Mrs. Dodge about it. Appears as though they owed a bill here at the mercantile, and they skipped out without payin' it." Collin looked down at Jack. "Mr. Grimly said, folks do that a lot. Can you imagine that?" he asked.

"Is Mr. Harris, the Constable, going after them?" Jack asked.

Collin shrugged his shoulders. "I don't think anyone knows where they lit off to." Collin sighed and said, "Well, I best be

Judy Lennington

getting' home. I still sweep up the furniture factory before I bed down for the night. See you tomorrow, Jack."

"Good night Collin," Jack said. Collin jumped off the porch and began running toward home. Jack glanced up at the setting sun one more time before he too jumped from the porch and ran toward home. As he was climbing the steps to the porch he saw his father approaching.

"Good evening, Jack. Did you work at the mercantile today?" Sheldon asked.

"Yes, Sir," Jack replied. "Today and tomorrow, father."

Sheldon rustled Jack's hair. "Good boy. Wellsville could use a couple more like you around here."

They had entered the kitchen. Jack shook hands with his grandfather and embraced his grandmother. "What did you have for supper, Jack?" his grandmother asked.

"We had fried cabbage and boiled potatoes, grandmother," Jack replied.

"Humph!" Delores said, with her back to Jack. "Sounds to me like we are going to be letting your pants out some."

Sheldon laughed and rustled Jack's hair. "He's growing like a weed."

Jack went outside to sit on the porch while his family ate their supper. Limpy laid on the porch beside him and Jack stroked the hound as he stared up at the night sky. As it became darker, the stars became more prevalent. Limpy was licking his hand when Sheldon came out to sit on the porch next to Jack.

"That old hound dog really likes you, doesn't he?" Sheldon asked.

Jack nodded his head. "Yes, he does, Father. He's a mighty good dog, too. He goes with me everywhere. I'm trying to train him to stay out of the house, but it is hard with the door being open all day. He sees me go in there and he doesn't understand why he can't. Then Grandmother gets after him with a broom."

Sheldon laughed. "Yes, I can remember her getting after our dogs with a broom too," he said.

"You had a dog when you were a boy?" Jack asked.

Sheldon nodded his head. "Yes, I did. Dallas and I both had a dog. Mine was named Lucky and I think Dallas' was named Brownie because he was all brown."

"Did grandmother get after them with brooms?" Jack asked.

"Oh, yes," Sheldon said, laughing. "So, did you have a good day, Jack?"

"It was fine, Sir," Jack replied. "How was yours?"

"Mine was long and hot," Sheldon said. "Does it bother you much that Mrs. McCauley is working at the store and you only get to work two days a week?"

"No, Sir," Jack said. "I like being able to play with Limpy. I am saving my money to buy something though."

"What would that be?" Sheldon asked.

"Mrs. Dodge showed me this contraption in an ordering book she keeps on the counter. It is something new and she said three people in houses on Water Street have ordered one. It's a cook stove. The dangest thing you've ever seen, Father. It's made of iron and it's real heavy. You build a fire in it and it heats up so you can cook on top of it and it has an oven box with a big door to bake in. I'm going to save up to buy one for Grandmother because she let me keep Limpy." Jack explained.

"Well, I've heard of those stoves. They were talking about that at the mill the other day. Appears as though one of the fellows at the mill was talking to someone who ordered one. He said they

Judy Lennington

are real heavy. Do you think that old floor in there would support the weight of one of them stoves?" Sheldon asked.

Jack looked behind him at the kitchen floor. "I think that old wood floor is sturdy enough," Jack replied.

Sheldon rustled Jack's hair again, "I think you're right. I think, I've a might to start saving too. Between the two of us, we ought to come up with enough money for one of them stoves. It would be a wonderful way to show your grandmother how much we appreciate all she does for us."

They sat quietly for a few moments, staring off into the stillness of the night and watching the stars. Without looking at his father, Jack mustered up the courage to ask, "Do you like Mrs. McCauley?"

"Of course, I like Mrs. McCauley," Sheldon replied. "Don't you?"

"Yes, I like her well enough, but that isn't what I meant," Jack said. "I mean, do you like her enough to marry her?"

"Marry her!" Sheldon repeated. "Where did that come from?"

"Well, you spent the entire day with her, Sunday, introducing her to all your friends and all," Jack replied.

"Well, that doesn't mean I want to marry her," Sheldon said. "I didn't want to leave her on her own amongst all those strangers." Sheldon looked down at Jack. "It wouldn't be very neighborly of us to invite her to accompany us to the church social and then abandon her and her children. She would have sat on a blanket under a tree and everyone would have passed her by. She wouldn't feel very welcome and I think it would have been rude."

"So, you walked around with her all day just to be neighborly?" Jack asked.

"Of course," Sheldon said, laughing. "What made you think I wanted to marry her?"

Jack shrugged his shoulders. "I don't know, I just thought of it. I think Collin thought of it too, because he seemed upset that you were spending so much time with her."

"Well," Sheldon laughed, "Collin has nothing to worry about. I have no plans to marry anyone. I'm not saying Mrs. McCauley isn't attractive or nice enough. I'm quite certain she would make someone a very nice wife, but not me. I had the best wife I could ever ask for. If I ever marry again, it won't be for a very long time." Sheldon placed his arm around Jack's shoulders.

"I'm happy to hear that. I wouldn't mind having Collin for a brother, but all those girls. Yuck!" Jack said. Sheldon laughed as he pulled Jack closer.

Jack slept soundly that night. He was comforted knowing his mother was not that easily replaced. As the days wore on, he worked two days a week at the mercantile and played with Limpy in the hills on the days he didn't work. His grandfather's health was failing and Jack found that Lester seldom left the house. When fall came Jack was happy to see his old friend, Collin, had returned to school. He was not alone, for his brothers and sisters also attended school, except for Tristan.

Mr. Dodge was back to his old self again and out on the floor of the mercantile. From time to time, he experienced headaches, and took to his bed, but they came less and less often as time passed. Mrs. McCauley worked full time at the mercantile, taking Tristan with her, and Mr. and Mrs. Dodge taught her how to cypher and run the register.

Melvin Riley was not present when school started. Without a side-kick to back him up, Anthony Patrone kept to himself. Harry Moser went off to college and Katherine took a part time

Judy Lennington

job cleaning houses for some of the elite on Water Street. By Thanksgiving, Harry and Kate announced their engagement.

Sheldon and Jack saved their money and they did buy a cook stove for Delores. It was put together at the mercantile and delivered one evening after Jack got home from school. Sheldon had split wood all evening, the night before, and filled the wood box on the porch. Mr. Grimly helped to install the stove and by the time Sheldon got home from work that evening, Delores had biscuits in the oven and stew on the stove. They all sat at the table eating and laughing together. Jack was happy, as he sat at the table looking at the smiling faces of those he loved around him. His legs dangled from the chair and rested on Limpy who slept under the supper table.